DANGEROUS ADVICE

As their kiss deepened, Matt's hands explored, sliding under her sweatshirt and cupping her breasts.

"You aren't playing fair," Paige murmured against his mouth.

"Is that what you want, Paige? For me to play fair?"

Under his touch, her skin grew hot and moist. Need, too long ignored, turned b??? smoldering lava. "???

Now that she had a??? slammed into her, ??? mind, bared of all c??? sensations coming f??? her still held back, a??? sensed it.

"Don't fight it, darling," he said as he skimmed her face with kisses. "Please don't fight it now." Then he said, "You're trembling."

She laughed, a short unsteady laugh. She wanted him so much, and yet . . . "It's been a long time. I mean, I haven't . . ."

He cupped her face and kissed her. "You'll do fine. Just follow your heart."

PASSIONS

She could never tell how far they would lead her . . .

PASSIONS

by
Christiane Heggan

AN ONYX BOOK

ONYX
Published by the Penguin Group
Penguin Books USA Inc., 375 Hudson Street,
New York, New York 10014, U.S.A.
Penguin Books Ltd, 27 Wrights Lane,
London W8 5TZ, England
Penguin Books Australia Ltd, Ringwood,
Victoria, Australia
Penguin Books Canada Ltd, 10 Alcorn Avenue,
Toronto, Ontario, Canada M4V 3B2
Penguin Books (N.Z.) Ltd, 182-190 Wairau Road,
Auckland 10, New Zealand

Penguin Books Ltd, Registered Offices:
Harmondsworth, Middlesex, England

First published by Onyx, an imprint of New American Library,
a division of Penguin Books USA Inc.

First Printing, February, 1993
10 9 8 7 6 5 4 3 2 1

For my mother, with love.

Give me that man
That is not passion's slave, and I will wear him
In my heart's core, ay, in my heart of heart.

Shakespeare
Hamlet

ONE

Istanbul, July 27, 1991

His tall, lean frame standing well above the crowd, his intense gray eyes searching past the endless row of shops, Matt McKenzie cut through the throng of people with the slow but steady stride of the hunter. The Grand Bazaar in Istanbul's old quarter of Stamboul was a territory he knew well. A self-contained city, gated, domed, walled, and mysterious, it was a labyrinth of twisted streets and alleyways, some so narrow only a very slim Stamboullu could get through them.

More than four thousand shops and hundreds of stalls bulged with merchandise for every taste and purse—brassware, alabaster, jewelry, fabric, fake antiques, and, of course, the largest assortment of Turkish rugs anywhere in the world.

As always in this late-afternoon heat, the air was foul. Already heavily polluted by industrialization and the constant waterway traffic on the Bosporus, the city's air mingled the smells of spices from the nearby Egyptian Market and the garbage that littered the streets. Beautiful, enigmatic Istanbul was also known as one of the dirtiest cities in the world.

He should have been exhausted. In the last twenty-four hours, he had traveled more than six thousand miles and had only dozed off for an hour or two. Yet except for a light stubble he hadn't bothered to shave, there was an alertness about him, a toughness that made other men instantly wary and compelled them to move out of his way.

He was accustomed to long trips. And he was accustomed to the hunt. It was one of the characteristics that made him so good at what he did: tracking down stolen art.

Over six feet tall, with muscular shoulders and a chest to match, he had inherited the McKenzies' light Scottish looks, the lean face, sandy hair, and watchful gray eyes. Normally his handsome features wouldn't have betrayed his anxiety, for his occupation demanded a cool head and total control of his emotions. But these were not normal circumstances. He wasn't here to find a stolen painting or a rare object d'art for one of his clients. He had come to Istanbul because Paige, the only woman he had ever loved, was in trouble.

When Tom DiMaggio, his friend and partner, had walked into their private investigation agency three days ago in New York and told him he suspected Matt's former wife of smuggling illegally excavated antiquities from Turkey, his first reaction had been one of absolute denial. Paige a smuggler? That was ridiculous. The girl didn't have a crooked bone in her beautiful body. Educated at the University of California at Santa Barbara, where she had graduated with a master's degree in fine arts, she had built her reputation as an art dealer on knowledge, good taste, and an unquestionable integrity.

But that was the Paige he had known. Now that she was engaged to San Francisco publishing tycoon Jeremy Newman, himself an avid art collector, who the hell knew what she was like? Or what motivated her?

He had excluded greed. Paige was a wealthy woman in her own right, and too much of an art lover to capitalize on it in a less than honorable way. Her clients, on the other hand, Newman included, had different visions of what collecting was all about. For some, it was a multimillion-dollar business, for others, the solution to an insatiable need to possess only the most exquisite and rarest of objects, no matter the cost, no matter the risk.

And the risks were plenty. In the last ten years, the antiquities trade, controlled by the Munich-based antiquities mafia, had become an international business with revenues close to a billion dollars a year. As the world's number-one supplier of classical antiquities—all illegal—Turkey had become the focal point for dealers and collectors all over the world.

Tom had been investigating the disappearance of a statue from the Antalya Museum in southwestern Turkey. In searching through a list of dealers connected with members of the antiquities mafia, he had come upon the name of Paige McKenzie. Intrigued, he had investigated further and learned through one of his many contacts in Munich that two weeks ago, a shipment labeled "plaster casts for dolls," but suspected of containing something else, had left Istanbul for the Bavarian capital. A few days later, Paige had arrived in Munich and made arrangements for that shipment to be sent to the States.

It hadn't taken Tom long to realize that the casts had been used as a "ghost" shipment, a ploy commonly used for transporting objects far more valuable than those declared.

Torn between his decision to stay out of Paige's life and his need to help her, Matt had thought about the matter for two days, furious at himself for still caring, for still wanting to protect her.

Over and over he'd told himself that Paige was a big girl. She knew the risks involved in this business as well as he did. If indeed she was in trouble, let that stuffy jerk she was about to marry get her out of the mess, since he was probably the one responsible for it.

Also, as Tom had pointed out, it was entirely possible that the smuggling operation would go undetected by the authorities, as so many of them did nowadays. But Matt hadn't shared his friend's optimism. Eleven years in the FBI had taught him that no matter how clever smugglers were, Interpol, as well as Matt's former colleagues in the bureau, were never very far behind. If caught and charged with illegal art dealing, Paige would not only lose her gallery, but she could face a two- to five-year prison sentence, depending on the nature of the theft.

In the end, Matt had decided to go to Istanbul and investigate the matter himself.

His first stop had been Munich. The Bavarian capital, because of its lax laws concerning stolen art, had been the center of smuggling operations for years. Matt had many friends there, all of whom had been helpful to him in the past. But only one had the connections he needed for this particular job.

He hadn't been disappointed. Keleb Arzan, a Turk of Kurdish extraction and one of Munich's most reliable art dealers, had provided him with the name of a man in Istanbul who might be able to help him.

"His name is Tariq Mazur," Keleb had told him. "He owns a brass shop in Istanbul's Grand Bazaar. The man has an incredible, and frightening, memory. Hardly any activity, legal or otherwise, is conducted without him knowing its most sordid details. He's a greedy man who makes his living by selling information to people such as you. But don't expect him to back anything he tells you in court or in front of a witness. And don't make the mistake of showing up with a tape recorder in your pocket. The man doesn't like to be crossed. You do, and he'll cut your heart out and have it for breakfast. It's that simple."

"Any weaknesses?"

"Only one—young girls. I can help you with that."

"How much money is he going to want?"

"Twenty-five thousand. Possibly more. Take fifty and see how it goes."

Matt had winced at the amount. He had only brought twenty thousand dollars with him, and the account the agency maintained in Munich for emergencies such as this had been depleted during Tom's visit. Fortunately, the New York banks were still open when he called, and four hours later, thirty thousand dollars, all the money he had in the world, had been transferred into the agency's account.

"Hey, mister," a merchant called out in English as Matt passed his display of hand-knotted rugs. "You want beautiful carpet duty free? Buy here. Look," he added, as he lovingly stroked a rug in vivid shades of red and orange, "made with the wool of six-month-old lambs. Soft as a woman's skin. Come. Touch. Very good stuff. And very cheap."

Matt ignored him, as he did the other merchants, and kept walking, following the directions a shopkeeper had given him earlier. At last he reached the Street of the Copperworkers at the bazaar's southern end, and found Mazur's shop, sandwiched between two others. Inside, a young boy with sharp brown eyes and tightly curled black hair looked up.

"I'm here to see Tariq Mazur," Matt told him.

Although Matt had spoken in Turkish, the boy, no more than thirteen or fourteen, lowered the Tarzan comic book he had been reading, gave Matt a quick but thorough appraisal, and answered him in English. "What do you want with Tariq?"

"It's personal. Tell him President Grover Cleveland and four of his brothers are here to see him." Keleb had told him to start with five thousand dollars and wait for Tariq's reaction.

"Wait here," the boy said.

Less than a minute later, he reappeared. Holding a green beaded curtain to the side, he motioned for Matt to follow him. The room Matt entered was smoky and smelled of the sickening jasmine-scented water the Turks used in their water pipes. As the boy disappeared, Matt waited for his eyes to adjust to the dim light.

Sitting on a cushion, drawing on a hookah, was a grotesquely obese man with a round, bald head, a bulging belly, and massive gold rings on eight of his ten pudgy fingers. He reminded Matt of a fatter, uglier version of the late actor Sydney Greenstreet.

Sucking on his water pipe, the man watched Matt through sleepy, half-closed eyes, then, removing the long contraption from his mouth and propping it against his chest, he clapped his hands twice. At once, a huge man built like a Sumo wrestler materialized and expertly frisked Matt before nodding to Mazur and disappearing.

The Turk smiled, exposing two gold teeth on one side of his mouth, and motioned to the cushion across from him. "Please sit down, Mr. Cleveland," he said in accented but excellent English. His greedy eyes gleamed as he spoke the name of the former American president. "Or do you prefer to be called something else?"

"I usually go by the name of McKenzie," Matt said. "Matt McKenzie." He started to extend his hand, but the man across from him didn't seem to notice the gesture, or chose to ignore it. Matt withdrew his hand, remembering Keleb's advice to be patient and play the man's game. "I appreciate your seeing me," he said, doing his best to sound respectful. "I know how valuable your time is."

The Turk picked up his pipe again and started to draw. "Let me see your credentials first, then I shall decide whether or not we can do business together."

Matt realized that Tariq expected a five-thousand-dollar advance with no guarantee that his information was worth the retainer. For a moment, he was tempted to hold back, then thought better of it. Although the oriental custom of bargaining for merchandise was expected in Istanbul, bargaining for information was taboo. Reluctantly, Matt pulled out five one-thousand-dollar bills from his breast pocket and handed them to the fat man.

Tariq quickly folded the bills and slipped them into his shirt pocket. "What do you want to know, Mr. McKenzie?"

Matt repeated what he had told Keleb a few hours earlier. For a moment he had thought of leaving Paige's name out of the conversation, thinking that it might give Tariq additional leverage once he made the connection. But Keleb had advised him against it.

"He probably knows her name already. And if he finds out you've withheld something he feels he should know, he'll throw you out and keep your money."

When Matt finished his story, Tariq shook his head in wonder. "Why would you want to help an ex-wife?"

"Because she's innocent and I don't want her to take the fall for someone else."

"Is that all?" Through a cloud of smoke, the man's shrewd gaze surveyed Matt.

"That's all."

"Or is it possible that you still love this woman?"

Matt shot the Turk a quick, speculative glance. The man's voice and eyes may have looked drowsy from all that sweet smoke, but his mind was crystal clear. "Yes," he said, surprised to hear himself admit something this private to a man like Tariq. "It's possible."

Tariq let out a soft chuckle that sounded like a gurgle. "You Americans. You amuse me. You all look so invincible, so sure of yourselves, as if the whole world were your harem. And yet you allow your emotions to rule you—always." He shrugged as he brought the pipe back to his fat lips. "But I'm a reasonable man. I understand about matters of the heart." He chuckled again. "I have a great fondness for women myself. But then I guess you already know that."

"I know you like pretty young girls."

Tariq bowed his head in silent agreement.

"In another thirty seconds," Matt continued, glancing at his watch, "your shopkeeper will come in to let you know that a young girl by the name of Zelah is here to see you. If you care to take a look at her before we start doing business, you'll find her more than satisfactory."

A visible shiver of pleasure coursed through the man's repulsive body, and for a moment, Matt felt sorry for the girl. He felt sorry for all the girls who had had to suffer the amorous exploits of a man like Tariq Mazur. But Zelah had not been forced to accept the assignment, and her services would be well rewarded.

Moments later, the young boy Matt had talked to earlier came in, squatted by Tariq's side, and whispered something into his ear. With a swiftness that was astounding for a man his size, the Turk stood up and wobbled toward the door. When he came back, his eyes gleamed with lust and a smile of satisfaction was spread across his thick face. Behind him, the huge bodyguard followed, carrying two cups of çay, the strong tea, which in the last few years had replaced coffee as the Turkish national drink.

"I'm quite familiar with the shipment you mentioned," Tariq said, taking back his place on the cushion and picking up one of the tiny, tulip-shaped cups. "But to hear what I know will cost you an additional twenty thousand dollars.

Matt had expected that much, but he hesitated, for effect, and to discourage the fat man from asking more. Then he sighed and removed another four stacks of bills from his pocket.

"Two weeks ago, a crate containing the item you described was sent to a Munich gallery by the name of Appolo," Tariq said. "However, I have heard that the contents were not a set of doll casts, but a marble carving of one of the twelve labors of Hercules, removed from an ancient sarcophagus found in a Turkish farm field in the mid-1970s. Over the years, all twelve carvings have been removed from the sarcophagus and sold to various collectors and museums for a great deal of money. To this date, only six of those carvings have been recovered by the Turkish government. The rest are believed to be in the hands of private collectors."

"What happened when the crate arrived at the Appolo Gallery?"

"The buyer's representative went to Munich, inspected the contents, and approved them for shipment to the United States—San Francisco to be exact."

"And that representative's name?"

Tariq let out a long stream of gray smoke. "Paige McKenzie of Santa Barbara, California."

Matt felt the sweat on his back turn cold. Tariq Mazur had just confirmed his worst fears.

TWO

"Well, Daddy, what do you think?"

Paige McKenzie propped the two watercolors she had brought from Beauchamp on the credenza of her father's study and took a step back to admire the effect. "The Boudin beach scene or the Van Pol fruit bowl?"

She spun around, her tumble of loose, dark curls swinging around her shoulders, one proud eyebrow lifting in that cool, aristocratic way she had of commanding attention.

Looking at her, Paul Granger felt an involuntary pinch in his heart as he was reminded of how much she looked like her mother. Not as classically beautiful as Ann, she nonetheless had that same proud carriage, that same long, elegant neck, that same wide mouth with the full, sensual lower lip. She even had the same raven-black hair. Only her eyes, clear blue like his, identified her as a Granger.

"You choose, darling," he said, enjoying her enthusiasm. "After all, you're the expert."

"But it's *your* birthday present. And you're the one who will have to live with it. Unless," she added, her eyes alight with humor, "you would like to impress that impressionist buff you've been dating, in which case I have a lovely Van Gogh watercolor at the gallery that I'm sure would dazzle her."

Paige's smile dissolved into a giggle as her father's handsome face pinked under the tan. Embarrassment wasn't an emotion one usually associated with Santa Barbara's most confident criminal judge. "Why, Daddy, I believe you're blushing."

"And you love it, don't you? You love seeing the old man flustered."

"What I love," she said, coming to stand in front of him and adjusting the Windsor knot in his tie, "is to see you happy."

"I am happy, darling. But not for the reasons you think. Sheilah Potts is just an out-of-town colleague I've been entertaining for a few days. That's all."

Paige didn't hide her disappointment. At fifty-four, with only a few lines around his eyes and a splattering of gray throughout his wavy brown hair, her father exuded strength and a youthful vitality many women in Santa Barbara admired. But although he'd had a few affairs over the years, none had ever been serious enough to incite him to marry again. Once she had hoped he and her Aunt Kate could have found happiness together. But Kate, whose only passion was her antiques gallery, hadn't been interested in a relationship with anyone and eventually, Paige had abandoned her fruitless attempts at matchmaking.

On an impulse, she hugged her father, something she didn't do nearly as often as she wanted to these days. "Oh, Daddy. Everything has worked out just fine for both of us, hasn't it?"

Paul returned the hug. A couple of years ago, when Paige was still married to Matt, he would have agreed with her. Now he wasn't so sure. In spite of her assurance that she was happy, this upcoming marriage to Jeremy seemed all wrong to him. But now wasn't the time to burden her with his doubts. "Yes, darling, it has." His eyes roamed over the beloved face. "Thanks to you, to the way you looked after me all these years, this old grouch turned out pretty well after all."

Paige squeezed his hand, proud to have inherited his strength, his zest for life, and his need to survive. Although her mother's unexpected departure twenty-four years ago had been a terrible shock to him and had forced him to pull out of the race for Santa Barbara's district attorney, he had rebounded quickly. As one of the state's most talented criminal layers, he had had too much pride, too much integrity, to allow his personal life to interfere with his professional obligations.

It had been different for Paige. Only seven years old at the time, her whole life had centered around her mother. For a long time after that fateful Christmas Eve, she had roamed through the Grangers' huge house, crying and blaming herself, certain that her mother had left because of some horrible deed on her part.

In time her anguish had turned to anger, and then to a burning hatred that had consumed her for years, well into womanhood. Matt McKenzie had changed all that. Matt was an expert at avoiding wasteful emotions. "Save your energies for love," he had told her once. "In the end, that's the only thing that will sustain you."

He had been right. Matt's love for her, and hers for him, had transformed her. In his arms, her hostilities toward a mother she no longer knew had been forgotten. Inhibitions had been shed like the clothes he so expertly peeled off her skin. He'd brought her pleasures and sensations she'd never experienced before and she had savored each one with great gusto, giving all she had in return—giving as she would never give again. Not even to Jeremy Newman, whom she would be marrying in a few months.

"Something wrong, darling?"

Her father's concerned tone startled her, and she silently scolded herself. Why, after two long years, did thoughts of her exhusband keep intruding with such intensity? What perverted pleasure did she derive from always associating the best times of her life with Matt McKenzie?

"Actually, yes, there is," she said, forcing her tone to be light and playful. "It's about my fiesta party on Saturday evening. I haven't received your RSVP yet." Knowing how he hated to give up his weekend fishing trips, she added, "You wouldn't be thinking of skipping it, would you?"

"And miss the best party of the year? Not a chance."

"Good. Because Jeremy and I will make our engagement official that night, and we want all those we love to be present." Although she pretended to look at the two watercolors still propped up on the credenza, she cast her father a covert glance. He had never tried to hide the fact that he thought Jeremy wasn't right for her, that deep down he hoped she and Matt, whom he loved like a son, would somehow patch things up and get back together.

Paul caught her gaze and held it. "Are you sure about this decision, darling? Sure you won't regret it later?"

Paige had asked herself that same question many times over the last few weeks, and each time, the answer had been a resounding no. Jeremy was a wonderful, loving man who made her feel wanted, and more important, he made her feel needed, something she hadn't experienced with Matt during the last half of their marriage. "Of course, I'm sure," she said with a laugh. "Would I have accepted Jeremy's proposal if I weren't?"

"And you are completely over Matt?"

Although the question brought another flush to her cheeks and she took a couple of seconds to answer, when she did, her tone was light and breezy. "Completely, Daddy." She brushed an invisible spec of dusk from his lapel. "And now, if you'll tell me which of those two prints you prefer, I'll take the other one back to Beauchamp and be on my way. I have a lunch date with Mindy and you know how she hates to wait."

Paul smiled as he continued to watch her. "I'll take the Van Pol."

Paige nodded and kissed him on the cheek. "Good choice." In a smooth gesture, she swept her purse from his desk, hooked it over her right shoulder, and walked toward the door in her usual brisk stride. Once there, she turned. "Enjoy your weekend, Daddy. But don't overdo it. You'll need your dancing legs for my party next Saturday night."

In an instant, she was gone, leaving Paul chuckling.

* * *

Spotting a parking space half a block from the Santa Barbara County Courthouse, Paige slid her 1959 red MG convertible along the curb, knowing she'd find nothing nearer Mindy's shop at this time of day. Opening the door, she swung her long, shapely legs out, noticing, with a certain pleasure, the admiring look they drew from a motorist driving by.

At thirty-one, Paige personified what people called the "California look." Unlike other art dealers who liked to dress for success, Paige dressed for her own pleasure, favoring modern clothes and colors that were nothing short of electrifying.

On this clear, sunny day, she had chosen to be nothing less than brilliant by wearing a hot pink lycra dress that revealed long, bare, and glorious legs, comfortable black, open-toe sandals, and a wide straw hat with its pink front rim turned up. Although her late grandmother had left her a safeful of expensive jewelry, Paige never wore it, preferring the versatility of costume jewelry, such as the green dolphin pin she wore on the rim of her hat, or the long black and pink glass earrings that shimmered with every toss of her head.

Walking in her breezy, easy style, she crossed the street, turned left at the art museum, heading south on State Street, where her best friend's furniture shop was located.

State Street was a broad, tree-lined artery that cut through the center of town, connecting Stern Wharf to Mission Santa Barbara north of the city. On each side of the street, city workers were already busy hanging flags, banners, and streamers in preparation for Santa Barbara's Old Spanish Days, a five-day celebration that would fill the streets with music, laughter, and endless parades.

Of all the places Paige had visited over the years, Santa Barbara remained her favorite. For awhile after her divorce from Matt, she had considered leaving California and moving to London, where one of her college friends now ran a successful art gallery. But in the end she couldn't bear to leave her hometown. There were too many memories attached to it, and although not all of them were happy ones, few places in the world could equal Santa Barbara for beauty and for what many locals simply called the "good life."

Nestled between the Santa Inez mountains and the Pacific Ocean, Santa Barbara is a sun-drenched vision of red tile roofs, palm trees, and flower-bedecked courtyards. As a beach community, it could have looked like dozens of others along the golden coast. But with its unique architecture and its decidedly Spanish flavor, it had become a pleasure of the senses, where beauty, both natural and man-made, prevailed.

Paige reached her friend's shop, appropriately named "For The Fun Of It," in less than five minutes. As she opened the door, a bell tinkled once.

"I'm in here," Mindy called out from the back.

Paige made her way around several groupings of postmodern furniture in a variety of rainbow colors, and into the atelier Mindy playfully called "the loony room." There, only a privileged few could see the artist at work.

The room, with two French doors that opened on a sunny courtyard, was filled with more of Mindy's quirky, flamboyant furniture—some finished, some awaiting a last coat of Day-Glo paint.

Although postmodern furniture had never attracted Paige, she had high regard for Mindy's free-spirited genius. Each of her designs was a one-of-a-kind creation that made shopping for furniture a visual experience people never forgot. If indeed tradition was nonexistent here, imagination was inspiring. It manifested itself in the chartreuse television cabinet in the shape of a puffy cloud, in the purple cubistic sofa, and in the fiberglass and bronze chest that a museum of modern art in Milan had just purchased for twelve thousand dollars and would display next month in its permanent exhibit of "Artists of the Nineties."

Smiling, Paige stood in the doorway, watching her friend. Shorter than Paige's five foot seven by three or four inches, Mindy Haliday was an attractive young woman with very short, black hair, large dark eyes and the flawless olive complexion she had inherited from her Hispanic ancestors.

The two women had been friends since the third grade and except for two short absences from each other—one when Mindy had been attending L.A.'s Chouinard Art Institute and the second when Paige had been married to Matt and living in New York—they had been inseparable.

Wearing paint-stained overalls, Mindy sat on her haunches, facing something that vaguely resembled a floor lamp. After scrolling her now famous signature on the round black base, she stood up and turned to Paige. "Well, what do you think?"

Paige studied the zigzag of neon tubes attached to a tall, black rod. "What is it?"

"Oh, come on, McKenzie. Use your imagination."

"A portable shower?" Paige teased.

Mindy heaved a heavy sigh. "You're hopeless. It's a floor lamp."

Paige kept a straight face. "You're joking."

"Watch." Bending, Mindy pulled a retractable electrical cord from the base and plugged it into the wall. The twelve tubes were instantly ablaze with vivid colors ranging from purple-blue to carnation red. It may not have been the most practical lamp to read by, but the effect was as spectacular as a California sunset.

"Do you really expect to sell this?" Paige asked, feigning skepticism.

Mindy gave her friend a smug look. "It's already sold, smarty-pants. An L.A. director bought it for twenty-five hundred dollars and asked me to design an entire bedroom set around it."

Paige sighed. "And I thought we were in a recession."

"We are. But people appreciate good, fun furniture. Not like in that museum of yours where one has to be a Rockefeller in order to afford one of your 'used' trinkets."

At Paige's exaggerated outraged expression, Mindy, who always enjoyed showing their disparity when it came to art, grinned, stepped over a tangerine clock she had been painting earlier, judging from the orange streaks in her hair, and kissed Paige on the cheek. "I couldn't resist that. Truce?"

"Only if lunch is on you—an expensive lunch."

"Deal." Mindy stepped out of her overalls. Underneath she wore multicolored leggings and an oversize white cotton blouse.

"How was the reunion between you and Larry?" Paige asked with a grin. Mindy's husband, a merchant marine officer, spent long periods at sea, and it wasn't unusual for the young couple to hibernate for days at a time when he came home.

Mindy fluffed up her hair, her eyes shining with glee. "Explosive. There's nothing more arousing than a man who's been at sea for six months. You ought to try it sometime."

Paige smiled, feeling that old familiar pinch in her heart. There had been a time when she had known exactly what passion did to two people. "Did you call me here to brag?" she teased.

"No. I asked you over because I found out something I think you should know."

"What?"

"I'll tell you over a crab salad and a tall, frosty glass of iced tea. Andria's Harborside okay? Or are you in the mood for something more exotic?"

"The Harborside's fine."

A few minutes later, they were settled at a table overlooking the marina. "So what's up?" Paige asked.

Mindy surveyed her friend for a moment, marveling at how self-confident and serene she looked these days. It was quite a change from the disillusioned young woman who had returned home two years ago, feeling she had failed not only herself but the entire world as well. In time, however, and in her own inimitable way, Paige had picked herself up again, brushed away the scars left by her divorce, and dived into her work with renewed passion.

Beautiful as well as successful, she didn't lack admirers, many of whom would have married her in a heartbeat if she had given them the slightest encouragement. But only the handsome, charismatic, and very persistent Jeremy Newman had been able to change her mind about men.

Mindy had never liked Jeremy. The man was too condescending, too rich, and too damned old. "Do you love him?" she'd asked Paige the day her friend had called to say she had accepted Jeremy's marriage proposal. "Enough to spend the rest of your life with him?"

Paige's answer had been rather evasive. She had talked of affection, trust, commitment, and said nothing about love, about passion, about excitement—all the emotions she had experienced with Matt.

"I've had enough excitement to last me a lifetime," she had told a skeptical Mindy. "And anyway, I like my life just the way it is now. Peaceful and pleasant."

And now, all that was about to change.

"Mindy," Paige said with a flash of annoyance in her blue eyes, for patience wasn't one of her virtues. "Stop watching me with that weird look on your face and tell me what's going on."

Mindy took a deep breath. "I ran into Rocky this morning," she said, watching her friend's face tense at the mention of the McKenzies' ranch foreman."

"And?"

"He told me Matt is coming back to California."

Paige wasn't sure which emotion she experienced first—shock, bitterness, or anger. In the crowded dining room, the sound of conversation faded into a soft buzz, and it took her a full minute before she could speak again. "By coming back," she said, watching the waitress place a glass of Chardonnay in front of her. "I assume you mean for a visit."

"No. I mean permanently. Rocky said Matt was tired of the rat race and was coming back to help his grandfather run the ranch."

"What about his job at Worldwide Investigations?"

"He quit."

So he had finally done it. He had finally taken her advice and followed his dream. She picked up her glass and sipped her wine.

Why now? she thought, remembering the many bitter arguments she and Matt had had concerning the job that took him away so much of the time. Why hadn't he made this decision to come back here two years ago when she had begged him to leave Worldwide Investigations? When the move could have saved their marriage?

"Paige, are you all right?"

"Of course I'm all right. What else did Rocky say?"

"That Matt's arriving on Saturday."

Saturday. The day of her party. The day she and Jeremy had chosen to announce their engagement. How perfectly timed. How perfectly . . . Matt.

To give herself something to do, she opened her purse and pulled out a gold compact. Thank God her coloring was back to normal, although her eyes were much too bright.

"Well," Mindy said, with a gleam of anticipation in her eyes. "What's the verdict? Are you happy? Indifferent? What?"

Paige snapped her compact shut. "Of course I'm not happy. Whatever gave you the idea I might be?"

"I just thought—"

"Matt is a troublemaker, Mindy. Surely you haven't forgotten that? Remember when he crashed my grandmother's Christmas party four years ago? I wouldn't put it past him to try to repeat the performance."

"He didn't actually *crash* the party, did he? And anyway, he behaved perfectly, if I recall."

Paige took a long soothing breath. Mindy had always had a soft spot where Matt was concerned. A lot of people did. Well, the McKenzie charm might work on some, but it wouldn't work on her. Not this time. Whatever Matt was up to, he would be wasting his time.

As for his return to California, why should she care that he had suddenly decided to become a gentleman rancher? It had nothing to do with her. The Santa Inez Valley might only be thirty miles from Santa Barbara, but for all she and Matt had in common these days, they might as well be from different planets.

Totally back in control now, she picked up her menu and gave Mindy a ready smile. "Shall we order? I'm famished."

Mindy didn't miss her friend's forced smile, the aloof lift of her eyebrow, a familiar expression that was as defensive as it was engaging. But she wasn't fooled for one second. She had known Paige far too long to believe this indifference was anything but an act. For in spite of the fact that she was about to marry Jeremy Newman, Paige was a one-man woman. And that man was Matt McKenzie. How Paige proposed to deal with his imminent return now that she was engaged to his archenemy was anyone's guess. But one thing was certain, Mindy thought as she opened her menu. It would not be boring.

THREE

Kate Madison sat in the elegant, antiques-filled living room of her Victorian home on Olive Street with her hands clenched and her mouth set in a tight line. On the coffee table in front of her was a copy of today's *Santa Barbara News Press*.

Like a magnet, Kate's gaze was drawn back to the photograph of Jeremy Newman and Paige as they smiled happily at the camera. Underneath the snapshot was a short caption. "San Francisco's most eligible bachelor still refuses to comment on his growing relationship with beautiful Santa Barbara art dealer, Paige McKenzie. Sources reveal, however, that wedding bells will soon be ringing for the lovely couple."

As a sob rose and caught in her throat, Kate closed her eyes. Even after all those years, all the misery Jeremy had put her through, the longing in her heart was so acutely painful, the memories of her past relationship so vivid, that for a brief moment they overpowered everything else.

Aware that another excruciating headache was beginning to build, Kate stood up and absentmindedly massaged her temples as she paced the room.

She found pacing soothing. She and her sister Ann had done a lot of it during their childhood. Of course, in those days the pacing had been due to their excitement as they shared each other's dreams. How young and carefree they had been then, both so hopeful, waiting for Prince Charming to come and take them away from their small New Jersey town.

She let out a small, shaky laugh. Her prince had come, all right. But instead of sweeping her away to his magic kingdom and loving her forever after, he had turned her life into a nightmare.

Kate stopped in front of a Queen Ann lowboy and glanced at her reflection in the French gilt mirror above it. Almost unconsciously, her hand went to her hair to straighten a wave, a gesture that was hardly necessary, since she was always perfectly groomed.

Although she was thirty pounds overweight and rather plain looking, fifty-two year old Kate Madison succeeded in projecting an elegant, sophisticated image, much of which was enhanced by her reputation as one of the country's foremost art and antiques dealers. She had close-set brown eyes, forgettable but cleverly made-up features, and short, mousy brown hair rendered thick and glossy through the magic of beauty salons.

She had never married, for few men knew her well enough to appreciate the passion that had once burned beneath that plain, rather passive facade. Whenever she needed someone to escort her to one of the many functions to which she was invited, she called on one of her male friends, or on her brother-in-law, Paul Granger, who was always happy to escort her anywhere she wished.

She had worked hard to get where she was today, studying, cleaning other people's houses, waiting tables, and allowing nothing to stand in the way of her dream.

She hadn't counted on love. A love so powerful, so destructive, that for awhile it had destroyed all her values, all she had ever believed in.

As always when she thought of Jeremy, her hand went to her throat, to the gold chain and antique Victorian locket he had given her years ago as a symbol of his love. How foolish and naive she had been then to think that a man like Jeremy Newman was capable of love. All he had ever wanted was to use her, to exploit her. And when someone else better had come along, he had discarded her like an old shoe.

Yet in spite of his rejection and the realization that he

no longer needed her, Kate had never lost hope that someday Jeremy would come back to her. Four years ago, when, thanks to Paige, he had agreed to do business with Kate's gallery again, that hope had soared. But the euphoric moment had been short lived. Paige was the one he had requested as his art consultant. And eventually, the inevitable had happened. Paige had fallen in love with him, and he with her.

In the mirror, Kate watched as her trembling fingers gripped the precious pendant, then, with a vicious tug ripped the chain from her neck. Opening her hand, she stared at the open locket and Paige's picture nestled in the tiny oval space. But it was no longer her niece's beloved face she saw, but that of the *other* woman, the woman who would soon be sharing Jeremy's bed, the woman who would be returning his kisses, responding to the touch of his clever hands, hearing his words of passion.

With a cry of rage, Kate tore the picture from the locket and flung it across the room. Then, almost immediately, she dropped to her knees, lowered her head in her hands, and burst into deep, wrenching sobs.

It was happening all over again, she thought, struggling against the wave of emotions that threatened to overpower her. She was losing control, losing all rationality, all sense of right and wrong.

She remained in that prostrated position for a long time. When, at last, the sobs subsided, Kate stood up, walked over to where Paige's picture and the locket had fallen, and picked them up. Her body, so rigid before, now trembled uncontrollably at the horrible, destructive thought that had flashed through her mind a moment ago.

"I won't let it happen, baby," she murmured, smoothing the picture and tucking it back into the locket. "I won't allow myself to hurt you. Ever."

A hundred and twenty-five miles northeast of Rio, on a small peninsula called Bùzios, Jeremy Newman gazed at the star-studded sky as he lay naked in front of the dark, silver-streaked Atlantic Ocean.

It was a splendid night. A night filled with warm, fragrant air and the muted sound of a samba drifting in from the chartered yacht anchored twenty feet away. It was also a night to celebrate, for two days from now, he and Paige would make their engagement official and announce it to the world. To commemorate the occasion, Jeremy had wanted to give his fiancée the rarest, most exquisite ring man had ever set eyes on.

He'd searched a long time for this particular black pearl. And as always, his patience had been rewarded. He'd found the ring right here in Bùzios, in the possession of a wealthy South American jeweler.

The Brazilian had bargained long and hard, reminding Jeremy that this particular pearl had come from the peaceful lagoon of Marutea in the Tuamotu archipelago, where the giant black-lipped oyster called the *Pinctada margaritifera* produced the largest and finest black pearl in the world.

Jeremy hadn't needed the sales pitch. He had brought with him a Sotheby's jewelry expert who had confirmed the pearl's rarity and estimated the value of the ring at half a million dollars—one hundred thousand more than the Brazilian was asking. Jeremy, who, in spite of his wealth, never passed up a bargain, had bought the ring on the spot.

Hearing a faint snore, he turned to look at the naked, coffee-colored girl lying on the chaise next to him. Alea had fallen asleep. Which wasn't too surprising considering they had spent the day swimming, diving, and making love.

Smiling, he brought a tall, frosty glass of rum and lime to his lips and sipped the tangy drink slowly while the fingers of his right hand stroked the woman's thigh. In a little while, he would wake her up. She might be tired, but he was in top form, and definitely ready for one last romp before he went back to the States.

At fifty-seven, Jeremy was a handsome, well-mannered

man who bore a certain resemblance to the late Cary Grant. His eyes, deeply set, were dark and alert, the eyes of a predator, eyes that could turn from caressing to ruthless in the time it took one to blink.

Proud of his lean, hard physique, he kept himself in excellent physical condition with two sets of tennis a day, jogging, and an active, although prudent, sex life.

He was a wealthy and powerful man, one of San Francisco's most enduring tycoons as well as the publisher of the *San Francisco Globe,* the multi-Pulitzer prize-winning newspaper his father had established at the turn of the century.

At one time, money and the power it afforded those who had a great deal of it had been foremost in his mind. But now, after nearly thirty-five years of undisputed success, he preferred to spend his time indulging in the finer things in life, such as sailing, raising polo ponies, and adding to his already immense art collection.

His art, which he displayed in all four of his residences as well as in his San Francisco museum, had an estimated value of over five hundred million dollars, although a rival newspaper had once hinted that it might be more.

Unlike the late Armand Hammer, described in *Time* magazine as "a man with a rage for fame and no eye for art," Jeremy's taste approached the sublime. He was known in the trade as a "truc collector," a man who acquired beautiful works of art not so much for investment, but for the sheer pleasure they brought him and others.

He was a formidable adversary, a man few dared to challenge—personally or professionally. A man, some thought, who might be able to put this country back on track.

But when the Republican Party had approached him regarding the possibility of becoming a senatorial candidate, Jeremy had turned them down. He abhorred politics. The power might have been fun, but he was too spirited to be governed by rules and ethics. Besides, at the time he had needed all his energy to woo his other passion—the beautiful Paige McKenzie.

McKenzie. Oh, how he despised that name. And how eager he was to have Paige change it. For awhile, his hatred for the McKenzies had threatened to extend to Paige simply because, by marrying Matt four years ago, she had taken the hated name.

Her marriage had been a severe blow to Jeremy's ego. But at the same time, he had understood how easy it was for an innocent young woman to be swept off her feet when a McKenzie came calling. Jeremy had experienced that destructive charm firsthand, thirty-six years ago, when his fiancée, Caroline Wescott, had left him for Matt's father only two months before she and Jeremy were due to marry.

The McKenzies had been his *bête noire* ever since. And when, six years ago, Matt McKenzie had burst into his house, accusing him of murdering his father, Jeremy had sworn that someday he would get even with him for all the humiliation he had put him through.

And now at last he was about to have the sweetest revenge of all by marrying the only woman Matt had ever loved. For although Paige had long since put her former husband out of her mind—and her heart—Jeremy doubted Matt had been able to do the same. No man could ever love a woman like Paige and then forget her.

Jeremy had never understood how men could lose their head over a woman. He certainly never had. And never would. Love hadn't been an essential part of his growing up. His parents had seemed quite content without it, and so had he. If he had missed it at all during his early childhood, he couldn't remember.

And so instead of concentrating on the complicated aspects of love, he had focused his attentions on needs, challenges, fulfillments, victories. The kind of victory he was experiencing at this very moment as he thought about Paige and the fact that she would soon be Mrs. Jeremy Newman.

The young woman who lay by his side now was nothing more than a pleasant and temporary diversion, for Jeremy was a virile, healthy man with needs and desires that had to be satisfied. And since Paige had insisted they wait until their wedding night before becoming lovers, Jeremy didn't see any reason to deprive himself of pleasures he considered vital to his well-being.

As his hand reached the furry triangle between the girl's thighs, she rolled over to her side, her long cinnamon leg lifting and clamping over his hand. At the sight of his growing erection, she laughed softly and reached for him, her fingertips moving expertly up and down his penis.

"Feel like a little swim, lover?" Her voice was as smooth as honey, her guttural island accent as arousing as her touch.

He turned around and kissed her right breast, taking the small, dark nipple into his mouth as the thrill of anticipation made his pulse race faster. But as his mouth started to move lower, the telephone that never left his side rang.

"Don't answer it," the girl whispered in his ear.

Her hot, moist breath was almost more than he could bear. "You go ahead," he urged. "I'll be with you in a moment."

As he picked up the receiver, he watched her superb body undulate slowly toward the calm shimmering water. "Hello?" he said, his eyes fastened on the round, firm buttocks.

"Mr. Newman?"

He recognized Chu Seng's voice instantly, and, knowing only an emergency would make his butler call him, he tensed up, wondering if something had happened to Paige. "What is it, Chu Seng?"

"I thought you'd like to know that Mr. Matthew Mc-Kenzie is coming back to California, sir. For good."

Jeremy's jaw tightened and his eyes grew hard. In the distance, the girl went out of focus. "What the hell are you talking about?"

"One of our stable boys at the ranch heard that Mr. McKenzie left Worldwide Investigation and is returning to the Santa Inez Valley to work with his grandfather. He's due in day after tomorrow."

For a moment, Jeremy sat very still, absorbing the news, yet unable to think. Then, pulling himself together, he glanced at his Louis Vuitton I world-time watch, which simultaneously displayed the current time in several major cities around the world. If he took the yacht back to Rio in the morning, he could take the two o'clock flight to San Francisco, rest a little, and then fly to Santa Barbara before McKenzie had time to do anything cute.

"Thank you, Chu Seng," he said at last. "I'll be back home as soon as I can. Please have whatever I'll need for my trip to Santa Barbara ready."

After he hung up, he gave himself a few more minutes before returning his attention to Alea, who was jumping in and out of the water, waving at him, her small, pointed breasts glistening in the moonlight. He waved back. Then, without a word, he stood up and went to join her.

The jet taking Matt back to his native California banked in a slow, steady angle of descent over the Sierra Madre mountains, giving Matt an uninterrupted view of Santa Barbara County, which spread from Guadalupe to the west to the small eastern town of Carpinteria at the end of the bay.

Highways, state parks, and expensive real estate now occupied the land Chumash Indians had claimed more than six thousand years ago, and in the channel, towering oil platforms had replaced the vessels that had brought the first Spanish settlers to California.

Just past the mountains was his country—the Santa Inez Valley, with its rich vineyards, its fields of golden wild oats, and thousands of acres of ranchland where herds of Herefords and Aberdeen Angus grazed on what used to be, before the long, devastating draught, rich, green pastures.

And farther down the slope, sprawling lazily toward the ocean, lay Santa Barbara, where he had spent some of the most magical moments of his life, in the company of the most beautiful, most fascinating, most exasperating woman God had ever created.

And now, after two years of silence, two years during

which he'd tried to forget her, tried to survive without her, their paths were about to cross once again.

As the large, blue expanse of Lake Cachuma came into view, he wondered what her reaction would be when they finally met. Would she be friendly? Sarcastic? Indifferent?

He smiled, remembering that indifference was a skill Paige had mastered. She had used it on him like a weapon four years ago, hoping it would bruise his ego enough to send him away. But he had fooled her. And in the end she had shed that cool, elegant composure of hers and let him see the burning passion beneath—a passion he had never forgotten.

He held back a sigh of regret. He had been a fool to let her go. And an even greater fool not to have noticed the first signs of trouble sooner, to have believed that no matter what, love would prevail.

He glanced out the window again and saw that the plane was over the ocean now, banking in a half-turn and coming back inland toward the Santa Barbara Airport. What would Paige say once his investigation was over and she found out he had returned not to help his grandfather run the ranch, but to clear her name? Would she mellow a little? Would she look at him in a different light?

Of course there was always the possibility that she was guilty, that she was in this mess up to her lovely little neck.

Matt sighed. What the hell would he do then?

Paige's quiet beach house had never seen as much activity as it did on the afternoon of August third, as cars and trucks continued to pull in and out of the driveway, unloading food, chairs, flower arrangements, and cases of assorted wines and champagnes.

Maria, the Grangers' long-time maid, whom Paige had borrowed from her father for the party, was equally busy, answering the telephone and dealing with last-minute RSVPs and requests from various society columnists to attend the party.

Paige had turned the press down. Her grandmother may

have enjoyed having dozens of reporters attend her fancy soirées, but Paige found no pleasure in widespread publicity. She'd had enough of it as a child to last her a lifetime.

Standing on the top level of the tiered deck, sipping iced tea, Paige watched two men from a downtown hardware store install windscreens and portable heaters around the deck, for even in August, Santa Barbara nights were known to be breezy and cool.

She hadn't planned to keep such an active interest in the moment-by-moment preparations, since Maria was doing such a good job of it, but the activity kept her from thinking about Matt and his ill-timed return.

Although she had managed to appear unconcerned in front of Mindy the other day, she had been in turmoil ever since hearing about Matt. Over and over, she had told herself that his return had nothing to do with her, and nothing to do with her engagement to Jeremy Newman. But Matt was an unpredictable man, a man who thrived on the unexpected, and who, once he had made up his mind about something, let nothing stand in his way.

"Would you like to take a look from down below, ma'am?" one of the electricians asked as he secured the last string of red and green lanterns along the roof overhang. "See if it looks all right to you?"

Grateful for the temporary distraction, Paige put her glass down and ran to the lower deck, which was level with the beach. Shielding her eyes from the blazing sun, she looked up. "It's fine," she called out.

A flock of screeching seagulls flew over her, flapping their wings. Keeping her eyes shielded, she turned to follow their flight as one of them detached itself from the group and took a smooth dive toward a wave, retrieving the catch of the day and flying away with it.

How peaceful and simple everything was out here, she thought, leaning against the railing and watching foamy waves roll in and out in a mesmerizing pattern. One could almost shut out the world and its problems. Almost.

She had bought the house five years ago after deciding

that, at twenty-six, the time had come for her to leave the family nest.

"But it's nothing more than a *box*!" her grandmother had exclaimed as soon as she had seen the tiny beachfront house set on a knoll a short distance from the Biltmore Hotel. "It has no style, darling, no room to speak of, and the deck looks as if a pack of vultures have been feasting on it for centuries." Shuddering delicately, Eve Granger had added, "And it has aluminum shutters."

Paige had laughed at her grandmother's skepticism and had gone to work. True, the house was small and shapeless, and sea air had all but eaten away the cedar siding and deck. But how could one ignore the tranquility, the breathtaking view that went on for miles, and the two acres on which she could expand at will?

Six months later, with the help of a local architect, the square box had been transformed into an octagonal redwood and glass structure, the old deck torn down and rebuilt on three levels, and the neglected garden, which Paige had turned over to one of Santa Barbara's most creative landscapers, become a fragrant array of night-blooming jasmine, lavender, and hibiscus.

She had filled the high-beamed interiors with comfortable sofas and chairs in soft turquoise, local pottery, and a wonderful mix of blond wood antiques and contemporary pieces.

Tonight's exciting gathering of friends was Paige's own version of Eve Granger's elaborate Fiesta Night. Years ago, the Grangers had been one of the first Santa Barbara families to host a party in honor of Old Spanish Days. By the time Paige was born, her grandmother's affairs had become as legendary as the history behind the celebration. Paige had loved the frantic preparations in their large Montecito home, the dozens of caterers rushing from one end of the property to the other, carrying dishes and tables, erecting tents and bandstands, stringing lanterns in the huge oaks and oleanders.

She remembered Eve's last Fiesta party. She and Matt had flown in from New York to attend. They had been so much in love then. If anyone had told her that a year later she would be divorced, she would have laughed in his or her face.

A gust of wind blew Paige's hair in a dozen directions and she brushed it back with her hand. Nostalgia filled her—so acute, so unexpected, that for a moment the present faded away and she felt herself drifting back to the past. So many changes had brought her to this point. And the wheels had been set in motion four years ago, before she met Matt.

FOUR

October 4, 1987

As Paige Granger had anticipated, the highly publicized exhibition of pre-Columbian art at the Jeremy Newman Museum on San Francisco's Ghirardelli Square had not only attracted well-known collectors and dealers from all over the world, but a few of the country's most prominent art advisers as well.

Not that Paige was surprised by the clout present. As one of today's most respected art collectors, as well as the owner of the artifacts on display, Jeremy Newman had an uncanny gift for attracting crowds. And today was no exception.

Pausing in the arch to the first exhibit room, Paige removed her sunglasses and surveyed the well-dressed, chatty crowd, recognizing among it Harry Parker, director of Fine Art Museums of San Francisco, James Wood of the Chicago Art Institute, and New York-based private art adviser, Norton Rosenbaum.

Although curiosity played an important part in her visit to the Newman Museum, Paige was here for only one reason—to woo Jeremy Newman back to Beauchamp, her Aunt Kate's art and antiques gallery in Santa Barbara, where Paige also worked as a dealer and a budding art consultant.

Once Beauchamp's most valuable customer, Jeremy had abruptly severed all ties with the gallery two years ago. When Paige, puzzled by her aunt's vague explanations of an irreconcilable disagreement concerning an acquisition, offered to act as mediator, Kate had reacted with unexpected sharpness.

"You will do no such thing, Paige."

"But Aunt Kate, Jeremy Newman is our best customer. We will lose tons of business if he leaves."

"We'll survive."

While Beauchamp had indeed survived, the loss of Jeremy's patronage, as well as that of several of his wealthy friends, had cost Kate a fortune in commissions.

Once or twice, Paige thought about approaching the San Francisco publisher on her own, hoping that by then, whatever had happened between him and Kate would have been forgotten. But each time she had changed her mind, afraid that her interference might do more harm than good. It wasn't until she saw him on a *Good Morning America* segment a week ago that the thought had crept back into her head.

As Jeremy Newman had talked about the collection he was about to unveil, Paige saw an unexpected side of him. Newman, who had been described in an unauthorized biography as arrogant and ruthless, had been warm, witty, and as excited about the forthcoming show as a small boy with a new puppy. Mesmerized, Paige had stood in the middle of her bedroom in bra and panties, listening to him. And liking him. However, whether or not he would agree to see her, considering she was Kate Madison's niece, was something else entirely. But she owed it to herself, and to Beauchamp, to try.

Anticipating a negative reaction on Kate's part, Paige kept her intention to go to San Francisco to herself. Later, if all went well, as she hoped it would, there would be plenty of time to tell Kate the good news.

She spent the next several days in the library, poring over dozens of articles about the publisher and talking to art dealers here and abroad who knew him well. This visit to the museum his father had founded in 1911 was the last phase of her research and one she looked forward to, since pre-Columbian art had been her favorite subject in college.

Fanning herself lightly with the program she had just picked up from a console, Paige made her way toward a large display case, nodding politely, but not encouragingly, to the handsome man who smiled at her as she passed by.

Paige was accustomed to heads turning. At twenty-seven, she had the slender body and energetic walk of a runway model, a mass of dark, pre-Raphaelite curls, and eyes as clear and blue as the purest lagoon. A long time ago, as she had made the difficult transition from child to teenager with little effort, people had begun to notice not only her beauty but also her striking resemblance to her mother, Ann Granger.

Although Paige had not found the comparison flattering in view of how she felt about her mother, she had nonetheless come to terms with her looks, and now prided herself that although she still looked very much like her mother, she was as different from her as night from day.

"Paige, what a pleasant surprise."

Forcing a smile, for she had recognized the sweet, insincere voice of Arlene Lassiter, owner of San Francisco's premiere antiques gallery of the same name, Paige turned around and found herself swept into a perfumed embrace. "How are you, Arlene?" she said, trying not to wrinkle her nose in distaste at the overpowering scent that was the woman's trademark.

"Marvelous." Arlene was in her early sixties, with dyed red hair and a plump figure that her well-cut Bill Blass black suit did its best to conceal. She had been a successful antiques dealer for more than three decades, a position she had earned more with her social savvy than her good taste.

Pulling away, Arlene lowered her glasses and took in Paige's outfit—the long, narrow red jacket, almost severe if not for the sprinkle of faux jewels on the lapels, the straight black skirt, the hem of which ended an inch or so above the knees, and the high-heeled red Guccis.

Paige smiled. The look of envy on Arlene's face exceeded any compliment the woman could have voiced.

"What in the world are you doing here today?" Arlene

asked, emphasizing that last word. "Weren't you invited to yesterday's grand opening?"

Although the remark was meant to make Paige feel unimportant, she shrugged it off. "No, I wasn't. And I'm glad actually, or I would have missed you, Arlene." Then, to veil the sarcasm, she leaned forward, adding in a tone that only a very keen ear could have found demeaning, "And running into you is always such a joy."

Her eyes narrowing, Arlene gave her an hesitant smile, not sure whether she had been complimented or insulted. "I didn't know you were interested in pre-Columbian art," she said, tossing away her momentary confusion with her usual flair.

"A client of mine is," Paige lied. She raised an inquisitive eyebrow. "And you?"

Arlene, always eager to show her clout, waived toward a small group that stood looking at several carvings hung on a wall. "Sir Lionel Blickens is in town for a few days, and I thought this would be the perfect opportunity to give him a taste of our American culture. He arrived late last night," she added with a smug smile, "which is the reason I was unable to attend the opening. Ah, I see he's looking for me." She turned to Paige, briefly touched her cheek with hers. "*Ciao*, darling. It was *so* nice to see you. Do give my best to Kate."

"I will." With an amused smile, Paige watched her disappear into the crowd, remembering the woman's unsuccessful efforts over the years to acquire Jeremy as a client. What would happen to that smug, patronizing expression of hers, Paige wondered, indulging in a rare moment of cattiness, if *she* were to succeed where Arlene had failed?

Hiding a smile of pure glee behind her program, Paige made a mental note to tell Arlene the good news as soon as it happened. Then, returning her attention to the contents of the room, she headed for the first display case.

The newspapers hadn't exaggerated. Besides various weapons, jewelry, and headdresses, the collection included an impressive gathering of Olmec jade heads, rare

wood carvings, and Mayan vessels, one dating as far back
as 900 A.D. Whoever Jeremy had commissioned to acquire this collection had done a superb job, considering
that Mexico and Peru, where most pre-Columbian artifacts were buried, forbade its exportation.

Up to a few years ago, however, thanks to the greed-
iness of some South and Central American officials, the
smuggling of ancient artifacts into the United States,
where such trading was legal, had been relatively easy,
requiring little more than imagination and money. It was
more difficult now, but since penalties were seldom, if
ever, enforced, the traffic of pre-Columbian art was still
a very lucrative market.

As Paige reached the second viewing room, she held
her breath. Assembled in that room was a collection of
Veracruz antiquities that until now, she had seen only in
Mexico's most famous museums. Mounted on black
granite stands were more than a dozen statues of various
gods and warriors, all of which she recognized as part
of a treasure that had been excavated from a site in Central Veracruz several years ago.

Astounded at the wealth around her, Paige continued
to move from one statue to another, her trained eye
studying each feature, each crack where the sculptures
had been purposely broken in several pieces and then
reconstructed—a common practice that facilitated smuggling.

It wasn't until she found herself face to face with the
statue of a hunchback, a figure that many pre-Columbian
people had revered as much as they had revered their
gods, that Paige felt her pulse quicken. Something about
this particular piece struck her as odd.

Her curiosity fully aroused now, she moved closer, her
gaze taking in the square-shaped face, the narrow hooded
eyes, the eager expression of eyes and mouth. It was a
striking figure, similar to many she had studied at UCSB.

Quickly, she flipped through her catalogue, but, as she
had expected, it only verified what she already knew—
that the statue was more than a thousand years old and

was one of the most important works of ancient art to ever enter the United States. It said nothing about provenance and had no documented history. Which wasn't too surprising. When it came to antiquities, dealers and collectors knew better than to ask too many questions about provenance and former ownership.

Still puzzled, Paige continued to study the statue until her gaze stopped at the hands. Because in pre-Columbian times artists had placed so much emphasis on the elaborate headdresses, the ornaments, and the facial expressions, few of today's experts paid much attention to other parts of the body.

A small gasp escaped her. The hands! How could she have missed something so obvious? There was a mobility to them that didn't conform to what she knew of Veracruz art. Two fingers of the hunchback's right hand were closed to form a circle, while his other hand, which rested against his thigh, grasped a corner of his loin cloth.

She turned to the sculpture nearest the hunchback, her eyes searching for a similar discrepancy, and found it. Her pulse racing now, she walked around the room once more, studying the statues' hands more closely. To her bewilderment, all the sculptures on display had hands that didn't match what she knew of true Veracruz art.

Holding her catalogue against her chest, Paige took a deep breath, staggered by the implication of what she had discovered.

All the antiquities in this room were forgeries.

Not trusting her opinion, Paige had immediately contacted Ávilar Corón, the curator of antiquities at the Selecal Archaeological Museum in Veracruz, Mexico. Intrigued, he had agreed to fly to San Francisco and take a look at the display.

Señor Corón, an expert on Veracruz art and a member of the archaeological expedition that had excavated the site years ago, had confirmed Paige's suspicions.

"You have a very good eye, Miss Granger," he'd told her as he studied each sculpture with great interest.

"Are you saying those *are* forgeries?"

"Indeed they are. It isn't just the hands that give them away, but the feet as well. Look at how the toes curl under instead of being straight out and molded together."

"I hadn't noticed that. But you're right."

"The workmanship is excellent, however. And at first glance, the materials used seem authentic. Of course I can't make a totally accurate statement until scientific tests can be conducted."

"But why hasn't anyone else noticed the discrepancies?" Paige asked. "This room has been filled with dealers, collectors, and scholars of pre-Columbian art all week."

Corón sighed. "Unfortunately, it isn't uncommon for good forgeries to go undetected, even when they bear such dissimilarities with the actual work. The reason is that with so few pre-Columbian sites having been excavated, there is still a great deal to learn about the iconography of the ancient Americas. The hands and feet we see here are wrong, but still look very authentic, and no one knows enough about this kind of art to dispute it."

Getting an appointment with Jeremy Newman, however, hadn't been easy. But Paige had persisted, calling his secretary two, sometimes three times a day, each time insisting that the matter she had to discuss was urgent and confidential. Finally, the publisher had agreed to see her.

Now, as she followed Jeremy's Chinese manservant through a well-appointed hallway in his Pacific Heights residence, Paige felt her first twinge of apprehension. Jeremy Newman was a man who prided himself on having an unerring eye when it came to art. He had built a solid reputation as a connoisseur and gained the respect of thousands of his peers. And now she, Paige Granger, had come to shatter that myth? To tell him his instincts had failed him? That a collection that had probably cost him several million dollars, and taken him years to assemble, was a fake? Her teeth clamped on her bottom lip. She'd be lucky if he didn't throw her out of his house after the first sentence.

"Mr. Newman will be with you in a moment," the butler said, showing her into a vast drawing room and closing the double doors behind him as he left.

In the immense museumlike room, Paige stood in total awe. In front of her was an assortment of paintings, decorative objects, and furniture that left her breathless. There were groupings of Louis XV sofas and chairs covered with pale green silk damask, Boulle cabinets, inlaid tables, Meissen clocks, and Goblin tapestries. Hanging from the ceiling Paige recognized a pair of Louis XIV crystal chandeliers that had been auctioned at Christie's last year for a mere 4.8 million dollars. The walls, painted a neutral ivory, were covered with Monets, Renoirs, and Rembrandts.

"Do you approve?"

Paige spun around, surprised, for she hadn't heard the door open. Jeremy Newman stood in front of her, dressed casually in beige slacks and a pale green crewneck sweater. Although he had seemed taller on television, she found him just as handsome and younger looking than most fifty-three-year-old men she knew, with the exclusion of her father. He had thick salt-and-pepper hair; the tanned complexion of the outdoorsman; and direct, watchful dark eyes that surveyed her with great interest.

"It's very impressive," she replied, not bothering to tell him that she found the room a bit ostentatious. "My aunt told me your home housed exceptional treasures, but I wasn't quite prepared for such a breathtaking display."

He gave her a pleased smile and came forward, his hand extended as if he had been waiting for her approval before committing himself any further. "Kate has trained you well."

He gazed at her unhurriedly. He had been a great admirer of her mother some years ago, and although Paige might not be as beautiful as Ann, there was something much more vibrant about this girl, a buoyancy and strength her mother hadn't possessed. Her voluminous curls reminded him of a Goya painting he had seen at the Prado Museum in Madrid once. Against them, her skin looked almost luminous, as if he were looking at her through silk-covered lenses. The eyes, of course, were extraordinary, as blue and direct as her father's and her grandfather's before that. The mouth may have been a trifle too generous and the jaw too wide for her to be considered a classic beauty. But had she chosen to be a model, he knew at least three agencies that would have signed her on the spot.

As the houseman reappeared and politely waited by the door, Jeremy asked. "May I offer you something to drink, Miss Granger? Chu Seng makes the best cup of tea this side of China."

Paige shook her head, reminding herself that what she had come to discuss was hardly conducive to tea and crumpets. "I came to talk to you about your pre-Columbian exhibition."

Again he looked pleased. "You saw it?"

"Last week. I've been trying to get an appointment with you ever since."

Although Jeremy's eyes grew suddenly wary, his smile remained friendly. "Oh. Why is that?"

Under his piercing gaze Paige tried not to fidget. "There is no other way to tell you this but come right out with it." She was pleased to see that at least her voice hadn't betrayed her nervousness. "I'm afraid I'm the bearer of rather unpleasant news, Mr. Newman." Then, after taking a deep breath, she added, "Your Veracruz exhibition is the work of a forger."

FIVE

Controlling his emotions was something Jeremy Newman had mastered long before Paige Granger was even born. It had helped him get the advantage in a number of difficult situations over the years, and would undoubtedly continue to do so for many more.

But this time, his control slipped. His heart lurched and as the shock sent the adrenaline rushing through his system, his hand gripped the chair near him for support.

"I beg your pardon?" he managed to say at last. His voice slurred a little as if he had been drinking.

Paige repeated her statement.

He swallowed, wondering if this was some sort of prank. He'd met his share of weirdos over the years, people who thought they could extract money from him by accusing him of various wrongdoings ranging from slander to corruption and even paternity.

But for some reason, he ruled out Paige Granger from that group. The girl had too much class, and too good a reputation for him to dismiss her as a common opportunist. "What in the world gave you such a preposterous idea, Miss Granger?" he finally managed to ask with just the right amount of outrage.

As she told him of her findings, her call to Avilar Corón, and the expert's visit to San Francisco, Jeremy watched and listened, his confidence slowly vanishing in the wake of her revelations.

He had been so damned sure they'd get away with it. When he and Carter Lawson, a San Francisco dealer of pre-Columbian art with whom he had worked for years, had discovered Ciero Valdez in Central Mexico, Jeremy had known this was a major step in his commitment to put together a unique collection.

Ciero Valdez was a young artist whose undiscovered talent lay in his ability to create Veracruz-style sculptures that were so like the real thing in look and texture that even Carter, an expert in Veracruz art, had believed they were the real McCoy.

Jeremy had immediately commissioned Ciero to create a series of sculptures that, although they would resemble those that had been excavated in previous years, would not be exact replicas. Carter had explained that exact copies of already-existing pieces would have been too easily recognized as forgeries, since the originals were prominently displayed in national museums throughout Mexico. But by adding a different headdress, another strand of beads, or a frown instead of a leery grin, the new work looked authentic enough to fool the experts. If Ciero hadn't gotten carried away with his clever artistry and changed the hands and feet as well, the ruse would have gone undetected forever.

When Paige was finished, Jeremy was silent for a moment. The girl was good. And she had done her homework before coming here. This wasn't some idealistic art student he could buy or sell at will. She was intelligent, proud, and determined to get to the truth.

"Well," he said, shaking his head and walking around the room as if in a state of shock, which wasn't all that difficult to do, considering the bomb the kid had just dropped on his lap. "I must say, I find your findings incredible." He turned to look at her. "And if you don't mind my saying so, beyond the bounds of reason. I only deal with the most reputable art dealers, Miss Granger. You should know that."

"I do. And I understand your reluctance to believe me, Mr. Newman. After all, you know nothing about me. But surely you've heard of Avilar Corón, haven't you?"

He hadn't. Although he had a feeling he would. Very soon. "Of course. But even experts can be wrong."

"Exactly. Which is why Mr. Corón feels that in the interest of the public, and you as well, the collection should be examined by scientists and other experts in the field as soon as possible."

Jeremy's jaw clenched. Damn this Corón. And damn her. He was tempted to dismiss the two of them and tell them to go and find something else with which to amuse themselves. But that would be unwise. And it would be equally unwise to try to bribe them. One only had to look at the proud expression in Paige's eyes as she talked, at the passion in her voice, to know that for the first time in his life, Jeremy Newman had met someone he couldn't buy.

He sighed. For a few glorious days he had been one of the most envied collectors in the world. But he had to put that behind him now and concentrate on getting out of this mess in a dignified manner. And with the least harm to his reputation.

"Very well, Miss Granger," he said, raising his arms and letting them fall by his side in a helpless gesture. "I'll take Mr. Corón's advice and have the collection examined. I don't like it and I don't think anything will come of it, except bad publicity for me. But I'll do it. As a lover of art, I can do nothing else but get to the bottom of this without delay."

Paige let out a sigh of relief. Although the news had come as a shock to him, Jeremy Newman had taken it with the kind of control and dignity one could only admire. Now that he had accepted the inevitable, there was a kindness and warmth about him that made whatever was left of her nervousness disappear.

She turned to look at him. Her expression was grave, her voice gentle. "I'm truly sorry to have been the one to bring you such distressing news, Mr. Newman. If it's any consolation, I hope with all my heart Mr. Corón is wrong."

"So do I, Miss Granger," Jeremy said emphatically. "So do I."

"I *know* the statues are forgeries, Carter," Jeremy Newman said into the telephone in the clear, patient tone one would use in talking to a slow-witted child. "What I'm trying to tell you is that I want a full-fledged investigation conducted just as if I *didn't* know they were forgeries. I want you to get in touch with the best experts in Veracruz art you can find and bring them to San Francisco."

"Oh . . . Well . . . In that case," the man at the other end of the line replied in an unsteady voice. "The curator Miss Granger spoke about, Avilar Corón, is the best."

"Fine. Fly him in then, along with those two scientists from UCLA, just to show our good intentions. I want this matter resolved quickly. By the end of the week. And of course, since we can't afford to have you accused of any improprieties, you'll have to come up with a fictitious Mexican art dealer who will have conveniently disappeared when he realized he had been exposed. I trust that won't be too difficult to arrange?"

"No, but we have a more serious problem on hand."

"What's that?"

"The artist, Ciero Valdez. Once this thing comes out, he might decide he'd like a little more recognition. Or he might try to blackmail us. Money for his silence."

Jeremy, who had already anticipated the sculptor's greed, folded his fingers over his palm and inspected his impeccably manicured nails. His expression hardly changing, he said, "He won't give us any difficulties when he's made aware of what I know about his younger sister."

"What's wrong with her?"

"She's an illegal alien, Carter. I understand Valdez is very devoted to her. I'm sure he would be devastated if someone suddenly threatened to tip off Immigration."

He knew there was no need to spell out what he wanted done. Carter Lawson, who owed his reputation to Jeremy's continued support over the years, was too greedy to allow scruples to stand in the way of a good deal—or in the way of self-preservation. In the twenty-some years Jeremy had known him, he had found the man to be shrewd and resourceful, two qualities Jeremy appreciated and rewarded with equal generosity.

"Just keep me posted," Jeremy added. Then, not bothering to say good-bye, he hung up and went to stand by his drawing-room window overlooking the bay.

This was his favorite time of day, that magic moment between dusk and night that the French so aptly called *l'heure bleue*. Nowhere on earth did it seem more magic than over the San Francisco Bay as the fog drifted out to sea and the studded evening sky and the bay turned an intense indigo.

But tonight, even the spectacular view failed to lift his spirits. Paige Granger had cost him a bloody fortune. Not to mention the loss of credibility with collectors all over the world. His judgment, his undisputed knowledge, and even his reputation were jeopardized. And all because of a schoolgirl's passion for Veracruz art, a girl with an eye so extraordinary that she had seen what experts had missed.

With a brusque gesture, he opened a black marble cigarette box near him, pulled out a Marlboro, and lit it with a solid gold butane lighter that lay near the box. He inhaled deeply, holding the soothing smoke in his lungs before releasing it.

After a few moments, his body relaxed and his anger began to fade. There would be other exhibitions, he reminded himself, other ways to dazzle the public. In the spring, the Washington National Gallery would feature a three-month exhibition of his collection of Impressionist paintings. And next December, his collection of Fabergé eggs, enameled gold boxes, and miniature jeweled flowers would be displayed at the Helmsley Palace Hotel in New York. Eighty-seven items in all, valued at more than sixty million dollars. Not even Malcom Forbes could boast a collection as rich as this one.

Pursing his lips in a satisfied expression, Jeremy turned around and walked across the room slowly, like a general reviewing his troops. His hands behind his back, he let his gaze drift from the paintings on the wall, to the two Boules chests flanking the ornate French mantel, to the twelve-foot glass cabinet that held his collection of rare books and manuscripts.

He couldn't remember a time in his life when beautiful things hadn't been his passion. As a small boy, frail in appearance and unpopular with other boys his age, he had shunned football and other such sports, content to stay home, surrounded by antique furniture, famous paintings, and fine porcelain.

His early love for rare things had been his escape from a world he found hostile, a world where grown-ups hardly ever noticed him, and where classmates scorned him. He was nine years old when he started his own ''museum'' in the attic of his parents' fifty-five room home on Washington Street in San Francisco. Gathering objects his mother had either discarded or stored away, he arranged them with an uncommon flair and then charged admission to his friends.

When an outraged mother complained to his father, rather than scold his son, Philip Newman roared with laughter, pleased that his only child had inherited his flair for business. From that moment on, Jeremy and his father had been inseparable.

Jeremy learned a great deal from Philip Newman during those early years. But one lesson he never allowed himself to forget was that money bought power. And that leaders, men like his father and his grandfather before that, men with guts and grit, controlled the world.

The rest he learned on his own, by observing, listening, and experimenting. Early in his training, he realized that in order to control people, it was essential to have a certain leverage over them.

For the next thirty-five years, Jeremy made it a point to learn everything about anyone in and out of his employ, from the most insignificant copyboy to the city's most powerful politicians. He knew their strengths, their weaknesses, and their most private secrets. But more important, he knew their hungers.

By the time he was forty-eight, Jeremy had expanded his father's newspaper into a publishing empire that included eighteen daily newspapers and magazines, a dozen radio stations, and a television network. It wasn't quite as much as what his former hero, William Randolph Hearst, had owned, but it was close. Very close.

Women found him fascinating and considered him a "great catch," either for themselves or for their unmarried daughters. But Jeremy, a confirmed bachelor, wasn't interested in marriage. In spite of the fact that he dated some of the most beautiful women in the state, he had never really gotten over losing Caroline Wescott, to whom he had been engaged when he was only twenty-one and had lost to Adam McKenzie.

After that all he had cared about was making money.

He stopped in front of a bronze statue of Diana and ran his hand along the smooth bare back, the muscled but delicately molded arm as it prepared to sink an arrow into an unsuspecting prey.

Oddly, his thoughts drifted back to Paige Granger, although this time he felt no anger. What sort of men did she favor, he wondered, the back of his finger tracing the taut line of Diana's lower back. Strong, confident men or the gentler type? Was she more likely to be attracted to wealth and power or to honesty and sensitivity?

Smiling, because he knew that whatever the game, he could play it, he gave Diana's backside a playful tap and turned away, heading toward the door. Someday soon he would seek an answer to this question. Right now, he had important matters to tend to and a press conference to prepare.

It took nearly two weeks for the three experts Jeremy had flown in from around the world to render their verdict and declare that indeed, Jeremy Newman's collection of Veracruz art was a forgery.

Assailed with requests for interviews, Jeremy delt with the press courteously and efficiently, blaming only himself for this unfortunate incident.

"I was a bit too eager," he admitted during the press conference he chose to hold at his museum, although not in the Veracruz exhibit room, which had been sealed off. "Too eager to bring the public a unique collection of art. And in my eagerness, I allowed myself to be careless."

In the front row, a young woman with an unsmiling face raised her hand. "Some people say you staged this forgery, Mr. Newman." Her probing eyes watched him closely. "And that you're powerful enough to get away with it. What do you say to that?"

"I say it's the most preposterous, and unkind, accusation I have ever heard," he replied, making it a point to hold her formidable gaze without flinching. "I love art too much, as you all know, to play such despicable games." He gave her his famous Newman grin. "And anyway, with all I have already, why would I even want to?"

The reporter's smile was slightly cynical. "Greatness?"

Jeremy was silent for a moment. The bitch had done her homework. She was, of course, referring to a statement he had made some time ago that a collector was better off having nothing until he could have great things, adding that *he* happened to have an eye for greatness.

"Achieving greatness," he said easily. "Isn't one of my priorities. Bringing pleasure through art, and educating the public are." His gaze encompassed the room and he smiled, showing he could take the hard line of questioning. "Although from now on, I'll exercise greater caution on how I go about bringing such pleasure to other art lovers."

"What is being done to find the forger?" another reporter asked. "Or the Mexican dealer who arranged for you to get the collection?"

"Everything. Unfortunately, and in spite of the Mexican authorities' diligent search, there has been no trace of the two men. But I feel confident they will be found very soon.''

The grilling went on for another ten minutes, but he could see by the way the reporters talked to one another as they left that they had been impressed by his poise and his courtesy, and more important, that they had believed him.

He waited until the publicity had died down before he called Paige at the gallery two weeks later.

''Well,'' he said, flattered that she recognized his voice before he had a chance to identify himself. ''Did I handle the matter properly?''

''Like a pro,'' she replied with laughter in her voice, as if she were genuinely happy to hear from him. ''But then I had no doubt that you would.''

''Thank you.'' Lowering his voice down to his most seductive pitch, he added, ''I don't suppose you hand out special rewards for special achievers.''

Her rich laugh sent a shiver down his spine. ''What sort of reward did you have in mind?''

''How about lunch tomorrow?''

There was a short pause before she spoke again. ''Oh, I think that can be arranged.''

During the next two months, Jeremy's relationship with Paige grew and strengthened both professionally and personally. Far from resenting her for exposing the forgery, he had praised her for her attention to details, as well as her courage.

''Not too many people would have come forward with this kind of information,'' he had told her during their first lunch together. ''But you did. And I applaud you for that, Paige.''

They had talked mostly about her, her interests in English furniture and French decorative arts, and her growing role as an art consultant.

Aware that hundreds of dealers claimed to be art consultants these days, he questioned her relentlessly, wanting to know who she represented, what she had bought for them and at what price. Paige answered his inquiries with charm and wit, never revealing anything about her clients that shouldn't be revealed—a detail Jeremy had seemed to appreciate very much.

Jeremy listened, astounded that one so young could know so much about art. She was also candid about Beauchamp, flattering him by telling him it had never been quite the same without him, and admitting, with a soft laugh, how she had hoped to bring him back.

"But that was before I discovered the Veracruz forgery, of course."

She had presented him with the perfect opportunity to develop their relationship. He didn't need another art consultant. And he certainly didn't need Kate Madison—not after their past history together.

But by the time their coffee arrived, Jeremy had asked Paige to act as his art adviser, if not for all his transactions, at least for a few. He didn't even argue with her when she told him she would be consulting with Kate from time to time, since she was so much more familiar with what he liked.

From that moment on, Jeremy found many pretexts to spend more time at his Santa Inez Valley ranch, where he raised polo ponies, calling Paige as soon as he arrived, and inviting her to lunch or to view an exhibit he wanted to see.

Because he was so well known, their relationship was regarded with a great deal of speculation by both the San Francisco and the Santa Barbara communities. Not surprisingly, Kate was the first to express her opinion on that subject.

"I don't think acquiring Jeremy as a client was a wise decision on your part, after all," she told Paige during a private moment at the Grangers' house, where both had been invited to Thanksgiving dinner. "The man is taking nearly all of your time. I wouldn't be a bit surprised if before long, he'll be asking you to represent him exclusively."

"No, he won't. He knows how much I enjoy the diversity of my job. As for spending so much time with him, Aunt Kate, I'm surprised you're saying that. You know what being an art adviser involves. I have to counsel him, present him with options, meet with him at a moment's notice.''

''And you don't think you're doing more for him than for anyone else?''

Paige pursed her lips in a thoughtful expression. ''A little, perhaps. But that's because I'm trying to develop a feeling of mutual trust between us. Haven't you always told me how important that was?''

''Not to that extent. And not with Jeremy Newman.''

''Why not?''

She saw a strange look pass through her aunt's eyes. ''Because I don't want you hurt.''

Before Kate could turn away, Paige grasped her arm. ''What did he do to you, Aunt Kate, that you're so bitter toward him? If it's anything that might help me serve him better, don't you think I should know?''

Her lips tightly pressed together, Kate shook her head. ''I've already told you. We had a falling-out, a professional difference of opinion.''

''What sort of falling-out? Regarding what?''

''Stop it!'' Kate's face turned pale and her body tensed in such a way that Paige released her instantly. ''I told you once that I never wanted to talk about it, and I don't appreciate this constant prying just because Jeremy is your friend now. If you think he's so wonderful, then fine. Let's leave it at that.''

Distraught, Paige watched as her aunt went to rejoin the others in the solarium, where Maria was serving coffee and pumpkin pie.

Hurting Kate was the last thing she wanted to do. After her father, she was the person Paige loved most in the world. It was Aunt Kate who had taken over the duties of mother when Ann had left, who had driven her to Girl Scout meetings and baked for her class, although the Granger household employed a full-time cook. It was

Kate who had taken her shopping, helped her experiment with new hair-dos, and told her about boys.

In later years, it was Kate who had introduced Paige to the wonders of art, explaining the history behind each piece in her gallery, talking about each painting in such fascinating detail that Paige couldn't wait to run to Beauchamp every afternoon after school. There, surrounded by precious objects, fine paintings and furniture that had belonged to kings, Paige had built her knowledge and shaped her future.

By the time she had graduated from college, Beauchamp was one of the most successful galleries in California, an accomplishment that was largely due to the business of one collector—Jeremy Newman.

Although Paige, like many Californians, knew a great deal about the San Francisco publisher, she had never met him. Most of his transactions with Kate were done over the telephone and in the strictest confidence.

She hated not having Kate's approval where Jeremy was concerned, and she wished that in time, her aunt would take another stand. But until then, Paige was thrilled and proud to be part of a small, elite group of art advisers who worked for Jeremy Newman. She was also a little apprehensive. She knew that the next few months would be a testing period for her, that her friendship with Jeremy, her talents, and her availability to fly to New York or London at a moment's notice, weren't enough to secure her position. Trust was the most important factor in their relationship, and until she earned that, she wasn't in all the way.

It wasn't until Jeremy called her on the evening of December fifth of that year, requesting a breakfast meeting at the Biltmore Hotel the following morning, that Paige realized their professional relationship was about to take a new turn.

There was a different tone to his voice as he talked to her, a touch of laughter and mystery she found intriguing. If her instincts were right, Jeremy was finally ready to give her an important assignment, one that, if properly handled, would mark the beginning of a new and brilliant career. It was important that she didn't let him down.

The sunny terrace of the Biltmore was already filled to capacity when Paige arrived on Sunday morning. All around her, towering palms, bright umbrellas, and gigantic pots of exotic flowers gave no hint that in some parts of the country, people fought snow blizzards and subzero temperatures.

Paige paused briefly by the open French doors, aware that the bright chatter of voices was momentarily interrupted as heads turned to look at her. Pretending not to notice, her gaze continued to sweep the terrace until she spotted Jeremy.

As he saw her approach, Jeremy folded his newspaper and stood up, a ready smile on his lips. "Good morning, Paige," he said in his well-modulated, self-assured voice. "It was very gracious of you to accept this last-minute invitation." His dark gaze swept over her in swift appraisal, taking in the olive suede suit and the vivid red blouse. "You look lovely." He waited for her to sit down before doing the same. "I took the liberty of ordering," he added, gesturing toward the platter of fresh fruit and croissants. "I hope this is all right."

"It's perfect." She waited until both had helped each other to a slice of cantaloupe and then, unable to wait a moment longer, she said, "So what was so important that you dragged me away from a perfectly boring Sunday morning?"

He laughed and when he did, the small lines around his eyes deepened, making him look very handsome.

"That's one of the things I like about you, Paige. You never waste time with small talk." Then, his face serious, he leaned over the table. "Have you ever heard of a man by the name of Ted Krugger?" he asked.

Paige's blue eyes narrowed in concentration as she searched her memory, aware that a successful association with Jeremy Newman depended not only on her knowledge of art, but on her awareness of those who greatly influenced the market.

"I'm sorry," she admitted at last. "I'm afraid I haven't."

"That's all right. And not at all surprising. Krugger is an American art dealer who now works and lives in Venice, Italy. Although he owned a few good paintings at one time, he was never a top dealer. And now my sources tell me that because of recent bad investments, he's forced to close his gallery and liquidate what he has left."

Paige took a sip of her coffee. "I take it he has something you want."

Jeremy nodded. "An early Toulouse Lautrec drawing he's been too damned stubborn to sell."

"Has he changed his mind?"

"Yes. He's now willing to negotiate. But he wants to do so rather quickly."

Paige was immediately cautious. "Why is that?"

"To pay some back taxes, I imagine. Or maybe he's trying to skip town before the government catches up with him. Frankly, I don't care. In fact, I'm rather pleased the man is in such a hurry. It could work in our favor, price-wise."

Paige felt a tug of excitement. It wasn't the sort of challenge she had expected, but it was a start, and her chance to show Jeremy she was as good a negotiator as any of his more established advisers.

Still, quick deals made her nervous. Not that she was totally against them. Some were quite legitimate. And, as Jeremy had pointed out, they could be to one's advantage. But she always felt more comfortable knowing as much as possible about a prospective seller before she engaged in a serious discussion with him.

"Did he call you himself?" she asked. "Or did he go through a third party?"

"He called me. He remembered the generous offer I made him a year or so ago and decided it was too good to pass up after all."

"How much did you offer him?"

"Two million dollars."

Paige nodded. "Of course, I would have to see the condition of the drawing to know if it's worth that much, but even if it is, considering he came to you this time, we might be able to get it for less."

Jeremy's eyes gleamed in appreciation. "Exactly." He picked up a croissant and delicately tore a piece off one end. "Anyway, I want you to go to Italy and negotiate that purchase for me. Once you've settled on a price, my lawyer will do the rest." He waited for the waitress to refill their coffee cups and leave before he continued. "Oh, and one other thing. The man is overly obsessed with privacy and asked that you follow a few simple instructions."

Paige raised an inquisitive eyebrow. "Such as?"

Jeremy shrugged. "He didn't tell me. All I know is that you are to check into your hotel and wait for his call."

Paige smiled and helped herself to a slice of papaya. "Will I have to give a password when he calls?"

Jeremy laughed. "I hardly think so. As I said, the man is probably knee-deep in tax problems and taking extra precautions to insure the government doesn't get wind of what he's up to. But that's not my concern. My concern is to get that drawing at the best possible price." He reached for her hand and squeezed it. "And after hearing about the great deal you made on that Seurat last month for Mrs. Butler, I'm convinced you're the person I want for this transaction."

She didn't ask how he had found out about the Seurat. Jeremy's network of informants was as legendary as the man himself. "Thank you, Jeremy. Although I must warn you, a few of Lautrec's early works can command great sums of money. I believe the last one of a circus performer went for 5.5 million at a private sale. Knowing that, Krugger could ask a lot more than the two million you offered him last year."

His face suddenly serious, Jeremy leaned across the table. "I'm prepared to pay whatever he asks."

She held his gaze. "I won't disappoint you, Jeremy."

Jeremy inhaled deeply and leaned back in his chair. He wasn't sure what pleased him more, her confidence or the fact that she was here, looking more beautiful and more desirable than any woman he had ever known.

More and more these days, he felt drawn to her, to her beauty, her intelligence, her grace. In many ways she reminded him of Caroline. She had the same class, the same elegance—an elegance that came naturally and effortlessly. She was more flamboyant than Caroline, more colorful. But it suited her. He had seen the way men and women had turned to look at her when she had approached his table earlier. He had felt a deep sense of pride then, as he always did when he was in the presence of something, or someone, beautiful.

Once again the thought entered his mind that she would make the perfect wife for him. She had everything a man of his status could want—beauty, intelligence, wit, and charm. And youth, he thought with a shiver of delight. One could hardly overlook that. Because of her, of that youthful energy and enthusiasm, he felt more vibrant, more virile now than he had in years.

Idly he began to imagine her in his house, entertaining friends, associates, and dignitaries. He imagined her sitting with him at night, sipping a brandy, or sharing a midnight swim in his Marbella home or his Barbados condo.

Ah, yes, he thought, feeling the beginning of an erection at the mere thought of all the delicious pleasures she could bring him, this was the woman he wanted to marry, *had* to marry.

"What are you thinking about?" Paige asked, breaking into his thoughts.

"Venice," he said, finding himself wishing he could go with her. "You leave tomorrow morning, by the way. I have chartered a jet for you, and my secretary made reservations at the Gritti Palace Hotel."

Paige observed him for a while as she sipped her orange juice. There had been no question in his mind as to whether or not she would go. He hadn't asked if she had other plans for the coming week, other clients to see or anything more pressing to do. He had simply assumed nothing else would matter. It wasn't the way she usually did business, for all her clients were equally important to her, but in this case, and because she wanted so much to please him, she would make an exception.

"Anything wrong?" he asked, catching her gaze.

She put her glass down and smiled, shaking her head. "No. Everything is just right."

They were interrupted by a waitress who came to tell Jeremy he had a phone call. After he excused himself, Paige watched him walk away, an elegant, imposing figure who could neither leave nor enter a room without the head of every female turning in his direction—as they did now.

Catching one of those glances, Paige held back a smile. How many of those women here today, unaware that all that existed between her and Jeremy was friendship, wished they could be in her shoes?

SIX

A foot of snow, followed by mild temperatures, had turned the streets and sidewalks of Manhattan into piles of gray slush that pedestrians, at least those with the Christmas spirit, did their best to ignore.

But at Rockefeller Plaza, where dozens of tourists had already gathered, the scene was all glitter and holiday music. Behind the golden statue of Prometheus, a seventy-five foot Norway spruce shimmered with hundreds of lights, while on the ice rink, skaters, wrapped in colorful mufflers and fancy tights, danced to the tune of Barbara Streisand's "White Christmas."

In a plush office thirty stories above the plaza, Matt McKenzie was on the phone, sitting at his desk and watching the activity below. At the other end of the line, his client continued to express her displeasure with a barrage of questions for which Matt had no answer.

This case was beginning to bore him. Taking abuse from a little old lady he had thought sweet and harmless was hardly his idea of earning a living.

He shouldn't have taken the damn job. The value of the missing vase wasn't high enough to justify the two weeks one of his best men had already spent on the case. But when the seventy-year-old widow had walked into his office in tears and begged him to find a Ming vase that had been given to her by her late husband on their twentieth wedding anniversary, Matt hadn't had the heart to turn her down. He knew all about objects of sentimental value. He had a trunkful of them—mementos of all sizes and shapes that had belonged to his parents and that no one but himself gave a damn about.

He picked up a crumpled piece of paper on his desk, aimed it at the miniature NBA basket on Tom's desk, and shot. He missed. "I realize it's been two weeks since your vase was stolen, Mrs. Ruznak," Matt said, as soon as his client gave him a chance to speak. "But as I told you yesterday, *and* the day before that, our trail ran cold a little over a week ago, and unless—"

He pulled the receiver from his ear and winced as he was bombarded with a storm of protests at the unspoken suggestion that he might abandon the search. He didn't think anyone would have blamed him if he'd hung up just then. Lord knows he was tempted. But he didn't.

At thirty-five, and after thirteen years in this business, Matt McKenzie had mastered the art of self-control.

It hadn't been easy. As a boy he had been undisciplined, impetuous, and a little more aggressive than most. He was the one who always wandered off and got lost on school trips. At camp, whenever a boat capsized, or someone fell off a cliff or crashed his bike, the name McKenzie immediately came to mind.

"You're just like your father," his mother had snapped one afternoon after he had fallen off his horse during a roping session with a mean and angry steer. "You're just as crazy."

He preferred to think of himself as a free spirit. It was that free spirit, combined with an insatiable need for adventure, that had led him to a career in the FBI after his graduation from New York University. But although initiative and self-reliance were qualities the bureau regarded highly, recklessness had no place in a structured organization like the Federal Bureau of Investigation. And since Matt had wanted to be a special agent more than anything in the world since he was fifteen years old, he'd had to learn how to follow rules. And to take orders.

The first two years of his career were spent moving from one field office to another, investigating cases such as white-collar crimes, domestic terrorism, and narcotics. It wasn't until he had distinguished himself on a particularly intricate art theft, where he had posed as a fence in order to catch a thief, that his superiors realized Matt's talents would be better used in the Bureau's special Art Squad in New York City.

But after eleven years with the FBI, Matt had needed a change, as well as more money. Knowing that his old friend, Tom DiMaggio, who owned an investigation agency that specialized in the tracking of stolen art, was always on the lookout for good agents, he had applied for a job. Tom had hired him on the spot at twice his former salary.

His reputation already well established, it hadn't taken him long to reach the top of his profession. While most experts agreed that only ten percent of all stolen art work was ever recovered, Matt's results were considerably higher.

Because of his reputation, he could afford to be selective about the cases he handled. Once in a while, however, he would take one simply because he found it intriguing, or, as he had with Mrs. Ruznak, because he felt sorry for the person.

His conversation finally over, Matt switched off his portable phone and, hearing a soft chuckle behind him, turned to see Tom DiMaggio standing in the doorway, one shoulder against the jamb.

"Your charming Mrs. Ruznak, I presume?" Tom said with a twinkle in his eye.

"She's going to be *your* delightful Mrs. Ruznak if Tony doesn't find her damn vase before I leave for Venice this evening." Pointing at the folder in Tom's hand, he added, "Is that the file on Paige Granger?"

"Yep." Tom, a six-foot-four, two-hundred-pound former NYPD detective with a gray crew cut and big, bassethound eyes, handed Matt the file before folding his tall, lanky frame into a blue-upholstered chair opposite Matt's desk. "It isn't much, but I think you'll find it sufficient."

Matt opened the folder. Inside was the usual assortment of photographs, press clippings, and background information that newspapers kept on file about people they felt were newsworthy.

The Grangers apparently qualified. Twenty years ago, Paige's mother, Ann, had abruptly walked away from her family a few weeks before her husband, Paul, was expected to be elected Santa Barbara district attorney. Foul play had been suspected at first, but when a private detective had traced Ann all the way to Rome and then later lost the trail, the police had assumed she didn't want to be found and filed the case away.

According to her personal file, Paige Granger was an art and antiques dealer who also acted as art adviser for three California collectors. She had graduated from the University of California at Santa Barbara with an M.A. in fine arts, was single, and Paul Granger's only child.

She was also stunning. With those thick dark curls, incredible blue eyes, and proud carriage, she personified breeding and privilege. She's probably spoiled as hell, Matt thought, noting the rather haughty lift of her eyebrow the camera had captured in all three snapshots. Those society girls always were.

The folder also contained a picture of Jeremy Newman, Paige Granger's third and newest client, as well as a man Matt had despised for years. As he stared at the all-too-familiar face, he felt an unvoluntary clench of his jaw.

Ever since Matt could remember, his family had been at odds with Jeremy Newman. It had begun before he was born, when his mother, then Caroline Wescott, was engaged to Jeremy. Matt's grandparents had owned the twenty-thousand-acre Canyon-T Ranch in the Santa Inez Valley, and Jeremy the smaller horse farm adjacent to it.

It was at one of Jeremy's glittering ranch parties that Matt's father, Adam McKenzie, had met Caroline Wescott. A few days later, the beautiful San Francisco socialite had broken her engagement and eloped with Adam, leaving behind an enraged Jeremy and a stunned community.

Then, two years ago, Matt's parents had been visiting

Jeremy at his ranch when their car had exploded, killing Adam on impact and critically injuring Caroline.

Jeremy, although deeply shaken by the tragedy, hadn't been able to offer any explanation for the bombing. He had admitted to having recently renewed his relationship with Caroline and having had an argument with Adam that night. But beyond that, and in spite of Matt's angry accusations, Jeremy swore he knew nothing.

"I had no reason to want your father dead!" he had shouted at Matt. "It was more the other way around. And anyway, do you think I'd be stupid enough to use a bomb, for Christ's sake? Or commit the murder in my own backyard? Or take a chance with Caroline's life?"

He was right. As much as Matt had hated to admit it. Someone else had wanted Adam dead. Someone who knew where Adam would be that night and hadn't counted on Caroline being there.

The sound of Tom's voice brought him back. "Great-looking gal, this Paige Granger. Did you ever meet her?"

Matt shook his head. "Her family and mine were acquainted once. But, no, I never met her personally."

"And you think there's a chance she's tied up with that stolen Goya you're after?"

Matt continued to study the girl in the photograph, lingering over the sensual mouth, the cool, almost aloof smile. "My guess is she is."

Tom smiled. "Guilty before proven innocent?"

"Guilty by virtue of association," Matt said sarcastically. "In this case, association with the worst kind. I'd bet a year's pay Newman is involved in some form of art trafficking. No one that obsessed with art is ever a hundred percent clean."

"You could be right. But my instincts tell me this business between Krugger and Newman is purely coincidental."

"When did you join his fan club?"

"I didn't. But don't forget he's sending his adviser to Italy to purchase a legitimate work of art."

"So what? They could be *pretending* to buy something

legit. And when Paige Granger gets there, she'll negotiate something else, perhaps the Goya, and use the legitimate drawing as a ghost shipment. Happens all the
time.''

Tom shook his head, still unconvinced. ''This young
woman doesn't fit the mold of a crooked art dealer. She's
got an impeccable record, a good education, and comes
from a wealthy, respected family. Why would she jeop-
ardize all that?''

Matt shrugged. ''Greed? Power? Who knows how rich
people think?'' He continued to study Paige's file, flipping through it, noting the fancy schools she had attended, her years as an honor-roll student, some of the
charities she sponsored.

Maybe Tom was right. Maybe he was letting his dislike
of Jeremy Newman influence his judgment again. For a
week now, he had been restudying this case, going over
old files, talking to people he'd talked to three months
ago when the Goya first disappeared, and no matter how
badly he wanted to pin this on Newman, he could find
no connection between him and Krugger except a casual
acquaintance. The fact that Newman was now buying a
legitimate work of art from the man Matt had been pursuing all those weeks, presented an intriguing possibility,
but it was hardly the evidence Matt needed to hang Newman.

The case had been a classic robbery—at least by Italian
standards. Two masked men had forced entry into the
Carlucceri Museum of Fine Arts in Venice, disconnected
the alarm, and gagged a guard, before removing Goya's
famous *Doña Antonia Zarate* from its frame and fleeing
with it.

The painting, whose value was estimated at ten million
dollars, had never been recovered. Hired by the museum,
Matt had followed one cold trail after another, traveling
to Switzerland, Austria, and France. His hunch, however, was that the painting, too famous to travel without
proper documentation, was still in Italy, perhaps even in
Venice, and that the thief was simply waiting for the stat-

ute of limitations on stolen goods to expire before trying
to sell it.

After an extensive investigation, Matt's chief suspect
was a sixty-year-old American by the name of Theodore
Krugger, now a resident of Venice and the owner of a
gallery there. Krugger had been an assistant curator at
the Carlucceri Museum some years ago, and although the
police had found no motive and no evidence against him,
Matt had stayed on the case.

Enlisting the services of an Italian investigator by the
name of Amerigo, he'd found out that Krugger was married and the father of three grown children, and that two
afternoons a week he visited a young, attractive dress-
maker by the name of Donatella Serapi, who lived in an
old, dilapidated palazzo on the seedier side of Venice.

According to the detective, the relationship was a
stormy one. ''They either spend hours making passionate
love,'' Amerigo had said with a chuckle after he'd found
out about Krugger's mistress, ''or they fight like cats and
dogs. Sometimes they do both. But one thing is certain,
my friend. The lady has expensive tastes. She's bleeding
the man dry.''

It was that information, plus the fact that several years
ago Krugger had been suspected of illegal art trafficking,
although never charged, that convinced Matt he was on
the right track.

There was only a handful of collectors in the world
who could afford the Goya. Jeremy Newman was one of
them. And when Amerigo, who had put a tap on Krugger's phone weeks ago, called to say Newman was sending one of his advisers to talk to Krugger, Matt had
decided to handle the next phase himself.

''I know you like to work alone,'' Tom told Matt as
he saw him get up. ''But if this guy is getting ready to
skip town and suspects you're on to him, he could be
dangerous. I want you to take Dennis with you.''

''As you say, I work alone.'' Matt's tone softened.
''Stop worrying about me, will you? Everything will be
fine.''

"Have you made arrangements for a gun?"

Matt nodded. "Amerigo will have one waiting for me."

Tom leaned back in his chair and watched his friend, and the best agent he'd ever had, close Paige Granger's file and throw it into his briefcase. The two men had met during an art theft investigation seven years ago and had been friends ever since. Beside the fact that Tom loved Matt like a brother, he admired his coolness and his logical mind, the quick way he reacted to a situation and always managed to stay one step ahead of everyone else, including Interpol.

Hiring him two years ago had started out as a favor to Matt, who had needed the extra money to pay for his mother's high medical bills at the California Trauma Institute, where she had been in a coma since the car bombing at Newman's Ranch.

But the way it had turned out, it was Tom who had come out the big winner. Matt was a natural. And when he had a hunch, as he did now, the man was relentless.

Tom stood up. "Need a ride to the airport?"

"Nah. I'll take a cab." Matt snapped his briefcase shut. "I need you here in case Mrs. Ruznak calls back."

"Now wait a minute! I said I'd help out. I didn't say I'd play nursemaid to her."

Matt gave Tom a wide, innocent grin, unhooked his navy London Fog from a coatrack, and threw it over his shoulder. "She doesn't need a nursemaid, Tom. Just a day-by-day report on Tony's progress."

Before Tom had a chance to protest, Matt was out the door.

SEVEN

"Look, Paige, I don't want to put a damper on your excitement," Kate said when her niece called to tell her about her upcoming trip to Venice. "But this Ted Krugger business is a little too strange for me. You know nothing about this man."

"I know he has a Toulouse-Lautrec drawing Jeremy wants and he's willing to sell it. That's enough for me."

"But all this cloak-and-dagger, waiting for instructions by the phone, like some B movie. It's totally ridiculous, not to mention dangerous."

"Oh, Aunt Kate, will you stop treating me like a little girl? Everything will be fine. I told you why Krugger is being so cautious. He's probably trying to avoid paying his taxes. And while I don't condone what he's doing, I agree with Jeremy that it's none of our business."

Kate sighed. It was no use trying to use common sense when Paige was this excited about an assignment. "Will you at least promise me to be careful?" she asked as a compromise, but only because she knew she had no other choice.

"I promise. And if it'll make you feel better I'll call you as soon as I have concluded my deal with Krugger."

"Thank you, darling."

But when Kate hung up, her face was somber. She didn't like the way this assignment was shaping up. It might be perfectly innocent, but she had done enough business with Jeremy in the past to know that with him, nothing was ever as simple as it seemed.

So many times she had wanted to tell Paige the truth

about Jeremy, how she too had fallen prey to his charms and believed he was a kind and generous benefactor, when in reality he was crooked and exploitive. *And* a consummate liar.

But to divulge such secrets meant having to admit the truth about herself as well, how she had helped Jeremy with dozens of illegal transactions over the years, buying stolen paintings and objets d'art for him, forging documents, even smuggling the goods herself whenever necessary.

Paige would never understand she had done it for love. And she would never forgive her. Feeling suddenly restless, Kate walked over to the well-stocked liquor cart and poured herself a brandy. Once she had been just as ambitious and idealistic as Paige. In those early weeks after she had first arrived in Santa Barbara to help Paul care for the child, her life had revolved only around Validia's, the antiques gallery where she worked, and her niece.

She had been so happy then, so full of hopes for the future. But the dreams she dreamed seemed so far away, so unreachable at times, that occasionally she lost track of them, even wondered if they would ever come true.

And then Jeremy Newman had walked into Validia's.

Of all the important collectors she had read about, Jeremy was her favorite. Not only because of his exquisite taste, but also because he regarded art not as materialistic possessions but as great works to be admired and enjoyed by all.

To her surprise, he told her he had come to see her on the recommendation of a friend. Within a few moments, they were talking about her background, her reason for coming to Santa Barbara, and her hopes for the future.

She had never told anyone so much about herself—certainly not a stranger. Yet something about the way Jeremy questioned her made her realize he wasn't doing so out of mere curiosity, but because he was genuinely interested in her.

They talked for nearly an hour, covering a multitude of subjects—furniture, old masters paintings, medieval art, antiquities. Jeremy's knowledge was immense for such a young man. But she could see that he was equally dazzled by hers.

Later, when he steered the conversation to more serious matters, asking her opinion on expensive artworks she didn't think would ever pass through her hands, she was able to answer his questions accurately and with great flair, the way she would have if he had been a client.

"You're very good, Miss Madison," he said at last. He came to stand directly in front of her, his eaglelike stare piercing right through to her very soul. "Very good indeed."

It was then that he told her about his plans to open an antiques gallery, not in San Francisco, as one might have expected, but right here in Santa Barbara. "The Beauchamp Gallery on Anapamu Street. You may have heard of it."

She had. The owner, a widower who had never recovered from his wife's death, had allowed the gallery to get hopelessly run-down, so much so that no one had been interested in buying it. Until now.

"I'm looking for a talented and ambitious dealer to run it for me," Jeremy added, watching her closely. "Someone like you."

Speechless, Kate could only stare at him.

"If you're interested," Jeremy continued, as if he hadn't noticed the look of shock on her face. "I'd like a commitment from you as soon as possible."

"I'm very interested," she managed to say at last.

Kate's life was never the same after that.

Within six months, Beauchamp was one of the most talked-about galleries in town, with clients coming from as far as Los Angeles, and, of course, San Francisco, to purchase one of Kate's exquisite pieces.

She began to travel all over Europe, the Far East, and Central America, making important contacts everywhere she went, building her clientele and her reputation, increasing her ever-growing knowledge.

More and more, Jeremy came to rely on her, asking

her advice, talking to her on an equal level, something he didn't do with many people. He admired what he called her "vision," the way she had of looking at Beauchamp not just as it was now, but as it would be five, ten, and even twenty years from now.

But success hadn't come without a price. For Kate, that price was her integrity. In 1970, during one of their weekly business lunches at the Biltmore, Jeremy asked her to go to Frankfurt as his representative and negotiate the purchase of a ruby and diamond–encrusted Fabergé rose for his collection of the designer's famous jeweled flowers.

Kate knew immediately he was talking about the St. Petersburg Rose, which had been stolen from its owner, a London businessman, only a few weeks before.

Kate's first impulse was to turn Jeremy down. Unlike many dealers who had found great financial rewards in the trade of stolen art, Kate had no interest in making money that way. Besides, what if she were caught? What if she lost the love and respect of her family and friends? What if she ended up in prison?

In a low, soothing voice, Jeremy told her she had nothing to fear, that he would never let anything happen to her. "It's done all the time, Kate, I assure you. And if I don't buy it, someone else will."

She was still battling with her conscience when he reached across the table and took her hand. Almost immediately, dozens of different and wonderful sensations speared through her body—sensations she had tried to ignore for many months.

"I'm going to have that rose," Jeremy continued as he stroked the inside of her hand. "If not with your help, then with someone else's." He gave her a long, suggestive look. "But I'd rather it be you."

By the time coffee arrived, she had agreed to go. But she didn't do so because he was her boss, or because she owed him so much, or even because he might regard her refusal as an act of disloyalty and fire her. Kate agreed to go to Frankfurt because she was desperately in love with Jeremy, and refusing him anything was totally beyond her power.

They became lovers that night. And although the thought crossed her mind that he was securing her loyalty, she ignored it and gave herself to him body and soul.

The relationship, which he insisted should remain secret, lasted fifteen years. Never once during that time did she delude herself into believing he loved her. She knew she wasn't beautiful enough or witty enough or sophisticated enough for him. She knew he played with her emotions the way one plays with the tender strings of a violin, and that he could be terribly cruel and vindictive when something didn't go his way.

She even knew he went out with other women. Although that realization had hurt her deeply at first, she had never confronted him or made a scene. The two evenings a month she spent with him in a hotel room—for he never took her home—weren't nearly enough for all the love she had to give, yet she felt secure in their relationship, knowing he needed her too much to ever break it.

A few years later, she was able to buy into the successful gallery, and by 1978, ten years after the beginning of her association with Jeremy, Kate owned Beauchamp outright.

But her greatest reward was not the wealth she had begun to accumulate, or her reputation as one of the country's foremost art and antiques dealers. Her greatest reward was that she had earned Jeremy's absolute trust. She wasn't only his lover, but his friend and confidant as well and the only other person beside Chu Seng to know about Jeremy's "secret gallery" beneath his San Francisco house. It was an incredible room, filled with paintings, sculptures, and jewels the world thought had disappeared forever.

It shocked her at first to find out the man she idolized was nothing more than a high-class crook, and that he was using her and others to satisfy his obsession. But her love for him was so powerful, her need to please and earn his praise so vital, that the mere thought of walking away from the relationship caused her to break into a cold sweat.

She experienced her first real fears in the summer of 1985, when Caroline McKenzie, who had been having marital problems with her husband Adam for years, came to California for an indefinite stay at the McKenzies' ranch in Los Olivos.

Caroline, she knew, was the only woman who could make Jeremy consider marriage. And the only woman who could take him from her, not for a night or for a week, but forever.

A few days later, Kate's fears were confirmed, and her wonderful world came crashing down like a house of cards.

"I can't see you anymore, Kate," Jeremy told her on the telephone one afternoon in July. His voice was so cold, so impersonal, she couldn't believe he was talking to her.

"What are you saying?" she asked, her whole body trembling.

"I mean it's over. It wasn't really meant to last this long anyway, and—"

"No!" Fighting back tears of hysteria, she gripped the phone with both hands. "Don't say another word, Jeremy, please. Not until we've talked. I'll come up to San Francisco—"

"No, you won't. I don't want you coming up here, or to the ranch. I don't want any more contact with you, Kate. Is that understood?"

He couldn't have hurt her more if he had sank a knife into her heart. "Jeremy, you can't end this relationship now. We have a life together, business deals, purchases that need—"

"My lawyer will handle all that."

After he hung up, Kate sat in her bedroom in a state of shock, staring at the telephone, hearing the monstrous words over and over again. *"It's over."*

She remained there for hours, in the dark, unable to think. She wanted to die. Or kill.

As night turned into dawn, her despair grew into a rage she could no longer control. "That bitch!" she screamed, pacing her bedroom in the same clothes she'd worn the day before. After all this time. After all the humiliations she put him through when she married Adam McKenzie, she had the gall to come back here and act as if she had done nothing more serious than play hooky for thirty-six years.

She continued to pace, tearing pillows, throwing perfume bottles against the wall, shouting obscenities, until, exhausted, she collapsed into a chair.

She stayed in that same position for the rest of the day, refusing the food her maid, Lisa, brought her, only getting up to call the gallery and tell Paige she had the flu and wouldn't be in.

She thought for hours—monstrous, frightening thoughts she pushed away. But they kept coming back, each time more fierce, more persistent than the time before.

By morning, her heart was as cold as stone and her body stiff from lack of sleep. But there was no question in her mind as to what she had to do. She had to get Jeremy back. And to do that she had to kill Caroline McKenzie.

Moments later, she went into the bathroom to shower, got dressed, and drove to Los Angeles to see an old friend.

Carlos Fuente was a wealthy Nicaraguan art trafficker with a dubious background, who had left Managua abruptly three years ago, after being implicated in the bombing of a government office.

Kate had met him in 1972, when she had been looking for Aztec artifacts Jeremy wanted to buy, and although Carlos wasn't the sort of man with whom she normally associated, she had liked him and the two of them had become friends.

When he had showed up on Kate's doorstep three years

ago, claiming she was the only person in the United States he could trust, and needed a safe place to say until his assets could be transferred, she hadn't turned him away.

"I owe you my life," he had told her a few weeks later. "If you ever need me for anything, remember, Carlos is here."

She had remembered.

Two days after her visit to Carlos's luxurious Beverly Hills house, Kate had what she wanted—a bomb that was easy to install and untraceable.

"You just place it under the seat with this end up," Carlos had told her, pointing to a diagram he had made on a paper napkin. "When the passenger sits down, the bomb will detonate."

That night, still in a half-daze, Kate drove to Newman's ranch in Los Olivos, where she knew Caroline now spent all her weekends. Her rented Jaguar was in the driveway, unlocked. Kate opened the driver's side and carefully placed the bomb under the seat, the way Carlos had instructed her. Then she closed the door without a sound and drove back to Santa Barbara.

The next morning, as she was getting dressed and listening to the television news, Kate stopped dead in her tracks as she heard the broadcaster make a staggering announcement.

"Late last night, a car bomb exploded outside Jeremy Newman's ranch house in Los Olivos, California, killing New York investment counselor Adam McKenzie and seriously injuring his wife, Caroline. An investigation is under way."

Kate stared blankly at the television set as her mind tried to comprehend what she had just heard. *Adam?* Had they said *Adam*?

Frantic, she started to turn the dial in search of another news flash. When she found it, the announcement was the same. But this time it was accompanied by a photograph of Adam and Caroline together, smiling at the camera.

Kate ran into the bathroom and had barely reached the toilet bowl when she threw up.

In the weeks that followed, the police investigated a number of leads and apprehended two suspects. Both men had been clients of Adam McKenzie's and had lost a considerable amount of money recently, due to his unwise investments. According to Adam's boss, in the last week, the investment counselor had received a rash of phone calls from the two men, threatening him with bodily harm, or worse, if Adam didn't find a way of recovering their money.

A few days later, both had been released on insufficient evidence.

The police had never suspected the bomb may have been intended for Caroline. In time, they had filed the unsolved case away with dozens of others.

Kate stared into her brandy, which she hadn't touched. Many times during the last two years she had asked herself how she could have done something so vile, so violent, and so totally against everything in which she believed. Love had been her only answer. Not love as most people knew it, but an obsessive, destructive kind of love that turned gentle, decent people into monsters.

At first, her anguish over what she had done had been so deep that she had considered turning herself in. But in the end, her survival instincts, those same instincts that had helped her get through her childhood, stopped her.

With a sigh, she put the brandy snifter on the table and sat down, filled with memories she wanted to forget and couldn't.

After a moment, she lowered her head into her hands and wept.

"He's falling for you, you know," Mindy said in that knowing tone of hers.

Paige glanced in the outside mirror of her MG and stirred the powerful little car into the fast lane in order to pass an eighteen-wheeler. Even at this early morning

hour, the traffic on Highway 101, which led to the Santa
Barbara Airport and then north, toward Big Sur and San
Francisco, was already heavy with commuters. "Well, I
hate to disappoint you, Miss Know-It-All," she said,
keeping her eyes on the road as she talked. "But you're
wrong. Jeremy and I are just friends."

"You're not disappointing me. You know I can't stand
the guy."

Paige threw her an amused glance. "This from the girl
who oohed and ahhhed all over his picture once?"

"Give me a break! I was sixteen. I thought he was just
about the most handsome man in the world then."

"And you don't think he's so handsome now, is that
it?"

"No, I still think he's a great-looking guy. But now
that I'm older and smarter, I can see he's obnoxious as
hell. So why can't you?"

"You just have to know him, that's all."

"No, thanks." Mindy paused before adding, "How
does Kate feel about Jeremy's growing interest in you and
your career?"

"She's not too happy about it." Paige shrugged. "But
she'll be all right. She needs a little time to adjust to the
idea, that's all."

"Want my theory on this?"

Paige smiled, knowing a negative answer wouldn't stop
Mindy, who was just as outspoken as she was. "I'm dying to hear your theory."

"I think Kate had, and may still have, a major crush
on Jeremy. And if you're not careful, you're going to find
yourself in the middle of a very touchy situation."

Paige was silent. Long ago, when Jeremy was still
Kate's client, she had suspected the same thing. And
when Jeremy had walked away from Beauchamp two
years ago and Kate had been so deeply affected, Paige's
suspicions were stronger than ever. But she had never
believed the two had been romantically involved.

"I agree with you my aunt may have been in love with
Jeremy once," Paige conceded. "But I'm certain that's

all over now. So even if I were interested in Jeremy in a romantic way, I don't think it would matter to Aunt Kate—not in that sense anyway.''

Mindy gave her friend a worried look. ''Are you interested in Jeremy?''

''Of course I'm not, you idiot!'' Bringing the car to a stop in front of the terminal, she stepped out, pulled her suitcase out of the tiny trunk, then tossed her keys to Mindy, who caught them in midair. ''Be kind to my baby, will you? She likes to take corners on all four wheels.''

Mindy gave Paige a light kiss. ''Don't worry about your car. Worry about yourself. Alone in Venice, surrounded by all those gorgeous modern-day Casanovas.'' She sighed and rolled her eyes upward. ''I hope you remember this is where you hang your hat.''

Paige laughed and waved good-bye. ''If I decide not to come back, you'll be the first to know.''

EIGHT

A cold drizzle had been falling over the area when Paige landed at Marco Polo airport on December eighth. But now, as the motor launch sped across the choppy lagoon toward the main island of San Marco, the rain stopped abruptly and the fog began to lift, unveiling the misty beauty of one of the most written-about cities in the world—Venice.

During the summer months, the Serenissima, as Venice was often called, belonged to the tourists—throngs of travelers who took the city by siege, hurrying from one palazzo to another and storming the souvenir shops, anxious to take a piece of Venezia back with them.

But in the winter, the pace slowed and the city was returned to its citizens—proper-looking children in school uniforms, old women arguing over the price of oranges, and gondoliers patiently waiting for a fare.

Paige had been to Venice twice before, once with Kate during the carnival and another time during Regatta Week in September, when hundreds of barges lavishly decorated made their way along the Grand Canal.

Each time, Paige had been awestruck by the addictive beauty of the ancient city. And at the same time she had been filled with a sense of hopelessness. For in spite of its endurance against a sea that was steadily biding its time, there was a vulnerability about Venice, a fragility that never failed to move her. Now, as it rose from the wind-whipped waters, looking proud and defiant, Paige was reminded of a regal old queen defending her crumbling empire until her last breath.

At last, the launch left the freezing lagoon and entered the Grand Canal, which wound its way through Venice. The sun had already begun to penetrate the morning mist, wrapping the maze of streets and crisscrossing canals in a gauzy light that had some of Paige's fellow travelers, possibly first-time visitors to Venice, open-mouthed with admiration.

Paige had been huddled in her coat, but now she lowered her collar and lifted her face to the pale winter sun. Thanks to her ability to sleep like a baby on long flights, she felt rested and eager to begin her assignment. She had never felt more confident, more certain of her success than she did at this very moment.

Venice, she knew, would mark a turning point in her career. And she couldn't wait for the fun to begin.

Her photograph didn't do her justice, Matt thought, as he watched Paige Granger walk out of the Gritti Palace in that loose, swinging walk of hers. He had been in the lobby when she had arrived earlier, and even after the long flight from L.A., she had looked radiant and full of energy. With her mass of dark curls tumbling about her shoulders, her youthful gait and long-limbed figure, she had had every man in the hotel lobby, including the wide-eyed desk clerk, totally mesmerized.

Keeping his distance so he wouldn't be noticed, Matt wondered if the note the clerk had handed her a moment ago was from Ted Krugger. Taking a look at it would certainly have simplified his task. But he hadn't dared to get that close to her. And attempting to bribe the Gritti's impeccable staff would have been as pointless as trying to make a Buckingham Palace guard crack a smile.

As a *vaporetto* glided to a stop outside the hotel, Matt saw Paige hesitate. Then, after a moment of reflection, she turned away from the boat and started walking in the direction of Piazza San Marco, looking more like a tourist on a sightseeing tour than someone on her way to an important meeting.

Well, no matter how long it took to get to Krugger,

he'd wait. Stalking, waiting, and blending with the crowd was something he did well. In fact, it was probably the part of his job he liked best. Other investigators lived for the adventure, the travel to exotic locales, the women. He liked the hunt. Not that it was something he intended to do forever. At thirty-five, a man had to start thinking of his future, of something more rewarding to do with the rest of his life than chasing art thieves. Like getting married perhaps, raising children, and working at the ranch with his grandfather. That last thought brought a moment of mild nostalgia, and he shook it away quickly. He couldn't think of that now. He couldn't afford to be distracted.

His attention still focused on Paige, he watched her stop in front of a gallery featuring a one-man show before she decided to go in. After a few seconds, Matt shrugged and did the same.

At the door, a smiling, well-dressed man with a goatee and thinning gray hair—presumably the gallery owner—greeted him in Italian and offered him a glass of champagne. Matt declined the drink but returned the greeting. Italian was one of the four foreign languages he spoke fluently, as well as being his favorite.

As he mingled with the crowd, striking up a conversation here and there, he saw that although *he* had passed unnoticed, Paige Granger had not. Underneath her red coat, which now lay over her arm, she wore a fake leopard skirt that revealed terrific-looking legs, a loose black sweater, and low-heeled black walking shoes. Besides her coat, the only splash of color was a bright red wool beret, which she wore at a jaunty angle over her dark curls.

As if to echo his thoughts, an older man with a beautiful brunette on his arm turned to give Paige an appreciative glance. But she didn't seem to notice. Or chose not to. She kept moving from painting to painting, looking at each canvas closely and with enough perplexity to convince Matt she wasn't a fan of abstract art any more than he was.

Oddly, he found himself wishing the circumstances were different.

Someone was watching her.

Holding a flute a waiter had just handed her, Paige took a sip of champagne and scanned the Armani-dressed crowd above the rim of her glass. Although a few heads had turned when she had first entered the gallery, the appraisals had been open and not at all offending. This was different. It was uncomfortable, irritating. And a little eerie.

Was it possible that in spite of the instructions that had been delivered to her earlier, Ted Krugger had changed his mind and decided to follow her and meet her here after all? Was he the one watching her? And if so, where was he? Why were they playing this silly game of cat and mouse with only half the players aware of what was going on?

She had been on her way to St. Marc's Basilica when she had passed the Scorcese Gallery. Noticing a poster in the window announcing a one-man show by a contemporary local artist, and remembering what Jeremy had said about Krugger liking contemporary art, she had gone in.

The sensation of being watched persisted. Trying to appear unconcerned, Paige took another casual sip of her champagne and let her gaze drift from one small group to another. All seemed innocent enough—elegant men and women greeting each other with the exuberance Italians were famous for, and a few serious art lovers who had come here not to be seen or to drink expensive champagne but to be inspired.

Her gaze had begun a second sweep of the room when she saw him. He was tall, at least six feet two, in his midthirties, and very handsome. Lean of face and body, he had the sandy hair and hazel eyes that were a Venetian's trademark; in his well-cut tweed jacket and impeccable gray trousers, she judged him to be affluent as well as attractive.

As their eyes made contact a shapely blonde in a black see-through blouse leaned over to say something to him and his interest in Paige vanished. Amused, Paige turned back toward the painting she had been studying earlier. It was just as well. Turning down the advances of a persistent Italian wasn't on her list of favorite things to do while in Venice. Her disastrous experience with an American romeo a few years ago was still too fresh in her mind for her to even contemplate having another.

Dismissing the man with a shrug, she tried to make some sense out of the painting in front of her. The artist had ambitiously titled it "Nude Dancing." But no matter how much she concentrated, she couldn't see anything but streaks of pink, blue, and yellow that vaguely, but only vaguely, resembled a rainbow.

"Personally, I prefer Modigliani's nudes."

At the sound of the low-pitched American-speaking voice, Paige turned around and found herself face to face with the stranger who had been watching her a moment ago. He stood with his hands in his pockets, looking perfectly relaxed, as though accosting strange women in art galleries were something he did every day.

At closer inspection she saw that he didn't look Venetian at all. Although he was tanned, he didn't have the olive-tone complexion of most northern Italians, and his eyes, which she had thought hazel at first, were in fact pale gray.

Every instinct told her to walk away. She knew his kind well. Rich playboys who roamed the jet-setting capitals of the world in search of thrills, men who lived off huge trust funds and thought the word "job" had been invented for others less fortunate. Yet something kept her riveted to her spot.

"From what I saw earlier," she said lightly, "your tastes seem to lean more toward live nudes."

He laughed a warm, friendly laugh, totally devoid of embarrassment. "A temporary distraction, I assure you."

"In that case, may I suggest you return to it?"

Matt was aware of cool blue eyes assessing him. Then, without warning, she gave a brief nod of her pretty head and started to walk away.

He hadn't planned to approach her this way. In fact, he hadn't planned on approaching her at all. But like a fool, he had let his guard down and committed the ultimate error in clandestine operations. He had allowed himself to be spotted. Now it was necessary for him to change his game plan. And he had to do it quickly, convincingly.

"At least allow me to apologize for staring at you so rudely before, Miss Granger," he said to the departing figure. Then, seeing the unspoken question in her eyes as she stopped and turned around, he added, "I recognized you from a recent photograph in the *Los Angeles Times* and couldn't resist coming over to say hello—like a good neighbor."

"Neighbor?" she repeated, puzzled.

He nodded. "My name is Matt McKenzie. My grandfather and your grandmother have known each other for a long time."

Although she had never met Josh McKenzie's grandson, Paige was instantly familiar with his name. Because of Matt's two flamboyant parents, Adam and Caroline, the McKenzies had been the subject of dozens of newspaper articles over the years. But it was Adam's tragic death two years ago at Jeremy Newman's ranch that had focused the eyes of the entire nation on Santa Barbara County.

She smiled. "Of course. The famous New York investigator. My aunt mentioned you once or twice. You're somewhat of a local hero in our part of the world, Mr. McKenzie. Especially after the recovery of the Van Dyck painting last month. Congratulations. That was a spectacular job."

"I had luck on my side. But thank you. And please call me Matt."

She moved to the next painting, Matt at her side. "Are you here on business?"

"Pleasure." The lie came easily, out of habit. And

necessity. Casting an amused glance at the rest of the paintings around the room, he added, "Although so far, pleasure has eluded me."

She took another sip of her champagne. "If you aren't fond of abstract art, what are you doing here?"

"I came because a friend promised me the most exhilarating show in town." He looked around, pretending to be searching for someone. "But I seem to have been stood up." He turned back to her. "And you?"

"I never get stood up."

Amused gray eyes assessed her. "I'm sure you don't. What I meant was what brought you to the Scorcese Gallery?"

She shrugged. "The sign in the window. And the fact that I had a few hours to kill."

"In that case." Before she could stop him, he took the glass from her and handed it to a passing waiter. "Why don't you and I discreetly slip out of here and find something more stimulating to do?"

From someone else, the remark could have been regarded as suggestive. From him, it was merely intriguing. But nonetheless, friend of the family or not, she had no intention of entertaining him any further. Let the bosomy Lorelei he had admired a moment ago stimulate him.

"Maybe some other time—"

She never finished her sentence. A flurry of activity, applause, and exclamations of pleasure broke out all around them as the artist, a bony, unsmiling man, arrived fashionably late. Dressed in black pants, a matching shirt, and a black coat casually thrown over his shoulders, he looked like a mafia don. A black Fedora completed the look.

"Dear Lord," Matt whispered in Paige's ear. "Let's get out of here before someone mistakes us for fans of his." Then, firmly taking her hand, he steered her through the now very thick crowd, using his body as a shield.

As they made their way toward the door, Paige was

conscious of several things—the way he moved, slowly but with a coiled, controlled energy; how some of the women allowed him to brush against them when they could have easily moved out of his way, and how her heart thumped madly and for reasons she couldn't fathom. What was happening to her? Why was she letting this man, whom she had just met, make her feel like a silly teenager about to go on her first date?

Once outside, Matt helped her back into her coat. "What I had in mind," he said, acting as if he hadn't even heard her refusal of a moment ago, "was an exploration of Venice on foot. Have you ever done it?"

She shook her head. "There's never been enough time." Why was she answering him? Leading him on when she had no intention of going out with him?

"I promise you, it's an experience you'll never forget. Afterwards we could go to one of those small, out-of-the-way trattorias and sample some of the local cuisine. What do you say?"

Paige sighed. It was obvious from the determined look on his face that he wouldn't leave her alone until she had said yes. All right," she said at last and against her better judgment. "But I'll have to pass on dinner. I'm meeting someone at eight."

For the next five hours, they did all the things people did when they came to Venice. They strolled through a labyrinth of streets, discovering tiny alleys that spilled into unexpected piazzas neither knew existed. They shopped for *Carnevale* masks at Il Prato, sipped Bellinis at Harry's Bar, and took an outrageously expensive gondola ride down the Grand Canal, giggling like children as they passed under the Bridge of Sighs, half-expecting to see Lord Byron waving at them from his balcony.

Later, they took a *vaporetto* to Piazza San Marco, where Caffè Florian, the piazza's center stage, had moved its outdoor tables inside for the winter. There, surrounded by the cozy aroma of hot chocolate, the hiss of espresso machines, and soft, intimate lighting, Paige listened to Matt's early dreams of becoming a cowboy.

"My grandfather was my first hero," he confessed, his eyes softening as he spoke about Josh. "And those first ten years at the ranch were the happiest of my life. I was devastated when we moved to New York."

"Is it true you knew how to ride a horse before you could walk?"

"Yes, ma'am. And I have my grandfather to thank for that. And for teaching me how to build barns, put up fences, and round up cattle."

"That's pretty hard work for a young boy."

"For some, perhaps. For me, it was a dream come true."

"What happened to it?"

The gray eyes locked with hers. "You mean the dream?"

Paige caught the brief sadness in his eyes and nodded.

Matt stared into his coffee cup. "Things change. Values change."

"It's never too late for dreams, you know."

A shadow, dark and swift, passed through his eyes and for a moment she felt as if he had retreated into a very dark, lonely place. Because the last few hours had brought her very close to Matt—closer than she had wanted to be—she thought about pressing him, then changed her mind. Some secrets, she knew, were too sad, too painful to share. "I'm sorry. I didn't mean to pry."

"You weren't." He waved away her apology. "Tell me about *your* dreams."

"I'm living them each day," Paige replied honestly.

"Is Jeremy Newman one of them?"

The question, spoken with a veil of sarcasm, startled her. "Professionally speaking, yes he is," she said with a defensive squaring of her shoulders. "Why do you ask?"

He shrugged. "I read a lot of press about the two of

you recently and I was just curious about your relationship with him, that's all.''

"I see. And has your curiosity been satisfied?"

"More or less." He motioned to the waiter for two more espressos and before the uneasy moment could turn into something more serious, he brought the conversation back to a lighter subject, and made her laugh with more tales of his childhood and of Josh, whom he seemed to admire more than he had his father.

When he asked about her life in Santa Barbara, her work, and her friends, she hesitated. Because of the painful memories left by her mother's abandonment, she had never been very good at talking about herself. But somehow, with him, it was easy.

Matt watched her as she talked. She was different from what he had imagined. There was a freshness about her, a candor that didn't fit the image of the sophisticated, spoiled rich girl he'd had of her at first.

As a fascinating side of Paige Granger began to emerge, he wondered why in the world she would want to get involved with an egotistical jerk like Jeremy Newman.

"Why are you looking at me this way?"

Realizing he had been staring at her more intently than he had meant to, Matt shrugged. "I was just enjoying our conversation, the way you have of telling a story— especially that last one about your grandmother. I remember Eve Granger as a stern-voiced, rather fearless woman. The way you talk about her, the things she's done, the charities she sponsors, you make her sound almost . . .''

Paige laughed. "Human?"

"Well . . . yes. But don't tell her I said so."

Matt listened to her deep, rich laugh. Foolishly he found himself wishing the stolen Goya wouldn't be at Krugger's house, that the American wasn't his man after all. And that Paige's transaction would go on as planned without her ever knowing the true reason for his presence in Venice.

It was dark by the time they left Florian's at six o'clock. The fog had already begun its slow drift across the lagoon, wrapping Venice in a soft blanket that distanced the fifteen-hundred-year-old city even farther from the rest of the world.

During the short boat ride back to the Gritti, where Matt was also staying, they sat close and exchanged secretive glances, like long-time lovers. It was obvious to both of them that a strong attraction had developed between them and that neither was quite sure how to deal with it.

"Good night, Matt," Paige whispered when the elevator stopped at her floor. She felt sad to leave him and relieved at the same time. "It was an unexpected but wonderful . . ."

The words died on her lips. Without warning, Matt pulled her to him and kissed her.

No one had ever kissed her that way before. It was a wild, electrifying kiss, a sensual invasion of all her senses and an awakening of her deepest desires. His mouth was hot and hungry, his tongue demanding, forcing hers to respond while his hands slid slowly down her arms, drawing her closer. Heat coiled through her body, melting away her resistance, sending each nerve tingling.

When she surrendered, his response was instantaneous. His hands were all over her now, circling her waist, drifting across her breasts, cupping her buttocks. "Let's go inside," he whispered in her ear.

"I can't." She meant to push him away, run into the safety of her room. Instead, she slid her hands inside his jacket, feeling the width of broad shoulders, the flexing of hard muscles. "My meeting . . . very important."

This wasn't in the scenario, she thought as she opened her mouth to receive another kiss. This was madness. She knew nothing about him, not even if he really was who he said he was. What about that foreboding she had had earlier at the gallery? That inexplicable sense of danger? Was she going to ignore it? Was she going to be swept into something she couldn't control, something she might regret?

Reluctantly, she pulled away. "I must go."

He nodded, catching his breath. "At least let me take you wherever you're going. I'll wait for you and bring you back here."

The thought of Matt waiting for her while she tried to negotiate a multimillion-dollar deal brought her back to reality. She needed to approach Krugger with a cool, level head, not with her hormones churning at the thought of what, and who, was waiting for her.

"I don't think so, Matt." She fumbled for her key, embarrassed at her sudden clumsiness. "And anyway, I don't know how long I'll be." She produced the key and gave him a weak smile. "Saved."

At the door, she glanced coyly over her shoulder. "Would you like to have breakfast in the morning?"

He nodded, knowing that by morning, she would hate him. "Sure."

Matt stood in the hallway long after she had closed the door. Emotions, more powerful than any he had ever felt, fought to stay in check. How in hell had he let things go that far? What sort of spell had she cast on him that for a moment he had lost track of everything except the siren he held in his arms?

Taking a deep breath, he jammed his hands into his pockets, turned around, and headed for the elevator. Whatever was happening to him, he'd deal with it later. Right now, he had a job to do.

NINE

The private *motoscofo* that had been waiting by the dock outside Paige's hotel at precisely eight o'clock moved briskly across small, silent canals. The fog was thicker now, the waters ink black, illuminated only by the boat's single headlight and the lights coming from apartment windows on each side of the canal.

Paige sat in the boat, huddled in a warm purple cape under which she wore a simple black dinner dress. She shivered, suddenly filled with an uneasiness she could only attribute to the shadows and to the quiet, although efficient driver.

They moved rapidly through areas of the city that were unfamiliar to her—waterways only a very small boat could navigate, and along buildings that were so decayed, so deeply rooted in water that no amount of restoration could save them.

The note from Ted Krugger had been short and precise. "A motor launch will be waiting for you outside your hotel at eight o'clock this evening and will bring you to my home for dinner. Respectfully yours, Ted Krugger."

At last the boat slowed down and started gliding toward a landing. As Paige stepped out on the dock, a skinny black cat who had been rummaging through a garbage bin stared at her with frightened yellow eyes before scurrying away. She glanced at the decrepit apartment house that loomed in front of her and again she shivered.

"Per favore, signorina."

Realizing the driver was waiting for her, Paige nodded and followed him along a narrow, foul-smelling path that skirted a dried-up, neglected garden. As she walked up ancient stone steps, she could hear the water lapping at the foundations, claiming another chunk of history.

A short, portly man with thinning gray hair and worried brown eyes opened the door. "Good evening, Miss Granger." He glanced beyond her as if to make sure she was alone, before adding, "Welcome to my home."

"Thank you for inviting me," Paige replied as he helped her with her cape and handed it to his driver, who apparently doubled as a butler.

Paige followed her host into a large but sparsely furnished living room and remained standing while he busied himself at a cart already set up with a bottle of sherry and two glasses. Everything in the room, from the Tiepolo ceilings and brocade-covered walls to the worn red Victorian sofas, indicated that Krugger's home had once been a sumptuous residence. But now, after centuries of wind and water damage, decay had settled in like a comfortable tenant.

Discreetly, Paige took in the directoire secretary, the Chinese twin lamps, the reproductions on the walls, and the worthless knicknacks. If this were the sum of Krugger's art collection, then Jeremy had been correct in assuming it lacked imagination. None of what she saw here impressed her as being of any great value. And judging from the run-down condition of the place, there was little doubt that Ted Krugger was in dire need of money.

"Several years ago, I thought of restoring this house," Krugger said, catching her glance. "But what would be the point? This city is doomed. All the millions of dollars that are being spent each year trying to save it are a waste of time and money." He handed her a glass. "That's why young people are fleeing Venice by the hundreds. Only the old remain here. And the rich."

"And the art," she reminded him, offended that a man who had made art his life could have become so insensitive to it.

Ted Krugger gave her a sharp look. Another idealist, he thought with disgust. There were many like her these days, well-educated young men and women, who, although they had made the dealing of art their profession, regarded it more as a teaching tool than a way to make money.

Not him. From the moment he had entered this business thirty-five years ago, he'd had only one thought in mind. To be rich.

But then, things hadn't been moving fast enough for him, and in 1957, he and his wife Claire had moved to Venice, where a friend of his, also an art dealer, had made a fortune dealing in stolen art. Ted had, too. Then, when sexy Donatella had entered his life three years ago, the money started to slip through his fingers like fine sand.

But how could he refuse her the furs, the jewels, the trips to Paris at collection time, or even the Ferrari, when she looked at him with those big brown eyes and wiggled her gorgeous ass in front of his face? After forty years with Claire, he deserved a little excitement in his life.

It wasn't until Donatella told him it was time for her to move out of this house and into a palazzo on the Grand Canal that he had decided to pull the heist at the Carlucceri Museum, where he had worked years ago.

Thank God, it had been easy. Except for an alarm that Luigi, his long-time associate, had quickly disconnected, everything inside the museum was the same. If it hadn't been for another guard sounding a second alarm, they would have walked out of there with fifty million dollars in artwork.

Instead, he could only take the Goya. He had cut that one out first because it was practically sold to a Japanese collector he'd done business with in the past.

Then, at the last minute, the bastard had pulled out of the deal. Ted had tried to sell the painting elsewhere, but no one had been willing to touch it so soon after the theft. Desperate for money, he'd had no choice but to liquidate the contents of his gallery, including the Lautrec drawing. It wouldn't bring enough to buy Donatella her palazzo, but it would bring enough to fly to South America, where Donatella had always wanted to go, and start fresh. Then, in a year or so, he'd sell the Goya to one of those rich South Americans and buy Donatella anything her little heart desired. Claire would have to manage with what was left in their joint bank account.

Krugger watched Paige Granger's eyes as she studied a reproduction of a self-portrait by Renaissance artist Andrea del Sarto and wondered if she was sharp enough to spot it as a copy, if she even knew that the original hung in the Uffizi gallery in Florence. If she did, she might worry about the authenticity of the Lautrec she had come to purchase.

She needn't. He had more sense than to play games with a man like Jeremy Newman.

"Pretty good for a reproduction, isn't it?" he asked, deciding to play it safe.

"Excellent. The brown hues are a little too vivid, though." Paige turned and gave him a pleasant smile. "Softer, more indirect lighting should correct that."

Krugger gave a short bow of his head. So the girl was knowledgeable as well as beautiful. Well, that shouldn't have surprised him. Newman was known to associate only with the very best.

That was fine with him. If she were that smart, she would know the Lautrec was well worth the three million dollars he intended to ask for it.

Paige, who never touched alcohol during a negotiation, put her glass down. "Could I take a look at that drawing now, Mr. Krugger?"

Krugger nodded and took another sip of his sherry before putting his glass down. "Certainly." With an affable smile, he led her into an adjoining room that was empty except for a few packing boxes that had been sealed and numbered.

In a corner, propped on an easel, with an indirect light that accentuated the charcoal shadings, was Lautrec's *La Goulue* in all her bawdy splendor.

Krugger chuckled. "Ah, I see from the flicker in your eyes that something of mine has finally impressed you."

Paige didn't reply. Although she was familiar with many of Lautrec's drawings, she had never seen any of his early works. This particular one was from a famous series of cabaret scenes, featuring *La Goulue*, a Parisian entertainer with whom the artist had been fascinated. In it he had captured the dancer's very essence, her restless energy, the knowing "come-on" of her gaze, coupled with a loneliness that never failed to startle.

"It's lovely," Paige said at last, backing away, not taking her eyes off the drawing. "May I ask why you're selling it?"

Krugger shrugged. "For the same reason one sells stocks. To make money."

Again, his comment offended her, but she resisted the impulse to make one of her own. "And how much are you asking for the drawing, Mr. Krugger?"

"Why don't we discuss this over dinner?" Gallantly, he offered his arm, which she took. "I'm not only hungry, but I find dinner conversation infinitely more suited to conducting business, don't you?"

Paige smiled and bowed her head. He was hungry, all right. For Jeremy's money. That's why he'd gone to him first, knowing Jeremy would give him the best price for his merchandise.

She smiled, wondering how outrageous Krugger's first offer would be.

Using a pencil flashlight to guide his way, Matt hurried up the back stairs of Donatella's apartment building, moving with the speed and stealth of a panther. Dressed in black from head to toe, he blended well with the night.

Taking a gamble Paige would be going to her meeting in a launch, he had hired a *motoscofo* to stand by and had given his driver a silent signal as soon as she had boarded her boat.

Following her had been tricky. Nightlife in Venice, especially at this time of year, was practically nonexistent, and as Paige's boat had wended its way in and out of deserted canals, remaining unnoticed had been difficult.

Halfway to their destination, he had realized they weren't going to Krugger's house but to Donatella's. Matt had been there before and had searched the place thoroughly, as he had Krugger's gallery and his home near the Rialto market. At the time, he had found nothing. But tonight, he had a hunch he would.

Getting inside the house was easy. He'd climbed dozens of balconies in his career, forced open twice as many windows, and distracted more servants than he could remember. He knew the local authorities wouldn't look kindly on this kind of behavior on their own territory, but Inspector Francesco Lippi of the Venice police, with whom Matt had been working on this theft, would be glad to close the file on the case.

As he peered through a window, Matt saw the man who had driven Paige's boat sitting at the kitchen table, watching a comedy show on a small television set. From time to time, he'd roar with laughter as he slapped his thigh repeatedly. There was no need to distract him. He'd be occupied for awhile.

Once he had located the back entrance, Matt let himself in, wincing as the warped, ancient wood door creaked open. But in the next room, the laughter went on uninterrupted.

After checking to make sure there were no other servants, Matt made his way toward the staircase. Krugger and Paige were deeply involved in their conversation and never saw his shadow flash across the hall.

Since he had been here before, he knew the apartment layout well and, rather than search every room, he went directly to the master suite, opening the door slowly. He didn't think Donatella would be in here, but when he found the room empty, he heaved a sigh of relief just the same. A screaming woman would have put a serious crimp in his plans.

He moved quickly and soundlessly toward an antique

armoire he knew concealed a small closet. It had been empty when he had first discovered it three months ago, and there was always the possibility it would be empty now. But he didn't think so. Three large suitcases sat at the foot of the four-poster bed, all closed and ready to go. Thrown over them was a man's navy cashmere coat. Had he had time to look for it, Matt knew he would have found a one-way airline ticket out of the country.

Using a small rug to slide the heavy armoire out of the way, Matt opened the closet door. There, standing upright against a wall, was a packing tube about two inches in diameter.

Holding his breath, Matt removed the cap, slowly pulled out the contents, and unrolled the canvas. Only then was he able to let his breath out. Although it had been cut from its frame to facilitate the theft, the Goya hadn't been damaged. Carefully, Matt rerolled the famous painting, slid it back into its container, and placed it back where he'd found it, shutting the closet door but not bothering to replace the armoire.

Moving toward the telephone on a night table, he picked up the receiver and dialed Francesco Lippi's number. While he waited for the inspector to come to the phone, he wondered how understanding Paige would be when she found out he had ruined her deal.

She wouldn't have rated the evening as one of the most exciting moments of her life. Krugger had turned out to be a pompous bore and a tougher negotiator than she had expected. Finally, after nearly an hour of dickering, they had agreed on two and a half million dollars for the Lautrec—a little more than Paige had expected to pay, but still a good price. Jeremy would be pleased.

Now, anxious to wrap up the deal and get back to her hotel, Paige turned down Krugger's offer of dessert and laid her napkin by the side of her plate. "If you have no objections, Mr. Krugger. I would like to call Mr. Newman's attorney right away so that we may finalize everything within the next twenty-four hours."

"I'm afraid that's not possible," a familiar voice said from behind her. "Your Mr. Krugger isn't going to be in a position to finalize any deals for a very, very long time."

TEN

Paige spun around in her chair just as Krugger bolted to a standing position.

"Who the hell are you?" he shouted, his face an angry red. "And how did you get in?"

Paige's astonished gaze swept over Matt's black pants, the jacket, the hat. "Matt! What in the world—"

"You know this man?" Krugger's eyes darted back and forth from her to Matt.

"I do, but—"

"My name is Matt McKenzie," Matt said. "I'm with Worldwide Investigations." In a gesture Paige barely noticed, he produced an identification case and flashed it open long enough for the dealer to see the credentials. "You are a difficult man to catch, Krugger."

"You stupid woman!" Krugger bellowed, hitting the table so hard a glass toppled over, spilling red wine over the white tablecloth. "You told a *detective* about this meeting? After all the trouble I went to, explaining—"

"She didn't tell me anything." Matt came to stand by her as if they were allies facing a common enemy. Two hours ago, she would have found the gesture reassuring, perhaps even endearing. Now a sixth sense told her *he* was the enemy.

"I knew she was meeting you somewhere in Venice this evening," Matt continued. 'And I followed her."

"You followed me?" Paige repeated in angry disbelief. "Why?"

"Because I've been after this man for three months,

looking for a stolen Goya he's got hidden in an upstairs closet."

"That's ridiculous! Mr. Krugger is a respectable art dealer. I'm here to do business with him."

"Your respectable Mr. Krugger is nothing more than a clever thief who was about to use Newman's money to finance a quick escape from Italy." He hadn't taken his eyes off the American art dealer. "Where were you off to, Krugger? South America? Or Japan, perhaps? Both have a relatively short statute of limitations, don't they?"

Krugger was swallowing rapidly and choking at the same time. "Out!" he shouted. "Both of you, out. I don't have to answer any of your questions. You have no authority here, McKenzie. And certainly no right to be in my house. Luigi!" he called, glancing toward the door.

"You mean Donatella's house, don't you? By the way," Matt asked, glancing around him, "where is she?"

In a state of half-shock, Paige said, "Who's Donatella?"

"Krugger's mistress. A very expensive mistress. She's the reason our friend here is in this mess, isn't it, Teddy?"

"I don't know what you're talking about. You've got me mixed up with someone else. Luigi!" he shouted again, louder this time. "Goddamn it, where is that man?"

Luigi ran in, a startled look on his face. As soon as he saw Matt, he came to a stop.

"Not a move or a sound from you," Matt told him in Italian. From his back pocket, he pulled out the nine-mm Beretta that Amerigo had given him earlier and waved it at a chair in a far corner. "Over there. Slowly."

As Luigi meekly did as Matt instructed him, Paige's gaze tore itself from the gun and shot back to Krugger, whose face had turned a sick shade of gray. She remembered the packed boxes in the next room, his instructions to Jeremy, his nervousness when she had first arrived. She had assumed he was worried about a government investigator, but judging from the trapped look on his face now, he was guilty of a lot more than tax evasion. "Is any of this true?" she asked, praying he would say no and make her believe it.

"Of course it's not true! I know nothing about a stolen painting." Picking up his napkin from the table, he wiped his forehead. "Yes, I have a Goya upstairs, but it's mine. Everything in this house is mine, bought in good faith."

Matt gave him a thin smile. "And Mussolini was an angel of mercy."

"Out of my house!" Krugger repeated, pointing at the hallway behind them with a shaking finger. "Or I'll call the police."

"I've saved you the trouble, pal." Matt glanced at his watch. "The police should be here any minute. Until then," he reached for a chair nearby, and slid it in Krugger's direction, "you sit quietly. Like your friend. And don't try anything funny unless you want to end up with a hole in your kneecap." Although Krugger gave Matt a hateful look, he too did as he was told.

Turning to Paige, Matt's tone softened. "I'm sorry you had to be involved in this."

"You're *sorry*? How can you be *sorry* when you planned this farce from the beginning?"

"I had no choice."

"Of course you had a choice. You could have told me the truth. I would have understood. I would have cooperated. Unless," she added, her tone turning sarcastic, "I too was under suspicion."

As Matt remained silent, fury, hot and wild filled her chest. "My God, that's it, isn't it? You thought I came to Venice not to buy the Lautrec, but the Goya."

Matt had the grace to look miserable. "I admit that I thought so at first, but not for long, Paige, I swear it."

"Then why didn't you tell me what was going on?"

"I couldn't afford to take any chances."

"So you set me up."

"Not exactly—"

"Running into each other at the gallery earlier?" she interrupted. "That wasn't by chance, was it?"

He held her gaze. "No."

"You knew I was coming here? To Venice?"

He nodded. "I've had Krugger under surveillance for some time now. That's how I knew he was planning to sell Newman the Lautrec. What I didn't know was where he had the Goya. Somehow, in the last couple of days, he slipped by my man—"

She wasn't listening to him. "It was all an act—the pretended friendship, the warm, amusing stories of your childhood. It was all meant to soften me up, to take me off guard, so I would confide in you, tell you where I was going."

"You're wrong about that—"

"No, Matt. *You* are wrong to think I'm going to stand here and listen to one more lie."

As she started to leave, he stopped her. "You can't go yet."

She gave a contemptuous glance to the hand that held her arm and waited for him to remove it. "Why not?"

"Because the police are going to want to question you too." Her body grew rigid. "It'll only be a formality, Paige. But it has to be done."

They were interrupted by the sound of footsteps echoing through the house. Moments later, a short, wiry man with black hair and shrewd brown eyes walked in. Behind him was a uniformed policeman who quietly took his position by the door.

"I see you've got everything under control," the plain-clothed man told Matt in an accented English. He glanced at Krugger, who was now prostrated in his chair, his eyes staring blankly at the floor. After a moment, the man returned his gaze to Paige. "Is she the accomplice?"

"I most certainly am not!" Paige cried.

Matt smiled. "This is Miss Granger, Francesco. You might say she's an innocent bystander. The one you want is over there." He pointed to where Luigi sat.

The Italian glanced behind him and nodded before returning his attention to Paige. "I'm Inspector Lippi," he said. "May I ask what you were doing here this evening, Miss Granger?"

Humiliation at the thought that he too had mistaken her for a thief brought a new flash of anger, but somehow she managed to control it. "Are you suspecting me of something, Inspector?"

"Not unless you give me reason to."

Paige squared her shoulders. "I'm an American art dealer. I came to Venice to purchase a drawing from Mr. Krugger."

"A legitimate drawing," Matt interjected. "I checked."

She threw him a scathing look before deliberately turning her back to him. "I would like to be allowed to conclude my transaction, if you don't mind." She didn't have much hope the policeman would allow her to do that, but she couldn't leave here without at least trying. "After all, the Lautrec has nothing to do with your case. Am I right?"

"Yes, that is correct. But I'm afraid what you ask is not possible, Miss Granger. This apartment and its contents will be sealed pending an investigation of Mr. Krugger's activities. Later, perhaps—"

"How much later?"

Lippi shrugged. "Who can say? This is Italy, Miss Granger. Red tape moves slowly here."

"I see." She tried not to think of Jeremy, of his reaction not only once he found out she had failed him, but at the realization that Matt McKenzie was the one responsible for this fiasco.

"Will you be in Venice long, Miss Granger?"

"I'm leaving tomorrow. Why?"

At those words, Matt took a step forward. "Paige, please stay another day. You and I need to talk."

Tossing her hair behind her shoulders, she gave the inspector a cool, questioning glance. "Do I have to answer any of *his* questions?"

Lippi glanced from one to the other with great interest,

his shrewd eyes quickly assessing the situation. "Not unless you want to. But I will need a statement from you."

"Do I have to do it this evening?"

Lippi shook his head. "Tomorrow morning will be fine." He handed Paige a card with his name and an address on Calle dei Fuseri. "Can you meet me at the station at eight o'clock?"

"Yes. Thank you. May I go now?"

"Certainly."

When she turned to leave, Matt was standing behind her, her cape in his hands, ready to help her with it. He had been as silent as a shadow.

"Give me this," she said, snatching the garment from his hands.

"You'll need a ride to the hotel. Give me a minute and I'll take you back."

"What I'll give you," she flared, "is five seconds to get out of my way."

Turning to the inspector who was still watching the exchange with fascinated interest, Paige nodded at him. Then she swung the coat around her, and ignoring Matt, stalked out of the room.

Matt stood in front of the bathroom mirror, shaving with nothing but a towel wrapped around his hips. From time to time, his left hand reached for the cup of strong Italian coffee he had balanced on the edge of the sink, and he took big gulps of it.

Despite the fact he had only slept four hours, his hand was steady, his stroke sure as he guided the razor through the thick lather. His mind, however, was elsewhere.

Without interrupting what he was doing, he glanced at his watch on the other side of the sink. Eight-thirty. Paige should be back from her meeting with Francesco in about an hour. The question was, would she agree to talk to him then, or would she take her phone off the hook and not answer the door the way she had done last night?

He tried to keep his mind on what he would say to her, but it kept wandering back to the two of them strolling through the streets of Venice yesterday, hand in hand. He thought of the way she had looked at Florian's, relaxed and playful, of the glances they had exchanged in the boat on the way back to the Gritti Palace. Had she realized then the effect she was having on him? Had *he*?''

With a sigh, he put his razor down, rinsed his face, and went in to get dressed. At nine-fifteen, unable to wait a moment longer, he dialed Paige's room. He tried again at nine-twenty and then again five minutes later.

''Damn you, Francesco. What the hell is taking you so long?''

By nine-forty-five, he called the hotel desk. Maybe she was back and wasn't answering the phone. If so, his job would be even more difficult than he had anticipated.

''Did you notice if Miss Granger came back yet?'' he asked the desk clerk after identifying himself.

''Miss Granger won't be back, sir. She checked out early this morning.''

''Checked out? Where did she go?''

''Back to the United States, I believe.''

Matt thanked him, hung up, and immediately dialed the airport. After the expected runaround, an Alitalia supervisor came on the line and agreed to bend the rules a little.

''Yes, we have a Miss Paige Granger booked on our Venice–London–New York flight, Mr. McKenzie. That plane leaves in thirty-five minutes.''

Two minutes later, Matt was boarding a *motoscofo* outside the hotel. ''I'll pay you twice the fare if you get me to the airport in half the time,'' he told the driver, who grinned knowingly.

Maneuvering the boat through the morning traffic wasted an incredible amount of time, but once they were out in the lagoon, in the open waters, the powerful boat raced toward its destination like a torpedo.

Once at the airport, Matt ran to the Alitalia's departure gates. A handful of passengers, tickets in hand, were getting ready to board a plane. But there was no sign of Paige anywhere.

"That London-bound plane," he told a startled airline representative at the desk. "I need to get someone off right away. It's an emergency."

The clerk shook his head. "You are too late, *signore*. It just took off."

ELEVEN

"Oh, dear!"

At his mother's exclamation, Paul Granger, who had been reading the transcripts of a murder trial case prior to sentencing, looked up across the dining room table. "What is it, Mother?"

"Why, it's Paige," Eve Granger said, turning her copy of the *Santa Barbara News Press* so her son could see the article that had caught her attention. "She's been involved in some dreadful Italian scandal."

"What!" Paul grabbed the newspaper. On an inside page was a photograph of his daughter and underneath the caption: "Santa Barbara art dealer involved in international art scam."

Paul's gaze shifted to the article below. According to United Press International, Theodore Krugger, an American art dealer living in Italy, had been arrested during an investigation conducted by private investigator Matthew McKenzie of New York City. Paige, who had been at Krugger's home at the time of the arrest, had been questioned and then released.

"Why didn't she call?" Eve said in a plaintive tone. "Why didn't she tell us she was in trouble?"

"Probably because she didn't want to upset you."

"But we could have helped. We could have stopped the newspapers from printing that story."

Paul laid the paper down. "Paige is a big girl, Mother. She's perfectly capable of handling every facet of her career—good and bad." He smiled. "Besides, I doubt that even *you* could have stopped UPI from doing their job.''

That wasn't entirely true. Even now, at eighty-five, with her snow-white hair and her occasional bouts with arthritis, Eve Granger looked as invincible and as capable of taking on an army of reporters as she had when she was half her age.

"Well, I find this news very distressing," Eve continued, undisturbed by Paul's remark and his mocking smile. "Paige's entire future depended on the successful completion of that deal for Jeremy Newman. It's bad enough it went sour. But to have Matt McKenzie, of all people, involved . . ." She shook her head, briefly closing her eyes for greater emphasis. "Jeremy isn't going to like that at all."

"But it isn't Paige's fault. She had no idea Krugger was a thief or that Matt McKenzie was investigating him. I'm sure Jeremy will understand that."

"Then you don't know Jeremy. He's going to be furious. Especially so soon after that Veracruz scandal." Dramatically, to make sure she would catch her son's attention, she fell back against her chair. "He's going to think Paige is jinxed."

Pouring himself another cup of coffee, Paul smiled and gazed fondly at the regal woman sitting across the dining room table.

Except for being older, she wasn't much different from the woman with whom he had grown up. Her hair, completely white now, was still combed in that tidy top knot, and her green eyes were as sharp today as they had been when he was a boy.

Although she was an incorrigible meddler, he loved her dearly. He loved her strength, the way she had held this family together during his father's long battle with cancer, and after his death more than twenty years ago.

And how could he forget how vital her love and support had been during the difficult weeks after Ann had left him? He'd been at his lowest then, ready to give up everything he had worked for, buried in his grief.

But Eve Granger was a woman for whom the word "defeat" was synonymous with "disgrace." "A Granger does not wallow in self-pity," she told him one evening as he sat in his room, his head in his hands. "As ill as your father was, he never allowed anyone to feel sorry for him. And he never allowed his illness to stop him from leading a full and enjoyable life. Right up to the end."

"I have no life without Ann."

"Nonsense. You have a brilliant career ahead of you. And you have a daughter who needs you."

She had been right. In time, and although he had never stopped loving Ann, his wounds had healed. A few years later, he had been elected district attorney, and had gone on to become one of the best criminal judges in the state of California.

Looking pleased that at last she had his undivided attention, Eve said, "You know, Paul, I may have found the perfect solution to our dilemma."

"I wasn't aware we *had* a dilemma."

Alert green eyes sparkled at him, full of sudden mischief. "What would you think of a Christmas party, darling? Something outrageous and glamorous to kick off the holiday season? I know it's short notice. But I'm sure Lucinda and her marvelous catering staff will be able to accommodate us somehow."

"What brought that on?"

Eve met her son's suspicious blue gaze without flinching. "Why, the spirit of the season, of course."

"Bull. You've got something cooking in that lovely head of yours, and I want to know what it is."

"Very well, if you must. I thought a party would be the perfect way for Jeremy and Paige to get closer."

Seeing the incredulous look in Paul's eyes, she added, 'Oh, come now, darling. Don't tell me you haven't noticed how simply perfect those two are for each other."

"By perfect, I take it you mean in a romantic way?"

"Why the shocked expression?"

"Because I can't believe you would even think of playing matchmaker between Jeremy and Paige. They have nothing in common, Mother, except their love of art. And he is twice her age.''

''I thought you liked Jeremy.''

''He's all right. But not as a potential son-in-law.'' At the sound of those words, Paul chuckled. ''Dear God, the mere thought of that is so ludicrous, I have a hard time keeping a straight face.''

''Does that mean you aren't in favor of a Christmas party?''

''I'm in favor of it only if you promise not to play Cupid and not to pressure Paige in any way.''

''All right, all right, I promise.''

Although the impatient wave of her hand told Paul she was lying, he resisted the impulse to press his point any further. His mother was getting old and she had been lonely since Paige had moved out of the house a year ago. Maybe one of her fancy parties was exactly what she needed to cheer her up. He would talk to Paige when she returned from Venice and warn her of what her grandmother was up to.

''I have to go,'' he said, tossing the transcripts into his briefcase. He stood up and downed the last of his coffee before kissing his mother on the cheek. ''See you tonight, beautiful.''

She straighted his necktie. ''You're handing down your sentence on the O'Malley case today, aren't you?''

Paul nodded.

''I hope you'll give him the maximum the law allows, darling. Santa Barbara has no use for a degenerate like him.''

Paul shook his head as he walked away. It always amazed him that although he had just turned fifty-three, Eve still tried to run his life the way she had when he was a boy.

Watching her son walk away, Eve Granger marveled at how much Paul looked like his father. He had the same handsome physique, the same energetic walk, the same curly brown hair and direct blue gaze. And thanks to her, he had become as good a criminal judge as Cabbot had been. Perhaps even better. And he would go farther, too. If he ever stopped being so stubborn.

In spite of Paul's occasional complaints that she was trying to run his life, she was proud to have played such an important role in her son's career. And she would continue to do so until the day she died. How else was he going to be elected governor of California?

Paul hadn't shown much interest in the idea when she had first suggested it to him. In fact, in the last few months, he had been talking about leaving the bench and taking time off to write a novel—a murder mystery, of all things.

Of course, retiring when he had such a golden future ahead of him was totally unacceptable. But she hadn't argued with him at the time. She knew once the Republican Party approached him, he wouldn't be able to turn them down.

Paul was a natural for politics. For awhile, he hadn't thought so. But that had been Ann's fault. She had held him back. With her lack of ambition and her narrow vision, she had been an albatross around his neck.

Well, thank God, that part of his life was over. Ann had been delt with discreetly and quickly, before she could destroy Paul's brilliant future.

Smiling now, because she took great pride in her resourcefulness, Eve picked up the green Sèvres teapot from a set that had been in the Granger family for generations, and poured herself another cup of Earl Grey, which her maid, Maria, always prepared the way she liked it—hot and strong. Then she stood up and, carrying her cup, she walked over to the open window, pleased to see that the gardeners were already busy stringing Christmas lights in the evergreens that lined the long serpentine drive.

She inhaled deeply. Those last two months of the year, November and December, were her favorite; partly because everything was so crisp and clean, and partly because they brought back such fond memories.

It was shortly before Thanksgiving that she and Cabbot had moved into this house. It had been only a modest two-story colonial then, built on the land her father, one of Montecito's early settlers, had given them as a wedding present. But as Cabbot's law career had expanded, so had the house, until it had become one of the most beautiful and most photographed estates in Montecito.

"Señora Granger?"

Eve turned around. "Yes, Maria?"

"You have a phone call," Maria said, handing her the portable phone. "It's Paige."

"Oh." Eve's face immediately brightened. "Paige, darling," she said into the phone. "Where are you?"

"Heathrow, Grandmother, I need you to—"

"You should have called sooner, Paige. There was no reason for you to go through this ordeal all alone. I'm sure I could have done something to prevent that awful story from appearing in all the newspapers."

"Grandmother, will you please listen to me. I can't talk right now. I'm about to board my flight, and I need you to tell Mindy that I'm coming in a day earlier. If she can't pick me up, tell her not to worry. I'll take a limo. Can you do that for me, Grandmother?"

"Well, of course I will, dear. But first I want to—"

"Can't now. Love you. Bye."

As the line disconnected, Eve, a look of disbelief on her face, contemplated the telephone for a moment as if she expected the instrument to give her an explanation of her granddaughter's strange behavior. Then, with a shake of her head, she turned the switch off. She'd never understand young people today. Always on the go, always in a hurry, never taking time for what really mattered: the family.

And she understood Paige least of all. With a little help from Eve, the girl could have been a curator at any of the state's greatest museums. She could have had a position of respect and prestige, been invited to all the right functions, sat on important boards. But she hadn't been interested.

"I'll be the one to decide where and how far my career will go, Grandmother," she had said in that half-mocking, half-serious tone Eve knew so well. "No one else."

Of course Eve knew perfectly well who was to blame for some of Paige's shortcomings. Kate. Although different from Ann in many respects, Kate had always been weak where Paige was concerned, spoiling her shamelessly, giving in to all her whims, allowing her to be a "free thinker," which in her opinion was synonymous with being a "hippie."

Not that Paige was a bad person. Far from it. She was beautiful, intelligent, respectful most of the time, and loving. But she was a wildcat. And once in a while, she needed someone to point her in the right direction.

And the right direction, Eve had decided, was Jeremy Newman. The man had breeding, status, and wealth, and he obviously adored Paige.

Eve smiled, remembering her earlier thought of hosting a Christmas party. It would be the perfect setting for a budding romance. Paul might disapprove of her meddling, but deep down he was just as anxious as she was to see his daughter settled.

Her hand, which was remarkable steady for a woman her age, went to touch the long rope of pearls that hung around her neck, for even at breakfast, Eve Granger insisted on being perfectly dressed, perfectly groomed.

After awhile, she turned around and looked directly across the room at the portrait of her husband that hung on the wall above the buffet table. She raised her cup in a private salute.

"Don't worry, darling. It will all work out in the end. You know I always do what's best for the family."

She had screwed up royally.

Sitting in the plane that was taking her back to New York where she would catch a connecting flight to Santa

Barbara, Paige tossed aside a copy of the *London Daily Mail*. That newspaper, as well as several other publications, had carried a complete account of her "Venetian Affair," as the press had been quick to label her unfortunate trip.

In spite of Inspector Lippi's promise to keep her name and Jeremy's out of the papers, the story had leaked out somehow. By the time Paige had arrived at Marco Polo Airport, the Italian press, with their usual flair for the dramatic, had turned the story into something that read like an Ian Fleming novel.

Jeremy would be furious. He would fire her. And after reading the dozen or so variations of the incident, including the one that had romantically linked her to Matt McKenzie and asserted that the two had conspired together to trap Krugger, the local press would hound her for weeks.

Leaning back, she tried to sleep, or at least doze off for a little while. But every time she closed her eyes, she thought of Matt, of how he had used her, lied to her, tricked her.

How could she have been so gullible? Allowing herself to fall for the oldest con game of all. Seduction. Like a schoolgirl, she had let herself be swept away by the magic of those cool gray eyes, the firm touch of his hand, the soothing, caressing sound of his voice. Fool, fool, fool.

"Miss Granger, would you like something to drink? Wine? Champagne? A soft drink?"

Paige met the flight attendant's friendly gaze and shook her head. Her stomach was a bundle of raw nerves and the thought of drinking or eating anything made her feel ill. With a sigh, she picked up a copy of *Newsweek* and flipped through it, hoping to find something that would distract her for the next hour or so.

As she scanned the art section, her gaze fell on an article about Zachary Calvert, a well-known Manhattan art collector. The photograph that accompanied the write-up showed him in front of his latest acquisition, *Taking the Bastille*, an exquisite Aubusson tapestry depicting the day French revolutionary troops had stormed the infamous prison. She had met the industrialist in New York City six months ago during a fund-raising benefit for the Metropolitan Museum of Art.

Calvert's art collection, although not as important as Jeremy's, had been written about in various magazines over the years. He was known as a man of strength and determination who enjoyed making headlines and being the envy of other collectors. His acquisition of the French tapestry a few days ago had made Jeremy furious.

"Do you know how long I've been after this tapestry?" he had fumed. "Ten years. I was willing to pay any price for it. And the bastard steals it right from under my nose."

As Paige continued to read the *Newsweek* article, a bold, incredible idea began to take shape in her mind, sending a tingle of anticipation up and down her spine. An idea that would salvage her career with Jeremy. Stunned that she would even think such preposterous thoughts, she told herself it would never work, that she would end up being in even greater trouble than she already was. And then again . . .

Turning around in her seat, she caught the attention of the flight attendant and asked for a telephone. Moments later, she was dialing Manhattan information for Zachary Calvert's number, praying it would be listed.

With a sigh of relief she listened to the recording as it gave her the number.

"Why in the world would I want to sell a work of art it took me years to acquire?" Zachary Calvert asked. "And to Jeremy Newman, of all people?"

Paige sat in the collector's elegant living room overlooking Park Avenue. He had not only remembered her but had told her he would be delighted to see her.

Calvert was in his late sixties, with thinning white hair, round, rimless glasses, and smooth, pink cheeks that made him look like someone's favorite uncle. Only his eyes, dark and shrewd, suggested a man of incredible strength.

"Because you are a dealmaker first and a collector second," she replied in answer to his question. "And the offer I'm about to make you is a fabulous deal. One that even a successful businessman like you doesn't make every day."

She saw the hint of interest in his eyes. "What kind of a deal?"

"I'll give you exactly what you paid for the tapestry, since we both know it's overvalued and you'd never be able to sell it for more, but I'll throw in something Mr. Newman has and that I know you want very much—as much as he wants your tapestry."

"What's that?"

"His Prince Rudolf hunting sword."

Except for a repeated flicker of his right eyelid, Calvert remained perfectly still. "Does Jeremy know you're using his precious sword as a bargaining tool?"

"No. He doesn't even know I'm here."

"Then you're a very brave young woman."

"I'm a desperate woman, Mr. Calvert. I'm sure you've read the newspapers."

"What if he turns you down? He hates my guts, you know."

"He won't turn me down," she said, choosing to ignore his last remark.

Paige watched Calvert walk to the window. Sixty-two floors below, Manhattan battled with its second rush hour of the day. But inside the plush penthouse, not a single street sound could be heard—only the hammering of her own heart.

When Calvert turned to face her again, the nervous eye twitch was gone. "You're a hard person to say no to, Miss Granger. "And Jeremy is a lucky man."

Relief washed over her. "Is that a yes?"

Zachary Calvert smiled, looking very much like a sweet old uncle again. "Yes, Miss Granger. A resounding yes."

TWELVE

From New York, Paige had flown directly to San Francisco to see Jeremy. Now, sitting in the vast drawing room and surrounded by all the things he treasured, she was filled with apprehension at the enormity of what she had done.

The sword, which had belonged to crown Prince Rudolf of Austria, wasn't Jeremy's most valuable item, but it was one of his favorites. Made of silver and decorated with bears, boars, and dragons, it had remained in the royal family for nearly two centuries before finally being made available to the public. Jeremy had bought it at an auction two years ago and kept it prominently displayed in a glass and mahogany case against the wall directly in front of her.

To give herself something to do, Paige picked up a teapot from a tray Chu Seng had brought in, and refilled her cup with the hot, fragrant brew. Behind her, a clock that had once stood on Mozart's mantel struck four o'clock.

She had been waiting for nearly ten minutes. Not a good sign. She knew Jeremy well enough by now to realize that this unnecessary wait was a form of punishment for her failure, a way for him to assert his authority, to clue her that she was no longer important.

Willing herself to stay calm, she continued to sip her tea, ignoring the sword, trying to convince herself that once she told Jeremy of the exchange she had negotiated, he would be so pleased, he'd forget about the Lautrec drawing.

The door opened. Jeremy, impeccable as always in navy trousers and a cream turtleneck, stood in the doorway, his dark eyes unsmiling, his mouth set in a tight, forbidding line. Paige resisted the impulse to stand. ''Good afternoon, Jeremy.''

He dipped his chin. ''Paige.''

For a moment, Jeremy didn't move, content enough to watch her. Although she looked tired and preoccupied, he had never seen her looking more beautiful or more desirable. She wore a winter white wool coatdress with a tapered waist and a large sunflower pin on the lapel.

Keeping his emotions under control, Jeremy marveled at how exquisitely she fitted into his surroundings. There was a racy elegance about her, a youthful vitality that made all the other women he had known, with the possible exception of Caroline, pale in comparison.

He imagined her in one of Caroline's gowns. The gold Givenchy perhaps, with the long, full satin skirt and the pearl-encrusted bodice. Paige would look wonderful in designer clothes. He thought of her walking around this room as his wife and hostess, entertaining his guests, discussing his priceless paintings, smiling that wide, seductive smile.

He hadn't wanted to make her wait this long. But it was important that she be made aware of her weaknesses. It would make her more vulnerable, more anxious to please him in the future.

He could tell by her relaxed facial expression, by the way she held her back, that in spite of all that had happened, she had lost none of her confidence, none of that pride he had so often admired.

If any of his other consultants had failed him this way, he would have fired them on the spot. He couldn't do that with Paige. He could no more walk away from her now than he could stop buying works of art. Her presence had become indispensable. She had become his most challenging quest, his master plan. Winning her was a thought so delicious, so utterly exciting that every time it entered his mind, he found himself in an extraordinary state of arousal.

Finally, he broke the awkward silence. "I assume you've seen the papers?"

Knowing how Jeremy hated meekness, Paige returned his steady gaze, measure for measure. "I'm very sorry about that, Jeremy. However, I never talked to a single reporter. You must believe that. As far as that ridiculous story about Matt and I being romantically involved, it's absolutely untrue." She hoped the slight falter in her voice as she spoke those last words hadn't betrayed her.

"I believe you." Jeremy was still standing, still looking at her. "What I can't understand is how you allowed yourself to be fooled by a man like Matt McKenzie."

The words, spoken through tight lips, were filled with venom and Paige realized that his anger stemmed more from the fact that a McKenzie had once again upset his plans than from losing the Lautrec or being talked about in the newspapers.

Paige sighed. "It seemed perfectly innocent at the time, Jeremy—two Americans, connected somehow, alone in a foreign city. I never thought for a moment that he was setting me up." She saw no need to tell him about the attraction she had felt for Matt almost from the start, about the wanting, the passion that had run through her hotly, making her lose her head.

"When it comes to the McKenzies, nothing is ever innocent," Jeremy continued. "You'll do well to remember that in the future. They have no scruples and no morals." His voice was thin and clipped and his dark eyes blazed like hot coals. "Promise me you'll never have anything more to do with that scoundrel."

"I promise. Although that's hardly necessary. I don't expect to see Matt McKenzie ever again." Smiling, she patted the space next to her on the sofa. "And now that I have been properly scolded," she teased. "Will you stop standing there like a general and come sit down? I have good news for you."

"About the Lautrec?"

"No, not about the Lautrec. I bought something else for you today. Something I hope will restore your faith in me."

A small frown creased his eyebrows. "Without consulting me? Without knowing if I'd be interested?"

"Oh, you are definitely interested."

"I'm listening."

"I went to see Zachary Calvert in New York and bought that French tapestry you like so much—*Taking the Bastille*."

The expression in Jeremy's eyes was a mixture of astonishment and incredulity. "You what!"

She laughed. "You heard me."

"You couldn't have. He told the *New York Times* a month ago he'd never sell that tapestry."

"I guess he changed his mind."

Jeremy's eyes grew cautious. "How much did it cost you?"

"I offered him exactly what he paid for it, but since that's hardly the kind of deal that would appeal to a man like Zachary Calvert, I threw in a bonus I knew he couldn't refuse."

"Oh. And what's that?"

Paige swallowed. "I offered him your Prince Rudolf sword."

For a moment, Jeremy's face seemed to solidify. In the stonelike features, only the eyes burned with a gleam she couldn't quite identify. Then unexpectedly, he threw his head back and laughed. It was a full, totally genuine laugh that went on for some time, leaving Paige baffled.

Maybe it was some sort of nervous reaction, she thought, not sure if she should rejoice or worry. Maybe the idea of what she had done was so ludicrous to him that his only option was to laugh. Paige remained seated, her hands folded on her lap, waiting for his laughter to end.

At last he was able to regain his composure. His eyes were still bright from the laughter, and he focused them on her. "You traded my Prince Rudolph sword? You actually committed my name—"

"And a hundred-thousand-dollar deposit. For good faith."

"Was that your idea also?"

"The deposit was. The amount was Calvert's. He said that as long as I had decided to play in the big league, I might as well play the game right."

Jeremy chuckled. "Yes, that's something Zachary would say. He always did fancy himself a big shot." He shook his head. Some of the starch had come off now and he seemed more like the Jeremy she knew. "You've got guts, Paige, I'll give you that. Of course I'm not bound to that deal, you know. In which case, you'll lose your hundred thousand."

"I realize that."

"And still you went ahead and did it."

"Kate taught me to always trust my instincts."

"I see. And what are your instincts telling you now?"

She returned his gaze. "You mean as far as our professional relationship is concerned?"

He nodded.

"That's not a fair question."

"Why not?"

"Because if that gleam of satisfaction in your eyes is any indication, I'd say you're rather pleased with me right now and that our relationship has never been more secure."

"And you'd be right, young lady. I wish half the people who work for me would show that kind of initiative."

"Then you're not upset about the sword?"

"Not too much. Although I'm not happy at the thought of that old gizzard owning it. I hate his guts, you know, almost as much as he hates mine."

Paige smiled. "He told me."

"What made you think he might want to sell the tapestry?"

"Because of something I read in *Newsweek* on the way back from Venice."

"I read that article. I didn't see anything in it about him wanting to sell the tapestry. In fact I got quite the opposite impression."

Paige smiled. "Sometimes, Jeremy, you have to read between the lines."

Jeremy watched her with undisguised admiration. Of all the dealers he had done business with over the years, few possessed Paige's boldness, ingenuity, and fearless determination. What a precious ally she'd be in years to come. And what a team they'd make once they were married.

"You are one remarkable woman, Paige Granger," he said at last. "And if you promise not to let my compliment go to your head, I'm damn glad to have you on my side." He glanced at his watch. "Chu Seng was about to serve a light lunch. I'll tell him to add another plate and to serve it in here." Not giving her a chance to turn him down, he added, "In the meantime, you can think of someplace where we can put my new acquisition."

"I don't have to think about it." Paige pointed at the white marble mantel above which a seascape that she hated held the place of honor. "Right there."

He followed her gaze. "Above the mantel? But that would mean . . . " He caught the expression in her eyes, and for a moment he stared at her in utter disbelief. Then, throwing his head back, he roared with laughter again.

Tom DiMaggio was waiting at Kennedy Airport when Matt arrived on the afternoon of December eleventh.

"Good work, kid," his friend said, giving Matt a solid pat on the back. "You've got every major newspaper in the country calling for an interview, and *60 Minutes* sent Morley Safer over. They'd like to do a segment on art theft and want your input."

"I hope you told them I don't give interviews."

"I told them none of us gave interviews—ever. But you know those guys. They always think you ought to make an exception for them."

Matt didn't smile. His face was grim, he carried his

suit bag over his shoulder and kept walking toward the exit at a brisk pace. He didn't give a damn what reporters thought. The only person on his mind right now was Paige Granger. How he had let her slip away from him.

He should have gone to her room that night after Krugger's arrest. He should have knocked at her door until she was forced to open it. Or he should have waited outside the hotel the following morning and gone with her to see Francesco. Instead, he had given her space, time to think for herself, to realize he wasn't such a bad guy.

And it had backfired.

"So where do you want to celebrate tonight?" he heard Tom ask. "Dinner somewhere? Joan has this friend she's been wanting you to meet. She's a great gal, terrific personality . . ."

Matt was only half-listening. From the loudspeaker, a female voice repeated an announcement that brought him to a dead halt.

"Announcing the immediate boarding of United Airlines Flight 273 to Denver and Santa Barbara."

"You'll have to celebrate without me, old buddy," Matt said, as he gave his friend a quick pat on the shoulder.

"Why? What's the matter? Hey!" Tom shouted as Matt suddenly made an about-face. "Where are you going?"

"Santa Barbara," Matt tossed over his shoulder. "I'll explain later. Meanwhile, put me down for a couple weeks' vacation, will you?" Then he broke into a sprint toward the United Airlines ticket counter.

THIRTEEN

Matt had been ten years old when he had left the Santa Inez Valley for New York City, yet every time he returned to the Canyon-T Ranch, he thought of it as coming home.

Now, as he drove his rented Jeep Cherokee up San Marco Pass, the scenic highway that connected Santa Barbara with the valley, he felt overwhelmed once again at the pure, fog-free air and the vistas of rolling hills that stretched from one barren canyon to the next.

This was the home of the big spread, of proud, hard-working ranchers who shared a rich history and a common love of the land. Many were descendants of the *rancheros* and *vaqueros* who had worked the Spanish land grants that once made up the valley. Others, like Josh, were sons and grandsons of early settlers, men and women who had come to California in search of a dream and had found paradise.

Some of the finest longhorns were being raised here, and the Canyon-T Ranch had once claimed one of the largest herds in the state. But a severe drought, now in its second year, had destroyed Josh's cattle-feeding operation and forced him to reduce his herd by half.

For years, several developers, as well as Jeremy Newman, had been interested in the McKenzie property. They approached Josh regularly, each time with a more attractive offer. But Josh was a cowboy born and bred, and the idea of doing anything other than ranching—even the idea of selling the land on which he had lived for the last seventy-two years—was unthinkable.

High in the cloudless blue sky, an eagle soared and then dove between two mountains at great speed, his wings casting a dark shadow. As Matt turned onto a rock-strewn pass just off Foxen Canyon Road, the Canyon-T Ranch came into view—twenty thousand acres of land and one of the largest single parcels left in the valley.

Straight ahead was his first home, a three-story farm-house Josh's grandparents had built themselves, beam by beam, adding on to it every time another child was born. Josh had outlived all four of his brothers and sisters, and although the house was much too large for him and his houseman now, he still insisted that all the rooms be kept open.

"That way they won't smell musty when my future great-grandchildren come to visit," he often quipped.

Josh, like other concerned grandparents, had hoped to see his grandson married and settled long before now. But although Matt enjoyed an occasional semiserious re-lationship, he had never considered marriage. He didn't think it was fair to ask someone he loved to share his life when his job required such extensive traveling and long absences from home.

As Matt brought the jeep to a stop, the front door flew open and his grandfather came out, waving and hurrying across the courtyard. At seventy-two, Josh McKenzie was the last of a dying breed of genuine, bow-legged cow-boys. As tall as Matt and as broad, he was fleshier, more powerful looking. But in spite of the extra pounds, he moved with the agility of a man half his age. He had thick white hair cropped short and laughing eyes the color of honey. A friendly, easygoing manner turned strangers into friends at the first handshake.

Matt ran to meet him. "Hi there, Gramps." His voice was husky with emotion, and he gripped the old man in a bear hug Josh returned with equal force. "Still light on your feet, I see."

"As light as any city slicker is," Josh retorted, wrap-ping a huge arm around his grandson's shoulder as they walked up toward the house. "And if you have any doubt about that, we'll saddle up and see which of us begs for mercy first. That is,'' he added with a twinkle in his eye, ''if you still remember how to ride.''

''Oh, I think I can remember a thing or two. After all, I learned from the best.''

Josh's big booming laugh echoed across the canyons. ''And don't you forget it.''

Once inside, Matt stopped, inhaling the unique mixed aroma of old wood fires, leather, and fine cigars that had impregnated the walls of his ancestors' home over the last century. Nostalgia filled him. He loved this house, the beamed soaring ceilings, the ancient stone floor, and the bright sunlight that poured in from every window.

It was a huge room, yet it felt cozy and warm. Groupings of white birch log furniture covered with burgundy upholstery were scattered throughout the room, in perfect harmony with the rich redwood interior. The pieces that had delighted him as a child were still there, waiting to entertain another generation—an old grain crusher that had been turned into a lamp, a saddle that had belonged to Teddy Roosevelt when he ranched the harsh Badlands of the Dakotas, and a pair of spurs with a history no one really knew.

''Good afternoon, sir. Welcome home.''

Nigel had kept the house running smoothly for the past thirty years, although he was more like a member of the family than a servant. He walked in carrying a tray of hors d'oeuvres that he placed on top of the birch bar alongside two glasses and a bottle of Jack Daniels. In his early sixties, he was short and slender and combed his black hair in the same slicked-back style he had worn when he had first come to work at the Canyon-T Ranch.

''Thank you, Nigel. It's good to be home.'' Matt gave the air an appreciative sniff. ''Game pie for dinner?''

The Englishman gave a pleased nod. ''Your favorite, if I recall.''

''You spoil me, Nigel. One of these days, when my grandfather isn't looking, I might just take you back to New York with me.''

Smiling, Nigel dropped two ice cubes into each glass, poured whiskey over it, and walked out as soundlessly as he had come in.

"Here's to you, son," Josh said, handing Matt a glass. "And to your recent tour de force." He chuckled as they clicked glasses. "I wish I could have seen Jeremy's face when he found out *you* were the one responsible for him losing that drawing he wanted." He tasted the whiskey and made an appreciative sound with his tongue before walking toward the sofa, the bottle of Jack Daniels hanging between two fingers. "And now, would you like to tell me what *really* brings you here?"

Matt laughed at his grandfather's perception. "You mean you didn't buy my story about needing a few days' rest?"

Josh leaned back against a plush burgundy cushion and shook his head. "You always were a poor liar."

For a moment, Matt lost himself in the contemplation of his drink. It had been a long time since he had confided in Josh about matters of the heart.

An involuntary smile tugged at the corner of his mouth. Now where had that come from? What he felt for Paige had nothing to do with the heart. He had been attracted to her, yes. And he had wanted her. Lord knows, he had wanted her. But to confuse lust for love was ridiculous.

"Have you ever done something right," he asked Josh at last, "but taken the wrong way about it?"

"Many times."

"What did you do to correct it?"

Slowly, Josh lifted one booted foot onto the coffee table, then the other, crossing his legs at the ankles. "Most of the time, I was too damned stubborn to do anything about it. Especially if it involved ranching, which I always believed I could do better than anyone else." He raised a bushy, still very black eyebrow in Matt's direction. "But we're not talking about work, are we, son?"

Matt shook his head.

"A woman, then? Is Paige Granger the reason you came to California?"

"It was probably a rotten idea," Matt said, more to himself than to his grandfather.

"Oh, I don't know. A lot of good can be said about impulses. It's the follow-through that most people manage to screw up."

Matt twirled his drink before taking another sip. "I already screwed up, Gramps. In a major way. Right now, I'm sure Paige Granger is wishing she'd never met me."

Josh's narrowed gaze settled fondly on his grandson. He had loved Adam deeply. But he loved Matt even more. Maybe because the boy was so much like him, full of spit and fire. But also because there was a gentleness about him most people didn't always expect, or notice. "Don't you go making too many assumptions about women. Some of them can be downright unpredictable." His chuckle sounded like a low rumble. "Your grandmother, rest her dear soul, was a fine example of that."

"Yet the two of you were the happiest couple in the valley."

"Anybody can be happy. You have to work at it, that's all." He held the bottle of Jack Daniels out to Matt, who shook his head. Then he splashed another inch of the liquor into his own glass. In the background, the sound of Nigel setting the table for dinner added a homey touch to their conversation. "Why don't you tell me what happened in Venice?"

Matt did as he was asked, leaving nothing out, not even the heated kiss he and Paige had shared. When he was finished, Josh was still watching him, but this time his expression was one of amusement.

"You've got it bad, haven't you son?"

Matt's eyebrows went up. "What? About Paige?" He shook his head. "I wouldn't exactly say that. But I do like her, and I would like . . . to set things straight between us."

"I see. Well, I don't know much about Paige except what you told me and the little bit I've read in the papers lately. But she impresses me as a smart, level-headed young lady. If you went to her and explained the situation now that she's had time to think, I'm sure she'd listen.''

''Maybe I should send you as my envoy. You've always had a way with the ladies.''

''In the old days I might have been able to help you. Things were simpler then. A lady was happy enough to be pampered and flattered. Nowadays, women want, and deserve, much more. In fact, if you think about it, they want the same things we do—love, sensitivity, trust, honesty.''

Matt made a disgruntled sound. ''I'm afraid I haven't fared too well with the last three. At least not as far as Paige Granger is concerned.''

Josh stood up and came to stand next to Matt. His smile had grown a little mellow from the liquor, but his step was sure and strong, his eyes shrewd and loving. ''That's because she doesn't know you like I do, son.'' He put his beefy hand on Matt's shoulder. ''It's up to you to let her see what the real Matt McKenzie is all about.''

That night, in the same bedroom he had occupied as a boy, amid football pennants, basketball trophies, and mementos he had long forgotten, Matt wondered if Paige Granger would even care to know what the real Matt McKenzie was all about.

Matt always experienced mixed feelings when he went to visit his mother at the California Trauma Institute on the outskirts of Solvang in the Santa Inez Valley. First there was hope that through some miracle he'd find her awake and well, and then there was fear that the worst had happened while he was away.

The car explosion that had killed Matt's father two years ago had thrown Caroline against a tree, causing her to suffer multiple brain contusions and an acute subdural hemorrhage. Although the latter had been corrected through surgery, she had remained in a deep coma for a week, after which she had slipped into what Dr. Rimer called a persistent vegetative state.

''I'll be honest with you,'' the chief neurologist had

told Matt on Caroline's first day at the Institute. "Most patients in this condition die within a few months or a few years. However, in rare instances, partial recovery has occurred. The fact that our tests show brain wave activity gives us hope, but I want you to be prepared for the worst because it could very easily happen."

Although CTI was one of the best neurological facilities in the United States, it was also one of the most expensive. Caroline's medical bills were astronomical, yet never once did Matt consider moving her to a more affordable facility, even when he had found out, to his shock, that his father had left no money in his estate.

"I'm sorry," the couple's lawyer had told Matt the day after Adam's funeral. "I thought you knew your parents were heavily indebted."

"But my mother was a wealthy woman. How could this happen?"

The lawyer had shrugged. "Bad investments, high-style living. I warned them many times, told them if they didn't stop their extravagant spending, they'd end up in the poorhouse. Your mother listened. Your father didn't."

Fortunately, the sale of his parents' Manhattan penthouse and Caroline's jewelry had enabled Matt to pay off their debts. But there had been virtually nothing left afterward for Caroline's medical care.

Josh, generous to a fault, had offered to put his savings at Matt's disposal, but Matt had refused. His grandfather needed all of his capital to keep the ranch going. And besides, Caroline was *his* responsibility. Whatever care she needed, *he* would provide.

The need for more money was the reason Matt had left the FBI and gone to work for his old friend at Worldwide Investigations. Tom DiMaggio had been delighted to take him on, and although Matt's new job involved foreign travel and less time to see his mother, his salary and substantial bonuses allowed him to keep her at CTI.

Now, waving at the guard who always recognized him, Matt followed the long tree-lined drive to the parking lot, slid the Jeep into an empty slot, and made his way toward one of the back buildings, where long-term patients resided.

Caroline lay in a pristine white bed, looking pale but peaceful, the same as she had been four months ago, when he had stopped over on his way to Japan. Even now, at fifty-six, her beauty never failed to move him. Except for a few gray strands through her brown hair, she hadn't changed at all over the last two years.

"Hello, Mom," he said at last. He leaned over to kiss her forehead, which felt soft and cool. "I've brought you a present."

He sat down on a bedside chair, reached into his jacket pocket, and pulled out a Murano glass necklace he had bought for her at Marco Polo Airport before he'd left Venice. The tiny beads were a light shade of green—Caroline's favorite color—and shimmered in the sunlight. Carefully, he slid the string around her neck and fastened it.

"They look gorgeous on you." He took her hand and held it. "Almost as gorgeous as that pendant I made for you in kindergarten one Christmas, remember? The purple clay heart that cracked on the way home?" He laughed, remembering the moment as if it were yesterday. "You and Dad were getting ready to go to a party a few nights later, and I was furious when I saw you weren't wearing my masterpiece."

He believed that his mother responded to his visits and conversations, so he always sat with her for hours, talking about whatever came into his head—his work, world affairs, their early life together.

He was still reminiscing about their last Christmas at the ranch when a stocky nurse in her early fifties, with short blond hair and a cheerful smile, came in. Her name was Mabel Greenwald and she had been caring for Caroline since the day she had been brought to the trauma center.

"So that's why all my nurses are buzzing like bees around honey today," she said in her gravelly voice, patting Matt's shoulder in form of a greeting. "Prince Charming is here."

"You give me too much credit, Mabel." He stood up to get out of her way.

"Hear that, Caroline?" Mabel said, attaching another bag to the small plastic feeding tube in Caroline's stomach. "Our Romeo here is being modest today. He's got every nurse on this floor fussing with their makeup and hitching up their skirts another inch and he pretends he knows nothing about it."

Matt caught her just as he walked by him and planted a resonant kiss on her cheek. "That's because you're the only woman in my heart, Mabel. You know that."

Mabel gave a lusty laugh. "Let me go, you maniac, before I force you to make an honest woman of me." Turning back to Caroline, she patted her hand. "You have a pleasant lunch, sweetie, and when you're finished, I'll come back and give you a nice rubdown."

"Thanks, Mabel," Matt said, his expression suddenly serious. "You're an angel."

"Sure, sure. That's what they all say." She moved toward the door. "Oh, by the way, stop by the nurses' station before you leave, will you, handsome? Lucille brought her baby boy for a checkup and she wants to show him to you." She smiled. "He loves the panda you sent him. Won't go anywhere without it."

After Mabel was gone, Matt sat holding his mother's hand for awhile, looking at her and remembering the vital, beautiful woman who had chaired committees, played tennis like a pro, and danced with royalty.

An all too familiar knot formed in his throat. She hadn't been the perfect mother. Far from it. And she was terrible when it came to priorities. No matter how many times he had asked, there always seemed to be something more important to do than attend one of his basketball games, or help him with his homework, the way other mothers did.

But he had adored her. He still did. Her flaws were the result of years of adulation, first from her doting parents, then from her many suitors, and finally, from the people in this valley, because they too had fallen under her irresistible spell.

For awhile, Matt's father had been the perfect companion for her and together they had been the toast of New York. Although Adam lacked ambition, he had the ability to charm and communicate, two attributes that had enabled him to make a fairly decent living as an investment counselor on Wall Street.

It wasn't until a couple of years ago that Caroline had grown tired of what she called their nomadic lifestyle.

"I'm getting too old to fly all over the world three, four, sometimes five times a year," she had told Matt one day during a visit to his New York townhouse. "I want more from your father than expensive flings to Capri and Gstaad. I want more attention, more tenderness. If he can't give me those things . . ."

She had left the sentence hang in the air and Matt, concerned that his parents' marriage might be in trouble, had gone to see his father.

Adam, who never took anyone's problems, including his own, very seriously, had shrugged off Caroline's remark with typical insouciance. "Your mother is going through a rough period right now,' he had said as he poured them both an inch of very old, very expensive Cognac. "Hormones, you know," he had added with a knowing look, as if that explained everything. "She'll be all right soon enough."

A week later, Caroline had left for the Canyon-T Ranch. When rumors that she was seeing Jeremy Newman again reached Adam, he flew to California to straighten the matter out and confront Jeremy. According to Josh, Caroline hadn't wanted to go with him, but Adam had insisted, and in the end she had given in. They had driven to Newman's Ranch together, in Caroline's rented Jaguar.

The following morning, wild with grief and certain Jeremy had killed his father, Matt had burst into the publisher's ranch house, and if it hadn't been for the two police officers who were already there, he would have killed Jeremy with his bare hands.

Later, when the police had shown him tire tracks from another car, a car that didn't belong to anyone at the ranch, Matt had realized he had jumped to conclusions a little too quickly.

"Someone else beside your parents drove to the ranch that night," the sergeant in charge of the case had told him. "Someone who knew your father would be here tonight, or followed him here. We're checking all the people he's had dealings with in the last few months, but it'll take some time."

Matt's first thought was to conduct the investigation himself. But as Tom had pointed out, criminal cases took time. And for Matt, time meant money—money he needed to pay for his mother's care.

In the end, he had given up on his one-man hunt and agreed to let the police handle the investigation.

They had never found Adam's murderer and eventually they had closed the file.

Matt sighed. It was four o'clock and time to leave. He kissed his mother's hand and stood up. "Good-bye, Mom. I'll be back tomorrow. And if you're very good, I'll bring you another present."

At the door, he gave her one last look, then gently, he closed the door behind him.

FOURTEEN

Half an hour later, Matt arrived in Santa Barbara, parked the Jeep by the courthouse, and walked toward Anapamu Street, where the Beauchamp Gallery was located.

Usually so sure of what to say, even in critical situations, he had no thought, no idea how to approach Paige. The impulse to follow her to Santa Barbara had been amusing at first, impossible to resist, but now that he was here, much of his earlier bravado had vanished.

The door of the gallery was open and Paige was alone, her back to him. He watched her pick up a rare San Cai porcelain dog figure from a secretary and move it to a walnut lowboy at the opposite corner of the room.

He waited, not wanting to startle her. Not that he thought she might actually drop the figure, but with a San Cai of this quality, one did not take chances.

Unobserved, he glanced at the store interiors, impressed but not surprised at the tasteful blend of seventeenth and eighteenth century furniture, objets d'art, and fine paintings. From the way Paige had described Beauchamp and some of her favorite pieces, he had had a mental image of the gallery immediately.

As Paige backed away to study the object in its new location, Matt let his gaze wander over the graceful line of her back. In that dress, she could make a man forget his own name. The garment, a warm caramel color edged in purple, was made of the finest knit and followed her curves without hugging them. The hem ended an inch or so above the knee, giving him once again a glimpse of those shapely legs, made even more attractive by the high-heeled purple pumps.

"Great piece," he commented when he felt it safe to speak. "It's from the Kangxi period, isn't it?" Closing the door behind him, he stepped inside.

Paige whipped around, a look of surprise and exasperation in her eyes. "What are *you* doing here?" Obviously, greetings were not on her agenda.

"I came to talk to you."

"Then you came a long way for nothing, Mr. McKenzie, because I have no desire to talk to you."

Her tone was a shade under glacial, her eyes as cold as an Arctic sky. This was no longer the shaken, angry young woman who had faced him at Krugger's house a few nights ago. She was very cool, very much in control.

"I was hoping that once you'd had time to think about what happened in Venice, you might understand my predicament a little better."

"Oh, I understood your predicament perfectly. It's the way you went about resolving it that I disapprove of."

Matt leaned against a Chippendale secretary and folded his arms. "Really? How should I have resolved it?"

The question took her by surprise. For a moment, she considered not answering him. Why should she waste her time playing his little game? Or risk Jeremy's wrath by engaging in a discussion of ethics with someone who obviously had none?

It was the challenge in his eyes that changed her mind. She had never been able to turn down a challenge.

"You should have told me the truth," she said, with less conviction than she would have liked. "I deserved that much. And I might have been able to help you. Together we could have found a way to trap Krugger."

"I see. Have you ever laid a trap for someone before?"

"You know I haven't."

"Right. Which means you have no experience, no idea how delicate a mission like this can be, or how quickly it can go wrong and turn on you if you're caught unprepared."

"I have very good instincts."

"Instincts can get you killed." He studied the tight, closed-up face, sensing that although a lot of the anger was gone, the resentment was still there. "You're not a professional," he continued in a softer tone. "No matter how hard you tried, Krugger would have seen through you in minutes."

"So what if he had?"

"He might have been desperate enough to kill us both if we had stood in his way."

"Aren't you being a little melodramatic?"

"Aren't you being a little unfair?"

She didn't answer. She didn't expect him to understand that betrayal wasn't something she took lightly. Early in her life, she had been deeply affected by it and had sworn she would never experience that kind of pain again. Of course, she had. And probably would again. But not if she could help it. "Have you said all you came to say?" she asked with studied detachment.

"No. I came to congratulate you on that tapestry you bought for Newman. I guess some good came out of that trip to Venice after all." He grinned. "Do you suppose I brought you luck?"

"You brought me nothing but trouble. Because of you I was nearly assaulted by a dozen paparazzi at Marco Polo Airport and had to be rescued by the police. Because of you and those lurid stories that were leaked to the press, I have lost one of my best clients and I'm on the verge of losing another. And if that isn't enough, a recent newspaper article referred to me as 'Jeremy's Jinx.' I'm lucky *he* didn't drop me as well."

"You might be better off if he had." The words were out of his mouth before he could stop them. He knew from the angry flush of her cheeks that attacking Jeremy had been a mistake. Although he still didn't believe there was anything between them other than a professional relationship, she was deeply loyal to him and would defend him to the end.

"That's really what this is all about isn't it? Jeremy. That's why you came to Venice—not to find your Goya, but hoping to implicate Jeremy in the theft."

"You have a very distorted opinion of me, Paige."

"I don't think so. I know about the feud between Jeremy and your family. But that's no reason to stage this vendetta against him."

"Is that what he calls it?"

"He doesn't call it anything. We don't talk about you."

"Good. Then we won't talk about him."

"We won't talk about anything anymore, because," she added, smiling at a woman who had just entered, "our conversation is over." She turned away from Matt. "Good afternoon, Mrs. Ledbetter," she said to the woman. "May I help you with something today?"

"I'll let you know in a moment, dear."

"Have dinner with me this evening," Matt said in a whisper.

"You've lost your mind." Still smiling, Paige watched as Mrs. Lebetter, a stout woman in her early seventies, gave Matt a sidelong glance before moving toward a scroll on the wall next to where they stood.

"Does that mean yes?" Matt pressed.

"It means no. As in never."

"Why are you refusing a harmless invitation to dinner?"

"Bluntly put, because I don't trust you."

Then as Mrs. Ledbetter's attention shifted from the scroll she had been pretending to admire, to their conversation, Paige turned her back to Matt and walked expectantly toward her client, leaving Matt no recourse but to leave. For now.

Paige had never met anyone as infuriating and bullheaded as Matt McKenzie. In the space of four short days, he had managed to throw her life into total chaos and make her feel as if she no longer had any control over it.

The day after his visit to Beauchamp, when she thought he had left Santa Barbara, he began appearing everywhere she went—at the opening of a friend's gallery in Monterey, at an auction in L.A., at another in San Diego. He had even shown up at an art dealers' luncheon, where he was, of all things, the guest speaker.

"I know he has people helping him arrange these supposedly coincidental meetings," Paige said to Kate on Monday morning after she ran into Matt at the garage where her car was being serviced and turned down his offer of a lift. "But it's not going to help him." She glanced at an enormous arrangement of pink roses—her favorite. "Where did those come from?"

Kate smiled as she bent down to take a whiff of the delicate flowers. "From Matt McKenzie. Aren't they lovely? Oh, and there's a card."

"Throw it away."

"The card?"

"The card, yes. *And* the flowers."

"Not on your life. They look lovely on this Sheraton table." She threw her niece an amused glance. "By the way, he wants to know if you'll be available for dinner this evening."

"You couldn't resist, could you? You had to read the card."

"I didn't think you'd mind."

Paige gave her aunt a disgusted look. "Are you enjoying this, Aunt Kate? Because if you are, you're playing right into his hands, you know. Men like him love an audience."

"Of course I'm enjoying this. I find the man totally fascinating. The whole town does."

"What do you mean, 'the whole town does'?"

"I mean there isn't a man or woman in Santa Barbara who isn't following this drama with bated breath as it keeps unfolding. Some have even taken bets as to which one will give in first."

Paige shook her head in wonder. "The things people will do to amuse themselves."

"Are you telling me you don't find him charming? Or refreshing? Or the least bit intriguing?"

"It takes a lot more than an obnoxious, persistent man to intrigue me, Aunt Kate. Although," she added with a meaningful glance toward her aunt, "I can't say the same for others." Picking up the morning mail, she went through it quickly, barely glancing at it. "Do me a favor, Aunt Kate, will you? Don't mention his name around me again. And don't encourage him if he should call. Maybe if we ignore him, he'll go away. Like a bad dream."

Pursuing women had never been his style. Even in high school, where all self-proclaimed red-blooded males made it a point to chase every girl in sight, Matt had always felt uncomfortable with the idea of forcing himself on a woman. Paige Granger had changed all that. Although he kept insisting he wasn't serious about her and only wanted a chance to apologize, his thoughts and actions told a different story.

Unfortunately, nothing he had done so far to break down her resistance had worked. The "accidental" meetings he had staged with the help of a few friends had accomplished nothing. Paige was unimpressed. And she continued to ignore him.

Soon he would be returning to New York, and unless something drastic happened within the next week to change his luck, he would have to admit defeat and get out of Paige Granger's life forever.

"Good evening, Nigel," Matt said as he walked into the kitchen on his fourth evening at the ranch. "What smells so good?"

"Veal Marengo, sir." The butler filled a pot with water and set it on the stove. "How did it go with Miss Granger today?"

At Matt's look of surprise, Nigel smiled and said, "I couldn't help catching part of your conversation with your grandfather at breakfast this morning."

Matt sighed and perched one hip on the solid pine kitchen table. "I'm afraid it's not going too well, Nigel. I seem to have lost my touch. Or maybe I never had it."

"Some women are more difficult to charm than others."

Matt smiled. "Is that an observation made from personal experience, Nigel?"

As Nigel lifted the lid of a red earthenware pot, the tantalizing aroma of mushrooms, wine, and veal stewing together filled the kitchen. "No, sir. With all due respect to my wonderful wife, it was *she* who pursued *me.*"

Matt laughed. "Good for you, Nigel."

"About your little problem," Nigel continued as he stirred the stew. "You might be interested in knowing that on Wednesday evening, Miss Granger's grandmother will be hosting the first Christmas party of the holiday season—a white and silver formal affair with a 1940 theme."

Matt folded his arms. "You don't say. Will the McKenzies be invited?"

Nigel smiled. "Your grandfather is."

"How interesting. A white and silver affair, huh?" Matt's expression was thoughtful for a moment. Then, without getting down from the table, he reached inside a drawer and pulled out a phone book. "Nigel, have I ever told you how truly amazing you are?"

"Many times. But it's always nice to hear it again. Would you like a beer before dinner, sir?"

Matt shook his head as he kept flipping through the yellow pages, stopping at Formal Wear. When he found the number he was looking for, he dialed.

"Good evening, Charlie," he said to the man who answered. "This is Matt McKenzie at the Canyon-T Ranch." After thanking the store owner for welcoming him back, he added, 'I know this is short notice, but could you find me a white tuxedo before Wednesday? Forty-two long, that's right."

He waited for a few moments, and when Charlie returned, he winked at Nigel, who was leaning against the kitchen counter and watching him with undisguised admiration. "Ah, splendid, Charlie. Thank you very much. No, that won't be necessary. I'll drive down and pick it up myself."

Hanging up, he flashed Nigel a big, boyish grin. "I'll have that beer after all, Nigel. And open one for yourself as well, will you? I hate to celebrate alone."

FIFTEEN

Although Montecito was famous for its glittering, sometimes extravagant social affairs, no one in the community could surpass the grandeur of Eve Granger's famous soirées.

It had been three years since she had last given a Christmas party, but this event, which Eve had modestly entitled "a gathering of friends," had clearly reinstated her as the grande dame of entertaining.

The house, inside and out, shimmered in a white and silver decor, the color theme she had chosen for this year's gala. Three twenty-foot Colorado blue spruces, each decorated with silver bells and white snowflakes, had been erected in each of the three main rooms—the solarium; the dining room, where the buffet table was set; and the living room, where a four-piece orchestra entertained the elegant crowd with 1940 tunes.

At Eve's request, the guests only wore white or silver or a combination of both, in a style that best reflected the mood of the forties.

The effect, Eve thought as she stood at the bottom of the staircase, was nothing short of sensational. As one stretch limousine after another pulled up at the entrance, women in de la Renta, Bob Mackie, and Scaasi gowns alighted, greeting one another with great excitement, for attending one of Eve Granger's parties always guaranteed large coverage in *W, Town and Country,* and all the important social columns.

Eve was glad to see that in spite of the short notice, nearly all of her important guests had come, including friends she hadn't seen in years, many of whom had interrupted their Florida or Palm Springs vacations in order to attend the bash. Even the Reagans, who were spending the holidays at nearby Rancho del Cielo, had promised to stop by.

Paige had been a little more difficult to convince. She hated large, elaborate parties and all the fuss that went with them. It was only after a great deal of coaxing that she had finally agreed to put in an appearance, promising to wear a white gown and not that ghastly red dress she had bought in Venice and that made her look like one of Al Capone's women.

Eve's gaze moved through the crowd, searching for her granddaughter, and stopped on Paul. With a twist of pleasure, she saw that he was talking to Beatrice Sheffield, heiress to the huge Sheffield oil fortune. It always pleased her to see her son associating with the right kind of women, and it had always been her secret ambition—well, not so secret, since Paul was aware of it—that he would someday marry Bea.

"They make a lovely couple, don't they?" said a man at her elbow.

"Yes," Eve replied, watching her son escort Bea to the dance floor. Then, glancing back at Alan Ratcliff, she realized her old friend wasn't talking about Paul and Beatrice at all, but about Paige and Jeremy, who stood in the solarium, chatting and laughing.

"Would you care to speculate about those two, my dear?" Alan asked.

Eve shook her head as her gaze lingered fondly on Paige's exquisite white satin sheath. With her hair parted in the middle and held at the sides by two white mother-of-pearl combs, she looked like a young Heddy Lamarr. "I would like nothing better, Alan. But you know my granddaughter. She's the umpredictable one in the family. Just when you think she's ready to settle down, she'll go and do something crazy."

Alan, who had two impetuous daughters of his own, smiled indulgently. "You don't have to worry about

Paige. From what I've seen of her, she's one of the most sensible, level-headed young ladies in this town. And frankly,'' he added with a discreet little chuckle, ''from the way Jeremy has been looking at her tonight, I doubt he's going to let her slip through his fingers.''

It was Eve's turn to smile. She had to agree with Alan. Jeremy seemed totally spellbound tonight. And he and Paige did make a lovely couple—he so refined, worldly, and powerful, and Paige beautiful and exciting, if a little untamed.

A warm glow of satisfaction enveloped her. This evening was turning out splendidly.

''Oh, my,'' Mindy whispered, her large dark eyes growing even larger. ''Now, *that's* what I call a hunk.''

Paige, who had managed to get away from Jeremy for a few minutes, turned around in order to see the object of Mindy's admiration. And almost choked on her salmon canapé.

Matt McKenzie, dressed in the required white tux and looking very relaxed, very much at home, stood under the archway that separated the solarium from the living room, his gray eyes scanning the crowd. It was obvious from the hands he shook and the cheeks he kissed that he knew half the people in this room.

''What is *he* doing here?'' Paige hissed.

Without taking her eyes off Matt, Mindy raised a quizzical eyebrow. ''You know him?''

''Unfortunately. It's Matt McKenzie. The gall of the man. Showing up here, uninvited.''

''*That's* the infamous Matt McKenzie?'' Mindy said in amazement. She turned to glance at Paige. ''I would never have recognized him from your description. Especially since you left out one tiny detail.''

''Such as?''

''Such as the guy is gorgeous.''

''He is not. And anyway, what difference does it make? He is still a pushy, assuming, ill-mannered moron.'' Seeing that Mindy's attention was once again focused on

Matt, she added, "Mindy, will you stop gawking and help me deal with this?"

Mindy threw her an amused glance. "Okay. What do you want me to do? Kidnap him? Stash him away in my bedroom until the year 2000?" She chuckled. "I don't think Larry would approve, but since this is in the name of friendship . . ." She glanced at a stunning blonde in a revealing silver mesh gown who was eyeing Matt with undisguised lust. "Although I may have to fight every female in this room just to get to him."

"Be serious, Mindy, please. Find Jeremy and occupy him while I get Matt out of here."

"Why? This party is just beginning to get interesting."

"It won't be once Jeremy sees Matt."

"Jeremy doesn't own this territory. And he doesn't own you."

"I know that. By why antagonize him? I have put too much time and effort into developing a decent relationship with him to have it destroyed now." She found herself wishing Kate were here. *She* would have known how to deal with this situation. But Kate, preferring not to find herself face to face with Jeremy, had declined the invitation.

"Look," Mindy suggested. "Why don't you just let fate run its course? After all, Matt is behaving like a perfect gentleman. Oh, oh," she added, giggling into her champagne. "I may have spoken too soon."

Paige turned around in time to see Matt slowly make his way across the room toward Eve and Jeremy.

He hadn't changed very much, Matt thought, keeping his eyes on Jeremy. A little grayer perhaps, but on him, it was becoming rather than aging. He was as lean and fit as he had been two years ago, and still generated more attention from the ladies than any other man in the room. It was easy to see why Caroline had fallen in love with him. The man exuded power and sex appeal. He always had. Even when he was young.

"Good evening, Eve."

Paige's grandmother spun around, her eyes wide, veiled with a trace of mild panic. "Matthew!"

"It's good to see you. You look wonderful." He bent to kiss her cheek and recognized the lovely scent of Shalimar. His mother had used it herself years ago. "My grandfather sends his regrets. And of course, his regards."

"Is Josh all right?"

"A little cranky." He tapped his shoulder. "His bursitis again," he lied, remembering how delighted Josh had been to find out he didn't have to attend what he called "one of Eve's boring shindigs." He added, "He'll be fine in a few days. I hope you don't mind my filling in for him."

"Of course not." She gave him a warm smile, for Eve was, before all, a gracious lady. Whatever displeasure his presence caused her, she concealed it with her usual flair.

Matt turned to Jeremy, who was watching the exchange with undisguised animosity. "Hello, Jeremy."

The older man nodded once. "Matthew."

"I hear you've just bought *Taking the Bastille* from Zachary Calvert. Congratulations."

"Thank you. Although Paige is the one who ought to be congratulated. She pulled off the coup without my knowing about it."

Matt's gaze swept around the room in search of Paige. "I'll be sure to do that," he said, pretending not to see the venomous look Jeremy gave him. Turning back to face the older man, he added, "I thought you might be interested in knowing that Ted Krugger and his butler have been formally charged and will probably be spending several uncomfortable years in an Italian prison."

"I'm always glad to hear that an art thief has received his due. However, you'll forgive me if I don't offer *you* my congratulations. I find the way you used Paige and risked her safety rather deplorable—as well as dangerous."

"You're the one who took a chance with her safety,"

Matt said, the lightness gone from his voice. "By sending her to do business with a man you knew was a crook."

"I had no such knowledge!"

Matt felt his old resentment flair anew. "The hell you didn't. You've known the man for years."

"I know a lot of people," Jeremy said, his face turning a bright, angry red. "That doesn't mean I do business with all of them. Besides, except for the Lautrec, Krugger's never had anything of any value."

"He had the Goya."

"Now just a minute, McKenzie! I resent your implication—"

"Gentlemen, please," Eve whispered, laying a hand on Jeremy's arm. "Not here. Not now." She turned to Matt, her voice imploring. "Perhaps it'd be best if you left, Matthew—"

Matt and Jeremy continued to stare at each other, like two predators about to attack each other for the same prey. Around them, conversations had fallen silent as heads turned around.

Matt was the first to regain his composure. Creating a scene was *not* the way to make Paige change her mind about him. He gave a short bow of his head. "I hadn't planned to stay long anyway," he said, addressing himself to Eve. "I'll go and say hello to Paul and be on my way."

Then, without another look in Jeremy's direction, he moved on.

Shivering, Paige wrapped her arms around her body, hugging herself. It was much too cold to be standing outside without a wrap, but taking refuge on the terrace was the best way she knew to avoid another confrontation with Matt.

She didn't know what he and Jeremy had said to each other, but from the look on Jeremy's face, it hadn't been good. Surely once Matt realized she was nowhere around, he'd assume she had left early and would go home. A sixth sense told her not to take any bets on it. If there was one thing she had learned about Matt McKenzie in the last few days, it was that he wasn't a man who gave up easily.

"Do you mind if I join you?"

At the sound of his voice, Paige took a deep breath and let it out slowly. "Would it make any difference if I said yes?" she said without turning.

"Not really. Although I'm not in the habit of sticking around where I'm not wanted."

He stood close behind her now, making it impossible for her to turn around and face him without their bodies touching. "Then why are you here?"

"Because you and I have unfinished business. And because I can't get you out of my mind."

She hadn't expected him to sound so humble or be so candid. It's a new tactic, she reminded herself, a switch to throw her off guard, to make her weaken.

"We never had any *business* together," she said, gazing at the stars. "As for your other predicament, I'm afraid I can't help you there." She felt a movement behind her, and the same after-shave she had smelled in Venice wrapped around her, like a caress. A wave of memories rushed through her senses, sending little signals she should have been immune to.

"Yes, you can. Have dinner with me. Or lunch. One hour of your time is all I'm asking."

From inside the house, strings playing *Moonlight Serenade* lent the night a sense of déjà vu. She sighed. "Don't you ever give up?"

"Not when someone is important to me. And you are important, Paige."

"Why? Because I've become a challenge?"

"No. Because we had something special in Venice and while we may never find it again, I'd like the chance to make things right between us—before I leave."

She should have been glad to hear that last part, but for some odd reason, she wasn't. "If I agree, will you leave me alone afterward?"

"Yes."

She turned around, slowly, barely managing not to touch him. In the glow of an overhead light, his eyes gleamed like melting pewter and his blond hair had turned silver. "No more embarrassing stunts on your part, no more phone calls or flowers?"

He shook his head. "I'll even call off the pilot."

She raised an eyebrow. "The pilot?"

He smiled. "I'll tell you about that another time. Do we have a date?"

"We'll have lunch. Do you know where Petronella is?"

"You can show me. What time do I pick you up?"

"You don't. I'll meet you at the restaurant. It's on Anacapa Street, next to Wells Fargo Bank. Twelve-thirty tomorrow."

He was still grinning when she left.

SIXTEEN

As always when Paige had reservations at Petronella, Alfonso, the ebullient owner she had known for years, came to meet her at the front desk. After the customary hug and a handshake with Matt, he escorted them to a shaded table in the patio, which was already crowded with tourists and local businessmen.

"Your usual white wine spritzer, Paige?" Alfonso asked as he centered a small pot of geraniums between them. "Or would you like something else today?"

"A wine spritzer will be fine, Alfonso, thank you."

"Make that two," Matt said. He waited until Alfonso had disappeared before returning his attention to Paige. In an ivory silk blouse and navy-striped pants, she looked both elegant and comfortable. She had tied her hair back, a style that brought her cheekbones as well as her eyes, into even greater focus. Whatever brilliant opening line he had planned to say in order to break the ice was forgotten.

"So what's taboo?" he asked, seeing she was just as lost for words as he was.

She hated it when he did that, startling her with questions or comments she didn't expect. "I beg your pardon?"

"We'll have to establish some sort of ground rules before we start, don't you think? Like what is safe for us to talk about and what isn't."

A small smile skimmed across her lips. "Oh." She pondered the suggestion for a moment, tapping her index finger against her chin. "Let's see, would you agree Jeremy Newman should be one of the unsafe subject matters?''

"Absolutely."

"And Venice?"

"*All* of Venice?"

She felt herself blush and laughed to cover her sudden embarrassment. "Yes. It's safer that way."

"Very well. He leaned back to let a waiter place their drinks on the table. "Of course, you realize there won't be anything to argue about."

"I'll chance it."

He had set the mood and she flowed into it, easily, surprised that her resentment was easing off with no effort on her part. If she had known it would be this painless to get rid of him, she would have accepted his invitation sooner.

Her only regret was that she had let Jeremy leave the party last night without telling him about her meeting with Matt. She had planned to call him this morning before he left for London on business. But by the time she had arrived at Beauchamp, Jeremy's secretary had left a message saying he had had to leave sooner than expected and would see Paige in about ten days.

Maybe it was just as well, Paige thought as she opened her menu. By the time Jeremy returned from England, Matt would be long gone and their lives would finally return to normal.

They were discussing the possibility of a crash in the art market when their crab salads arrived. All traces of awkwardness gone, they ate hungrily as they talked, and even laughed. If it hadn't been for the blueness of the sky and the warmth of the early-afternoon sun, they could have been in Venice, continuing the conversation they had started at Florian's.

The first hour passed quickly, without either Matt or Paige noticing it. It wasn't until they were sharing Petronella's famous mile-high mud pie that Paige realized she was talking about a time of her life which until now she had only shared with Mindy and Kate—her involvement with Brad Tishner.

"I suppose one could say that I loved him," she mused as she cut through the chocolate desert with the side of her fork. "In a wild, idealistic sort of way. I was fresh out of college. He was handsome, charming, and successful."

"And married."

She looked up. "How did you know?"

He shrugged. "Like you, I have very good instincts."

Paige nodded. "Yes, he was married. A little detail he failed to mention."

"When did you find out?"

"When I saw him shopping at a downtown store with a beautiful woman on his arm a few days before Christmas. I was devastated. Later, when I confronted him, he didn't even try to deny she was his wife."

"Would you have wanted him to?"

She hesitated, remembering how much she had wanted to keep him at the time. "I was in love, ready to believe anything." She paused, put another forkful of pie into her mouth. "As it was, he lied to me anyway. He told me they had agreed to a divorce but were staying together over the holiday so as not to disrupt any family plans, and that right after the first of the year, he'd start divorce proceedings and marry me."

"And you believed him."

She looked away, staring at nothing in particular. "I was very naive in those days."

"That's permitted when you're in love."

She looked at him, squinting a little as the sun shifted. He was as handsome under the California sun as he had been in the gray mist of Venice. Here his eyes looked softer, his hair blonder. "Were you ever?" she asked.

"Naive and in love? I suppose so. My most memorable experience was in the third grade when I developed a huge crush on a bus patrol girl three years older than I was."

"Ah, the older woman syndrome."

Matt laughed, a genuine, lusty laugh that chased away her somber mood. "Something like that."

Another hour passed. The patio was empty now, and a team of efficient waiters scurried around, cleaning tables, topping each with clean, crisp white table cloths and fresh flowers. Nearby, a gardener hummed the tune of *Guantanamera* as he weeded a flower bed.

"I'd like to offer you another cup of coffee," Matt said, "but I'm afraid we might wear out our welcome. Would you like to go somewhere else? A walk on the beach, perhaps? Or do you have something pressing to do at the gallery?"

He was very smooth. And very tempting. Her loyalty to Jeremy, the thought that she was betraying her promise to him, stopped her from taking Matt up on his invitation. "I can't. I have a three o'clock appointment."

"Then how about a movie tonight?"

She laughed and shook her head. He was persistent, like many of the boys she had known in college. But there was something different about Matt, a candor and a hopeful look in his eyes she found charming, almost impossible to resist. "I don't think so."

"Tomorrow, then? We could go out for Chinese afterwards?"

"I hate Chinese."

"Pizza? Buritos? Anything you want."

Nearby, a waiter, his hands and chin resting on a broom handle, watched them, a silly grin on his face.

She felt herself weaken. "Call me," she said.

She lay in bed for hours that night, unable to get Matt out of her mind.

Although they had agreed not to talk about Jeremy, and both had kept their promise, at one point Matt had talked about his mother, the excellent staff at the California Trauma Institute, and his hopes that she would recover soon. His tone was light and upbeat, but once in awhile, that same brief shadow Paige had seen in Venice crossed his eyes as if another part of him knew what he refused to admit, knew the inevitable.

At last she fell asleep, with visions of Matt in her head and thoughts of Venice in her heart.

He called early the next morning, inviting her to dinner that night, but she had to decline.

"I have to do inventory with Kate," she told him, cursing herself because she had been the one to suggest that date. Then, after a moment of reflection, she added, "But you could stop by the house later on if you'd like, for coffee? I should be home no later than nine."

"I'd like that very much."

She was silly and a little absentminded all day, a mood that caught Kate's attention right away.

"Is there anything you want to tell me, Paige?"

"No, why?"

"Because you've just put the Chesterfield wine cooler in the window."

"So?"

"So, we sold it to Mr. Cadman yesterday afternoon. He should be here any moment to pick it up."

Blushing, Paige went to retrieve the silver pail. "I had forgotten."

"Obviously," Kate said with an amused smile.

Matt arrived at nine-fifteen and handed her a box from a bakery on State Street. "Pumpkin pie to go with the coffee."

"Thank you. It's my favorite."

"I know." In answer to her raised eyebrow, he added, "I called your Aunt Kate earlier. She's charming. I'd like to meet her someday."

Paige didn't answer. Instead she busied herself with the coffee maker, aware that her hands shook as she went through the familiar ritual of spooning coffee into the filter.

"Do I make you nervous?" Leaning against the door jamb, his eyes followed her as she moved about the tidy yellow and white kitchen. She had changed into tight-fitting jeans and a red sweatshirt.

She glanced at him over her shoulder and saw that he watched her with bold, open admiration. She had noticed that same look at the restaurant, but she had felt safe there, less vulnerable. "Should I be?"

"No." He continued to watch her. She had a dancer's body, long, lean, and graceful. Remembering how it had felt in his arms outside her hotel room in Venice, his pulse quickened. What would she do if he followed his instincts right now and kissed her again?

"I like your house," he said, fighting the urge to do just that. "It suits you."

It was true. Although he had only glimpsed the living room and dining room when he had first arrived, what he had seen—space, light, bright colors, and the blue of the ocean—reminded him of Paige.

"Thank you." She pulled a container of cream from the refrigerator and filled a small yellow pot. "Tell me where *you* live."

"Not much to tell. It's your typical bachelor's apartment—small and efficient."

"Don't you miss space?"

"Once in awhile. Usually after a stay at the ranch. But since I'm so seldom home these days, my needs are very basic."

Paige turned to look at him. "What is it like, being away from home so much? Moving from one country to another?"

"Lonely." He shrugged. "But you get used to it after awhile."

"Somehow, I can't imagine you being lonely very often."

"Then you imagine wrong."

Without being sure why, she felt relieved. He had told her very little about his private life, and although she hadn't pressed him, she had been curious. He wasn't the kind of man a woman could easily resist. She decided their new friendship entitled her to a little prying. After all, she had told him about Brad. "You mean there's no one special in your life right now?" she asked, taking the pie out of the box and setting it on the counter.

Pulling away from the door, he came to stand behind her. "Would I have kissed you the way I did in Venice if there were?"

When she didn't answer, he ran his hand down the length of her hair, feeling an almost irresistible urge to sink his fingers into those soft, shiny curls. "Answer me, Paige."

She turned around and saw that the humor was gone from his eyes. Suddenly awkward, she struggled to find her voice. "I don't know you well enough to answer that."

"I think you do. You're just afraid to admit it." He paused as if waiting for her to protest. When she didn't, he added, "There hasn't been anyone special in my life for a long time. And even then, it wasn't all that special. Long-term travel can be trying on a relationship."

His gaze shifted to her mouth, which was only a breath away, then returned to her eyes in a slow, caressing motion. Paige felt momentarily spellbound. It was with great effort that she moved past him, opened a cabinet, and retrieved two mugs. "So where will you be going next?"

He smiled, amused that she was nervous enough to want to bring the conversation back to a safer subject. "Are you asking me to divulge professional secrets?"

"Why not? I divulged some of mine."

"You told me about a rare George III silver teaset you're trying to locate for a client, and, if I recall, *I* told you where to find it."

Paige smiled as she filled the mugs with steaming coffee. "Is that your way of telling me that I owe you?"

Before she had a chance to pick up the mugs, Matt took her by the shoulders and turned her around. "It depends on what kind of payoff you had in mind."

"Won't the best coffee in town do?"

"Not really." He pulled her to him. "But this will."

She was vaguely aware of warnings flashing through

her mind, of words of caution, reminders of another time when she had been just as vulnerable.

But the moment his lips touched hers, all caution disappeared, replaced by sensations so powerful no amount of common sense could compete with them.

As he tugged her closer, Paige felt her breath quicken. In silent accord her lips opened to the teasing of his tongue. She found herself reaching for him, clinging, experiencing the passion all over again, feeding the hunger with open-mouth kisses that left her gasping and wanting more.

He took everything she gave greedily, while his hands explored, slid over her sweatshirt and brushed her breasts.

"You aren't playing fair," she murmured against his mouth.

"Is that what you want, Paige? For me to play fair?"

Under his touch, her skin grew hot and moist. Need, too long ignored, turned her blood into smoldering lava. "No."

Now that she had admitted the truth, emotions slammed into her, making her head spin. Her mind, bared of all caution, filled with him, with sensations coming from him. And yet a part of her still held back and he sensed it.

"Don't fight it, darling," he said, as he skimmed her face with kisses. "Please don't fight it now."

His hands went to her face, framing it as he looked into her eyes. It was that look, that gesture, that moment of absolute tenderness that won her in the end, for tenderness wasn't something she had known with Brad. With a sigh that seemed to have come from her very soul, she wrapped her arms around his neck.

His lips were soft, moving expertly against hers, but now, rather than deepen the kiss as he had before, he touched his mouth to hers for only a moment, just enough to tease her. When she tried to take more, he didn't let her.

The game made her wild for him, but she played it

gladly, learning as she went, nipping at his lower lip, allowing the heat within her to build. Closing her eyes, she let herself absorb every sensation, every tingle as her body pressed against his, began to move.

She heard him suck in his breath, and this time, his mouth was no longer playful, but more urgent. Then she was aware of being lifted, carried up the stairs, of Matt's warm breath along her cheek. She guided him to her room, turned on the light.

"You're trembling," Matt said as he put her down.

She laughed, a short, unsteady laugh. It had been years since she had made love to a man. And even then, she had never considered herself very good at it. She wanted him so much, and yet . . . "It's been a long time. I mean, I haven't . . ."

He cupped her face and kissed her. "You'll do just fine. Just follow your heart."

She did, knowing that to follow her heart was to lose it. Shedding whatever inhibitions she had left, she fumbled with the buttons of his shirt, clumsily at first, then with more confidence until she had the garment open.

Her fingers were hesitant as they moved over the broad expanse of skin and hair, felt the hard muscles, the wild beat of his heart. Boldly, she pressed her lips to that very spot, and made small, wet circles with her tongue, moving toward his nipple with a calculated slowness until she reached her target.

She heard him groan, and the sound inflamed her more than anything else he could have done. All at once, everything changed. There was a stir, a shift of control from him to her. Playfully, she hooked two fingers at the front of his belt and pulled him farther into the room, toward the bed, unfastening the buckle as she walked backward.

The hunger was almost unbearable now. Where had it come from? Was it because of the lack of men in her life all those years? Or was it because of the man who was here now?

"Undress me," she whispered.

Smiling at her bravado, Matt tugged at the sweatshirt, and let it drop to the floor before he unhooked her blue lacy bra. Her breasts were small but exquisitely shaped. Half-wild with the need to taste her, he bent to kiss them, pushing them together so he could lick each nipple in turn and watch them turn into hard peaks.

He had never thought it would be so difficult to keep his own desire in check. He had done it dozens of times. But it was different with Paige. Each sigh, each ragged breath she let out, played havoc with his senses. Her needs became his needs, her urgency, a delicious aphrodisiac that sent his blood racing to his loins.

Holding her to cushion the fall, he pushed her down onto the kingsize bed, his mouth pressing against the hollow of her neck, inhalling her fragrance. He drew down her jeans, kissing every inch of skin revealed, peeling off the blue panties, before he tore off his own clothes with shaking hands.

"God, you're beautiful, he whispered, quickly returning to her."

She felt his hands skim over her, slide down to her thighs, parting them. She knew what pleasure could do, how it could dull the mind and rack the body, turning it into a mass of sensations. But she didn't know it could be like this, that the wanting could be so powerful, that wherever he touched her, a pulse would beat, a nerve would respond, heat would burst.

He felt her need, the tug of her hands as she tried to pull him back to her. But he was determined to drive her higher still, and so, ignoring his own desire, he let his mouth continue its exploration, slowly, lovingly. He marveled at the softness of her breasts as he kissed them, at the slenderness of her waist as he wrapped his hands around it, at the flatness and smoothness of her stomach. Further down, her skin was even softer, lightly scented with lavender.

"No!"

The alarm in her voice stopped him. He looked up, saw the panic of the unknown in her eyes. He cursed himself for not being more tuned to her needs, for having rushed her. "Tell me what you want, Paige."

She pulled him to her. "You."

That's all he needed to hear. In one smooth motion, his body covered hers, center to center, heart to heart. Slow and easy. He said the words to himself over and over, aware that soon, they would be meaningless. Still, the thought that he could wait this long, that he could tease, torture, and still want to give more, was a revelation.

"What have you done to me?" he murmured, gazing into the cool blueness of her eyes.

"I don't know. Tell me."

"You make me forget the promises I've made to myself, the rules I've set."

Her hands slid along his hard hips, followed the softer contours of his buttocks and pressed him against her. "Is that bad?"

Matt shuddered. "God, no. Not when breaking the rules feels like this."

She started to say something else and then caught her breath. He had slid into her, rock hard. She arched her back, responding at once. They moved slowly at first, then with mounting speed. As the urgency grew, the sound of their breathing filled the room.

A moment ago, Paige had been conscious of the roar of the ocean, but now the world seemed to dissolve. Only the sensations remained. And the excruciating pleasure. "Matt, I . . ."

He entered her just as she cried out his name, filling her, making her want to move faster, desperate to take all he could give. The heat was unbearable. She could barely breathe, didn't want to breathe for fear of breaking the spell.

Her climax tore into her, so potent, so complete, that for a moment she thought she would faint. But he was there for her, his hands groping for hers, his fingers interlacing with her fingers as his passion was released into her.

* * *

He woke up to the roar of the ocean and the tantalizing aroma of bacon. Glancing at a bedside clock, he saw that it was seven o'clock. So, like him, Paige was an early riser.

He padded to the bathroom in search of a towel to wrap around him and found a neatly folded dark green terry robe on the top shelf of a white wicker cabinet.

Hoping it would be roomy enough for him, he pulled it out and saw from the label that it was a man's robe. His first instinct was to put it back. Then he changed his mind and slipped into it, smiling at the thought that he had experienced his first stab of jealousy.

They had awakened twice during the night, each time more hungry for each other than the previous time. Paige was like a child in a candy store—wide-eyed at the wonders still to be found and eager to savor those she already knew. Her imagination, he had discovered, was endless. She was a newly born vixen, anxious to test her wings. And like him, eager to give. Later they had gone downstairs and feasted on pumpkin pie and a large glass of milk. Then, hand in hand, they had gone back to bed.

As he came down the stairs, he paid more attention to the lower portion of the house and again it was impossible for him to imagine Paige living anywhere else. Everything here was strictly vintage California, from the turquoise sofas and chairs that seemed to be an extension of the sea, to the collection of local pottery in soft pastel shades. On a far wall, a large bookcase, drenched in sunshine, soared all the way to the cathedral ceiling, crammed with well-read books, framed photographs, and other mementos.

He found her in the kitchen, standing in front of the island and whipping some sort of batter with a fork, while on the stove, bacon sizzled gently. In her powder-blue sweats and ponytail, she looked like a schoolgirl.

"Need any help?"

She spun around, ponytail flying. Her face had been scrubbed clean, and except for the intimate, slightly wicked expression in her eyes, she looked nothing like the passionate woman he had held in his arms through the night.

"Good morning. I see you've found Daddy's robe." She didn't miss the look of relief in his eyes and was pleased that he had cared enough to wonder. "My father spent a lot of time here when the house was being renovated."

She handed him two plates stacked with silverware and crisp green napkins and pointed to a coffee table in front of a roaring fire in the living room. "He painted all the rooms."

Matt took another look at the ivory walls with the turquoise border near the ceiling. "Very nice."

"I'll tell him you said so."

He set the dishes side by side on the coffee table, topping each with a napkin. When he came back into the kitchen, Paige had piled bacon, enough for twelve hungry men, onto a platter. She handed it to him.

"Mmmm. Domesticity suits you, Mr. McKenzie."

"You think so?"

"Definitely." She followed him into the living room. "What else can you do around the house?"

"What is this? A test?"

"Are you afraid of tests?"

"I'm not afraid of anything," he said, with exaggerated pride. "Let's see, I can chop wood."

She glanced toward the fire in the living room. "Mine comes already chopped."

"And fold the laundry."

"Not *do* the laundry?"

He snatched a slice of crisp bacon from the tray and bit into it, realizing he was famished. "Sorry. I have someone who comes in once a week to do that. She also prepares little homemade dinners for me, which she puts in small plastic bags, then throws in the freezer until I'm ready for them."

"So in other words, you are rather useless?"

She was playing with the belt around his waist as she

talked, making it very difficult for him to concentrate on food. "I wouldn't exactly say that." He pulled the rubber band from her hair and watched as it tumbled in loose, glorious curls. "I have a few other attributes." He kissed her lightly, teasingly. "You already know some of them."

"Mmmm, it's been so long, I'm afraid I have forgotten."

Blue eyes he had never thought could smolder gazed up at him, setting him on fire. "Would you care to refresh my memory?"

SEVENTEEN

Paige had known from that first moment in Venice that she was destined to fall in love with him. What she hadn't realized was how quickly, how recklessly, she would surrender her heart.

Aware that Matt had to be back in New York by December twenty-seventh, she had decided to spend every moment of the next few days with him.

Braving Santa Barbara's chilly mornings, they rented bicycles and rode them on Cabrillo Boulevard, sailed to the Channel Islands at noon, and sometimes joined college students at East Beach for a game of volleyball.

At night, Matt came to the house, where he dazzled her with his only culinary specialty—marinara sauce, which he poured over spaghetti one night, rice and shrimp the next, omelettes, or whatever Paige happened to have in the refrigerator.

But it was Paige's first trip to the Canyon-T Ranch a few days later, and her introduction to Josh, whom she had met briefly at her grandmother's house years ago, that would remain one of the highlights of that week.

As she stepped out of the Jeep on the afternoon of December 22, Josh came out to meet them, appraised Paige with those smiling and irresistible golden eyes, then, folding his arms against his barrel-like chest, he said to Matt, "Now, son, that's what I call a thoroughbred."

Paige laughed, partly to hide her embarrassment and partly because no compliment had ever sounded so genuine or been delivered with so much charm.

Later, as they sipped strong, black coffee and sampled warm slices of Nigel's famous Christmas stollen, Paige found herself drawn to Josh and his wonderful sense of humor. Like all cowboys she knew, he was a wonderful storyteller; but he was also straightforward, loyal, and proud, and it was easy to see why Matt adored him. When it was time to leave and Josh asked her to come back to the ranch anytime, even after Matt was gone, she knew the offer was sincere and promised she would.

"So what do you think of my grandfather?" Matt asked her later as they were driving back to Santa Barbara.

"He's a wonderful man—honest, generous. And very handsome," she added, throwing Matt a playful glance. "Like all the McKenzie men."

"You forgot crazy." He threw her the same glance. "Like all the McKenzie men?"

Paige laughed. "Only one of them is crazy. Which reminds me," she added, "you·never did tell me what prank you had planned the other day before I accepted your lunch invitation." She turned around in her seat, and faced him. "Something involving a pilot?"

"Oh, that." Matt chuckled. "I haven't forgotten. I just wasn't sure you were ready for it."

"Considering how upset I was with you then, I'd say I'd be more inclined to be amused now than I was a few days ago." Placing her hand on his thigh, she shook it gently. "So come on, tell me."

After glancing at the clock on the dash, Matt took the next exit and pulled over to the side of the road. "All right, if that's what you want." Turning off the engine, he picked up the car phone and dialed a number. "Johnnie?" he said, when his party answered. "McKenzie. Is it too late for you make that run now?" He glanced behind them. "I'm on Modoc, a couple of miles north of La Cumbre Country Club." He laughed. "Thanks, buddy. I appreciate it."

He hung up, looking mysterious and a little sheepish. "It'll only be a few minutes."

"What is this all about, Matt? Who did you call?"

"Patience, darling, patience."

A few moments later, the rumble of a plane directly above them make them look up. But when Paige started to look away, Matt stopped her. "Pay attention," he said, leaning toward the window and pointing at the sky.

Squinting against the setting sun, Paige looked up. Trailing behind the plane, a long, pink banner spelled out the message: "I love you, Paige. Will you marry me?"

Her eyes wide and incredulous, her mouth open in shock, Paige could only stare at the sky. When she turned back to Matt, her eyes were filled with contained laughter. "Tell me you weren't going to have that plane fly over Santa Barbara with those words trailing behind it."

Matt watched as the plane turned around, getting ready for another pass. "Desperate moments call for desperate actions, my love. I had to do something to get your attention."

"I could have had you arrested for harassment."

He leaned over and stole a kiss. "No, you wouldn't have."

"Mmmm. Pretty sure of yourself, aren't you?"

"Not really. But I always try to accentuate the positive when I'm nervous. It throws people off."

"Why would you be nervous now?"

"Because you haven't given me your answer yet," Matt said, his expression solemn.

Paige's smile faded. Inside her chest, her heart lurched. "What are you talking about?"

"I'm talking about you and me getting married. I'm talking about the fact that I love you, that I have loved you from the first moment I saw you in Venice."

She fell back against her seat, as if a bomb had hit her. High above them, the plane made one last pass, dipped a wing in farewell, and then disappeared, the pink banner flapping in the breeze.

Until now, she had tried not to spoil whatever time they had left together with thoughts of tearful good-byes and promises to call every day. She knew how Matt felt about marriage, knew that the best she could hope for was one of those long-distance relationships—apart during the week, together on weekends.

She looked at him, expecting to see that teasing smile of his. She didn't. "You can't be serious," she said, still doubtful.

He took a curl that had gone astray and pushed it back into her hair. "I've never been more serious in my life."

"But a few days ago, you said—"

"I said a lot of things. I thought I meant them. I thought I knew what I wanted out of life." He pulled her to him. "But that was before I met you."

"Are you sure marriage is what you want?"

He ran his hand along her cheek, her neck, smiling when she moistened her lips with her tongue. She always did that when she was nervous. "Very sure. I know, it'll be difficult at first. But we can make it work, darling. I'll *make* it work." A momentary shadow dulled the brightness in his eyes. "The question is, do you love me enough to do the same?"

Unable to cope with the sudden burst of joy, she threw her arms around Matt, laughing and crying at the same time. "Yes!" she said, just before his lips crushed hers. "Yes, yes, yes!"

Jeremy took a sip of his chilled mimosa and nodded approvingly at the excellent proportions of orange juice and Roederer Cristal. No matter how good the first-class service on most aircraft was, nothing equalled the sheer luxury of having your own private jet.

He was in a fitting mood this morning. And for just reason. Not only had he finalized his deal to buy the *London Meteor* from British newspaper mogul, Harrisson Blythe, but he had spent one of the most exciting weeks of his life in the company of the very pretty and very sexy Lady Sarah Wyatt.

There had been a time when he had considered marrying the royal-blooded Sarah. But after further consideration, he had decided against it. She didn't have the right style, or the intelligence necessary to mix with the people in his high-powered circle. At twenty-three, Sarah Wyatt's main interests revolved almost solely around the discovery of the latest nightclub, or the decision to wear long instead of short at the next social bash.

Jeremy was considering ordering another drink when the attractive flight attendant walked toward him, a portable telephone in her hand. "Your houseman is on the line, Mr. Newman."

Surprised, for Chu Seng seldom called during a flight, he took the receiver from her hand. "Yes, Chu Seng, what is it?"

"I'm sorry to bother you with this, sir. But something has happened with Miss Granger I feel you ought to know before you talk to her."

At the mention of Paige's name, Jeremy set his glass down. "What's wrong with Paige?"

"While you were gone, Miss Granger and Mr. Matthew McKenzie became engaged, sir. The wedding is scheduled for January ninth."

Jeremy's whole body went rigid. "Where did you hear that nonsense?"

"On the twelve o'clock news, sir. And from several reporters who have been calling here all afternoon."

For a moment, Jeremy's mind was unable to deal with the shock. Only rage, swift and lethal, filled his head. That vermin! That no-good, double-crossing vermin. He was just as unscrupulous as his father, after all. He had that same pirate blood running through his veins, that same arrogance.

"Miss Granger also called," Chu Seng continued. "She wants to talk to you as soon as it's convenient."

He hesitated, too stunned, too angry to decide on an immediate course of action. He needed time. He needed a clear head. "Tell her I should be home within a couple of hours, but explain that I'm tired and won't be able to see her until tomorrow."

He hung up and took a deep breath, waiting for the hammering in his heart to subside, for his thoughts to settle into some sort of logical order. But all he could think of was that once again, a McKenzie had taken away the woman he wanted to marry.

That fucking son of a bitch. He had been trouble from the very beginning. It hadn't been enough that he had humiliated him two years ago in front of the entire country by accusing him of murder, and that he had ruined his deal with Ted Krugger. Now he had to steal Paige from under his nose, the way his father had stolen Caroline.

His first impulse was to stop the wedding somehow. He should be able to think of something between now and January ninth. Perhaps he could kidnap Paige, tell her he did it for her own good. But that thought was as childish as it was impractical. And Paige would never forgive him. As for his alternate brainstorm—finding some sort of dirt on McKenzie and having him thrown in jail for a year or two—he had already tried that two years ago. The man was as clean as the virgin snow. One would think that after all those years of dealing with millions of dollars in art, some sort of payoff money would have passed through his hands somehow, that he would have succumbed to the temptation, like any normal human being.

But he hadn't. Self-righteous bastard. Always acting like some superior son of a bitch, when in fact he was nothing but a low-life wanderer like his father.

It took Jeremy a long time to calm down, to think about this wedding in a rational manner, to see it as a temporary setback rather than a defeat.

By the time the flight attendant came to tell him that San Francisco Airport had given them clearance to land, he was in complete control of his emotions again.

He knew Paige too well to believe she would settle for a part-time husband. And with Matt's professional obligations and his frequent trips out of the country, that was exactly what he would be—a part-time husband. Paige would hate it. She was accustomed to having those she loved around her, not thousands of miles away six months of the year. No matter how much they loved each other, the distance was bound to put a serious strain on their relationship.

A thin smile drifted across Jeremy's features. And when that happened, he would be right there to lend Paige his support. After all, what were friends for?

Jeremy stood just inside his drawing room, watching Paige, who seemed lost in the contemplation of the San Francisco Bay. As always, her presence filled the room. And his senses. The thought that soon she would be on another coast, bringing pleasure to another man, made him want to do terrible things to McKenzie. Forcing his fists open, he walked across the room, stopping a few feet behind her. "Paige?"

She turned around, cheeks flushed, blue eyes shining, as if she had been miles away. They're lovers, he thought, bitterness and jealousy making his mouth taste sour. Only a woman in love could look like this.

Making an enormous effort to keep a welcoming smile on his lips, he greeted her with his hands extended, as he always did. "How are you, my dear?" He drew her close and kissed her on the cheek. "You look wonderful." He waited for her to sit down before doing the same.

She didn't thank him for the compliment, didn't ask about his trip or if his business had gone according to plan. In typical fashion, she went right to the heart of the matter.

"I'm afraid you aren't going to be pleased with what I have to tell you."

He leaned back and folded his arms. "If it's about you and Matt McKenzie, I already know." The direct approach was something he had decided at the last minute, knowing that with a woman like Paige it was the kind of scheme that would work best.

"Oh." Momentarily thrown, Paige just stared at him. Jeremy never failed to amaze her. Now perhaps more than ever. She searched the familiar face for signs of bitterness, of anger, but other than a slight look of disapproval, which wasn't all that surprising, he was as friendly as ever. "How did you find out?" she asked.

"Chu Seng. He called me on the plane yesterday and gave me the news."

"I have to admit, I expected a different reaction."

"Really? Why?"

"I thought you might see my marriage to Matt as an act of disloyalty."

He shook his head, making every effort to look caring and compassionate. "I could never feel that way about you, Paige. Oh, I won't pretend that I'm happy about this decision of yours. I'm sure it's no secret anymore how I feel about you."

"I'm sorry," she said, realizing too late that Kate and Mindy had been right after all. "I never meant—"

He raised a hand. "I know. Please understand that I hold no bitterness toward you, Paige, no anger. Actually, right now, I'm much more concerned about your happiness than about my wounded ego."

"You don't have to be concerned about me, Jeremy. I'm very happy."

"Of course, you are." He permitted himself a sarcastic laugh. "McKenzie sells charisma by the pound. He is also totally untrustworthy."

"You don't know him."

"And you do? After what? Eight, ten days? Isn't what happened in Venice an indication of how little you do know him?"

She held back the urge to snap at him. Losing her temper now wouldn't be very smart—not if she wanted him to stay with Beauchamp after she was gone. "I don't expect you to understand. Or to approve."

"What about your career? What about Beauchamp and all you had planned for it?"

"Beauchamp will survive without me. As for my career, there is no reason why I can't start a new one in Manhattan. After all, New York is the art center of the world." She smiled. "Or so New Yorkers claim."

"It won't be the same and you know it. You are a free spirit, Paige. You'll never be happy working for someone else. As for Manhattan," he gave a knowing shake of his head, "you'll be bored with it within three months."

"I'll take my chances." She paused, held his gaze. "I hope you and I can remain friends, Jeremy."

Jeremy had always known when to give up. He retreated now, making it a point to be graceful about it. "You can always count on that," he said, giving her hand a brotherly pat.

She watched him closely, trying to gauge his mood, trying to determine if this was the right moment to mention the gallery. Unsure, she decided to chance it anyway. "Will you stay with Beauchamp, then? Will you try to make things work between you and Kate?"

The question caught him unprepared, and he almost turned her down. Then, as he saw the anxious look in Paige's eyes, he realized he couldn't pass up this opportunity to do one more favor for her. He hated the thought of working with Kate again. But one or two transactions a year wouldn't hurt him. He wouldn't even have to see her. He sighed. "It's a lot to ask. But . . . yes, Paige. For you, I'll do it."

After she left, he went to stand by the window, watching her cross the street toward an airport limousine that had been waiting for her. McKenzie was getting himself a prime piece of property there, he thought as the chauffeur rushed to open her door. And the man was too stupid even to realize it.

Dressed in a black Nolan Miller suit that she had accessorized with a three-row pearl choker and matching earrings, Kate hummed happily as she walked around her elegantly set dining room table. It wasn't every day she brought out her personal *Compagnie des Indes* china, or her high-stemmed Baccarat glasses and monogrammed silver flatware. But tonight was a very special occasion, and she wanted everything to be perfect for Paige's and Matt's engagement dinner.

So far, so good, she thought, leaning over the table to move a water goblet a fraction of an inch to the right. Now if Eve would keep her dissatisfaction with this wedding to herself and behave, all would go well.

Like Eve, Kate had been skeptical at first. As much as she liked Matt and had been elated at the thought of having Jeremy out of Paige's life once and for all, marriage wasn't a decision one made in two short weeks. The fear that her impetuous niece might once again end up with a broken heart had frightened her very much.

But after seeing them together, after realizing how sincere, stable, and loving Matt was, Kate's fears had been laid to rest.

Her only regret was to see Paige move so far away. For the past twenty years, the two of them had been like mother and daughter, never apart from one another for more than a few days. And because she couldn't bear the thought of that separation being final, she had refused to buy Paige's shares in the business.

"There's no reason why we can't remain partners," she had told her. "In fact, with you in New York our association might prove to be even more interesting."

Still humming, Kate gave the table one last look. Then, satisfied that it was perfect in every way, she took a slow walk around the room to insure that all was in place.

As she reached the console by the window, her gaze stopped on a grouping of old family photographs, settling on one in particular.

It was a faded, black-and-white snapshot of Kate and her sister, Ann, taken a few days before Ann had left for New York to find fame and fortune. Ann had been seventeen, Kate fifteen. Their arms around each other, they were laughing at the camera. Although to the careful observer, the sadness in their eyes would not have passed unnoticed, on the surface they looked carefree and happy, their broad smiles full of youthful expectations at the wonderful future that awaited them.

Her heart suddenly aching for her sister, Kate picked up the antique silver frame and let her fingers trail over the glass. "You should be here, too, Ann," she whispered. "You should be part of this celebration."

She remained there for a long time, staring at the photograph through a veil of tears, remembering the closeness the two of them had shared, the way they had always comforted each other through their difficult childhood. And she remembered the day Ann had called to say she was getting married.

"I found my Prince Charming, Katie. He's almost too good to be true." Emotions had been too much and she had had to wait a moment before adding, "I love him so much, Katie. I don't know how I've lived without him all these years."

It had been a fairy-tale marriage. No couple on earth had been better suited for each other, more appealing to watch, more in love.

The news that they were expecting a baby had made their happiness complete. For nine months, Ann had been in a state of total bliss, singing as she prepared for the baby's arrival, wallpapering the nursery herself, and calling Kate every day for an updated report on her pregnancy.

"She's going to have a wonderful life, Katie," Ann had whispered almost fiercely the morning of Paige's christening. "She is never going to know terror, like we did, or the loneliness of not being loved, not being wanted."

Seven years later Ann had forgotten that promise and walked out on her child.

Even though Kate had finally heard from Ann and found out she lived in Italy, her sister had never revealed to her her reason for leaving Santa Barbara so abruptly.

For the past twenty years, they had communicated only by mail. Kate wrote twice a month, addressing the letters to a post office box in Rome, as she had been instructed in Ann's first letter.

"You must give me your absolute word, Katie," Ann had stressed in that letter. 'That you will never tell anyone where I am and that I have written to you. If I find

out you betrayed me, I'll move somewhere else and you'll
never hear from me again.''

And so Kate had kept Ann's secret. She had written
hundreds of letters over the years, telling her all about
Paige, sending photographs, news clippings, little things
she knew Ann would appreciate. In return, Ann told her
about the beautiful house where she lived, the kind and
wonderful man who had offered her sanctuary and whom
she had eventually married, how she had learned to paint
and to play the piano. But in spite of Kate's many attempts to learn more about that fateful Christmas Eve,
Ann had remained silent.

''Miss Madison?''

Still holding the picture, Kate turned her head. ''Yes,
Lisa?''

''Miss Granger and Mr. McKenzie have arrived.''

''Very well. Thank you, Lisa. Tell them to make themselves comfortable. I'll be right out.''

Dabbing at a tear that had caught in the corner of her
eye, Kate replaced the picture on the console. Then, her
heart pounding at the thought of the decision she had just
made, she squared her shoulders and went to greet her
two guests of honor.

EIGHTEEN

Of the seven hills on which the eternal city of Rome was built, the twin-peaked Aventine, the oldest, is by far the most beautiful and the least frequented by tourists. Surrounded by tranquil piazzas, pebble-path gardens, and baroque churches, it seems removed from the downtown frenzy and the impossible traffic congestion for which the Roman capital is so famous.

Inside her Renaissance villa on Via di Sant'Anselmo, Ann Ludicci, once known as Ann Granger, sat with her eyes closed. All around her the sounds of Mozart's *Piano Concerto No. 9* drifted from the concealed stereo system, while on the mantel a clock struck the hour.

Even now, only weeks away from her fifty-first birthday, she was a striking woman, with the same beautiful dark eyes, sensual mouth, and rich, curly black hair that had charmed Santa Barbarans twenty years ago. Her body had grown more mature, more voluptuous, but she was still elegant, even in the comfortable slacks and sweaters she now preferred to wear. There were fine lines fanning around her eyes but one could hardly call them laugh lines, for Ann Ludicci rarely laughed. Even when she smiled, there was a sadness about her, a longing that one sensed at once and that no amount of time had erased.

She was content to have found peace. A peace she owed largely to this house. And to her husband, Marcello. Opening her eyes, she allowed her gaze to move slowly across the room, as if to seek comfort from it. Villa Assumpta, which had been named after Marcello's mother, was a magnificent structure of seventeenth-century architecture, surrounded by lush gardens and three terraces, each commanding a spectacular view of Rome. Inside the villa, the luxury was even more breathtaking—sumptuous rooms, handpainted ceilings, marble columns.

Throughout the house was an astonishing collection of rare objects from around the world. But it was Marcello's Italian heritage that prevailed in almost every room—Sicilian pottery, brass from Sorrento, Tuscan furniture, Neapolitan figurines, even an intricate banister from Naples.

This room, which Assumpta had called the Blue Salon, was one of Ann's favorites. Decorated any other way, the size would have made it seem austere and cold. But with its colorful fireplace made of eighteenth-century tiles, its comfortable pale blue sofas, settees, and chairs, its painted boiserie and diffused lighting, the effect was warm and inviting, rich without being ostentatious.

Today, however, the quiet, elegant surroundings failed to work their magic. Not even the thought of Marvcello's portrait, which she had started yesterday, a present for his seventy-second birthday next month, could generate any excitement. A sigh escaped her lips and Ann lowered her gaze to the letter she still held in her hand—Kate's letter.

Over the years, news from her sister had arrived with comforting regularity—two letters every month. Each was filled with Kate's easy chatter, news of Paige along with little anecdotes that made Ann smile, but more often made her cry and long for her daughter even more.

Today's letter had brought on a new kind of anguish. Paige was getting married. Kate's delight poured out of every page as she talked in detail about the handsome future groom, Matt McKenzie, and all the frantic, last-minute preparations that surrounded the upcoming event. But it was her sister's closing paragraph that had driven right through Ann's heart.

I debated telling you about the wedding. [Kate wrote with her usual honesty] because I was afraid it would cause you too much pain. But the more I thought about it, the more I realized that I had no right to keep your daughter's most important day a secret from you. The wedding is scheduled for twelve noon on January ninth at Montecito First Presbyterian Church. You should be there, Ann. Regardless of what happened twenty years ago, of what drove you away, this is one moment you can't afford to miss. Think about it. Lovingly, Kate.

A sob rose to Ann's throat. Decisions had always been easy for Kate. She had always been the strong one, even though she was younger. She was the one who never cried when they were beaten, who never flinched when their parents screamed insults at each other in the room next door. It had been different with Ann. She had been the tender one, the romantic one, the one who had needed nurturing, guiding.

"Is something bothering you, *cara*?"

At the sound of Marcello's concerned voice and the gentle pressure of his hand on her shoulder, Ann turned around, covering his hand with his.

At seventy-two, former symphony conductor Marcello Ludicci had remained one of Italy's most talked-about men. He was tall and elegant, with fine, almost angular features and deep, dark eyes that few women, even now, could resist. His hair, almost entirely white, was thick and combed in that old-fashioned but becoming wavy style he'd worn for years.

He was a man of great strength. It was that strength, and his kindness, that had made Ann's grief more bearable over the years. And it was his strength she counted on now. Without a word, she handed him Kate's letter.

Marcello took it, read it, and came around the sofa where he sat down next to her. "You must go at once, of course," he said in the positive tone she had come to cherish. "I'll tell Noemi to make the necessary arrangements—"

"No!"

She could tell by the neutral expression in his eyes that he had been expecting her refusal. "Why not?" When she didn't answer, he took her hand in his. "It's been a long time, Ann. Twenty years."

"I made a bargain with Eve."

"And you kept it. You walked out of the Grangers' lives, left everything that was dearest to you in order to spare them a scandal. But this," he added, glancing at the letter still in his hand, "is something else entirely. No one could ever fault you for wanting to attend your daughter's wedding."

"Eve would."

"Eve Granger doesn't own Santa Barbara."

"You don't know her power, Marcello. She would have me run out of town the moment I stepped off the plane."

"Not if she didn't know you were coming. Not if no one recognized you."

Ann frowned. "You mean . . . I should wear a disguise?"

"Why not, if you'd rather stay incognito? It wouldn't have to be anything drastic. A large hat and a pair of dark sunglasses should be sufficient."

For the first time since Kate's letter had arrived with the morning mail, Ann allowed herself a glimmer of hope. "But what if she recognizes me anyway? Or if Paul recognizes me?" Doubts began to sway her again. "What if the truth comes out?" she asked in a small voice.

"Maybe it's time it did, *cara*. Paige is a big girl now, a woman about to be married, ready to start a family of her own. I think she can take the truth."

"But the press—"

"Al diavolo con la stampa!" Marcello exploded in a rare show of anger. "Who cares what they think? Or print? What matters now is you, Ann. You and your daughter getting back together."

"She'll never understand. From what Kate has told me over the years, Paige still harbors a lot of bitterness toward me."

"Bitterness goes away."

She stood up and walked over to the fireplace, where a warm fire had been burning since early this morning. Extending her hands toward the crackling flames, she thought of Kate's words: "This is one moment you can't afford to miss."

Yes, it would take courage to face her daughter, to face all of them. But not nearly as much courage as it had taken to walk away twenty years ago.

Her timid smile growing stronger, she turned toward her husband. "I'll do it, Marcello. I'll go."

After he had left to give her maid, Noemi, the necessary instructions, Ann walked over to the French window that overlooked the topiary gardens. In the distance, St. Peter's famous dome was shrouded in a light mist, and farther still, heavy rain clouds were forming.

The approaching storm reminded her of her childhood in New Jersey, of all the times she had stood by her bedroom window, waiting for the rain to end and the rainbow to appear. When it did, Ann always closed her eyes and made a wish, while Kate, who didn't believe in secret wishes, told her she was being foolish.

Perhaps if she hadn't filled her head with silly dreams, if she had been stronger, like Kate, her life might have turned out differently.

But what else was there in those days? How would she have even survived the first seventeen years of her life without those dreams to cling to?

She had been raised in Trenton, New Jersey, by two drunken parents who took out their frustrations on their two little daughters almost daily, and made their childhood a living hell.

Too ashamed to have friends over, she and Kate found comfort in each other by sharing their dreams and talking about the kind of life they would have when they grew up. Kate's dreams had changed many times over the years, but Ann's never did.

From the time she saw her first Ginger Rogers movie, she knew she wanted to be a dancer—a Broadway dancer. But there were no outlets in Trenton for such an ambitious dream. And so, at seventeen, too impatient to wait until she had graduated from high school, Ann moved to New York City, promising Kate that when she became rich and famous, she would send for her and they would live in a beautiful apartment overlooking Central Park.

But a few weeks later, Ann realized Manhattan wasn't the magic land she had imagined. Although she found a waitress job in a snack bar on Eighth Avenue, jobs on Broadway were rare, and reserved for those with training and experience.

Food and rent took nearly every cent she made, and when her roommate, a sixteen-year-old runaway from Omaha, told her Elmer, a nightclub owner she knew, was looking for another dancer, Ann ran to the interview with new hope in her heart.

Lolita's was a dingy nightclub down in the seedier part of the Village, and looked more like a bordello than a place where Ann could forge a dancing career. Gyrating in front of a rowdy crowd dressed in black fishnet stockings and a skimpy costume was hardly her idea of stardom. But the pay was twice what she made at the snack bar and would allow her to take those much-needed dancing lessons.

Although being nice to the male customers was expected, sleeping with them was usually left to the girls' discretion. Ann's determination to do her dance routine every night and then leave didn't bother Elmer until one of the men threatened to go elsewhere because the "Ice Queen" acted like she was too good for him. The following day, Elmer told her that if she didn't change her snooty ways, he would have to let her go.

She had hated sex from the very first day. She hated the groping, the noisy, wet kisses, the way some of the men shouted obscenities while pumping into her, paying no attention to her tears of shame and despair.

After awhile, she learned to block it all out, and although she had a reputation for being a "lousy lay" and wasn't much in demand, she managed to make enough money to eventually move into an apartment of her own.

She never gave up on Broadway. Braving the cold in the winter and the scorching heat in the summer, she continued to make the rounds of local theaters, sometimes waiting hours to audition, before being turned away at the end of the day.

It was in July of 1960, while she sat on a Central Park bench, massaging her tired feet, that she met Paul Granger.

With his light brown hair, striking blue eyes, and friendly smile, he was the most handsome man she had ever seen. He talked in a gentle, refined way, and when he looked at her his gaze was direct and warm, not hungry and sly like most men she knew. As he fed the squirrels, he told her he lived in Santa Barbara, California, where he practiced law. He had come to New York for a convention.

Too ashamed to admit what she did for a living, she told him the same thing she had told her landlady—that she worked as a secretary in a doctor's office while waiting for her big chance on Broadway.

"You should be a model," Paul said. His eyes traveled the length of her long, slender body. "You look like one."

"I do?"

"Absolutely. You are very beautiful, you know. Beautiful enough to be in *Vogue*."

She blushed, for no one had ever paid her such a compliment before. "Thank you."

The following day, they met at the same place, and this time he took her to lunch in an elegant restaurant on Forty-sixth Street, where waiters in black tuxedos waited on her like a princess. After a few sips of wine, she began to loosen up a little. They laughed and talked about things she had never discussed with anyone before—John F. Kennedy's chances of becoming the next president of the United States, the winter Olympics, which Paul had attended in Squaw Valley, and a new musical, *Camelot*, scheduled to open in a few months and in which she hoped to get a small part.

That night, she and Paul became lovers. And although she had dreaded it at first, knowing how bad she was, and how much she hated it, making love to him was the most wonderful, most arousing experience of her young life. Paul stroked her with a tenderness that made her tremble with desire. She responded by touching him in various places and watching his face to see if she was doing it right. It was the first time she had ever cared if she were doing it right.

Two months later, they were engaged and Ann was on her way to Santa Barbara. Before she left New York, she made sure the trail she left wouldn't lead to Lolita's, but to a genuine doctor's office on Lexington Avenue, where the manager, a friend of hers, had agreed to cover for her if anyone came to investigate.

Eve Granger, a tall, alluring woman, with eyes that looked as if they could see into one's very soul, greeted her politely but cautiously. Later that day, she queried Ann at length about her life in New York, her family, and her education, wrinkling her nose in distaste when Ann told her she hadn't gone to college.

"Mother isn't the easiest person to get to know," Paul offered later as a form of apology. "But once the two of you become better acquainted, it'll be different, I promise."

Paul's hopeful prediction never came true. For days after Ann's arrival in the Grangers' beautiful Montecito home, she lived in mortal fear of Eve Granger discovering her lie. But as the days passed and the date of the wedding grew nearer, she began to relax, secure in the knowledge that her horrible past was just that—past.

It wasn't until eight years later that Ann's beautiful world came crashing down.

During a fund-raising dinner for Paul, who was running for district attorney at the time, she came face to face with one of Lolita's most devoted customers, a building contractor who had taken pity on her one night, given her twenty dollars, and told her to go home.

The man, whose name she had forgotten, recognized

her immediately, and, unaware she was the guest of honor's wife, came over to say hello. Ann almost fainted from the shock, but recovered quickly. Taking him aside, she begged him not to say anything and heaved a sigh of relief when he agreed.

When Ann turned around to rejoin her husband, she saw that Eve, who always watched her like a hawk during those social functions, had seen everything.

A week later, on the afternoon of December 23, 1968, Eve summoned Ann into her study. The moment Ann saw the open folder on her mother-in-law's desk, with Ann's police record in plain view, the knot she'd had in her stomach all week, thinking the building contractor might decide to blackmail her after all, tightened. She had completely forgotten about that arrest.

It had happened about a year before she met Paul. Ann and three other girls had been entertaining a group of traveling salesmen backstage at Lolita's when the police arrived. Because two of the girls were caught having sex with some of the customers, all three dancers had been arrested, taken downtown in a police wagon, and booked for prostitution until Elmer's attorney had come to bail them out.

"You've been keeping secrets from us," Eve said, her green eyes showing a hatred Ann had never suspected before.

Ann swallowed to give herself more time. "Secrets?"

"Yes. It would seem that the story you told us eight years ago and the story in this file are quite different." This time, her voice was filled with contempt. "I had you figured out for a cold-blooded fortune hunter from the start, you know. I even thought about having you investigated. But Paul wouldn't hear of it." She gave Ann a disdainful look. "Of course, I did it anyway. Pity I wasn't thorough enough."

"Why do it now, Eve? After all this time."

"Because when I saw you talking to that contractor last week, I knew there was still a lot about you we didn't know." She straightened her back, her gleam triumphant. "And I was right."

Ann's first impulse was to confess everything and beg for mercy. But weakness was not a character trait Eve admired. Strength was her only hope now, the only language Eve would understand. And respect.

"Well," Eve urged. "What do you have to say for yourself?"

"Nothing that can help me now, Eve. Yes, I lied to Paul and I lied to you, but I did it because I was afraid to lose him. I loved him so very much, you see. Almost as much as I love him now."

"Then it's true? You were a . . . prostitute?" The way she spoke the word, Ann doubted she had ever said it before.

"I was hired as a dancer. I didn't realize until later that I would be asked to . . . to . . . "

"Sleep with the customers?"

"I was very young then, Eve, and very frightened."

"But very clever. Clever enough to fabricate this phony secretarial job and then lie to all of us."

Forgetting her promise to be strong, Ann begged Eve to forget what she had found out, pointing out it would only destroy the lives of the people they both loved.

Nothing worked. Her voice low, almost monotonous, Eve told Ann about the career Paul had so carefully built for himself, and how quickly it would end once the press found out about Ann's sordid past, not to mention her police record.

"But why would they go looking for anything now?" Ann cried in desperation. "If they wanted to find some dirt on me, they would have done it long ago, when I first arrived in Santa Barbara."

Eve shook her head. "Paul was only an attorney then, not important enough for them to waste their time. It's different now that he's running for public office." She glanced with distaste at the folder in front of her. "It will only be a matter of days before they uncover this ugly truth. And when they do, they'll drag Paul through the mud, ruin any chance he has of becoming district attorney.''

"Stop it! You're trying to torture me."

"And what about Paige?" Eve continued mercilessly. "Do you have any idea what this scandal will do to her once it hits the papers? She'll be ridiculed, hounded by the press, scarred forever.'' In the tall, straight-backed chair, Eve seemed to grow taller, more threatening. "If, on the other hand, you should leave Santa Barbara, the press wouldn't be nearly as anxious to dig into the past of a woman who was no longer part of Paul's life.''

A chill went through Ann's body. "They would never believe I left Paul. Everyone knows how much I love him.''

"They would if we leaked out you and Paul were having marital difficulties. There'd be a flurry of interest for a week or two after your departure and then it would all die down.''

Without taking her eyes off Ann, Eve pulled out a thick manila envelope from a drawer in her desk. "One hundred thousand dollars, Ann," she added. "That's what I'm offering you to get out of our lives forever.''

Ann's horrified gaze moved from the bulging envelope to the cool, composed woman who sat across from her. "My God, you've got it all figured out, haven't you?"

"I'm a practical woman, Ann. You know that.''

"You are a monster! You have no moral fiber, no compassion, no heart.''

"Political careers aren't built on heart, my dear. They are built on guts and brains. I'm proud to say that I possess both.''

Although Ann knew she was no match for a woman like Eve, she stood up, her body trembling from head to toe. "I won't do it! I won't leave my family.''

"Then you'll lose them. You know Paul as well as I do. You know how he hates deception. Once he finds out how you duped him all these years, he'll never forgive you. He'll divorce you and take full custody of Paige. And don't think he can't do it. The name Granger carries a lot of clout in this state. There isn't a judge in Santa Barbara County who won't side with him once they know the truth about you.''

Each word rang in Ann's head with dreadful finality. It was true that Paul could be unforgiving at times. Deception was something he had never tolerated from anyone. And he wouldn't tolerate it from her.

That night, convinced that the only way to save Paul and Paige from a scandal that would destroy them both was to leave Santa Barbara, Ann packed a few clothes and a picture of Paul and Paige together, wrote Paul the note Eve dictated, and left.

She hated herself for taking Eve's hundred thousand dollars. She wished she could have been strong enough to throw the envelope at her face. But she had no money of her own, and she was too ashamed to go to Kate for help. And anyway, Eve had told her to stay away from Trenton, since that would be the first place Paul would go looking for her.

At first, she considered living in New York because it was familiar, and because it was also big and impersonal and one could spend a lifetime there without ever being found. But when a reporter recognized her at the airport and ran after her, demanding her version of the separation, Ann panicked and fled. The following day, she purchased a one-way ticket to Rome, where a man she had met long ago lived. She didn't know if he would remember her, but she went anyway. She had nowhere else to go.

She had met Marcello Ludicci ten years before at a fancy party she had attended with one of Lolita's better customers. For some reason, he had taken a liking to her and had drawn her into a friendly conversation. Although she didn't think he believed she was a secretary and that she had come to the party with a coworker, he gave no indication that he had guessed the truth.

The following morning, at his request, she had met him for breakfast at the Pierre. It was then that she had told him of her dream to someday become a Broadway dancer. He had listened with great interest and had written down the name of a choreographer he knew. Before they parted, he had given her his card and made her promise that if she ever needed help of any kind, she should contact him.

Although the choreographer hadn't been able to do anything for her, Ann had never forgotten Marcello. And he had never forgotten her. When she called him from the Rome airport the morning she arrived, he immediately sent a car for her.

With the same interest and kindness he had shown in New York ten years before, Marcello listened to her, comforted her, and offered her everything he had for as long as she wanted it—his home, his servants, his cars, his money. He had demanded nothing in return, although she knew he was falling in love with her.

It wasn't until three years later that she began to show interest, and a certain talent, in painting. Marcello, delighted she had found something to occupy her during those long weeks when he was on tour, commissioned one of Italy's most famous artists to give Ann art lessons.

Within a few years, her paintings, which depicted the everyday life of ordinary people, became the rage of Italy.

"Signora Ludicci?"

At the sound of her maid's voice, Ann jumped and turned around. "Yes, Noemi?"

"About your trip, signora. Would you like to take something other than the slacks and blouses I usually pack for you?"

"No, but you may want to add a light coat," Ann replied, remembering the cool Santa Barbara evenings.

Suddenly, for reasons she couldn't explain, her mood changed, lifted. She was going to a wedding. Her *daughter's* wedding.

Her cheeks flushed with excitement, she pulled herself tall. "And something dressy, too," she added. "My green suit, perhaps. Yes, definitely the green suit. And some jewelry to go with it. Oh, and that new Gucci perfume Signor Ludicci gave me for Christmas.''

Then, eager to be on her way, Ann, who never rushed anywhere these days, ran upstairs to get ready.

NINETEEN

Because of the rumors that had surrounded Paige's relationship with Jeremy Newman those last couple of months, and the publicity her upcoming wedding to Matt had already generated, Paige had kept the guest list small and had chosen to have the ceremony at Montecito Presbyterian Church on San Ysidro Lane.

The press too had been kept to a minimum, much to Eve's displeasure. Having finally reconciled herself to the fact that Paige and Jeremy would never be married, she had hoped to give Paige a wedding worthy of the Granger name.

Standing in a small chamber adjoining the nave, Paige took one last look at her reflection in the mirror before turning to face her small audience.

"Well, guys, what do you think?"

"You look perfect," Kate said, her misty gaze taking in the glamorous, narrow ivory silk gown, the small, perky white hat, and the mass of dark curls underneath.

Mindy sighed. "I agree. And I feel sorry for Matt. How is the poor man supposed to remember his vows when he sees you coming in looking like this?"

Beaming, because taking Matt's breath away was exactly what she had had in mind, Paige turned toward Eve, who hadn't said a word. "Grandmother?"

Pleased that someone had finally bothered to ask her opinion, Eve came forward, chosing to hide her own emotions under a slightly reproachful tone. "Well, personally, I would have preferred to see you walking down the aisle in something a little more traditional and a little less . . .''

"Harlowish?" Paige finished.

Eve was gracious enough to manage a smile. "I was going to say dramatic. But I suppose Harlowish will do."

"Harlow had nothing that my beautiful daughter can't top."

At the sound of her father's voice and the sight of his happy face peeking through the door, Paige smiled expectantly. "Hello, Daddy. Are they ready for us?"

"Just about." Taking his mother's arm, Paul escorted Eve toward the door. "Time for you to take your seat, Mother." Then, seeing the pinched look she never concealed in his presence, he added. "Come on, Mother, cheer up. This is Paige's wedding, not her funeral." At the slight flutter around her lips, he squeezed her hand. "That's better."

He watched Rocky, Josh McKenzie's foreman, escort Eve toward the church's front row before returning his attention to Paige. Taking her hands in his, he spread her arms out in order to take a better look at her. "You're beautiful," he murmured.

He didn't add "as beautiful as your mother on *her* wedding day." But he thought it, for Paige had never looked more like Ann than she did now. The only difference was that she didn't have her mother's timidity, or that awful fear that she would never fit into the Grangers' circle of friends.

There was no such look in Paige's eyes. She radiated confidence, self-esteem, and love. Above all, she radiated love. "I'm going to miss you, Princess."

"I'll call you every day."

He laughed. "You'll be too busy being a bride."

Only then did he see a shadow pass through her beautiful eyes. "Oh, Daddy, I want so much to be a good wife to him."

He kissed her forehead. "And you will be. Oh, I know you have a few doubts, with Matt's job demanding so much of his time, and having to adjust to a new town, a new lifestyle. But remember, honey, Matt isn't just your husband. He's also your best friend. Whatever you feel, whatever you're afraid of, talk to him. Don't try to solve all your problems by yourself.''

He hadn't meant to get so serious. But the words had just blurted out, brought on by a frustration he still felt from time to time. If only someone had given that same advice to Ann on *her* wedding day, she would be with them right now. Instead she had run away, leaving behind only a note saying she was tired of Santa Barbara, of its politics, and that she needed to have a life of her own. There had been nothing more, not a thought for Paige, not a word of apology, nothing.

From the door, Mindy's voice rang loud and clear like a wake-up call. ''Okay folks, they're playing our song. Get in position.''

Paul's somber mood lifted and he turned to Paige, offering her his arm. ''Ready, Princess?''

Paige beamed. ''Ready, Daddy.''

One of the newest of the area's churches, Montecito Presbyterian had been built in the early 1930s on a four-acre wooded estate that had been donated to the church by former railroad magnate Andrew Hatburry. With its lush gardens, flower-bordered paths, and delicate iron-work, the Spanish structure looked more like a private residence than a house of worship and had quickly become the wealthiest parish in the community.

Standing outside, hidden behind a large rhododendron bush, Ann watched her daughter, now Mrs. Matt McKenzie, come out of the church.

Despite her fears, Ann's arrival in Santa Barbara had passed unnoticed. Even Kate, who had expected her, hadn't recognized her when she had showed up on her doorstep—not until Ann had removed her hat and sunglasses.

Their reunion had been emotional but happy and they had talked until three in the morning like two school girls. Not even the revelation of Ann's secret, which she hadn't been able to keep from Kate any longer, had lessened their joy of being together again.

The following day, with her disguise and the invitation Kate had given her, Ann had passed through Eve's security men without any difficulty.

She had sat in the church's last row, next to a couple she vaguely knew. But they had only nodded to her without any indication that they had recognized her. Then, before the receiving line had had a chance to form, she had quietly slipped out of the church and taken her position behind the large bush.

At last everyone was gone except the newlyweds and Paul. Ann hadn't been able to see him very well during the ceremony, but now that he stood only a few feet from her she felt a tightening in her chest. He had hardly changed at all. His figure was as trim as it had been when she had first met him, and his gray temples gave him a sophistication he hadn't had in his younger years.

An unexpected sob rose to her throat and she stifled it quickly as she watched all three make their way toward the double iron gates. No one would ever know she had been here.

"Go with God, darling," she whispered to Paige's retreating back. "And someday, find it in your heart to forgive me."

Paige wasn't sure what made her turn around. A sixth sense? Curiosity as she heard the faint rustle behind her and saw a figure quickly retreating behind the greenery? Whatever it was, it felt odd, disturbing, more powerful than any sensation she had ever had.

When she saw the woman's still, watchful figure, Paige stopped. Could she be a late guest who hadn't wanted to disturb the ceremony? she wondered. If so, why hadn't she come through the receiving line like everyone else? And why wasn't she coming forward now?

Frowning against the sunlight, Paige peered into the shadows. The woman was about Kate's age, well-dressed, and wore a large black hat and dark sunglasses that concealed most of her face.

"Darling, what is it?" Matt asked, wrapping his arm around her waist. "Did you forget something inside?"

She shook her head, unable to explain the feeling that kept her riveted to that spot, kept her staring at that woman. Without a word, she freed herself from Matt's hold and moved toward the stranger, slowly, like someone in a half-sleep. As each step took her closer, the woman's face became clearer, the square, model-like jawline more pronounced, the mouth wider, fuller.

The woman was frozen in shock now. And although behind the dark glasses her eyes were inscrutable, Paige knew that the woman's stare was as intense as her own.

A ripple went through her. Three feet from the woman, she stopped and swallowed, her throat suddenly dry. The antique diamond necklace her grandmother had insisted she wear today choked her, making it difficult to breathe. In the distance she heard her father call out her name. But she blocked it out. She blocked out everything. Except herself. And the woman.

She was close enough now to see that beneath the dark glasses, tears streamed down the softly rounded cheeks and onto the expensive green suit, staining the sequined lapels with dark, wet blotches.

"Mama . . ." It was no more than a whisper. Yet the single word seemed to echo across the hills as if someone had turned on an amplifier.

Paige stood transfixed, waiting for a denial, for someone to come and take her away.

The woman was the first to move forward. In the bright afternoon sunlight, her bejeweled suit gleamed and twinkled, as if to remind them that this was a festive occasion, that more fun was yet to come.

Slowly, the woman removed her sunglasses. "Paige. Oh, Paige, my beautiful little girl . . ."

Paige reeled back, almost falling from shock. It couldn't be. Her eyes and ears were playing tricks on her, as they had so often in the past. This woman who stood there, looking and sounding remarkably like the woman she used to call mother, was just another illusion.

Matt's strong arm steadied her. He didn't speak, only held her. She was aware of footsteps crunching the gravel, coming closer. She heard her father's sharp intake of breath, followed by another frozen silence before someone pushed a button and the world began to revolve again.

"My God, it *is* you!" Paul gasped

"Paul . . ."

"How dare you?" He came to stand by Paige, his arms by his side, rigid, his hands balled up into tight fists. The tanned face had turned a dull shade of gray, the blue eyes as cloudless as the sky a moment ago, now glinted with an expression that hovered between anguish and hatred. "How dare you show your face here? Now?"

Surprised that he could talk at all, Paul stopped and took another deep breath. The shock of seeing her here had speared through him with such force that it had taken all common sense away. His first impulse, crazy and wild, had been to run to her, to take her in his arms, to shower kisses on the beloved face and thank God she was all right, that she had come back to him.

She was beautiful. As beautiful as she had been the morning he had kissed her good-bye twenty years ago. Her hair had been longer, worn in a fashionable pageboy, and her face and figure not as full as they were now. But the eyes—oh, those dark, intense eyes that had turned his head in Central Park that summer morning—shone just as bright now. Although it was obvious that she had been crying, there was a calmness about her, a serenity that shocked him even more. It was as if the pain he had known all these years had passed her by.

"Paul, I know you're angry with me. But please hear me out. I . . . I hadn't meant it to happen this way. But since it has, I want to explain—"

"It's too late for an explanation. I can't even fathom where you found the gall to come here."

"Paige is my daughter. And she is getting married. I have a right to be here."

"You have no rights. You gave those up long ago."

Next to him, he heard Paige's trembling voice. "Where have you been all these years?"

"Rome. I . . . I knew someone there . . ."

Paul's eyes fell on the gold band around her finger. "And you married him."

"Eventually, yes."

At those words, Paul felt a stab of fresh pain. Why, he wondered? Had he expected her to remain unattached, the way he had, although he had divorced her? Had he hoped that after this mess was over, they would get back together?

"How did you find out about Paige's wedding?" he asked.

"From Kate." At the shocked look on Paul's face, Ann quickly added, "Don't be upset with her, Paul. Yes, she has known all along where I was, but I threatened to move to a new location and never contact her again if she breathed a word of my whereabouts to anyone. And I never told her the real reason for my leaving Santa Barbara. Not until last night."

"The two of you have been in touch all these years?" Paul's tone was aghast.

Ann nodded. "Only through letters. I never dared to use the phone, afraid that if I heard her voice, or if Paige answered, I'd lose my nerve and come back."

"Don't you think I deserved the same courtesy?" Paul sneered. "A letter, an explanation other than the one you left me?"

"I was scared, confused—"

"And I was out of my mind! I refused to believe you had left me. I suspected foul play and drove the cops crazy with theory after theory. Even after they traced you to Kennedy Airport, to the Alitalia counter where you bought a one-way ticket to Rome, I wouldn't believe you had left me. I hired a detective to try to find you. It was only when he called to say there was no Ann Granger in Rome and that you had probably changed your name, that I believed you had actually engineered this whole thing.''

''If you'll only let me explain—''

''I'm not interested in what you have to say, Ann. Not twenty years after the fact.'' He laid a hand on Matt's shoulder. ''I'll be in the car.'' Then without another glance in Ann's direction, he walked away.

Ann's gaze, blurred by tears, followed him until the door of the limousine closed behind him. Then she turned back to Paige, who had stood motionless and silent during the exchange between her and Paul. ''Don't walk away from me, too,'' she pleaded. ''Not yet.''

Paige felt Matt's grip loosen and when she reached for his hand to keep him there, with her, he bent down and kissed her cheek. ''It'll be all right, darling, I promise. You have to do this alone.''

As if through a fog, she heard her mother speak. ''I know what's going through your mind now, darling— confusion, shock, anger. But I promise you it will go away after I explain.'' Then as Paige remained silent, she added, ''Please, darling, say something.''

''Say something?'' Paige's voice, weak and strangled, sounded like that of a stranger. ''After twenty years of silence, you expect me to say . . . what? Hello, Mother, did you have a pleasant trip?''

''Then, let *me* do the talking. Let me try to explain—''

''There is nothing to explain. It's all painfully clear. You got tired of us, tired of me, and you left. You threw me away without a second thought, and without remorse.''

''No!''

''How fortunate that you could turn your life around so quickly, so easily,'' Paige continued in that flat, monotonous tone that sounded so unfamiliar to her. ''It wasn't quite the same for me, you see. I kept waiting, sometimes for hours at a time, sitting alone at my window, waiting for you to come back so you could take me in your arms and tell me I'd just had a nightmare.''

Ann's hand went to her mouth to stifle a sob. Now that Paige's anguish was put into words, she found her own even more unbearable. "Oh, darling, I wish I could have come back. I wish I could have been strong enough—"

"I spent years thinking it was my fault," Paige cut in. "Wondering what I had done to make you leave me, to make you stop loving me."

"Oh, my God . . ."

Paige's sarcastic chuckle died in her throat. "You sound surprised."

Tears welled up in Ann's eyes again. She shook her head. "It's just that I didn't think . . . had hoped . . ."

"That I wouldn't have been so deeply affected?" Paige cried. "How could you have hoped for that knowing how much I loved you?"

"I loved you, too, Paige. And I still do, more than you'll ever know."

Spear-straight, her arms by her side, Paige appeared not to have heard her. "I held you on a pedestal so high," she continued. "No one could touch you. In my eyes you could do no wrong. You were the perfect mother, the one I tried to imitate, the one all my friends envied. I worshipped you. More than Daddy, more than my favorite doll, more than anything in the world."

Paige heard her voice crack, but went on anyway. "Do you remember the weeks preceding that last Christmas? When you and I sat for the portrait we were going to give Daddy for Christmas?"

"Don't—"

"I never felt so proud as I did during those few weeks. It was such a wonderful ritual for me each morning, the two of us slipping into identical red velvet gowns, having Marietta comb our hair in the same glamorous upsweep. It was the first time in my life I was ever able to keep a secret." She ignored her mother's tortured look. "Why don't you ask me what happened to that portrait, Ann?"

"Stop it," Ann sobbed.

"Maria didn't know what to do with it," Paige continued. "So she took it from behind the Christmas tree, carried it to the attic and covered it with a sheet. She wouldn't tell me where it was, so one afternoon, I went looking for it. And I found it.''

Paige was breathing harder now, feeling the same hollow chill she had felt years ago. ''I took a kitchen knife with me and I slashed the canvas over and over. I probably would have kept stabbing it forever if Maria hadn't heard my screams and come to get me.''

Ann's tears flowed freely now. There was nothing she could say to mend her daughter's heart, nothing she could do. The pain was too deep.

Paige took another step forward, her gaze hard and unforgiving. ''Whatever your excuses for leaving me were, I don't want to hear them. Go back to Rome, Ann. Go back to your husband and to your family, if you have one. But leave me alone.''

Then, turning to Matt, who had stood up from his sitting position on a rock nearby, she extended her hand to him, and as he took it, she headed for the limousine.

TWENTY

Huddled in an old faded blue robe that was anything but glamorous, Paige sat on her living room floor, her back against the sofa. As Matt threw another log into the fire, there was a hiss and a burst of bright orange flame that wrapped the darkened room in a warm, golden glow.

In spite of the heat, Paige shivered, unable to chase away the chill she still felt inside. In order not to disrupt the wedding reception at the Grangers' house, she and her father had agreed to postpone telling Eve about Ann's visit until later. But acting happy and carefree after the emotional encounter at the church had been a difficult task for Paige.

Still crouched in front of the fireplace, Matt glanced back over his shoulder, his smile reassuring and tender. He had changed into a pair of shorts and an L.A. Rams tee-shirt, and looked like a football player in training. "Warm enough yet?"

She nodded. "I'm getting there."

He came to sit next to her and stretched out his long legs in front of him, crossing them at the ankles. "Kate called while you were changing. She's worried about you." He wrapped his right arm around her shoulders. "I told her you were in good hands."

Paige smiled and continued to gaze into the fire. "Did she believe you?"

"Of course. Between you and me, I think your Aunt Kate is madly in love with me."

"Between you and me, I think you're right." Then casually, she asked, "Is that all she said?"

"No. She told me your mother will be staying with her until Tuesday."

Paige's laugh was short and bitter. "Why so long? Is Ann hoping I'll change my mind and agree to talk to her?"

"I'm sure the possibility crossed her mind."

"Then she's greatly mistaken."

He glanced at her. "Still angry?"

"Angry, hurt, disillusioned."

"What can I do to help?"

She lay her head on his shoulder, glad for his presence, for the strength he brought her. "You're doing it. Just don't take my anger away."

Because he understood, he tightened his hold and said nothing. He knew how it felt to hate with such intensity. He had experienced it the night his father had died. Although his rage had been directed at Jeremy, whom he hardly knew at the time, it had made the pain more bearable.

"For months after she left," Paige continued in a voice that tore at his heart, "I waited for the moment when she would come back. I used to imagine how it would be, what I would do when she finally appeared on our doorstep." Her laugh was short and bitter. "I had all those different scenarios written out in my head, and once in awhile, I'd act one of them out, just to see how it felt. Each time, I ended up in tears."

He saw that tears were running down her cheeks now and he didn't try to stop them. She needed to cry, needed to let it all out. He drew her closer to him, and as he did, a small sigh that was more like a sob escaped her throat.

"I'm not sure exactly when I stopped loving her and started hating her. But when I did, the pain went away and only then was I able to face the fact that she would never come back."

"Couldn't you try to accept that she did come back?" he asked, his lips resting on the top of her head. "That she's been just as tortured as you have?"

He felt her tense. "What would be the purpose of that?"

"To forgive her?"

"Never!"

She looked up and met his gaze. The light from the fire was reflected in her eyes, making them gleam like blue topaz. Her emotional pain was so starkly evident that he felt it, deep in his own heart.

"I hate her for what she did, Matt. And I hate her for coming here today, for ruining my wedding day. And my wedding night."

She sounded so sad, so certain the day had been a total shambles, that in spite of the serious moment, Matt smiled. "Our wedding day will always be special, Paige. Because *we* made it special. As for our wedding night . . ."

She wiped the tears on her face with her sleeve. "What about it?"

Sensing she needed comfort right now, he lifted her chin and, very gently, kissed her lips, then her throat. As he did, he drank in her scent, which he had recognized earlier as *Opium,* the haunting Yves Saint Laurent fragrance she had worn in Venice. "I suppose I could try to salvage it."

Paige's face remained solemn. "In the mood I'm in, it could take you all night."

"Mmmm. I'm counting on it."

The promise in his eyes had a melting effect on her. She felt the anger drain as her love for Matt filled her heart. She watched him take her hand and bring it to his lips. Tenderly, his eyes never leaving her face, he kissed each finger.

It was something he did often, for he knew she liked it. But tonight the effect was devastating. Desire coursed through her like a flame. Not wanting to give into it too soon, she remained motionless.

Smiling, as if he guessed her inner struggle, Matt turned her hand and pressed his mouth to her palm, then to the inside of her wrist. Paige held her breath as she watched him, watched his lips and the occasional darting of his tongue. She imagined him doing all sorts of wicked, delicious things to her, things she had never allowed him to do before.

"Kiss me," she said in a seductive whisper.

He came to her quickly, sensing her need, and took her mouth. She tasted of vanilla icing and champagne. As he drew her to him, he felt her heart hammer against his chest. Yet he resisted the urge to deepen the kiss. He wanted her to relish this moment, to enjoy it beyond any point she'd ever reached before.

Her arms coiled around his neck. "Is that the best you can do?"

Her tone was husky, challenging. In her eyes, he caught the same sexy, playful gleam she had given him when she had walked down the aisle earlier. That look had driven him half-wild with desire then, and it was doing a damn good job now.

Responding to the challenge, he took her in his arms again, and this time he didn't hold back. As he thrust his tongue inside her mouth, he felt her tremble. He knew from the way she clung to him, the way she returned the kiss, the way she kept coming back for more, that the fire inside her raged just as furiously as his own. He knew she was ready.

Holding her shoulders, he leaned into her until her back touched the thick rug beneath them. Slowly, knowing how quickly she reached a simmering point, he untied her belt and pushed open the robe, only enough for him to skim his fingers over a pale, rounded breast and hear the small catch in her breath. Then, inch by inch, as he continued to stroke her, he slid the garment off her shoulders, until she lay naked in his arms.

Paige was lost in the sensations, in the sound of his voice as he murmured loving words, in the touch of his fingers as they probed, caressed, and drove her wild.

She moaned a protest as he pulled away to remove his clothes. Lips parted, her anticipation growing with every breath, Paige watched as he pulled his tee-shirt above his head and stepped out of his shorts and underwear. She never tired of watching his body in action. Under the taut skin, his well-developed muscles were visible but did not bulge. His broad chest, with its high, firm pectorals, tapered to a slender waist and narrow, rock-hard hips. His legs were magnificent—strong, muscular, and perfectly molded—the legs of a runner.

"Much better," she murmured when he came back to her and took her mouth again. She felt his erection press against her and reached for it, closing her fingers around it.

With a tortured groan, Matt touched his lips to the hollow of her throat where the pulse was strongest, stayed there for a long, agonizing moment before moving down to her breasts.

This time when he moved lower, she didn't stop him. The sensations were too delicious, the pleasure too intense, too intoxicating. As his tongue began to trail along the tender skin of her inner thigh, working its way to the very core of her, she gripped his shoulders.

"Matt . . ." She tried to pull him back to her. But he wouldn't let her. This time his fingers wrapped around her wrists and held her still while he continued on his wild, passionate journey.

He felt the change in her, the response, timid at first, then more brazen as her hips began to move, rising to meet him. Her body, as taut as piano wire a moment before, relaxed as her legs opened wider. He felt himself go wild. She tasted sweet. So sweet he couldn't get enough of her. Gripping her hips to steady her, he dipped his tongue deeper. Need, hot and urgent, hammered inside him. Still, he continued to give, continued to drive her higher.

"Oh, God." She felt her climax rising, peaking. Pleasure and sensations exploded, burst after burst, convulsing her body, making her take big gulps of air, until her lungs felt as if they too would explode.

"Come inside of me."

Although the command was said on a ragged breath, Matt heard it. And obeyed it. He filled her, barely able to breathe himself, watching her as he rode her, hard and fast. The heat had built to a pitch he could no longer control, and when she wrapped her legs high around his waist and cried out his name, release poured out of him and into her, as he was carried over the edge.

Although Ann didn't really believe Paige would change her mind at the last minute and show up at the airport, she kept glancing at the terminal entrance as travelers came through the doors.

"Why don't you stop making yourself miserable and tell Paige what happened?" Kate said, catching one of Ann's glances. "If you don't think you can do it, then let me. Believe me, nothing would make me happier than to expose Eve for the bitch she really is."

Ann shook her head. "No, Katie. It's best to leave things as they are. Anyway, I've accomplished what I set out to do, haven't I? I saw my daughter getting married." She gave Kate a brave smile. "And who knows? She might come around one of these days after all, without any coaxing from anyone."

"So, you're determined to let Eve get away with this?"

A young mother carrying a baby in her arms walked past them, and Ann's gaze followed them until they were out of sight. "My only concern right now is to pick up my life where I left it a few days ago, and make the best of it." Seeing the look of disapproval in Kate's eyes, she added, "Once I would have taken great pleasure in the thought of getting even with Eve. But now it would only disrupt Paige's and Paul's lives further, bring even more hatred into their hearts." She shrugged. "And anyway, revenge was never one of my priorities, Katie. You know that."

It was true. Ann had always been too soft, too forgiving, too quick to accept the blame. Even when she was little and suffering those vicious beatings from their father, Ann was convinced she deserved them. In time, she had forgiven her parents and sent them money and presents.

Not Kate. From the moment she had realized what was happening to her, hatred and resentment had built within her, year after year, hardening her, giving her the strength she needed to withstand the pain and the humiliation she suffered every day. But she had never forgiven her mother for being weak, or her father for his viciousness. Not even after they died.

The scars of her childhood might no longer have been visible, but they were still there. And at times, when she expected it the least, the memories still hurt.

"Katie? What's the matter?"

Shaking her head, Kate stared at Ann. "Nothing. Why?"

"You looked so strange for a moment, so far away." Ann's eyes were filled with concern.

Kate ran a hand through her hair. "I was thinking about what you said."

"You understand my point, don't you?"

"Frankly, no, I don't."

"But you'll respect my wishes and say nothing to Paige, or Paul, or anyone."

Reluctantly, Kate nodded. "Yes, Ann. I promise."

As the plane for Denver and New York was called, Ann hugged Kate. "Thank you, Katie. For everything. And remember about my offer. The villa is open to you at any time and for as long as you want. So please come and see me soon. Marcello would love it."

Kate nodded, wiped a tear. "I will. As soon as I can replace Paige at the gallery."

It wasn't until her plane was thirty thousand feet in the air that Ann removed her hat and sunglasses. Tossing them on the empty seat next to her, she sighed. In spite of her earlier optimism, she held little hope that Paige would ever be able to forgive her. The message in her daughter's eyes when both had stood outside the church had been painfully clear.

Paige never wanted to see her again.

TWENTY-ONE

They rediscovered Manhattan together, the way lovers do. Arm in arm, wrapped in duffle coats and bright wool scarves, Paige and Matt walked the streets of the city from Central Park to Washington Square and back with the exuberance of two young children.

New York had changed since Paige had last explored it in depth. It had a new convention center, a revamped seaport, a sprinkle of new hotels, and scores of new, fashionable boutiques. And, of course, it had Trump Tower.

Her impressions of the city had remained the same, however. She still found it too big, too noisy, and too impersonal. But she loved its energy, its mix of the old and the new, its fascination with "old money," and its spirited Greenwich Village, the closest thing to Paris's Latin Quarter she had seen anywhere.

Matt, who seldom did anything in New York but travel to and from work, hadn't set foot in lower Manhattan in years. But he followed Paige happily from one funky shop to another, while she shopped for old placemats, antique frames, or some other trinkets for his apartment—their apartment now.

On Sundays, they went to museums; watched the skaters at Rockefeller Center, sometimes even joined them; or had dinner with the DiMaggios, who lived in a big rambling house in Brooklyn with their teenage son, Sam, and three overfed Siamese cats.

Evenings were spent at home, cuddled up on the sofa. Paige loved Matt's apartment. It was part of a three-story luxury townhouse on East Sixty-third Street that had been divided and sold as separate units. Small and convenient, it had everything a modern-day bachelor could want—a tiny but efficient kitchen, a bathroom, and a living room—dining room that transformed itself into a bedroom with the simple pull of a sofa bed.

Instead of the expensive antiques and artwork Paige had expected, Matt had decorated the multifunctional room simply, making the most of the small space—a dark green leather sofa, two matching chairs, a couple of light oak tables, and one authentic Persian rug. On the walls he had hung several framed movie posters from famous black and white films—*Casablanca, Citizen Kane, The Lost Weekend,* and Paige's absolute favorite, *Gilda.*

As an additional wedding present, Tom DiMaggio had given them the most precious gift of all—time. For the next two months, Matt's activities were restricted to the New York area, allowing Paige and Matt to do all the things newlyweds did—spend long weekends in bed, eat whenever they felt like it, and get to know each other.

It wasn't until mid-March, when Matt resumed his travels, that Paige decided it was time to look for a job. Although New York boasted an abundance of antiques galleries and Paige's credentials were excellent, the Manhattan art community was much more structured, more formal than that of Santa Barbara or even San Francisco, and breaking through the barrier wasn't easy. But Paige was determined. By the end of the fourth week, she had found a part-time position in an uptown gallery that specialized in seventeenth- and eighteenth-century furniture.

Adjusting to Matt's frequent absences, even now that she was working, was more difficult than she had anticipated. Weekends were long and lonely. She offset them by going for walks in the park, watching television, and occasionally going to a movie.

Nothing helped. Everywhere she went she saw young couples laughing together and she felt even more miserable. To cheer herself up, she called home often, talking to Kate and the rest of the family, pretending all was fine and wonderful.

Jeremy, whose excellent personal reference was responsible in part for Paige's job, came to New York regularly. When he did, they met somewhere for lunch, or he would stop at Specter, the gallery where she worked, invite her to lunch, and whisk her away in his limousine.

Matt had hated Jeremy's visits at first. But after awhile, he had more or less resigned himself to the fact that, since Jeremy was still one of Beauchamp's most important clients, Paige could hardly cut him off without jeopardizing that relationship.

"I take it McKenzie is treating you well," Jeremy asked Paige one balmy April afternoon in 1988 as they lunched at Le Cirque.

She watched as he neatly dissected his grilled trout. "Matt is wonderful. When he's home, that is."

Fork and knife poised, Jeremy gave her a quick, inquisitive glance. "Problems?"

Embarrassed that he had caught her in a rare moment of self-pity, Paige shook her head. "No. No problems. It's just that when he's investigating a complicated case, I hardly ever see him."

"You mean like the Consolidated Mutual case?"

It was her turn to be surprised. "How do you know about Consolidated?"

He sighed. "Because I recommended Matt for the job. You see, the president of Consolidated and I are old friends. And when he mentioned that recent robbery at the Bittenberry Museum, which is insured with his company, I immediately told him that if he wanted to recover the paintings, he should forget about his in-house investigators and hire Matt."

"But you hate Matt."

Dabbing his mouth with a crisp white napkin, Jeremy took a sip of his Pouilly Fumé before answering. "I don't like him very much. And I certainly resent him for taking you away from Beauchamp. But that doesn't change the fact that I have a great deal of respect for his abilities."

Looking contrite, he added, "If I inadvertently caused you a problem, Paige, I'm very sorry. Had I known—"

"Jeremy, don't apologize. That was very kind of you to recommend Matt. As a matter of fact, he was delighted to get that job."

Jeremy held back a smile of satisfaction. He had debated telling her about his little intervention at first. Then, on the flight to New York, he had changed his mind, knowing that his unselfish gesture would earn him a few points. He had been right. "I'm glad," he said, with a small sigh of relief. "I wouldn't want to be responsible for bringing more tension between you and Matt."

She gave him a puzzled look. "There's no tension between Matt and me. Whatever gave you that idea?"

He shrugged. "I'm not sure. Perhaps because you seem so serious and pensive these days, much more so than when you first arrived in New York." He paused. "Unless of course, something at work is bothering you?"

She shook her head. "No. Nothing at all is bothering me."

That wasn't quite true. And Jeremy, in his own inimitable way, had read her like a book. Although she would never admit it to him, her problem was that she resented Matt's long absences and didn't know what to do about it.

She had thought about discussing the matter with him, but what could she say that wouldn't sound selfish? She had entered this marriage with her eyes wide open. Did she have any right to make demands now?

Aware that Jeremy was watching her closely, she smiled. "Will you stop looking so worried, Jeremy? I told you everything is fine. I couldn't be happier—at work *and* at home."

She wasn't sure when the trouble began. It was too subtle at first for either of them to notice. But as the weeks and months passed and Matt's cases continued to take him away for long periods of time, Paige found it increasingly difficult to be as understanding as Matt expected her to be.

She was lonely, and tried to tell him so from time to time without sounding unreasonable. But invariably the discussion would get away from her and she would end up sounding resentful and angry.

"I'm afraid I don't have much choice about my cases," Matt told her one night after Tom had called to brief him about a Minneapolis robbery that needed to be investigated right away.

"Of course you have a choice," she blurted out. "You can quit."

Stunned, Matt looked at her. "I can't quit. Investigating is the only job I know."

She blocked his way to the closet where he kept his suitcase. "That's not true. You know ranching."

Matt laughed. "I'd hardly call what I did when I was ten years old ranching."

"I thought you said that your dream was to go back to California some day and work with Josh."

"It is, but that's years down the line, Paige."

He didn't like the direction this conversation was taking. He had never told Paige how badly he needed this job, that without it, he would never be able to keep his mother at the California Trauma Institute. Paige had always assumed Adam had left enough money in his estate to more than cover those expenses. And that was exactly what he wanted her to keep on believing.

Josh had disagreed. He had warned Matt that secrets, even honorable secrets, had no place in a marriage. But Matt had waved the advice aside. Paige had a huge and generous heart. Once she knew the truth about Matt's financial situation, she would insist on paying for Caroline's care. And that's one thing he would never consent to. He had too much pride to allow anyone, especially his wife, to take over his responsibilities.

"Why does it have to be years down the line?" Paige insisted. "Why can't it be now?"

Taking her by the shoulders, he gently pushed her aside

and opened the closet. "Because I'm not ready to make such a drastic change just yet."

Paige threw him a murderous look and stormed out of the room. Cursing himself for not having thought of a better answer, he followed her into the kitchen. She stood looking out the window, her back stiff, her arms crossed in front of her chest.

"I'm sorry," he said, putting his hands on her shoulders and massaging them gently. "I know you hate these long separations. I hate them too."

"I bet."

"What does that mean?"

"It means," she said, spinning around, her eyes bright with tears, "that this job means more to you than *I* do."

"What?"

"You heard me."

"Paige, that's the most ridiculous thing I've ever heard you say."

She didn't answer him.

"I love you, baby. You know that, don't you?"

"You have a strange way of showing it, spending days, sometimes weeks away from home."

Ignoring her resistance, he pulled her to him and held her tight. Many times in the last few weeks he had considered asking Tom to give him a desk job, something that would keep him based in New York. Each time he had changed his mind. Without the field work, there would be no bonuses, and without those he would never be able to keep his mother at CTI.

"I'll tell you what," he said, putting his finger under her chin and lifting her head toward him. "What would you say about you and me taking that long-delayed honeymoon when I get back from Minneapolis? We've talked about it before, remember?"

She stared at a point behind his shoulder. "You always have something better to do."

"I won't this time. I promise. We'll fly to California, spend some time with our families, then continue on to Hawaii. What do you say?"

"Just the two of us?"

He laughed. "Of course just the two of us. Who else does one take on a honeymoon?"

They chose the island of Lana'i, Hawaii's most private hideaway. The bungalow they had rented was miles away from civilization and overlooked the crystal-clear waters of Hulopo'e Bay.

It was the most magical time of their lives. For a whole week, nothing existed but the two of them, the warm Hawaiian sun, and their love for each other.

Matt rose early each morning and went for a run along the beach while Paige cut pineapples and squeezed oranges for their breakfast. The rest of the day was spent swimming, fishing, and sailing. At night, they made love under the stars.

"I love you, Paige," Matt murmured as he held her in his arms on their last night on the island. "Don't ever forget that."

Paige sank deeper into his arms. She had never been more in love with Matt than she was at that very moment. How foolish of her to have doubted his love. And how unfair to have made things so difficult for him, to have pressured him to leave his job when he loved it so much. From now on, she would try harder. She would be more sensitive to his needs instead of concentrating on hers.

"No, darling," she said, smiling blissfully. "I'll never forget it."

It was in early January of 1989, during a long weekend in Palm Beach where the DiMaggios had a house, that Paige started to give serious thought to having a baby.

She and Matt had discussed raising a family, and although she had agreed to wait a couple of years until he was able to spend more time at home, Paige was beginning to have second thoughts. She longed for a baby, for a tender little body to love and cuddle and keep her company when Matt was away.

But more important, she wanted a baby because she

was certain that once she was pregnant, Matt would find a way to spend more time at home without necessarily having to leave Worldwide Investigations. He was too committed, too family-conscious to accept the role of temporary father.

And so that night, as Matt was waiting for her to get ready for bed, Paige threw away her birth-control pills. She knew it was wrong, sneaky, that it even bordered on despicable. But she convinced herself she was doing it for all the right reasons.

When the last of the pills had been flushed down the toilet, Paige went in to join her husband.

Matt was in Madrid when Paige found out she was pregnant. It was a blustery, windy mid-March morning, but the moment the doctor called to say she and Matt were expecting a baby at the end of October, Manhattan took on a rosy glow that not even the threat of an approaching snowstorm could dull.

A baby. Paige said the words out loud a hundred times that day, at the gallery when she was alone, and at home, glancing in the mirror from time to time, studying her profile to see if her figure had changed, even pushing her belly forward to see how she would look once she started to show.

Her first impulse was to call Matt and tell him the news. But she quickly dismissed that thought. She wasn't sure how he would react to the fact that she had made such a serious decision without discussing it with him first. And besides, news like this needed the proper setting. It needed the right ambience—candlelight and soft music. All the romantic trappings, she thought with a giggle, too excited to worry about anything else.

To keep herself busy until Matt's return a few days from now, she learned lullabyes, read books on Lamaze, and shopped for soft, wonderful baby clothes. She even bought a book in which to record their baby's first words, his first tooth, his first everything.

Although Dr. Conlan had warned her she might soon

experience nausea, she had never felt better in her life. She was a woman reborn, delirious with happiness, lighter than air. It was as if this new life growing inside of her had given her wings.

On the eve of Matt's return home, Paige shopped for his favorite dinner, had her hair done at Jacques Dessange on Park Avenue, and scrubbed the apartment from top to bottom, even though Mrs. Johnson, the housekeeper, always left it spotless.

She was cleaning the bathroom vanity when the first pain hit. It was sharp enough to take the wind out of her and force her to lean against the vanity. Dear God, what was *that*? she thought, dropping her sponge and staring at her pale, frightened face in the mirror.

Taking a long, steadying breath, she told herself not to panic. It was just a cramp, nothing to worry about. Maybe she had overdone it today. Or the excitement and anticipation had given her a nervous stomach. Nothing a little Maalox wouldn't cure.

She opened the medicine cabinet and took out the bottle of antacid. Her stomach felt queasy and her face was bathed in perspiration.

With a trembling hand, she uncapped the bottle and took a short swallow directly from the bottle. "There," she said, taking a deep breath. She tried to smile at her reflection. "I feel better already."

The second pain drove her down to her knees.

TWENTY-TWO

The first face she saw when she woke up was Jeremy's.

"What happened?" she asked, hearing her voice through a fog.

Jeremy took her hand in his and leaned forward, resting his elbows on the bed. "You're in the hospital, Paige. But you're all right now."

Everything came into focus then—the sterile hospital room, the pulverizing pains she had experienced earlier, the way she had slid to the floor, had crawled to the telephone. Panic rose to her throat and she began to retch.

"Take it easy, Paige. Breathe slowly, deeply. That's it."

"My baby . . ."

Clasping her hand between his, he brought it to his mouth and held it there. "You've had a miscarriage. You were brought here by ambulance."

The grief was instantaneous. It engulfed her in a great, cold wave that had her shaking and crying. She was aware of Jeremy taking her in his arms, rocking her, and stroking her hair. But, like a baby who couldn't be soothed, she continued to sob, deep wrenching sobs that went on forever.

She didn't know how long she cried or how long she kept her face buried against Jeremy's chest. She was aware of nothing, of no one, except her pain.

"Matt?" she managed to say at last as she pulled away from Jeremy.

"He's on his way. I called Tom DiMaggio at Worldwide Investigations and told him what happened." At first, Jeremy had thought about keeping the news to himself so Matt would be delayed indefinitely. Then he had decided against it. In the end, it would be his compassion and thoughtfulness Paige would remember. "Does Matt know you were pregnant?" he asked.

Paige shook her head.

"Why not?"

She was silent, not sure she should confide in Jeremy about something so personal.

"He doesn't want a child, does he?" Jeremy pressed. "That's why you didn't tell him."

Biting down on her lip, Paige nodded.

"Oh, Paige, I'm so sorry. No wonder you've been under such stress lately."

Stress. The word brought a chill to her heart. Her friend Angie in college had lost her baby because of undue stress. Was that what had happened to her? Had Matt's long absences from home, coupled with her apprehension about how he'd take the pregnancy, brought on this miscarriage? Turning to Jeremy, she asked, "How did you know I was here?"

"I came to New York to see the Ruthland exhibit at the Met. When I called the gallery to invite you to lunch, Mrs. Lodin said you had taken the day off. It was only after she told me Matt was out of town that I decided to stop by the apartment to make sure nothing was wrong. Your upstairs neighbor told me you had been taken to the hospital."

Paige closed her eyes and covered her face with her hands. How could so much have happened in such a short time? This afternoon, she was a mother-to-be. She was singing, buying baby clothes, leafing through a book of names. Now she lay in a hospital bed and her baby was gone. "It's all my fault," she murmured. "I was tired, but I ignored it. I did things I shouldn't have . . ."

"That's not true. I talked to your doctor. Miscarriages occur for a number of reasons, many of them unexplainable. Sometimes stress has a lot to do with it. Or it could be that the fetus just wasn't strong enough to—"

"Don't call it a fetus!" She hit the mattress with her fist. "He was my baby."

"Of course." With a featherlike touch, Jeremy took a tissue from the box on the nightstand and blotted her tears. "I'm just sorry I didn't get to your apartment sooner. If I had, I might have been able to get you to the hospital in time."

Matt could have too, she thought bitterly. *If* he had been home.

"I think we should call your family, let them know what's happened."

"No." She wiped her face with both hands and shook her head. "I don't want anyone to know about this. Not yet."

"They're family, Paige. They can help you."

"I can't deal with them now. Later perhaps . . ." Fresh tears pressed behind her closed lids. She turned away, burying her face in the pillow.

After awhile, she heard Jeremy slip quietly out of the room.

It was nine o'clock the following morning when Matt arrived at Columbia-Presbyterian Medical Center where Paige was hospitalized. His eyes were bloodshot from lack of sleep, and inside his stomach, a cold fist clutched him with an ironlike grip. After inquiring at the nurse's station which room was Paige's, he headed toward it, ignoring the visiting hours sign on the nurse's desk.

Paige slept, and although he approached her bedside without a sound, she opened her eyes instantly. They were red and swollen, her face pale and drawn.

"Paige. My darling." He gathered her in his arms and held her close to him. "Thank God you're all right." He tried not to break, but emotions he'd never had to deal with before began to choke him.

"Let me go," she whispered.

Surprised by her tone, he hesitated before finally releasing her. "I came as soon as I heard. I . . ." He frowned, realizing she wasn't listening, but staring straight ahead at the blank wall. "Paige, please darling. I want to help. Talk to me."

"What do you want me to say?" Her voice was flat, as empty as the expression in her eyes.

"Why didn't you tell me you were pregnant?"

She kept staring at the wall. "Because I wanted to create the perfect moment. I wanted to make it a celebration. I wanted to see the look on your face." She turned to him, her expression unchanged. "Would you have been happy, Matt?"

He hadn't expected the question. He had barely had time to think of anything except of what Paige had gone through and that he hadn't been there to comfort her. "I don't know."

He saw her eyes fill with tears. "Yes. Yes, of course I would have been happy," he added quickly. "But we'll have another baby, darling. Lots of them."

Too late, he realized how inappropriate that remark was. She didn't want to hear about other babies. She was grieving for the one she had lost. He sighed. "I'm sorry. I'm not handling this very well, am I?"

Paige looked at him. There was no reproach in his eyes or in his voice. It hadn't occurred to him that she had tricked him into this pregnancy, that she had needed something more than his love. "I made the decision to become pregnant two months ago," she volunteered, watching for a change of expression in his eyes. "I threw my birth-control pills away while we were in Florida—without telling you."

Matt had suspected that much but didn't tell her that. "That's not important now, darling. What matters is you. Us."

Us. She almost laughed. How could she even think of the two of them as one when she had mourned the death of her baby in another man's arms?

"I'll go talk to the doctor," Matt said, kissing her cheek and standing up. "I'll find out when I can take you home. Would you like that?"

She didn't answer him. She continued to stare at the

wall. What difference did it make where she went, and with whom? Something dear and wonderful between her and Matt had been broken and she didn't know if she could fix it. Or even wanted to.

In the days that followed her return from the hospital, Paige busied herself with daily tasks meant to help her adjust to her loss. Dry-eyed, she packed the few baby things she had bought and gave them away to Goodwill. She talked to friends and family and did small chores the doctor had permitted. She also took long walks, most of them with Matt, who had taken a few days off and wouldn't let her out of his sight.

He bought her books, flowers, tapes of her favorite movies. Day by day, her physical strength returned and her mental outlook improved. But somehow the distance between her and Matt kept widening, with neither one knowing what to do about it.

"I think I should go away for awhile," Paige said one night as she and Matt were finishing dinner. She looked up, saw the puzzled look on his face, and added, "Alone."

Matt rose from his chair so fast that it fell back, crashing against the wall. "Why would you want to do that?"

"Because I need a change."

In two long strides he was standing in front of her, pulling her out of her chair, forcing her to look at him. "Paige, you've got to stop this. I know losing the baby hit you hard, but it's over now. You've got to concentrate on the future. Our future."

Before he had a chance to pull her to him, she slipped away. "I'm doing that."

"By going away?"

"It won't be for long."

"That's not the point, Paige. The point is that you belong here. With me. And anyway, where would you go?"

"Home."

How easily she had said the word. As if this apartment

and the last fourteen months had been nothing more for her than a temporary arrangement.

"*This* is home, Paige. And I'm your husband. I'm the one you should turn to." Then, willing to do anything to help her get through her misery, he added, "If you really want to go to Santa Barbara, I'll come with you. I'm sure Tom will give me a few additional days off—"

"I want to go alone."

A chill went through him. After awhile, he walked out, slamming the door behind him.

Although Matt was in and out of New York on business, he talked to Paige every day. He had hoped that the separation would mellow her, make her realize how much she missed him, but it didn't, and their telephone conversations were getting shorter all the time, as if she couldn't wait to hang up and return to whatever she was doing.

He knew from Mindy that Jeremy came to see Paige often, and although Matt resented his interference, he kept his feelings to himself. He tried to be patient, to understand her need to heal in familiar surroundings, at her own pace. But after two weeks, he couldn't stand the situation any longer. Taking Paul's advice that he and Paige had to settle this matter before it grew worse, he flew to Santa Barbara, intent on bringing his wife back.

He found her at the beach house, sitting on the lower deck and looking at the sea. She wore the same jeans and sweatshirt she always wore at home, and her hair, loose and shiny, whipped around in the breeze.

She was surprised to see him there, since he hadn't told her he was coming, but she showed no other emotions. Politely, she asked if he wanted some iced tea or a sandwich.

"I've got chicken, roast beef, ham."

He had promised himself that he would remain calm and logical, that she had gone through a great ordeal and needed his understanding and not his anger. But something about the way she greeted him like some out-of-town guest, made him snap.

"Will you stop with the good hostess crap?" he bellowed, his pain so acute he could almost taste it. "I don't want your goddamned sandwich. And I'm sick of your perfect manners, of the chill in your voice when you talk to me."

"You don't have to shout, Matt. I can hear you."

"Then hear this. I've had it with this martyr attitude of yours. You think you're the only one who hurts? You think I don't feel for you? For the baby we lost? For myself?"

Her eyes flared. "I don't want you to talk about him, do you hear? You didn't want him. You don't know what it felt like to carry him inside of you all those weeks. And you don't know what it felt like to lose him. *You weren't even there!*"

She spat the last sentence. So that was it. She blamed him for not being with her when she lost the baby. She might even blame him for the miscarriage, for all he knew. "All right, I wasn't. How many times do I have to apologize for that?"

She looked away as if she hadn't heard the question. It hit him then that maybe she didn't love him any more. Otherwise how could she have come back here, picked up her former life exactly as she had left it a little over a year ago, and gone on as if he had never existed?

"What do you want to do?" he asked, feeling more helpless than he ever had before.

"I want you to let me have a little space. Is that so hard to understand?"

"You've had space. Two whole weeks of it."

"I need more time."

"To do what? Grow farther away from me? And closer to Jeremy?"

"Don't bring Jeremy into our problems."

"He *is* our problem, Paige. Can't you see that? You keep me out of your life, yet you see him every day."

"I don't see him every day. And anyway, what if I

did? Jeremy is my friend. God knows what I would have done at the hospital if he hadn't been there.''

"Yeah. That was very touching. And clever. What better time to put ideas in your head than when you're vulnerable and your husband is thousands of miles away.''

"Stop making him sound like some manipulative monster.''

"And stop talking about him as if he were some sort of god.'' In his brain, a bright red light flashed a warning. But he was too angry and too hurt to pay attention to it. "In fact, I want you to stop seeing him altogether. No more phone calls, no more cute, impromptu visits while I'm away, and no more of his fatherly advice.''

Holding the deck railing behind her, Paige raised a defiant chin. "Is that an ultimatum?''

"Take it any way you want. Just stop seeing Newman.''

She gave him a look that was charged with anger. "I think you'd better leave, Matt. Now.''

"You're making a mistake, Paige.''

"It won't be the first time.''

For a moment, he held her hard gaze, hoping she'd realize she was being unfair and ask him to stay. When she didn't, he turned around and left.

That evening, when Jeremy, who had been playing in a local polo tournament all weekend, stopped by, he found Paige quiet and withdrawn. "Something happened?'' he asked.

"Matt was here,'' she told him.

"Oh.'' Pulling up a deck chair, he sat close to her. "I take it it didn't go well.''

Paige shook her head and looked away. "He left almost right away.''

Jeremy held back a smile of satisfaction. He had been worried that a visit from Matt would convince Paige to go back to him, but judging from the somber look on her face, all she needed now to make her sever all ties with her husband was the right amount of sympathy and a little gentle persuasion. "You want to tell me about it?"

"There's nothing to tell. I thought he had come here ready to make concessions. But I was wrong. All he brought with him was anger and accusations."

Jeremy sighed. "I'm sorry, Paige. Truly sorry. But perhaps it's for the best. Now that you know where Matt stands, you can start looking toward the future, think of yourself for a change."

She turned to him, her eyes wide, a little frightened. "What are you saying?"

He leaned forward, chosing his words carefully. "I'm saying that it's time you made a decision about you and Matt. This limbo you're in now is killing you, Paige. Until today, I truly thought your marriage was worth saving. But now, seeing how deeply his visit affected you," he said, shaking his head, 'I no longer believe that."

Before she had a chance to answer, he stood up, gave her a cheerful smile and held out his hand. "My team won today. Would you like to see our trophy? It's in the car."

Paige nodded and took his hand.

Three weeks after his trip to Santa Barbara, as Matt returned from a short overnight trip, a thin young man with rimless glasses and a bright red parka approached him as he was unlocking his front door.

"Mr. McKenzie? Mr. Matthew McKenzie?"

Matt gave him a sour look. Courtesy wasn't one of his priorities these days. "That's me. What do you want?"

"This is for you, sir."

Matt took the brown manila envelope, glanced at the attorney's name on it and the Santa Barbara address and felt that cold familiar grip clutch his gut. Putting his suitcase down, he turned the envelope over in his hands.

He knew what was inside before he even opened it. Divorce papers.

It took Matt two days to decide on a course of action that would save his marriage. He had no idea what was going on inside Paige's head, and although at first he had thought she was just being bullheaded, the fact that she had started divorce proceedings changed all that.

He didn't want to divorce Paige any more than she wanted to divorce him. Therefore, he would go to Santa Barbara once more, and this time he would tell her what she wanted to hear. He would talk to Tom and request a desk job. He didn't like it. It meant taking a reduction in pay, making difficult adjustments. He might even have to move his mother to another medical facility. But if that's what it took to keep Paige, he'd find a way to make it all work. Somehow.

Paige wasn't home, so he went to Beauchamp, where Kate's assistant told him that Mrs. McKenzie was out of town, although she didn't know where, and that Miss Madison was in Los Angeles for the day.

Determined to find Paige, to wait until she returned if he had to, he went to see Mindy at the furniture shop.

"Matt!" Paige's long-time friend rushed into his arms and hugged him. "It's so good to see you." In spite of her bubbly reception, she looked uncomfortable. "Are you visiting Josh? Or just passing through?"

"Neither. I've come to take Paige home."

"Oh." Mindy turned away, pretending to center a lamp on a hot pink table in a shape he couldn't identify. "Where is she, Mindy?"

"Out of town, I believe. For a few days."

"Where?"

"I don't know—"

"Yes, you do."

Mindy knew a determined man when she saw one. And she knew this one very well. She had seen him in action, seen the way he had pursued Paige a year and a half ago, how he had braved the mighty Eve Granger and even Jeremy Newman. Here was a man who would fight until his last breath for a cause he thought just. A man who knew how to wait, how to wear one's strength down, how to extort information if he had to. She didn't think he would use force on her, but then again, with a man like Matt Mckenzie, one could never be certain.

"I'm not leaving here until you tell me where she is, Mindy."

Mindy sighed. "She's in Spain."

"What the hell is she doing in Spain?"

Mindy hesitated. She could lie, tell him Paige had gone to Europe for a client. But the way Matt continued to stare at her, with those hard gray eyes, convinced her that the truth was best. "She went to spend a couple of weeks in Marbella. With Jeremy."

The words drove right through his heart. In Marbella with Jeremy. How cozy. Here he was, beating his brains out looking for ways to save their marriage, and she was on the Costa del Sol partying with Jeremy and the rest of his phony friends.

What a jerk he had been.

His jaw set, he pulled the folded divorce papers from his jacket pocket and gave them one last glance. Two days ago, in a moment of anger, he had retained a lawyer and signed the damned things.

Then, when he had made up his mind to go to Santa Barbara, he had taken the papers with him, ready to tear them to pieces the moment Paige said the word.

"She's due back home in a couple of days," Mindy said. "Why don't you—"

He knew what she was thinking and didn't give her a chance to finish. "Good. When she comes back, tell her I hope she had a terrific time." He tossed the papers on the hot-pink table, ignoring Mindy's look of dismay. "And give her these."

Then, before Mindy could see the tears in his eyes, he left.

TWENTY-THREE

Although the Costa del Sol stretched for some 120 miles along Spain's southern coast, it was the western part of the area, starting just east of Marbella, that had emerged as Europe's most glamorous getaway.

Here, nestled between the Sierra Bermeja and the sunny Mediterranean, lay some of the most expensive real estate in the world—vast villas, Andalusian villages that looked as if they had been carved out of white marble, and ultrachic *urbanizacións* that only the very rich could afford.

Relatively unknown for years, except to local vacationers, Marbella and its chic surroundings shot into notoriety in the early 1950s, when people like Princess Soraya, King Farouk, and other members of the royal set began to drop anchor in its blue waters. Soon after that, the area now known as the Golden Mile had become the favorite playground of the rich and the titled, and the only resort in the world where nonstop parties were considered daily routine.

Jeremy's house, a sunwashed villa not nearly as ostentatious as Paige had expected, was built in the traditional Andalusian style—rosy tile roofs, splashing fountains, and grand stucco terraces shaded by palm trees and purple bougainvillea. Close to the beach, it was high enough on a hill so that even on a rare misty morning the bluish flanks of North Africa's Atlas Mountains could be seen.

Paige hadn't wanted to come. But Jeremy had insisted that Marbella was exactly what she needed to chase away her blues.

"You won't have to talk to anyone or attend any parties unless you feel like it," he had promised. "The house is yours to do as you wish and Pilar, my housekeeper, will be delighted to have someone else to spoil besides myself."

True to his word, Jeremy left her alone to do whatever she pleased, joining her occasionally for breakfast or afternoon tea when everyone else was observing Spain's most sacred ritual—the afternoon siesta.

Her days were slow and lazy, without pressure or intrusion of any kind. She swam, took long walks along the beach, and enjoyed Pilar's delicious cooking and tender loving care. The nights were restful, and although Marbella's beautiful people thought it declassé to go to bed before seven in the morning, Paige usually fell asleep at ten in the evening with the sounds of a distant party drifting in through the open windows.

At first, she tried not to think about Matt and the sad, unexpected turn their marriage had taken. But as she began to recuperate, he kept intruding into her thoughts with increasing regularity.

She missed him. Considering all they had shared, the revelation hadn't come as a total surprise. What did surprise her, however, was the guilt she experienced whenever she thought of their breakup.

She remembered his look of anguish at the hospital and how patient and tender he had been afterward as she recovered, spending every minute with her. But mostly, she remembered the last time they had been together, when he had come to Santa Barbara.

She had never seen him as angry and frustrated as he had been that afternoon. Or so frightened. Why hadn't she understood his grief then? Had she been that blind? Or had it been easier *not* to see?

Now, as she sat on the beach, watching the sun rise over the little town of Mostril, she thought of all the sunrises she and Matt had watched together, of all the promises they had made to each other—for better and for worse. She thought of the laughter, the cold winter evenings spent at home watching old movies together. How was it possible for two people who had been so close to have grown so far apart?

"Is this a private moment? Or may I intrude?"

At the sound of Jeremy's voice, Paige turned around and forced a smile. He took so much pride in the fact that she was getting better and stronger every day, she didn't want him to think that the famous "Newman Remedy," as he called it, wasn't always working. Besides, she enjoyed his company, his attentions, and the way he made her smile when she felt the least like it.

Another man would have taken advantage of her present state of mind and of her vulnerability. Not Jeremy. Although she sensed that he was still very much in love with her, his attitude toward her was always the same—friendly and respectful.

"You're not intruding, Jeremy. And anyway, what kind of houseguest would I be if I tried to claim all this scenic beauty for myself?"

Smiling, Jeremy ran down the last couple of steps. He wore a pair of Bermuda shorts in a vivid orange and red print, and a large straw hat. It wasn't the kind of attire one easily associated with the mighty Jeremy Newman, yet here, in these exotic surroundings, it suited him perfectly.

"I'm glad you're enjoying yourself." He sat down on the blanket, facing her. "It shows, you know," he added letting his gaze slide up and down her body. "You look resplendent."

"Thank you. And thank you for insisting that I come. I feel like a new woman already."

A frisson of desire ran through Jeremy's body. It was getting increasingly difficult to pretend she didn't affect him. In that black bikini and with her hair still wet from a recent swim, she looked like a goddess who had been sent down to earth with the sole purpose of driving men mad.

But this wasn't the time to lose his head, he reminded himself. Pushing her now would be unwise. She was still bruised, still in love with McKenzie. A few months from now, it would be different. But for the moment, he had to content himself with being her friend.

"Then do you think this new woman would like to do me a favor? Since this is our last night in Marbella?"

"What kind of favor?"

"I need an escort for this evening. Someone beautiful and fascinating. And I could think of only one person who fits the description."

"Oh, Jeremy, I don't know . . ."

He plucked a grape from the cluster she had brought down from the house and popped it in his mouth. "Look, I know I promised not to pressure you, but you'll love this group. The invitation came from my old friends, the von Pantzes," he added, as if the name should bring instant recognition on her part. "Terry is giving one of her famous dinner parties and she'd be shattered if I didn't bring my mysterious houseguest."

"I didn't bring anything to wear," Paige said, already dreading the thought of going shopping.

"Not to worry." He stole another grape, but this time, he put it into *her* mouth, making it impossible for her to protest. "I'll have something delivered to you by two o'clock this afternoon, which will give you plenty of time to exchange it if you don't find it suitable."

She didn't have the heart to turn him down. Not after all he had done for her. "Oh, why not? I guess I've played the recluse long enough." She didn't add that a party might be just what she needed to take her mind off Matt.

Jeremy gave her a light kiss on the cheek and stood up. "Good. Rest up. Cocktails start at ten-thirty."

As Marbella's most legendary hostess, Baroness Hubert von Pantz gave the kind of parties people talked about long after the season was over. Whether it was a luncheon for twenty, an elaborate dinner for eighty, or one of the baron's open houses, the event was always a sparkling affair, complete with live music, tons of exotic flowers, and elegant poolside tables.

Terry von Pantz's guest list was the most diversified and interesting in the community. She thought nothing of mixing blue bloods like Princess Sofie von Wurtemburg and Count Rudi Schönburg with social beach bums, or even *dodgerati*, those charming rogues on the lam Marbella found utterly fascinating.

Thanks to Jeremy, Paige didn't have to worry about not measuring up to the rest of the well-dressed crowd. Her gown, which had come from the Valentino boutique in Puerto Banús, was simple and stunning—something Paige would have chosen for herself. Soft folds of chiffon in a vivid shade of fushia folded around her in a long, breezy column that bared her shoulders and whispered with every step. Remembering her fondness for costume jewelry, Jeremy had added a necklace of pink and white glass beads and a pair of white high-heeled sandals in her exact size.

The moment they stepped on the terrace, they were greeted by two of Jeremy's close friends, the Duke of Chelsam, who owned the opulent Moorish mansion down the hill, and Lorelei Simpson, Marbella's resident social columnist.

"So *this* is Paige McKenzie." Giving a short bow, the duke took Paige's hand and brought it to his lips. "How clever of you to keep her all to yourself, old chap."

"I'm so thrilled you could come," Lorelei Simpson said. Did Jeremy tell you I have many friends in Santa Barbara?"

"Beware of Lorelei," Jeremy warned. "She is a master at extracting people's most deeply rooted secrets. And what she can't find out, she'll make up."

"Oh, Jeremy, what an incorrigible tease you are. He's lying, of course," Lorelei added with a coy smile. She took a sip of her champagne. "Is it true that your soon-to-be exhusband works for Interpol?"

Paige held back a smile. How typical. She had come

here to forget Matt and already he was the subject of conversation. "Actually, he is a private investigator."

"You weren't married very long, I hear?"

"Now that I think of it," the duke interjected, gallantly coming to Paige's rescue, "wasn't he the one responsible for poor Jeremy losing that Lautrec a year or so ago? Of course," he added, seeing a sour look on Jeremy's face and taking great pleasure in diverting the attention to his old friend, "I remember now. The lad actually *crashed* a dinner party and exposed the crook just when our Paige here was about to finalize the deal for Jeremy."

Lorelei Simpson shivered with excitement. "How exciting," she cooed. "He'd fit beautifully around here, wouldn't he, Jeremy?"

"I doubt that very much." Then, taking Paige's arm, Jeremy led her away from the chatty duo. "I'm sorry about this, Paige. I had no idea anyone would bring up Matt's name."

Paige patted his hand and glanced around the torchlit terrace, trying to appear unconcerned. "That's all right. I suppose I'll have to get used to hearing his name mentioned from time to time."

Dinner, which found her seated between one of Hollywood's sexiest leading men and Saudi Arabia's King Fahd, was more pleasant than she had expected. But when Jeremy came to invite her to dance later, she slipped into his arms gratefully.

"Glad you came?" he asked.

She nodded, not wanting to hurt his feelings. "Delighted. It's a lovely party, Jeremy. And your friends are charming."

It was then that the band switched to the languorous tune of "Unforgettable." Although she showed no reaction and kept on dancing, the rich timber of Nat King Cole's voice swept her away in a wave of memories that kept her fighting to keep the tears away.

"Unforgettable" had been her wedding's theme song. When she and Matt had walked into her grandmother's

solarium after the church ceremony and the band struck
the first few chords, she had forgotten the traumatic experience with her mother and danced as if she and Matt
were the only two people in the room. After that she had
never been able to hear the melody without her eyes misting.

What was he doing at this very moment? she wondered, closing her eyes and swaying to the music. Was
he thinking of her? Wondering where she was? With no
warning at all, another question sprang into her mind, so
quick and unexpected that she lost her step. *Was it too
late for them?*

It's the music, she thought, shaking herself out of her
trance. It's making me feel nostalgic, sentimental. I'll be
all right as soon as it stops.

But later, as she stood by her bedroom window,
breathing in the fragrant air, watching an anchored cruise
ship illuminate the late-night sky, the feeling she had
experienced at the von Pantzs' was just as powerful, just
as demanding of an answer.

Thoughts, crazy and wild, scrambled through her head.
Had she been too hasty with those divorce papers? Jeremy had been so sure that only a clean break would bring
her peace of mind. But that hadn't been the case. If anything, she was more miserable now than before.

Would it be totally out of place for her to call Matt
and tell him how she felt? Or to surprise him with a visit,
the way he had surprised her?

Because, unlike Matt, she never did anything on impulse, she weighed each thought carefully, pressing her
hand to her chest as she felt the excitement grow. Perhaps
they could reach some sort of compromise. Wasn't that
what marriage was all about? Making compromises?
Wasn't that what Matt had been trying to tell her all
along?

She remained standing at the window for a long time,
thinking, remembering, making decisions, discarding
them, making them all over again. By four o'clock in the
morning, only three hours before she and Jeremy were

scheduled to return to the States, she had made up her
mind. She would call Matt from Santa Barbara and tell
him she was coming to New York to talk to him.

They would tear up those divorce papers together.

"Jesus . . ."

At the sound of his grandson's groan, Josh, sitting in
a chair by the window, lowered his morning paper and
threw an amused glance toward Matt, who lay sprawled
on the sofa, fully dressed and badly in need of a shave.
"You're in pain, boy?"

Matt opened one eye. Then the other. The effort sent
a searing pain through his head. His mouth felt as if
someone had jammed a fistful of cotton balls into it and
he felt nauseous as hell. "What time is it?" he asked,
barely recognizing his own voice.

"A little before noon." Josh stood up, picked up a
thick, milky drink Nigel had just brought in, and took it
to Matt. "Here. This will make you feel better."

Matt took one look at the sickening-looking brew and
turned his head the other way. "Don't want it."

"I can't say I blame you. But you're going to drink it
anyway. Because you're not in any shape to do otherwise." Feeling sorry for the kid, he held his arm and
helped him sit up. Slowly.

Matt held back another string of groans and steadied
himself by gripping the sofa with both hands before
glowering at the drink in Josh's hands. He had had only
one other hangover in his life, and it had happened right
here, during a visit to the ranch, where Josh had thrown
him a high school graduation party. He had never forgotten that night. Or the morning after. Or Nigel's foul
remedy. That alone had made him vow to never get drunk
again. Until last night.

"Would you like to tell me what happened?" Josh
asked when Matt put the empty glass down.

"There's nothing to tell."

"In that case, why did you go and get roaring drunk?
If all you wanted was one of Nigel's little pick-me-ups,

you only had to ask. He would have gladly whipped one up for you.''

Matt leaned back on the sofa. His eyes felt like they'd been rubbed with sand paper. But he didn't dare close them again. He didn't dare do much of anything. ''Paige filed for divorce.''

Josh sighed. He had hoped until the end it wouldn't come to that. ''And you couldn't talk her out of it?''

''I never got the chance. When I went to see her, she had already left for Spain. With Jeremy.''

Josh walked over to the bar. It was too early for Jack Daniels, so he poured himself a Perrier. ''So you did the only sensible thing that came to mind. You went to the nearest bar, got smashed, and picked up a floozie.''

Even though the pain nearly made him cry out, Matt snapped to attention. ''What are you talking about?''

''I'm talking about being dumb, son. The binge is one thing. But the woman . . .''

''Oh, God.'' It was all coming back to him now. He had left Mindy's shop in a lousy mood, and on his way to the ranch, he had stopped at Miguel's Tavern in Los Olivos. He had been a third of the way into a bottle of Jack Daniels when the blonde had approached him. She was pretty, well-endowed, and friendly. But he wasn't interested. So after a brotherly peck that somehow had turned into a fiery kiss, he had sent her off. He had no idea how Josh had found out. A nosy neighbor, no doubt.

''Relax, Gramps,'' he said, understanding Josh's concern. ''Nothing happened with that woman—or with any woman.''

Josh heaved a sigh of relief. 'I'm glad to hear that. Now, what about some food to steady that stomach of yours?''

Matt waved his hand. ''I don't want anything right now, Gramps—except to forget about last night.''

''I doubt you'll be able to do that.''

''Why?''

Josh walked back to the chair where he had been sitting earlier, picked up the newspaper and came back. Without a word, he tossed the paper on Matt's lap.

Matt, an incredulous look on his face, stared at a snapshot of himself kissing the blonde, and the blaring headline above it: "Overworked Local Boy Comes Home for a Little R & R."

"Oh, dear God!"

The terminal was nearly deserted when Paige arrived in Santa Barbara. The Newman jet had made a brief stop to let her off before continuing on to San Francisco.

Spotting Mindy, who always insisted on acting as her chauffeur when she flew in and out of town, Paige hurried toward her. "Hi, there."

Mindy lowered the newspaper she'd been reading and jumped out of her seat. "Wow!" she exclaimed as she hugged her friend. "Don't you look terrific!" She pulled away and gave Paige another admiring look. "Does the Costa del Sol bottle whatever you're taking? Or is this new glow your own doing?"

"Let's just say that the old Paige is back." Then, seeing the effort Mindy was making to conceal something behind her back, she added, "What have you got there? A welcome-home present?"

To her surprise, Mindy, who never blushed, turned a vivid shade of red. "No . . . It's nothing like that."

Amused, Paige leaned sideways, trying to steal a peek. "Then what is it?"

Cursing herself for not discarding that damned newspaper sooner, Mindy shrugged. "Just a crossword puzzle I was working on while waiting for your plane to land."

"Crossword puzzle?" Paige's amused expression was replaced by one of puzzlement. "You don't *do* crossword puzzles, Mindy. In fact, you despise them."

"Oh, what the hell," Mindy said with a sigh of resignation, handing Paige the newspaper. "You're bound to find out anyway."

"Find out what . . ."

Whatever Paige had meant to say, died on her lips.

Her mouth open, her eyes wide with shock, she stared at a photo of Matt holding a curvaceous blonde in a passionate embrace and kissing her full on the mouth. Above the snapshot, the headlines in big bold letters, burned a hole right through her heart. "Overworked Local Boy Comes Home for a Little R & R."

"That bastard!" Paige hissed when she was finally able to talk. "How dare he put himself on display like this? Embarrassing me. Leaving me wide open to ridicule."

"Paige, calm down."

"I *am* calm."

"You're turning purple."

"Wouldn't you? This is a deliberate slap in the face, Mindy. Matt and I are still married, in case you've forgotten."

"I haven't. But *you* seem to have forgotten a small detail.

Paige gave her a blank look.

"You filed for divorce, kiddo, remember? And you went to Spain with another man."

"A *friend*, Mindy. I went to Spain with a *friend*. And you don't see *our* picture plastered all over the papers, do you?" With a disgusted shake of the head, she threw the paper on the seat Mindy had occupied earlier. "Where is he?"

"If you mean Matt, he left this morning. But he stopped by the furniture store day before yesterday. He was looking for you, Paige. I had to tell him where you were."

"So? I never intended to keep it a secret." She gave Mindy a sour look. "What did he want?"

"He didn't say. But he left me this." She reached into a large canary tote bag and pulled out the set of divorce papers Matt had left with her.

Paige's heart gave a leaping thud. She took the thick sheaf, flipped to the last page and saw that Matt's signature was on it. Wasn't that just terrific? While she was trying to figure out ways for her and Matt to reconcile, he and the chesty blonde had been having an early celebration. Right here. In Paige's own backyard, no less. How tasteful. But then what could one expect from a McKenzie?

With a curt nod, she folded the documents and put them into her own bag. "Well, I'm glad that's over and done with." She flashed Mindy a quick smile, hoping her watchful friend wouldn't notice how close she was to bursting into tears. "Now maybe I can get on with my life."

TWENTY-FOUR

Jeremy, who had heard about Matt's public display at Miguel's Tavern from his foreman at Newman's Ranch, waited until the investigator had returned to New York before calling on Josh McKenzie as he so often had in the last couple of years.

It had been only a few weeks since he had come by and made Josh another offer on his ranch, and although the old fool had turned him down again, Jeremy knew that with the drought persisting the way it did, it'd only be a matter of time until Josh would be forced to sell.

Ideally, he liked to wait three or four months between visits, thus giving Josh enough time to realize that offers like his didn't grow on trees. But too many hungry developers were scouting throughout central California these days, hoping to turn this valley into prime residential communities, and Jeremy didn't want the McKenzie property to slip through his fingers when he wasn't looking.

Years ago, he had decided that Josh's land would be the site for the most spectacular house in the world—even more spectacular than the one his role model, William Randolph Hearst, had built in San Simeon. Jeremy was only a boy when he had first seen Hearst Castle, but he had never forgotten the experience.

"One day I'll have a house just like that," he had told his father when they had returned to San Francisco after a few days' stay at the millionaire's house. "I'll call it Newman Castle."

Philip Newman had burst into his deep, rolling laugh.

"You know something, son? You're just the one who can do it."

Finding the right land on which to build his dream, however, hadn't been easy. Jeremy had hunted up and down the California coast, searching as far inland as Ojai, but the only property that was perfect in every way was the McKenzie ranch, which was adjacent to his own horse farm outside Los Olivos.

Now, as he brought his silver 500 SL to a stop a few feet from Josh's front door, Jeremy stepped out of the Mercedes and allowed himself another sweeping glance at the land he hoped would soon be his. Thousands of acres spread out for miles in all four directions, all rolling hills and wide pastures, intercepted every now and then by thick clusters of evergreens.

The only drawback was an inadequate water supply. Until three years ago, the water, supplied by the ranch's own creek-fed lake, had been more than ample. But with the drought that had begun in 1986 and continued to devastate central and southern California, the creek had dried up, leaving Josh's lake empty.

Like other cattle ranchers in the area, Josh had spent a fortune in the last two years drilling all over his ranch for another water source. But four years and two hundred thousand dollars later, he still hadn't found it.

Six months into the drought, Josh had come to him for help. But although Jeremy could have realized a handsome profit selling water from his spring-fed lake to his less fortunate neighbor, he had turned Josh down. Without a proper water supply, the Canyon-T Ranch would go broke in a year, and Josh would have no choice but to sell.

But something had gone wrong with that scenario. By giving up his feed business, selling half his herd, and making other major adjustments, Josh had managed to keep the ranch going. *And* he had kept the developers at bay.

Well, Jeremy thought, making his way toward the

house, old Josh wouldn't be able to turn him down this time. Not with this new offer.

Nigel, Josh's only servant, opened the door and showed him into what Josh's wife, Millie, had nicknamed the ''great room,'' probably because of its size and fabulous view of the valley. Jeremy had been a guest of Josh and Millie many times in the past, although not in recent years—not since Adam had been killed at Newman's Ranch four years ago.

Josh stood at the bar, wearing his standard uniform— faded blue jeans that accentuated his famous bowed legs and a plaid shirt with the sleeves rolled up to the elbows. His white hair was trimmed short and although his tanned face was deeply lined, he looked fit and much younger than his seventy-four years.

He was pouring himself a Jack Daniel's, the only liquor he ever drank, when Jeremy walked in. Reaching behind the bar, he pulled out another glass. ''Will you join me, Jeremy?''

''Gladly.'' He waited until Josh handed him his drink before adding, ''It was good of you to see me in the middle of the afternoon, Josh. I know you like to work until your men go home.''

Josh leaned one elbow on the bar surface. He wasn't in the habit of drinking with people he didn't like, or even having them in his house, but these visits of Jeremy's were something he had come to enjoy. There was nothing quite as rewarding as seeing an old adversary grovel. ''I figured it had to be important for you to come all the way from San Francisco in the middle of the week.''

Jeremy took a sip of his drink and let his gaze drift around the room. In the forty-some years he had been coming to the ranch, he had never seen this room, or the rest of the house, look any different than it did now. It was a cowboy's house—comfortable, unpretentious, and boring. But he wasn't here to pass judgement on Josh's taste in interior design. He was here to do business.

''I guess we've known each other too long to waste

time on pleasantries, so I'll come right to the point.'' He put his glass down. ''I've come to make you another offer on the ranch, Josh. One I hope you won't be able to turn down this time.''

''Then I guess I'm going to have to disappoint you again, Jeremy. Because what I told you four weeks ago still stands. I was born on this ranch and, God willing, I'll die on it.''

''At the rate you're going, working as hard as you do, you'll die sooner than you think.''

Josh threw him an amused glance. 'Worried about my health, Jeremy? Or are you just wishing out loud?''

''Don't be ridiculous. I've never wished you any harm and you know it. As a matter of fact, I admire you and the way you've kept this ranch going in spite of the drought.''

''No thanks to you.''

Jeremy waved an impatient hand. ''There's no point in rehashing all those ill feelings now. Instead, why don't we put our energies into more constructive matters—like making you a rich man.''

Not bothering to ask Jeremy if he wanted another drink, Josh splashed two fingers of whiskey in his own glass. Two drinks a day was all he allowed himself these days, but he didn't have any fast rules on how close those drinks could be. ''What do you want my ranch for, anyway?'' he asked. A few years ago he had heard a rumor about the publisher wanting to build another Hearst Castle somewhere in this area, but Josh had never relied on gossip much. ''You never did tell me.''

''I've been thinking of retiring,'' Jeremy lied. ''City life is beginning to get a little too fast-paced for me. I want to relax, to get more involved with my horses, raise some cattle maybe. My ranch isn't big enough for all that.''

''Well, I'll be damned. I never thought I'd hear the day when Jeremy Newman admitted he couldn't keep up with the rest of the world.''

Jeremy smiled, gazed thoughtfully into his drink.

"Time catches up, old friend. With the best of us."
Then, looking up, he added, "I'm prepared to pay you
top dollar, Josh."

"I'm sure you are."

"How does thirty million sound?"

"Damn good, if I were in the market to sell."

"You're being bullheaded again, Josh."

Josh saw Jeremy's complexion turn a shade redder and
held back a chuckle. "And you're getting hard of hearing
in your old age."

Jeremy slammed his glass down. "Dammit, Josh!
That's two million over what I offered you a month ago.
You won't get a better deal, and you know it."

"I'm not looking for a deal."

"What perverse pleasure do you get from working so
hard for so little?"

"You wouldn't understand."

Jeremy wasn't sure what he found more frustrating, the
old man's refusal, or the way he taunted him, as if he
actually enjoyed playing tug of war with him. "You're a
foolish man, Josh. And I'm almost tempted to withdraw
my offer." He sighed. "But I won't." He downed the
rest of his whiskey and put the empty glass down. "I'll
be at the ranch for a couple of days. Give me a call if
you have a change of heart."

"I'll do that." Josh walked him to the door and stood
on the threshold as the sleek Mercedes headed down the
winding road. It would have been so easy to let the man
have his way this time, to take the thirty million and
enjoy the last few years he had left on this good earth.
But Josh had a dream, too. And that dream was to pass
on this land to his grandson. Oh, he knew the boy wasn't
ready to come home yet, to settle down, but someday he
would be. And when that happened, he wanted this land
intact.

Paige had never believed in self-pity. But there were
times when a healthy dose of it was good for the soul.
This was such a time. During the week following her

return from Marbella, she did nothing but watch soap operas, eat junk food, and ponder what she considered to be a useless, miserable, unexciting life. The only exception she made in her daily routine was when she came out of her dark mood long enough to curse Matt McKenzie and the day she had met him.

Except for a few phone calls from her family and from Jeremy, she shut out all communication with the outside world. She had also resisted all attempts on Kate's part to discuss future career plans, even when Kate told her Lisa wasn't working out and would be leaving at the end of the month.

Mindy was the only person she permitted to enter her sanctum. Day after day her friend came to see her, her yellow bag filled with miracle workers—her famous chilis rellenos, which she smothered in cheese and salsa, bags of Amaretto coffee beans and special teas, warm croissants from a French bakery in Pasea Nuevo, and lovely, fragrant roses Mindy picked daily in her garden. But most important, she brought her love and her unconditional friendship.

"You've been cleaning," Mindy commented one morning as she stopped for one of her daily visits before going to her shop. Sniffing the air, she grinned. "And baking."

"Cinnamon rolls. I figured you fed me so well this past week, it was time I did something for you."

Mindy followed her friend into the spotless yellow and white kitchen and perched herself on a stool while Paige busied herself with mugs and plates. "Does this sudden domesticity mean you are finally ready to rejoin the rest of us poor working mortals?"

Paige picked up a roll, plucking a fat walnut from the sticky top and eating it with great gusto. "You could say that."

"Hey, that's great! Kate must be thrilled."

"She doesn't know yet."

"Why not? . . ." Mindy's pleased expression vanished. "Oh, Paige, don't tell me you've decided to take Jeremy up on his offer."

Paige shook her head. "No. The thought of Jeremy buying a San Francisco gallery and asking me to run it was flattering, but to tell you the truth, I wasn't even tempted. Beauchamp and I go back too far. And besides, I love working with Kate."

"Then why all the secrecy?"

"Because I've been toying with something, an idea, and I wanted your input before I approached my aunt."

Mindy's eyes grew wary. "The last time you had an idea, you created an uproar in the San Francisco art community."

Paige poured them both steaming cups of fragrant Amaretto-flavored coffee, and smiled, knowing Mindy was referring to Jeremy's forged Veracruz exhibit. "I realize that. But this is different. I want to do something significant for Beauchamp. Something that will put us in direct competition with important galleries all over the country."

"I thought Beauchamp was doing fine."

"It could be doing better. But then, none of the other galleries in town are setting the world on fire either."

"Is that what you want to do? Set the world on fire?"

Paige ignored Mindy's mocking smile and took a sip of coffee. "I want collectors all over the country to start looking at Beauchamp the way they look at William Doyle Galleries or Christie's."

"You're talking about giants here, kiddo."

"You don't become a giant by waiting for things to happen, Mindy. Doyle and Christie were small once, but they made things happen for them. If they could do it, so can we." Carried by the excitement, Paige began to walk around the island, stopping every now and then to break off a piece of cinnamon roll, which she ate as she talked. "What would you say if I, and other local art dealers, decided to hold an important antiques fair? Right here in Santa Barbara?"

Mindy put her mug down. "By antiques fair, I take it you don't mean some sort of artsy sidewalk sale."

"Of course not. I mean an event on the order of Grosvenor's Fair in London or the Paris Biennale des Antiquaires."

"I'd say you're crazy."

Paige didn't seem to have heard her. "Imagine an event so rich, so glamorous that important dealers from all over the world would beg to attend. Imagine all three ballrooms of the Biltmore Hotel crammed with the finest antique furniture the world has ever seen, old masters paintings, and precious objets d'art. Imagine a committee so prestigious that it could only be headed not by one famous art dealer, but by two."

Mindy's dark eyes shone with amusement as they attempted to keep up with Paige's erratic pacing. "And who might those two gods be?"

Paige stopped in front of Mindy, a look of triumph on her face. "Richard Prentiss of England, and Jean Lafont of France."

Mindy shrugged. "I'm afraid I've never heard of them. But if they're as big as you say, how would you go about convincing them to attend this little bash of yours?"

"I would start with the friends I made in Marbella. Many of the people there are important art collectors and attend all the big fairs. If I can persuade even a few to come to Santa Barbara, I can almost guarantee that Lafont and Prentiss won't turn me down. Their egos won't allow it."

"And you haven't mentioned any of this to Kate?"

Paige shook her head. "I need to work out the details in my head a little more first." With one swift, graceful movement, she sat on the island. "So what do you think?"

"I say go for it, kiddo. It's a wild idea, but knowing you like I do, you'll make it work."

Paige kept developing her brainstorm long after Mindy had gone. With each new thought came another. Tons of legwork would have to be done. She would have to enlist the support of every art dealer in town, solicit funds, talk to insurance companies, airlines, and hotels, including of course, the Biltmore, where the event would take place.

By the time Paige had put all her thoughts in order, it was midnight—an ungodly hour to expect someone, even Kate, to absorb all she had come up with in the last day. But she was too excited to wait until morning.

"Hello, Aunt Kate?" she said when her aunt answered the phone. "Put on a pot of coffee, will you? I'm coming over."

The next sixteen months were the most frantic, frustrating, and exhilarating Paige had ever experienced. Driven by a momentum not even an early rejection of her idea on the part of the town could slow down, she traveled across the United States and to Europe, talking to antiques dealers, collectors, and organizers of other important fairs. Even Kate, who had been difficult to convince at first, was coming up with new ways to solicit funds and enlist the help of not only art dealers, but the entire community as well.

But in spite of Paige's efforts and her powers of persuasion, Jean Lafont and Richard Prentiss had turned down her offer to cochair the fair. "I'm afraid I might as well forget about them and start looking for someone else," she told Jeremy during one of their lunch dates in January of 1991. "They're just not interested."

"Or," Jeremy replied, sipping his Chardonnay and watching her above the rim of his glass. "You could stop being so stubborn and let me talk to them."

"Absolutely not. You've done too much already. Anything more would be an exploitation of your friendship, and I simply won't allow it."

But Jeremy hadn't listened to her protests. Things hadn't gone as well as he had hoped in the last year and a half where he and Paige were concerned. Although she seemed to be over her divorce from Matt and was grateful to Jeremy for all his support, she had remained immune to his subtle advances and had given him no indication that she wanted their relationship to go any further than where it was now.

Yet she had feelings for him. He was certain of that. He could tell that by the way she looked at him from time to time, from the way she laughed with him, told him secrets about herself she had never told him before.

It was true that he had done more toward the success of the Santa Barbara Fair than he had done for any other event in the past, even those involving his art collection. But apparently it hadn't been enough. He needed to do something more—something that would make her realize how indispensable he had become and awaken all those feelings she kept so well hidden.

Two weeks later, Jeremy walked into Beauchamp, carrying a bouquet of pink roses. "They'll do it," he announced, handing her the flowers with a flourish. "Lafont and Prentiss would love to cochair the Santa Barbara fair and want to meet with you sometime next week to discuss the details."

Paige's hands flew to her mouth. Then, with a cry of sheer joy, she threw herself in Jeremy's arms. 'I can't believe you did this for me. You are wonderful. An absolute angel."

Delighted at her reaction, Jeremy laughed as he held her close. "I thought you didn't want me to interfere."

She pulled away from him, her eyes shining as she gazed at him fondly. "I know. And I meant it then, but now that they're actually *coming* . . . Oh, Jeremy, don't you see what this means? The fair won't just be successful, it will be *immensely* successful." She took his hands in hers. "And I owe it all to you."

"Aren't you exaggerating my powers just a little?" he asked, managing a modest smile.

She shook her head and hugged him once again. "Dear Jeremy. What would I do without you?"

Behind a door that had been left ajar, Kate watched them. Her eyes were brimming with tears, but they weren't tears of joy. As Jeremy's arms encircled Paige's waist, pain and rage, those familiar demons, once again filled her heart, blocking everything else.

Closing the door, she leaned her forehead against it, and wept.

TWENTY-FIVE

On March 23, 1991, Eve Granger suffered a massive heart attack and died. Her death came as a great shock to the Santa Barbara community. Even though she had been old, no one had ever thought of her as an old woman with an old woman's failings.

It was as if a piece of Montecito history had died with her, and many who came to her funeral felt she would never be replaced. Only Kate, who hated Eve for ruining Ann's life years ago, had rejoiced at the thought that the old woman had finally paid her dues.

The bulk of Eve's estate had been left to Paul. Her jewelry and the sum of five million dollars, went to Paige. Twenty thousand dollars had been left to each of the servants, as well as monetary gifts to all their children. The Velasquez painting in the solarium, valued at a quarter of a million dollars, had been left to Kate, who had admired it many times in the past. "For services rendered to this family," the will had read. Kate later donated the painting to the Santa Barbara Art Museum.

There had been other surprises—one of the two Bentleys had gone to her elderly chauffeur who had served her so well for more than forty years; a generous donation had been bequeathed to each of the charities she had sponsored; and her IBM stocks, worth over two hundred thousand dollars, had been left to her hairdresser, a single mother of two, with instructions that half of it be earmarked for her sons' college education.

Long after her death, Eve Granger continued to be remembered as a grand and generous lady.

* * *

The first Santa Barbara International Antiques Fair, held from June 5 to the 15th, 1991, was an event the town would never forget. More than half a million people attended, and even those who had been skeptical until the end agreed that it had been a success beyond their wildest expectations.

By the time the fair ended, every art dealer present had already signed up for next year's event and dozens of others were calling to be included.

"Well, how does it feel to be an overnight celebrity?" Jeremy asked Paige as he drove her home the evening of the fair's closing.

"Exhilarating. And exhausting." Leaning back into the Mercedes's plush maroon leather seat, Paige closed her eyes, thankful that the madness was finally over. "But I'm totally drained. I just want to go to bed and sleep for three straight days."

Jeremy held back a suggestive answer. This moment was too important to screw it up in any way. He glanced at her. With her eyes closed and her body in a state of semiabandon, she was more desirable than ever, and it took all his willpower to keep his hands off her.

By the time he pulled the car up in front of her house, she was sound asleep. He shut off the engine and turned around to face her. Her lips were slightly parted and the skirt of her narrow pink suit had ridden halfway up her thigh, exposing the lacy top of a sheer ivory stocking. Unable to resist the pull, Jeremy leaned over and covered her mouth with his.

From the soft cocoon of sleep, Paige felt a stirring, faint, yet unmistakable. Suspended in a state of semiconsciousness, she responded to the wonderful sensation and opened her mouth. Her tongue met another, and she sighed and strained forward. Visions of Matt, of his hard, lean body, of his hands, his mouth, made her moan.

She felt herself floating on a small wave that grew larger, warmer, and more turbulent. Her mind was hazy with fatigue and sleep, and she couldn't quite comprehend what was happening to her, only that she didn't want it to end.

Clever hands moved over her body and she felt the hard punch of arousal and responded by coiling her arms around her assailant's neck as she opened her eyes.

"Jeremy!" She bolted up, her cheeks flushed. "My God, what are you doing?"

"What I've been wanting to do for a long time. No, don't pull away," he added. "Not now. Not when you want me as much as I want you."

The need had been too real, the wanting still too evident, for her to deny it. What wasn't totally clear was who she had wanted.

"I lost my head," she said, pushing the hand that still rested on her thigh.

"I know." He cupped the back of her neck and pulled her to him. "And I loved every delicious second of it." He kissed her again, gently this time, glad that although she was now fully awake, she didn't push him away. "I love you, Paige. Surely you don't doubt that."

"No."

"And have I been wrong in assuming that you have feelings for me, too?"

Paige felt herself blush. In the past several months, she had been aware that her feelings for Jeremy were changing, and although she didn't love him the way she had loved Matt, she was deeply attracted to him and thought about him more often than she cared to admit. "No, you haven't been wrong."

The look of relief in his eyes, and the exuberance in his voice when he spoke made her smile. "Then marry me, Paige. Marry me and I swear I'll make you the happiest woman on earth. I'll shower you with love and attention. You'll not only be my wife, but my friend and my partner as well. Together we'll fill the house with the sound of laughter and happy children. As many children as you want." He grinned. "At least enough for a polo team."

Deep within her, something stirred. Once she would

have given anything to hear Matt say those words to her. Now a dear and wonderful man was saying them, and she wasn't sure she deserved them. "You're very sweet, Jeremy."

Bringing her fingertips to his mouth, he kissed them. "No one has ever described me that way before. But from you, I'll accept it as a compliment." Then, his gaze deep and intense, he added, "I hope that was your way of saying yes."

Paige sighed, aware that he was arousing feelings in her she thought had died long ago. Yes, she had doubts. But were they realistic? Did she need to love someone the way she had loved Matt in order to be happy? Wasn't what she felt for Jeremy—sexual attraction and a deep affection—enough?

He pulled her to him and in the confinement of the car, she felt his body against her—vibrant and eager. "Will you marry me, Paige?" he repeated, his voice a whisper against her cheek.

Soft lips touched hers, barely skimming them, drifting along her throat.

In a voice that was a little breathless, she said, "Yes, Jeremy. I'll marry you."

"Jeremy has asked me to marry him," Paige said the following morning as she was rearranging a Ginori porcelain teaset in the window of Beauchamp.

The sudden crash behind her almost made her drop the cup and saucer she was holding.

"Aunt Kate!"

Horrified, Paige stared at the shattered Meissen plate at Kate's feet. "What happened?"

"It slipped." Kate's voice was low and harsh, her face stony. Then, swearing under her breath, she crouched down and with short brisk movements started to pick up the broken pieces.

Paige rushed forward. "Aunt Kate, don't! You'll cut yourself."

The warning came too late. As Kate swept a large fragment into her palm, the sharp porcelain sliced through her skin, drawing blood almost instantly.

Without a word, Paige ran to the bathroom and pulled out a small emergency kit from the medicine closet. When she came back, Kate was standing, holding her hand and staring at it vacantly while blood dripped on the hardwood floor.

"Come here." Gently, Paige lead her to a chair, made her sit down and started working on her cut the way Kate had done with her years ago. "It's all right. You won't need any stitches." Glancing up, she saw the distraught look on her aunt's face as she saw what was left of the Meissen. "Don't worry about the plate. The insurance will cover it." In a slightly scolding tone, she added, "I'm much more concerned about your carelessness in handling those broken pieces. Whatever happened to all that sage advice you used to give me when I was little?"

"I guess I wasn't thinking."

Her task done, Paige held her aunt's bandaged hand in hers. "That was my fault, wasn't it? I startled you with my announcement."

Kate stood up. As the shock began to wear off, her composure returned, and with it, enough wisdom to know that arguing with Paige any further about Jeremy would only arouse suspicions and possibly alienate her. "I must say, you don't pull any punches." To give herself something to do, she stooped and carefully picked up the broken pieces. "I suppose your answer was yes."

"It was." Taking a newspaper from a desk, Paige spread it on the floor and watched as Kate tilted the pile of broken china onto it. "I know you don't approve of my relationship with Jeremy. But you're wrong about him, Aunt Kate. He's not the man you once knew. He's changed."

In control again, Kate stood up. "Really? How?"

"In many ways. He isn't so competitive any more. He is more appreciative of little things around him, his priorities have changed." Determined to make Kate change her mind about Jeremy, she added, "He's asked me to participate in the Solstice Parade with him next week. The committee is one couple short for the jitterbug number and he signed us up.'' She laughed. ''Can you believe it? Jeremy Newman taking time for a parade? Would he have done that years ago?''

How would she know? Kate thought bitterly. He had never taken her anywhere but business lunches and out-of-the-way motels for their biweekly rendezvous. She shook her head. ''I doubt it.' Then, putting on the brightest, cheeriest smile she could manage, she opened her arms. ''I guess congratulations are in order.''

''Oh, thank you, Aunt Kate,'' Paige said, rushing into her aunt's arms and embracing her. ''You don't know how much having your blessing means to me.''

Later, long after Paige had gone home, Kate sat at her desk, fingering the locket around her neck. Inside she felt as cold and empty as she had the day Jeremy had called to say they were through.

''I won't let you marry her, Jeremy,'' she whispered fiercely as her hand tightened around the locket. ''I won't let you marry anyone.''

Although Kate had decided to keep her feelings about Paige's plans to marry Jeremy to herself, when Jeremy called at the gallery the following morning, she made no attempt to disguise the chill in her voice.

''Paige isn't here, Jeremy. I don't know when she'll be back.''

''I don't want to talk to Paige. I need to talk to you. Are you available for lunch tomorrow?''

Kate couldn't hold back a short, contemptuous laugh. They hadn't said a civil word to each other in over six years and here he was, acting as if nothing had happened, as if he still owned her. ''No, I'm not available for lunch tomorrow, Jeremy. Or any day after that. I know this is difficult for you to understand, but you're not the only one whose time is valuable.''

There was a short silence at the other end of the line as if Jeremy were trying to collect himself. But when he spoke again, his tone was just as courteous as it had been a moment ago. "Look, Kate, this wasn't my idea. But it's a *good* idea, so why don't you and I put our differences aside for a moment, and think of Paige?"

So that was it. He wanted to make peace with her, for Paige's sake. Well, why not go? It might be amusing to see how he proposed to win her over. "All right, Jeremy. I suppose I can spare you a few minutes."

"Good. Noon then? At the Biltmore?"

She smiled. Some things never changed. "The Biltmore will be fine."

Kate was already sitting at an outside table that had been reserved for them when Jeremy, punctual as always, arrived.

The moment she saw him, walking toward her in that brisk, confident stride, she felt her own self-assurance disappear as a rush of emotions ranging from love to hate threatened to betray her.

Tucking her trembling hands under the table, she continued to watch him. He hadn't changed. He was still the same handsome, alluring, confident Jeremy who had walked into Validia's twenty-four years ago and filled her head with dreams.

"Kate." Smiling affably, he took the chair across from her. Behind the dark glasses, his eyes were inscrutable. "You're looking well."

Feeling some of her poise return, she gave him a cynical smile. He was as smooth as ever. "Thank you, Jeremy. So are you."

He motioned to a waiter and ordered two glasses of Chardonnay. It amused her to see that he still liked to be in charge, still assumed that his choices need never be challenged. In a way, he reminded her very much of Eve Granger. Perhaps that was the reason they had had such an affinity for one another.

"Thank you for coming, Kate," he said, removing his sunglasses and tucking them neatly inside his jacket pocket. "I'm glad that we're both mature enough to handle this—"

"Cut the bull, will you, Jeremy, and come to the point. As I said on the phone, my time is valuable."

The smile faded, but only slightly. No matter how critical the situation, Jeremy was very good at saving face. "Very well. I'll say this as succinctly as I can. Paige doesn't know about our past relationship, and I would like it to stay that way."

"Keeping secrets from your future bride already, Jeremy?"

"I prefer to call it being practical. However, Paige has made it clear to me that she wants you and me to reconcile. In fact, she's been rather persistent about it."

Kate didn't say anything. Paige had made those same allusions to her many times in the past, and although Kate had been able to dismiss them, even ignore them, it was only a matter of time until her niece decided to be more direct.

"Well," Kate said with a shrug, "that's your problem rather than mine, don't you think? I was always willing to talk to you, if you recall. But your orders were very specific. No calls, no visits, no interference of any kind."

"I'm willing to change that now. After all, we can't keep on avoiding each other indefinitely without arousing suspicion. If we don't make at least an effort to get along, everyone will wonder why we are prolonging this feud now that we're about to become family."

That last word, and the instant image it conjured—happy relatives gathered around a Christmas tree, exchanging presents and singing Christmas carols—was so ludicrous that she laughed out loud. "Don't count your chickens before they hatch, Jeremy. You aren't married to my niece yet."

For the first time, she saw the flicker of uncertainty in his eyes, perhaps even a soupçon of fear. She liked it.

"What does that mean?" he asked.

She shrugged. "It means that anything can happen. Isn't that one of your favorite dictums, Jeremy?"

He licked his lips. "Look, I know you and I have had our differences in the past." He looked away for a moment, toward the ocean, as if searching for the right words. "And I know I have behaved somewhat unfairly toward you—"

"You behaved like a lousy son of a bitch."

He shot a quick worried glance around him. But no one was paying any attention to them. "I guess I deserved that," he said, returning his gaze to her.

"You're damn right, you do." She had imagined this scene a hundred times. But never like this. Never with this objectivity, this self-control. "You treated me like a piece of garbage," she continued. "Worse. After fifteen years of love and devotion, both of which you took gladly, you walked out of my life as if I had never existed."

"I'm sorry."

Startled, she stared at him. She had never heard him say those words before. Sorry was simply not in Jeremy Newman's vocabulary. The apology confused her. But only for a moment. Only until she looked into the dark, watchful eyes and saw the gleam of fear.

Jeremy was scared. In spite of his money and power, in spite of the hundreds of people he had intimidated over the years, he was terrified of what she knew, of what she could do to him.

She had the power to destroy him.

For a wild, insane, exhilarating moment, the thought was so irresistible, so utterly delicious, that she actually considered following through with it. How glorious it would be to see the mighty Jeremy Newman exposed to the world as a fraud, a thief, a blackmailer, to see him stripped of his precious halo. Oh, sweet, sweet revenge at last!

But too soon, Kate's euphoria was doused with a sobering dose of reality. By admitting that she had been Jeremy's lover and accomplice, and that she had been rejected for another woman, she could become the prime suspect in Adam's murder. This glorious, triumphant moment could never be—except in her imagination.

Unsuspecting of the inner battles she fought, Jeremy shot her an anxious glance. "Do you think we can make it work, Kate? Let bygones be bygones? I'm willing if you are."

It was her turn to feel smug, to feel as if she had the world by the balls. She laughed, a low, secretive laugh that brought a startled look to Jeremy's face. "No, thanks, Jeremy. Your offer comes a little too late."

"Kate, be reasonable."

"Why should I?"

"I told you. For Paige's sake."

"Paige is a big girl. She'll figure out the truth sooner or later. Or perhaps I should spare us both the suspense and tell her the truth now," she bluffed.

For a moment, their eyes locked. Jeremy seemed to be measuring her, matching her will to his, waiting for her to flinch. She didn't.

"You're bluffing," he said at last, his knowing gaze narrow and mean. "You don't have the guts to tell Paige the truth about us. And even if you did, it wouldn't make any difference. Paige would still marry me. *And,* she would finally see you as what you are—a pathetic, bitter, jilted woman."

The words hit her like a slap in the face. Although she had promised herself she wouldn't let him hurt her ever again, she was fast losing the battle. An intense rage filled her, making it difficult for her to breathe. Through the haze of tears, she saw him smile—the smile of the victorious.

"You bastard," she hissed between clenched teeth. Then, not trusting herself a moment longer, she stood up, gave him one last scathing look, and walked away.

TWENTY-SIX

It was a beautiful day for a parade.

From the corner of State Street and Ortega, where the parade was scheduled to begin, to Alameda Park, where it would end, the sidewalks were jammed with spectators, many of whom had been waiting since early morning.

Started by a Santa Barbaran fourteen years ago to celebrate the first day of summer, the Solstice Parade, a cross between Mardi Gras in New Orleans and Halloween, was one of the most colorful, spectacular events of the year, a day when flamboyance and joie de vivre reigned and when imagination knew no bounds.

Kate stood in her bedroom in front of a full-length mirror. She wore a long Hawaiian muumuu over jeans and a red polo shirt and comfortable black moccasins. In her hands she held an oversized papier-mâché dragon mask she had bought from a local craftsman yesterday.

Although she had planned to participate in the parade three days ago, she had not registered with the event organizers. Like many spectators, she would wait until the parade had reached Micheltorena Street, two blocks from the park, before joining the other marchers.

Bringing the mask to her face, she slid the elastic strap behind her head and positioned the two small holes over her eyes. Motionless, she stared at the grotesque figure in the mirror. But it was no longer her reflection she saw. It was Jeremy's. Jeremy, with his face shattered and bloody, Jeremy, as he crumpled to the ground while all around him marchers continued to mimic and dance, trampling over him.

She had been haunted by those images for three days, ever since Jeremy had mocked her at the Biltmore, humiliating her and reopening scars she thought had healed long ago.

With that smug little smile and hard, watchful gaze, he had reminded her of her father, of the way he had looked at her as he unbuckled his belt, slowly, waiting for her to beg for mercy, the way Ann always did. But Kate hadn't begged. And she wouldn't beg now.

After years of torment, years spent watching the man she loved slip farther and farther away from her, she had finally realized that to free herself of her obsession with Jeremy she had to kill him.

The Solstice Parade, in which Paige and Jeremy were participants, was the perfect place for her to carry out her task. With thousands of people crowding the streets and sidewalks, no one would notice her. No one would even hear the shot.

Stiffly, Kate moved toward her nightstand and opened the drawer. There, resting on a white handkerchief, was a Smith and Wesson .38-caliber revolver. She had bought it a couple of years ago when her neighbor, Mary Creswell, alone and asleep in her house, was robbed and nearly killed. Kate abhorred guns. But she had made herself learn all about them. And she had learned how to shoot.

She had expected to feel frightened. To feel some sort of emotion at the thought that she was about to kill the man she had loved for so long. But there was nothing. With that last insult three days ago, Jeremy had stripped her of all feelings.

Slowly, her fingers closed around the gun.

It was the last half-hour of the parade. As marchers, dancers, and floats continued to move toward Alameda Park, where the festival portion of the parade would take place, high-spirited spectators joined in, some in costumes, some not. But at this point it no longer mattered.

Her gun safely tucked inside her jeans pocket, Kate stepped into the madness. Next to her, a man in a black spider costume bowed deeply in front of her and extended his hand. After a brief hesitation, she took it. Then, following his lead, she strutted forward, improvising as she went. Putting herself on public display had never been one of her favorite endeavors. But she felt safe behind the mask. Safe and invisible.

Up ahead, Jeremy and Paige, along with a dozen other dancers, had come to a stop and were entertaining the crowd with a lively jitterbug routine they performed to the tune of Elvis Presley's "All Shook Up."

Kate had waited for this moment purposely, counting on the throng of marchers and the growing frenzy to lessen her risk of being noticed. But she would have to strike soon, before the jitterbug dancers reached the park. Once there, she'd never find them.

Still dancing, now to the rhythm of a rumba, Kate moved forward, ignoring the effort of the spider man to keep her with him.

She was less than thirty feet from them now. In order to kill Jeremy and not hurt anyone else, she would have to shoot him point blank. And she would have to do it with one shot. Crowd or not, she wouldn't get a second chance.

The heat was unbearable. Under the heavy mask, rivulets of sweat dripped into her eyes and along her cheeks. She ignored them. Soon it would all be over. She would be free. Free of Jeremy's sarcasm, his contempt, his pity. Never again would he taunt her with his conquests. Never again would he call her pathetic.

Ten feet. She could see the back of Jeremy's head, the neat haircut, the slender neck. He was a great dancer, light on his feet and graceful as he swung Paige away from him, spun her around, then took her waist again. Their dance finished, the twelve couples bowed to the crowd and continued their march toward the park.

Kate strutted closer. Five feet.

It was now or never.

As she prepared to reach for her gun, a hand closed around her wrist. With a cry of surprise, Kate whipped around. A man in lime leotards and war paint over his face grinned at her, ignored her protests, and pulled her into a circle of dancers.

"No!" she cried. "Let me go!"

But her words were drowned by the music, and within moments, a second dancer had taken her other hand. Not wanting to attract attention to herself, Kate skipped along, allowing herself to be drawn toward the center of the circle and then drawn back.

Glancing frantically over her shoulder, she saw Paige and Jeremy get farther and farther away from her.

At last, she was able to break free from the circle. Spotting one of the jitterbug dancers' black and white costumes, she ran toward him, shoving people aside, no longer caring about dancing her way through.

As she reached Alameda Park and searched the crowd, tears of frustration stung her eyes.

Jeremy was gone.

She had run all the way home. Now, exhausted from the run and overcome by emotions, she leaned against the closed door and slid to the floor.

Sometime between the park and here, she had realized the enormity of what she had almost done, the risks she had so foolishly taken. Her body shook with delayed fear. Fear for Paige, who could have been hurt, even killed. And fear for herself.

In her haste to seek revenge against Jeremy, she had overlooked the most important priority. Her own safety. What had made her think she could get away with murder? That she wouldn't be caught? That a woman running through the crowd with a gun in her hand wouldn't be noticed?

She took a deep breath, then another. Little by little, her mind cleared and her sanity returned. Hadn't this nonsense lasted long enough? she thought, removing her mask and staring at it. Wasn't it time she took control of her life? Forget about vengeance and past hurts? And above all, wasn't it time to forget Jeremy and go on?

"I can't do it!"she cried, throwing the mask across the room.

But deep within her, another voice, the same one that had helped her conquer her fears as a child, told her that she could, that she was strong and proud, that Jeremy wasn't worth going to prison for, not worth losing Paige's love.

It would take time. And willpower. But she could do it. She could free herself of Jeremy without destroying her life and the lives of the people she loved.

After awhile, Kate wiped her tears and stood up.

Matt, just back from a trip abroad, stood at his kitchen counter, debating which of Mrs. Johnson's two saran-wrapped dinners to pop into the microwave—beef bourgignon or chicken cacciatore.

Tonight the prospect of eating alone was even less appealing than usual. Maybe he should have accepted Tom DiMaggio's invitation to join him and Joan at the French Shack for dinner. Matt had been tempted, but in the mood he was in, he was certain he would have spoiled his friends' wedding anniversary celebration.

Earlier this evening, Josh had called with the news of Paige's engagement to Jeremy. "No wedding date has been set yet," Josh had added with a chuckle that failed to warm Matt's heart. "So until that little band is around her finger, it isn't too late to stop her, son. If you want to, that is."

Matt wanted to do a lot more than that. But this was a civilized country. And anyway, why should he blame Jeremy for the engagement? Paige had accepted his proposal, hadn't she? No one had held a gun to her head.

In disgust, he threw the two frozen dinners into the sink and left them there. Then, picking up his can of Bud from the counter, he went to stand by the living room window.

A summer storm had come and gone. Across the street, a toddler in a yellow slicker and matching boots ignored his father's warning and jumped into a puddle, clapping his hands in delight as water sprayed all around him.

The boy was about the age his child would have been if he had lived. His child. Matt had said those two words often during the last two years, wondering what kind of father he would have made. He knew the basics. He had learned them from Josh early in his childhood—love, kindness, patience, honesty. Had he learned them well enough to be a good role model for a young child?

Matt brought the can to his mouth and took a long swallow. He would never know now, would he? Those dreams, along with many others, were gone. Even his job had lost its sparkle. Oh, the drive was still there, and the motivation. But the pleasure and self-satisfaction he had always experienced at the close of a successful case were missing. Now all he cared about was the money.

Tom and Joan did their best to cheer him up by inviting him to the house often, and occasionally, a beautiful warm body shared his bed. But his heart wasn't in it.

"You're expecting too damned much," Tom had told him a few days ago as the two men shared a pizza in a restaurant on Seventh Avenue. "You've got to give a woman a chance to make her mark on you. And you've got to stop comparing everyone to Paige."

Was that what he was doing? Had he set her so damned high no one could touch her?

Before he could answer, the telephone rang, but he ignored it. It was probably Tom hoping to change his mind about dinner. But when he heard the voice of Dr. Rimer from the California Trauma Institute on the answering machine, Matt ran to pick up the receiver.

"I'm afraid I have bad news, Matt."

Matt's throat went dry. He closed his eyes while inside, his heart broke. For six years he had tried to prepare himself for this moment, and now that it was here, he found himself unable to face it, unwilling to accept it.

His hand tightly gripping the receiver, Matt held his breath and waited for the dreaded words.

"I'm so sorry, Matt," Dr. Rimer continued in his gentle, fatherly tone. "Your mother passed away a few minutes ago."

She had died of pneumonia, a common occurrence with patients in her condition.

Matt, who had come to CTI to say good-bye to the staff, hadn't wanted any of the dozens of presents he had bought Caroline over the last six years—perfumes she had loved, pretty jewelry, books he had read to her, a cuckoo clock that played *Bridge on the River Kwai*, her favorite tune.

"Give them away," he told a red-eyed Nurse Greenwald.

He kept the funeral small and simple. Jeremy hadn't been invited, but he came anyway, arriving halfway through the graveside services.

"What the hell is he doing here?" Matt muttered under his breath, watching the publisher take his place among the handful of mourners.

Josh's thick hand gripped Matt's shoulder. "The same thing we're all doing, son. Saying good-bye."

"I want him out of here."

"Now, Matt—"

"He's responsible for this, dammit. Maybe not directly, but he's responsible all the same. If he hadn't seduced her all over again, my father would never have needed to . . ." His voice broke.

"Easy, son." Josh's comforting grip tightened. "Easy."

After the services, as Josh talked to a valley rancher, Paul Granger came to offer Matt his condolences.

"I'm very sorry, Matt," he said, clasping his former son-in-law's hand with both of his. "If there's anything

I can do—anything at all—you'll let me know, won't you?''

"Yes, I will. Thank you, Paul." Matt's gaze moved through the dispersing crowd. "Paige didn't come with you?''

"She's in London. I couldn't reach her, but I left word at her hotel. I'm sure she'll call you as soon as she hears.''

Matt's heart sank a little lower. The thought of seeing Paige again, knowing she'd understand his grief, maybe even share it, had brought him an unexpected comfort. Besides Josh, he couldn't think of anyone he needed more right now.

He said good-bye to Paul and started walking back toward the waiting limousine.

"Matt?''

He turned to see Kate approaching. She wore a pale gray suit and a small matching hat. She had been crying, which surprised him, considering she hadn't known his mother.

Without a word, with the same gentleness he had witnessed when she had comforted Paige at the time of Ann's visit four years ago, Kate opened her arms and then folded them around him. The warm, motherly embrace was so acutely painful that all the feelings he had kept deep within himself for the last three days rose to the surface. Closing his eyes, he held on to Kate fiercely.

"Oh, Matt,'' she whispered. "If only I could take all the pain away. If only I had the power to change everything.''

He let her go but kept her hands in his. "Thanks Kate. And thanks for coming. It means a great deal to me to have you here.''

At those words, Kate felt as if someone had ripped her heart in two. Ever since learning about Caroline's death three days ago, she had spent her nights reliving the nightmare moment by moment, wondering when the suffering would finally end.

"Come,'' Matt said gently, still holding her hand. "I'll

walk you to your car. Unless you want to drive to the ranch with Josh and me. We're having a few people over. Nigel could bring you back later to pick up your car.''

Kate shook her head. She felt incapable of playing this charade a moment longer. Coming here had been difficult enough. Even more difficult than facing Jeremy, whom she hadn't seen since the near-disastrous Solstice Parade last month. "I have an important appointment, Matt. But I could stop by before you leave for New York. When will that be?''

"Tomorrow.''

"Then I'll say good-bye now.'' She hugged him again. "Take care of yourself, Matt. I love you.''

As she pulled her gray BMW from the curb, Kate saw Matt standing on the sidewalk, watching her, a small sad smile tugging at the corner of his mouth. Feeling a huge sob rise to her throat, she bit on her bottom lip and drove away.

By the time Paige returned to Santa Barbara a week later, Matt had already left.

"He's away on an assignment,'' Josh told her when she called the Canyon-T Ranch. "But I'm sure his office in New York will know where you can reach him, if you want to.''

"I don't think that will be necessary. I called to offer my condolences. I would have done it sooner, but I didn't get my father's message until a couple of days ago.''

"Would you like me to give him a message? He usually calls on Sundays.''

She was vaguely disappointed to have missed him, but after a moment of reflection, she realized it was just as well. Why reopen scars that had finally healed?

"No, no message, Josh. I'll send him a card.''

TWENTY-SEVEN

Of all the famous sidewalk cafés in Rome, none offered a more vivid and dynamic picture of what the city was all about than Doney's on Via Veneto at six o'clock in the evening.

Every day at this time, Roman motorists took their sense of the theatrical and their fiery tempers to the streets, creating not only the most extraordinary traffic jam in the world, but a spectacle not even ancient Roman gladiators could have equaled.

Ann Ludicci had witnessed this scene dozens of times during the last twenty-four years, yet she never tired of it. And now that Marcello was gone she had an even greater affinity for the city her husband had loved so much. She seldom went out these days, but meeting an old friend at Doney's for an *aperitivo* still remained one of her favorite pastimes.

This evening she had come to meet Ed Branigan, Marcello's long-time friend and attorney. Although Ed was retired now, he still looked after Ann's immense fortune and advised her as he had Marcello during his lifetime.

It was a warm July evening, and as they sat at a small table enjoying Rome's unique sights and sounds, Ed, who was usually so talkative, stared pensively into his Campari and soda.

"Have you told anyone else about this?" he asked at last, returning his attention to Ann.

She shook her head. "No. And that's the way I want it to stay, Ed. No one must know. Not even Kate."

"She's your sister, Ann. Why wouldn't you want her to know you are ill?"

"Because I don't want to burden her with my problems. She's got enough of her own right now with Paige marrying a man so totally unsuited to her." She looked away. "And besides, I don't want Kate's, or anyone's, pity. It was difficult enough telling you."

"Pity is *not* what I'm feeling for you, Ann. And Kate wouldn't either."

"You must give me your word, Ed."

As she talked, she gave him one of those deep intense gazes he had found so compelling years ago. He still did. With a sigh, Ed nodded. It wouldn't do any good to argue with her. Ann Ludicci was no longer the timid, tearful young woman he had first met. Pain and longing had long since eroded that facet of her personality. She had grown into a strong, self-confident woman who knew exactly what she wanted and how to go about getting it. "You have it," he promised.

"And you'll take care of my will right away? Write it exactly the way I told you?"

Again Ed nodded. "Word for word. First thing tomorrow morning. I'll call you when it's ready for your signature."

Ann leaned back into her chair, feeling better already. She had debated whether or not to tell her old friend about her illness, afraid it might be too much for him to accept so soon after Marcello's death. But when she had learned her brain tumor was inoperable and that she had only a few weeks left to live, she had felt it imperative to put her affairs in order.

She felt no anger or bitterness at the thought that soon she would no longer be part of a world she had come to love. And oddly, she felt no fear. Only a great sadness that Paige hadn't found it in her heart to forgive her.

"I expect my daughter will fight you on this," Ann warned. "She's quite strong, you know. And stubborn. Like her father." She smiled, reached across the table and patted his hand. "So I count on you to be firm with her, to convince her to do as I asked."

Ed, his throat too tight to say another word, covered her hand with his. Her strength astounded him. Marcello, who had adored her, had shielded her from every possible hardship over the years, allowing her to do very little for herself. Any other woman would have been lost after his death, incapable of taking charge of her life.

But from the moment Marcello had become ill, Ann had shown more strength and courage than anyone Ed knew, relying on no one but herself. He would miss her terribly.

He sighed, feeling helpless. "I wish there was something more I could do."

Ann smiled, a tender, serene sort of smile, as if for the first time in twenty-four years, she had finally found peace. "Just be there for me."

An explosion of profanities momentarily diverted their attention and Ann saw that in both directions of Via Veneto, cars, mopeds, and city buses had come to a complete stop. Everywhere men and women stood beside their vehicles, fists pounding the air, while their shouts and curses were drowned in the blaring of horns and wailing police sirens.

Perhaps because of the horrendous noise, Ann felt the pain in her head a little more than usual this evening. Taking advantage of Ed's distraction, she reached inside her purse for the pill she knew would bring her instant relief. She swallowed it quickly, washing it down with a little Coca-Cola, and by the time Ed turned back to say something about the traffic jam, she was able to smile back at him.

"But darling," Jeremy said when Paige stopped by his house on the morning of July twentieth, "I assure you there is absolutely nothing to worry about. This purchase is perfectly legitimate. Yes, those doll casts are very old, but I repeat, they are *not* classical antiquities."

"The fact remains that Henrick Zummer deals in illegally excavated antiquities, Jeremy. Doing business with a man of his reputation is unwise and dangerous.''

''A little controversy doesn't frighten me, Paige. You know that.''

Paige sighed. It was like talking to a mule. ''Then at least let me go to Munich and take a look at those casts.''

Jeremy felt a trickle of cold sweat run down his back. Christ, this was turning into a disaster. ''What for?'' he asked, struggling to hide his growing fear. ''You'll have the opportunity to inspect them when they arrive in a week or so.''

''I want to make sure they're what Zummer claims they are. And I want to make sure he's not playing games, using your name to smuggle illegal merchandise into the country. Don't look so shocked. It's been done before.''

Jeremy held back a sigh of impatience. This was his own damn fault. Not realizing Paige was in the next room, he had left the door to his study open and she had overheard part of his conversation with Henrick Zummer.

Although he had quickly covered up his carelessness by telling her he was only buying a set of antique doll casts from the German art dealer, her mistrust of the man had brought an immediate response from her. To argue any further would only arouse her suspicion more. She might even decide to share her concern with Kate. And after the murderous look the woman had given him last month at the Biltmore, he wouldn't put it past her to investigate the matter with all of her resources. Therefore, he had no choice but okay Paige's trip to Munich. Later tonight, after she was gone, he would call Zummer and warn him she was coming. Henrick would know what to do.

''I suppose there's no harm in your going to Munich,'' Jeremy conceded at last. Walking around his desk, he came to stand in front of her and gave her an apologetic smile. ''I'm sorry if I snapped at you a moment ago. But the thought of you being thousands of miles away from me, even for a couple of days, makes me crazy.''

Flattered, Paige coiled her arms around his neck, her tone light and teasing as she allowed him to draw her close. "Better to be separated for a few days than me being left at the altar while they drag you to prison for art trafficking."

"Have no fear. Only a SWAT team could keep me away from you on our wedding day. And even that is doubtful."

Paige laughed, but as she watched him walk back to his desk and make her reservations on the next flight to Munich, she felt a mild sense of unrest. She didn't like this new obsession of Jeremy's. It was true that antiquities excavated from the Turkish soil had become the rage of collectors all over the world in the last few years, but Turkish authorities were beginning to crack down on violators more and more, imposing large fines and in many instances bringing lawsuits against the perpetrators.

Paige had found out about Henrick Zummer's illegal activities three years ago when he had made headlines for smuggling a collection of rare Greek coins into the United States, where it had been bought by a wealthy Philadelphia collector. Although the collector had been heavily fined, Turkish authorities had been unable to touch Zummer.

As one of the oldest members of the antiquities mafia, Zummer and his brother, Wolf, were assisted by a network of powerful businessmen, collectors, and racketeers, whose wealth and connections knew no equal. It was that network that kept Zummer and his brother safe from Turkish authorities and even from Interpol.

"You're all set," Jeremy said, coming back and taking her in his arms again. "Your tickets will be waiting for you at the Santa Barbara airport. I wish I could pick you up when you get back, but as you know, I'm leaving for Rio at the end of the week." He took her left hand and gazed at it lovingly. "And just think, when I get back, I'll be able to slip an engagement ring on this lovely finger."

Paige laughed, touched that he cared enough to go all the way to South America to find the exact ring he wanted. "I still think Brazil is an awfully long way to go for an engagement ring."

He kissed her fingertips. "Not if you want the very best."

Munich's skies were heavy with thunderclouds when Paige arrived in the Bavarian capital on the morning of July twenty-third. As her cab sped along broad, tree-lined avenues, she peered out the window, amazed to see how, despite the addition of several modern skyscrapers, the city had managed to retain most of its former Baroque charm.

Munich, which had been no more than a small settlement in the Middle Ages, had prospered quickly over the years, thanks mostly to its salt trade. But it was its art, the legacy of kings, that had earned it its rightful place in the world, eventually attracting not only collectors and curators but traffickers and smugglers as well.

Zummer's gallery, Appolo was located on the elegant, tree-lined Maximilianstrasse, and attested to the man's success and indisputable good taste. The front room, where he greeted Paige, was filled with Greek and Roman antiquities, some legal, others probably not. But then again, in Munich, the difference was inconsequential.

Henrick Zummer, whom Paige had called earlier this morning, greeted her with German formality, clicking his heels as he shook her hand. Sleek, dapper, and cultivated, he presented the picture of the perfect businessman and seemed to be as much a pillar of his community as Jeremy was in San Francisco.

"I hope you aren't taking offense at my visit, Herr Zummer."

"Not at all. I'm sure that under the circumstances I would be doing the same thing." As he talked, he watched her. Jeremy had warned him on the telephone yesterday that she was shrewd and knowledgeable. And while he agreed that a man, perhaps many men, could lose themselves in those beautiful blue eyes, Henrick reminded himself that beautiful women almost always spelled trouble.

"May I be the first to offer you my congratulations on your success?" he said, leading her into a backroom where two men were unpacking wooden crates. "I followed the Santa Barbara Fair with great interest last month. I would have gladly participated, but, unfortunately, I had a previous engagement that week. Perhaps next year."

Paige held back a smile. Since the Greek coins scandal, his activities and business travel had been restricted to Germany. Should he attempt to cross any border, he would be immediately arrested.

Zummer stopped in front of a crate and snapped his fingers at the two men, indicating he wanted this one opened. "As I told you on the telephone earlier," he said, turning back to Paige. "The casts arrived yesterday and I haven't had a chance to check them out yet. But I'm certain everything will be in order. The people I deal with in Istanbul are very reliable."

As Paige had expected, the contents of the crate revealed exactly what Jeremy had described—a pair of exquisite doll casts dating back to the seventeenth century.

Without Paige asking him to do so, Zummer went to a desk, sorted quickly through a stack of papers, and came back holding several documents for her to inspect. Everything, from the bill of lading, to export permits, to value declaration forms, was in perfect order, dated, signed, and sealed by half a dozen Turkish and German officials.

Paige handed everything back to him and nodded. "I'm glad to see that everything is in order. I take it the casts are ready to go?"

Zummer nodded.

"Very well. In that case I'd like the crate to be resealed and taken to the airport immediately." She watched Zummer's face closely for a suspicious reaction on his part. But other than a legitimate concern for the artwork, there was none.

"But Mrs. McKenzie, the cargo flight to San Francisco won't leave for another three days. The thought of a shipment of this value sitting in an airport storage room—"

"It won't. I've made arrangements with airport officials to keep the crate under twenty-four hour security until it leaves." She gave him a sweet smile. "You have no objections to this sudden change of plan, do you, Herr Zummer?"

"None at all." His expression hardly changing, Zummer said a few words in German to his men, who immediately stopped what they were doing and started sealing Jeremy's crate.

Paige's intentions had been to take the crate back to the States with her, or arrange for it to be shipped soon after that. But with an air-traffic controllers' strike that had gone into effect a few hours ago, dozens of flights had already been canceled, including her own. While she had been able to make arrangements to drive to Zurich and return to the States from there, Jeremy's crate, a lower priority, would have to fly out as originally planned.

"Thank you, Herr Zummer," she told him as the two men carried the crate outside, where her limousine was waiting. "I appreciate your help."

Zummer bowed his head as he shook her hand. Her request was only a minor inconvenience. It would require another trip to the airport later on, and another bribe to get the crate reopened and Jeremy's actual purchase, a scene of "Hercules' Twelve Labors," substituted.

Considering he had just made a five-thousand-dollar commission for a day's work, he wasn't going to worry about another hour or two.

That same afternoon in New York, Tom DiMaggio, who had just returned from Munich himself, where he had been investigating the disappearance of several pieces of antiquities, walked into Matt's office looking somber.

"I just found out something while I was in Munich I think you ought to know," he told Matt.

Seeing the serious expression on his friend's face, Matt dropped the file he had been studying back on his desk. "I'm listening."

"It's about Paige."

Matt fought to keep his expression unchanged. "What about Paige?"

"I'm afraid she might be mixed up with Henrick Zummer."

Matt, who knew about Zummer's reputation as a smuggler and a high-ranking member of the Munich antiquities mafia, sat up. "That's impossible!"

When Tom had finished telling him about his findings, Matt thought about it for an entire day. He told himself it was none of his business. Paige was out of his life. Gone. Why should he give a damn about anything? And besides, if she was stupid enough to play those dangerous games, she deserved to be caught.

At four o'clock the following afternoon, he called the TWA reservation desk at Kennedy Airport and asked to be booked on the next flight to Munich.

TWENTY-EIGHT

August 3, 1991

The sun had disappeared behind the horizon and a cold gust of wind blew across the private beach. Paige shivered and glanced at her watch. Almost six-thirty. In a little over an hour, the first of her guests would be arriving, and she had been sitting here all this time, daydreaming about Matt.

Running the fingers of both hands through her hair, she rested her forehead on top of her drawn-up knees, unable to shake off the nostalgia. What was it about her past that she couldn't forget it? That it kept coming back to her in small doses? Or, like today, in large doses.

Why couldn't she get it through her head that the part of her life that had belonged to Matt was over? She had to concentrate on Jeremy now, on the new and many challenges that awaited her—like running the Newman Foundation, which Jeremy had asked her to do a few days ago.

She had been astonished, and flattered, by the offer, by the fact that Jeremy had enough faith in her to give her such an important job. The responsibilities no longer frightened her, as they had at first. She knew she could do it. She already had dozens of ideas on how to change the organization's structure so it would run more efficiently, ideas she couldn't wait to share with Jeremy.

Of course, being president of the Newman Foundation was a full-time job and would seriously curtail her activities as an art consultant. But so what? Weren't new challenges what life was all about? Wasn't the foundation worth any job?

Dammit, she thought, hitting her knee with her fist. Why couldn't she muster a little more enthusiasm? What in the world was *wrong* with her tonight?

"Paige!"

She looked up. "Yes, Maria?"

"Telephone. It's Señor Newman. He is back from Brazil."

"Thank God," Paige muttered, standing up and brushing off the sand from the seat of her pants. The thought of him being so far away was probably what had put her in that strange mood. Now that he was back, everything would be fine. Everything would fall back into place.

Feeling her mood lift already, she smiled and ran upstairs to take the call.

Old Spanish Days, held every August during the harvest moon, was a Santa Barbara tradition that had begun more than half a century ago. Since then, Fiesta, as locals called it, had grown into a full-fledged festival, a four-day, fun-filled event that recalled the legendary days of the Spanish dons and the region's colorful history.

Paige, in an ecru lace dress that had belonged to Mindy's Spanish grandmother, stood on the lower deck, happy to see that her efforts of the past few days had paid off so well.

It was a wonderful night for a party. With the ocean only a few steps away and a west breeze blowing, the air smelled and tasted of the sea.

On the upper deck, the buffet table brimmed with American and Mexican specialties, and of course, Maria's famous chili, without which no family gathering was complete. From the glowing barbecue, the aroma of sizzling prime steaks permeated the night, while on the beach, guitar players in Mexican costumes strolled, entertaining the more than one hundred guests.

All had come in their finest attire—the men in *ranchero* or *vaquero* costumes and the ladies in elegant Spanish gowns.

"It's a lovely party, Paige."

Before she could turn around, she felt the gentle pressure of Jeremy's hand on her back, sliding down to rest just above the swell of her hip.

She smiled. "Mmmm. Praise from the master. I'm flattered."

"Oh, I'm afraid my talents as a host pale in comparison to yours, my dear." He moved closer, his arm now encircling her slender waist. "Look at those people. Even the help are having fun."

Paige followed his gaze and laughed as Congressman McDermott, an old friend of her father, took hold of Maria as she passed by. Ignoring her protests, he led her into a lively paso-doble while the crowd clapped in time with the music.

Jeremy let his gaze return to Paige. How lovely she looked tonight, he thought, studying his fiancée's perfect profile and feeling his desire for her grow. She was as seductive and mysterious as Michelangelo's Mona Lisa, as elusive as a rare jewel.

"I've missed you," he murmured.

Paige gave his hand an affectionate pat before extricating herself from his hold. "I'm glad you were able to get back in time, Jeremy. It wouldn't have been the same without you."

"And Rio wasn't any fun without you, my love." He brought her left hand to the light. "Have I told you how spectacular this ring looks on you?"

Smiling, Paige glanced down at her finger, half of which was concealed by an enormous black pearl, no doubt one of the rarest varieties, surrounded by twelve full-cut diamonds. It wasn't a ring she would have chosen for herself. But then her lack of appreciation for fine jewelry was legendary.

"It's lovely," she said, thinking her grandmother would have approved. Then, feeling the wind shift and grow colder, she shivered.

Jeremy wrapped an arm around her shoulders. "Are you cold?"

"A little." On the top deck, Maria was already turning on the outdoor heaters.

"I'll go get your wrap."

She stopped him. "No, let me. I need to talk to the
caterers anyway." She kissed him. "Why don't you go
say hello to my father? He's just arrived. I'll be right
back."

Jeremy watched her walk away. With that thin, lacy
dress clinging to her delicious curves, she had every head
turning, every male in sight fantasizing.

Soon, he thought with a little chuckle, Paige would be
Mrs. Jeremy Newman, and then at last *his* fantasy would
become a reality. And when they returned from their
honeymoon, he'd concentrate on building their dream
house—his dream house.

Now that he had purchased the Smith property, from
which Josh McKenzie bought his water—or should he say
used to buy his water—it wouldn't be long until the
Canyon-T Ranch began to show signs of real trouble.

In another few weeks, Josh would be *begging* Jeremy
to buy his ranch.

Watching her reflection in her bedroom mirror, Paige
adjusted one of her grandmother's shawls around her
shoulders, feeling a twinge of regret that Eve wasn't here.
She would have been proud tonight. Proud of the tradition Paige was carrying, proud of the way she looked, of
the man she was about to marry.

Idly, her hand went to smooth her hair, which she had
pulled back in an old-fashioned Spanish chignon and secured with a large tortoise-shell comb. *The man she was
about to marry.* What an odd way to put it. Why hadn't
she simply said "Jeremy"? Or "the man she loved"?

"Hello, Paige."

The sound of Matt's voice behind her had the effect of
an ice-cold shower. Or a bomb. She wasn't sure which.
Drawing a sharp intake of breath, Paige spun around. He
stood just inside the French doors, his tall shape framed
against the night sky, looking the same as he had two

years ago. With those snug blue jeans, white crewneck sweater and his inseparable L.A. Rams hat perched on the back of his head, it was as if time had stood still.

"What are you doing here?"

"Looking for you." Although his voice was steadier than Paige's, deep down Matt's emotions were on a roller coaster. His decision to crash his exwife's party had been another one of his impulses. One he had regretted the moment he had seen Paige and Jeremy standing together on the deck, embracing.

He had been about to leave when he had seen her make her way toward the house. Unable to resist the urge to see her, to talk to her, if only for a moment, he had followed her.

Watching as she took a step back, he found himself fighting another urge—that of taking her in his arms and kissing her senseless. Even with that severe Andalusian hairstyle, she looked fabulous. And with that flush in her cheeks and the mild panic in her eyes, she looked soft and vulnerable. Like the Paige he knew. The Paige he loved.

"This is a private party, Matt. By invitation only. And I don't recall inviting you."

"Now is that a way to greet a neighbor at Fiesta time? What happened to the motto *Mi casa es su casa?*"

Paige watched him step into the light. As he pulled off his hat an unruly strand of blond hair fell over his forehead. With a gesture that was as ineffective as it was familiar, he raked his fingers through it and grinned— that same slightly lopsided grin that had worn down her resistance four years ago in Venice. Chosing to ignore his question, she said, "What do you want?"

He shrugged. "To say hello. To see how you are. To let you know I was back."

"Why should I care?"

"No reason, I guess. I just thought since we were bound to run into each other sooner or later, we might as well meet on familiar ground."

"Why?"

"I thought it'd be less awkward." His eyes swept over the room, taking in each detail, which was forever engraved in his heart—the solid and simple blond pine furniture, the huge wool wall hanging they had bought together in the Napa Valley, the king-size bed where they had spent the first three days of their honeymoon, only coming out to shower and eat.

"I see you haven't changed anything."

She blushed, because for months now she had been meaning to redecorate, to rid herself of everything that reminded her of him, but for one reason or another, she had kept putting it off. "I haven't had the time." Her tone brittle, she added, "And now that you have taken your little trip down memory lane, will you please leave so that I can return to my guests?"

"What's the matter, darling? Is Old Money Bags keeping you on a time clock?"

"I'm not going to discuss Jeremy with you, Matt."

As she spoke, Matt's gaze fell on her ring. God, how could he have missed it? It was the ugliest, most obnoxious ring he had ever laid eyes on. How could she even think of wearing something like this for the rest of her life? Paige hated flashy jewelry. Her taste had always leaned toward the unexpected, the quirky. Never the ostentatious.

"When is the big day?" he asked casually.

She didn't miss the mocking light in his eyes as he finally pulled his gaze from her left hand, and for a wild moment she was filled with an irresistible urge to laugh with him. "Jeremy and I are getting married on November eleventh."

"Armistice Day. How romantic." He gave her an ironic smile. "Your choice?"

"Not that it's any of your business, but the decision was mutual." Why was she lying? What difference did it make that Jeremy had picked the date?

He leaned against her dresser. He was close enough now for her to smell his after-shave. Paco Rabanne. It was the fragrance she had bought him shortly after arriving in New York. Intrigued by the suggestive magazine ads she had seen in *Vogue*, she had stopped at Bergdorf one Friday afternoon after work and had bought it for him.

"It's made for you," she had told him after she had splashed a little of the crisp, lovely fragrance on his face.

He had given her one of his slow, lazy smiles, the kind that always led her astray. "And why is that?"

"Because it's bold and sexy—like you."

They had spent half the night making love, and in the morning, when she had awakened, Matt was standing by the side of the bed, a breakfast tray in his hand and a red rose between his teeth. By the time they had remembered the western omelette, it was cold.

Matt picked up a small, silver-framed snapshot of Jeremy in polo gear from the dresser and looked at it for a few seconds. "Do you love him?" he asked as he put the photograph back.

She was so startled by the question that she took a second or two to answer. "Of course I do. Jeremy is everything I want in a man. He's strong, reliable, protective."

"Sounds like you're describing a bulwark, darling, not the man you love."

He pulled away from the dresser, and came toward her, his step unhurried. "You shouldn't wear your hair that way. It makes you look much too serious."

She took a step back. "I stopped asking your opinion on how to wear my hair long ago."

"A pity." He reached out and pulled the comb from her careful chignon, gave her hair a light tousle with his hand until it cascaded around her shoulders. "There, that's much better." Then, without warning, he wrapped one arm around her waist and yanked her to him.

"Have you gone completely mad?" Paige gasped. "Let go of me!"

Before she could stop him, his mouth crushed hers. His fingers sank into her hair, pulling her head back, forcing her to bend backward and strain against him.

Furious, she tried to break free, but he was holding her in an ironlike grip. Breathless, she opened her mouth and immediately met the velvety softness of his tongue. Heat speared through her, making it impossible for her brain to transmit the proper messages to her body.

Needs and sensations invaded her instead—desire, stirrings, a quiver that began at her fingertips and jolted down to her toes. Crushed against his chest, she could feel his heart hammering. And hers.

Her hands, which had been balled up into fists against his chest, ready to pound on it, relaxed and opened.

And then he let her go. The release was so sudden, so unexpected that she staggered back, met the edge of the bed and fell on it.

"Tell me that old fart downstairs gets that kind of reaction from you and I'll believe you love him." Then, walking toward the dresser, Matt picked up his Rams hat and put it on his head, sliding it back and forth a few times until it fit snugly, at the right angle. He smiled, looking as unruffled as if he had just finished a quiet round of bridge. "See you around, darling."

Paige sat on the bed and watched him walk across the room and out the French doors in his long, easy stride. With trembling fingers she touched her mouth, still feeling the burning stroke of his lips, smelling the familiar after-shave. She was filled with an inexplicable sense of loss. As the roar in her ears subsided, she heard the din of voices, the sound of laughter and music coming from outside. A moment ago she had felt like dancing.

Lowering her head in her hands, she felt the tears come.

TWENTY-NINE

It was funny, Matt thought as he hung up the phone in his grandfather's upstairs study, how much one could learn with the slightest bit of ingenuity. In the last forty-eight hours, he had come across some interesting information regarding Jeremy Newman, information that more and more strengthened his belief that San Francisco's most upstanding citizen was up to his neck in the dealing of stolen art.

It wasn't anything he could use as concrete proof—unless one counted innuendos and disparaging remarks from envious collectors and art dealers who weren't important enough to be part of the Newman network. Nonetheless, the data helped him form a clearer picture of the real Jeremy Newman and gave him an idea of how far he might go to fulfill his ambitions.

It was with great reluctance that Matt had dismissed Kate as a possible source of information. Once, he had wondered about Paige's aunt and the part she had played in Jeremy's quest for greatness. But by the time he had met Paige, Kate's association with the publisher had been over for two years and Matt hadn't given it another thought.

He had no doubt that her past friendship with Jeremy would have brought a new slant on his investigation, but to question her now, even subtly, would be too dangerous. If she were guilty of past fraud, she wasn't about to tell him anything he could use. If she weren't, she would most likely mention his visit to Paige and his cover would be blown to bits.

Fortunately, he had found an excellent, and most willing, ally in the person of Arlene Lassiter of the Lassiter Gallery in San Francisco. Remembering what Paige had once told him about the woman's bitterness toward Jeremy for ignoring her all those years, Matt had paid her a visit on the pretext that he wanted to take a closer look at a set of antique coasters he had seen in her window.

She had recognized his name instantly and had sauntered out of her back office, charm oozing out of every pore, her sharp little eyes taking him in from head to toe. Before he could think of a way to steer the conversation toward Jeremy, she had opened that door herself.

"I was so sorry to hear you and Paige were divorced," she told him in that syrupy tone Paige despised. "The two of you made such a handsome couple. And Paige seemed so happy in those days, so relaxed and carefree. Much more so than she is now, with Jeremy."

Matt had bought the coasters, and somehow they had ended up at the Fairmont Hotel for a drink. There he had learned about Carter Lawson, the San Francisco art dealer who had helped Jeremy put that Veracruz collection together four years ago. The same collection Paige had exposed as a forgery.

"Of course, no one was ever able to prove Lawson had anything to do with the actual fraud," Arlene told him over a second very dry martini. "But I always thought the disappearance of that forger *and* the Mexican dealer as well was just a bit much. Besides, there's something about Carter Lawson I don't trust."

Investigating the Veracruz forgery might have proved interesting, but it wasn't Matt's field. And it would have taken too much time. His number-one priority at the moment was to expose Jeremy for the thief he was and get him to admit Paige's innocence in his most recent purchase—the antiquity piece from Istanbul. One of his first thoughts had been to search Jeremy's house and find where he hid the stolen goods. But Josh had quickly discouraged him.

"You'd have about as much chance of setting foot into

that fortress unnoticed as you would getting into Fort Knox,'' he had told him.

Trying to bribe Chu Seng, who had been in Jeremy's employ for over thirty years, or interrogating gallery owners who might alert Jeremy, would prove equally futile. Another alternative was to wait until the man made a mistake, but Matt hadn't liked that idea any more than he liked the others.

Resting his elbows on the desk, Matt raked his fingers through his hair. Was he too close to this case? he wondered, trying to remain objective. Was he trying too hard, not seeing the obvious? What good were these bits of information he kept unearthing, if he couldn't put them all together and solve the damn puzzle?

On his desk was a yellow pad where he had jotted down notes and drawn diagrams only he understood. It always helped him to look at a case on paper, see who was connected to whom and how. But today, the familiar exercise failed to light that much-needed spark. As he stared at the pad, all he saw was a combination of diagrams and notes that led nowhere.

The only positive news he had received since starting his investigation was that the crate containing the Turkish antiquity had been safely delivered to Newman's house an hour ago, without Interpol finding out about its true contents. For the time being, Paige was safe.

Feeling restless, he stood up and walked over to the window. Maybe he should step back from the case for a day or two, give himself time to see it more clearly. He wasn't in any hurry, was he? Tom had told him to take all the time he needed. And besides, Matt thought, suddenly remembering he'd promised Josh to help him with that broken fence in the south pasture, he was beginning to like it here. Very much.

Standing in his foyer, trembling with an excitement that had been building for days, Jeremy watched as Chu Seng unsealed the crate that had just been delivered.

In spite of the ill-timed air-traffic controller's strike in

Germany, everything had gone like clockwork. After Paige's visit to Henrick Zummer's gallery two weeks ago, the German art dealer had waited until she had safely left Munich before returning to the airport. There he had bought the cooperation of two airport officials, both of whom he had worked with before, reopening the crate and switching its contents.

Explaining to Paige that he had canceled the doll casts order was trickier. For a moment, her eyes had been filled with a mixture of surprise, irritation that her time had been wasted, and suspicion. It was only after he told her he had decided to take her advice after all and not do any more business with Zummer that she had mellowed.

"Careful, Chu Seng, careful," he said now as his servant reached down into the heavy straw packing and retrieved a large Styrofoam box.

Holding his breath, Jeremy waited until the box was on the floor before lifting the lid. For several seconds, he stood transfixed. Under his eyes lay the exquisite white marble carving of Hercules' third labor—the capture of the Arcadian stag.

"Marvelous," he whispered, not daring to pull the heavy object out of the box, but trailing his fingers over its surface. "Look at it, Chu Seng. Not a mark on it."

Chu Seng, a diminutive man with a weathered Oriental face and a few wisps of gray hair on his head, nodded. "It's very beautiful, Mr. Newman. Congratulations." Then, as Jeremy continued to admire the carving, he asked, "Do you want to keep it in the drawing room for awhile, or will you be taking it downstairs right away?"

"Oh, no, I can't keep it up here. It's too dangerous." He stood up. "You bring it down, Chu Seng. My hands are shaking too much."

With Chu Seng in tow, Jeremy hurried down to the basement and along a short hallway at the end of which was an intricately carved black lacquer Chinese secretary. Reaching inside one of its many drawers, he pressed a button and almost immediately the heavy piece of furniture slid to the side, revealing a door to which only he and Chu Seng, whom he trusted with his life, had a key.

Pulling a set of keys from his pocket, he selected one, opened the door, and reached for a light switch on the wall. He had been coming into this room every week for the last thirty years, yet everytime he entered it, he felt the same breathless excitement; the same exhilaration; and sometimes, although rarely, an almost irresistible urge to tell the world of the wonders that lay within those four walls.

It was shortly after he had acquired his first stolen painting, Van Gogh's *Breton Women*, that he'd had the idea of transforming the forgotten storage room into a secret gallery. Chu Seng's uncle, who had died five years ago, had done all the work, installed the track lighting, a mirror to give the room a sense of space, and a special air-conditioning system that kept the interiors dust and moisture free.

His chest swelling with pride, Jeremy let his gaze roam across the room for a moment. On the walls were paintings from the world's greatest artists—da Vinci, Rembrandt, Monet, and Picasso. But there were other treasures as well—a Fabergé column clock carved from Siberian jade, a porcelain cake basket made for Catherine the Great in 1777, a Sèvres bust of Louis XV. On a small table in the center of the room was Jeremy's favorite item to date—a pair of eighteen-karat candelabras that had mysteriously disappeared from Versailles the night Marie Antoinette had fled from the revolutionary troops and that had surfaced again two centuries later in a Vienna art gallery.

In a corner of the room was the first piece of classical antiquity he had purchased from Henrick Zummer—a life-sized statue of Eros, excavated from the Roman city of Aphrodisias in southwestern Turkey.

"Over there, Chu Seng. Next to Eros," Jeremy said, pointing to a spot next to the Greek God. "Later I'll decide how to best display it."

When he went back upstairs twenty minutes later, Chu

Seng had already cleaned out the foyer and removed the crate. Whistling happily, Jeremy went to get ready for a reception the San Francisco symphony was giving in his honor.

Life had never been so good.

Sitting in her father's chambers, Paige watched him slip out of his black robe and hang it on a hook. Although he had greeted her with his usual cheerfulness, there was a preoccupied look in his eyes, which, she suspected, was the reason for his phone call earlier today.

"I hope you don't mind my asking you to stop by," Paul said, turning back to her. Ignoring the big leather chair behind his desk, he came to sit directly across from Paige. "I know you're a busy lady these days."

Paige smiled. "If that remark is meant to remind me I don't come to see you as often as I should, I plead guilty."

"Never plead guilty, darling. It puts good lawyers out of business."

"All right. In that case, I *have* been busy. Between the preparations for the wedding and the honeymoon, which Jeremy left entirely up to me, I hardly have time to put in a decent day's work at the gallery."

Paul watched her in silence. Jeremy was exactly what he wanted to talk to Paige about. But now that she was here, sounding and looking so happy, he felt like a meddling old fool.

"Daddy, what's the matter?" Paige asked. "Why the serious look?"

Seeing no reason to delay the matter any longer, Paul met his daughter's inquiring gaze. "I had lunch with an old friend of mine yesterday. You may remember him. Ben Johnson?"

She nodded. Ben, one of her father's classmates at Harvard, was now a successful Santa Inez Valley attorney. "Don't tell me. He bragged about his son the neurosurgeon the whole time, and wouldn't give you a chance to brag about me."

The quip failed to bring a smile to Paul's lips. "On the contrary. We talked about you a great deal. And about Jeremy."

Paige stiffened. Her father had never hidden the fact that he disapproved of her marriage to Jeremy, and although he had more or less resigned himself to the fact that it was going to happen, she knew that deep down, he wished it wouldn't. "Does Ben know Jeremy?" she asked cooly.

"Not personally." He paused briefly before adding, "Did you know that Jeremy had bought the Smith Ranch?"

Paige gave him a startled look. "No, I didn't. When did he do that?"

"This past Wednesday. Ben represented Arnie Smith in the transaction."

Paige smoothed a pleat in her navy skirt. "Why are you telling me this, Daddy?"

"Because this purchase is affecting someone for whom you care very much—Josh Mckenzie."

More puzzled than ever, Paige looked up. "How?"

"Five years ago," Paul continued. "When Josh's water supply dried up due to the drought, he went to Jeremy and asked if he could buy his excess water. Jeremy refused."

Although she didn't miss the implication in that last remark, Paige chose to ignore it. "The drought has affected everyone, Daddy. I'm sure Jeremy didn't turn Josh down because he didn't want to help him, but because his own supply had diminished as well."

Paul shook his head. "Jeremy gets his water from a spring-fed lake, which in all probability will never run dry. He's always had plenty of water. Enough to supply a farm ten times the size of his. When Josh realized he'd never get water from Jeremy, he went to Arnie and the two men made a deal—an expensive deal, but it allowed Josh to save what was left of his cattle and keep the ranch going."

"Is there a point to all this?"

Paul's gaze didn't flinch. "The point is, now that Jeremy owns the Smith Ranch, he has refused to continue the arrangement Josh had with Arnie. Which means that without water, Josh will be bankrupt within a couple of months."

Paige was stunned. Although she was aware that the drought had affected the Canyon-T Ranch hardest because of its size, she had never suspected it was that serious. "Why will Josh go bankrupt? Why can't he just sell his cattle and wait out the drought the way many other ranchers are doing?"

"Because he borrowed heavily over the last few years, perhaps more than he should have. Until now, it wasn't a problem, but without his income from ranching, he won't be able to repay his latest loan, which is substantial, and due in sixty days."

"What are you saying?"

"I'm saying that Josh is going to be left with only two options—to let the bank foreclose on his ranch. Or to sell."

"What about Matt? Can't he help his grandfather?"

"I suspect Matt doesn't have the kind of money Josh needs, or he would have already paid off Josh's loan."

Paige fell back against her chair, absorbing the shock. "I had no idea Josh was in such trouble." When she looked up at her father again, her eyes were filled with reproach. "But to hold Jeremy responsible, to think that he would turn away from a neighbor in need, is ridiculous." As if to reinforce her own convictions as well as her father's, she shook her head. "No, I don't believe for one moment Jeremy would do anything so heartless."

"He would if he had something to gain."

"Like what?"

"Like the Canyon-T Ranch. According to Ben, Jeremy has been trying to buy that property for years. But Josh has kept turning him down. Jeremy has no use for the Smith Ranch. He bought it for only one reason—to cut off Josh's water supply so he would go bankrupt and be forced to sell."

Paige sprang out of her chair. "That's a damn lie!"

"No, darling. Ben—"

"Stop it! I won't hear another of your malicious accusations." Her eyes filled with tears. "I'm so disappointed in you, Daddy. To think you would stoop this low just to get me to break up with Jeremy . . ."

"Paige, believe me, that wasn't my intention."

"Oh, please don't try to deny it. You've never liked Jeremy. And you would do anything for this wedding not to happen. Well, your little stunt won't work, Daddy. Regardless of what your friend told you, *I* don't believe Jeremy would willfully drive Josh Mckenzie—or anyone—to bankruptcy."

"I don't deny that I have reservations about you and Jeremy. But, dear God, do you think I would make up something like this just to get you to change your mind?"

"Then why did you tell me?"

"Because it's too important for you not to know—considering how you feel about Josh."

"Did it ever occur to you that Jeremy might have wanted to tell me himself?"

Paul shook his head. "I don't think so, Paige. This is one transaction he wouldn't have discussed with you until *after* the wedding."

Paul saw the angry look in her eyes, and knew he had gone too far. But it was too late to back down now. "You will ask him about it, won't you? Soon?"

"And embarrass him? Let him see just how much this family hates him?" She shook her head. "I don't think so." Yanking her purse from his desk, she stalked across the room and toward the door, waiving him aside as he tried to stop her. "If you have any more dark revelations about my fiancé, save your breath. I'm not interested."

"If you won't talk to Jeremy, then at least talk to Josh. Will you do that? He'll tell you if what I told you is true or just idle gossip."

Paige gave him a withering look. "That's exactly what I intend to do."

Then, with a curt nod rather than the usual kiss, she walked out.

"You're not eating your fish, girl," Josh said, smiling at Paige across their table as they ate lunch at Alexander's Copenhagen Inn in Solvang. "Not that I blame you," he added, cutting through a thick, juicy steak. "Nothing beats a good piece of beef for taste and nutrition."

Paige smiled. "Spoken like a true cattleman."

"And don't you forget it." He gave her another thoughtful look as he ate. "Are you going to tell me what's bothering you?"

"You know me too well, Josh."

"That I do. You and I have been friends for a long time, Paige. You were much more to me than Matt's wife, you know. In a way, you were the daughter Millie and I always wanted." He took a sip of his whiskey and soda. "If only she'd had a chance to know you, I guarantee she would have loved you as much as I do."

Paige's smile felt tight, unnatural. "I love you too, Josh." She was silent for a moment, pushing her broiled flounder back and forth on her plate. "I went to see my father yesterday," she began.

"How is the good judge?"

"Fine." She watched him lather a thick slice of sourdough bread with butter. "He was talking to a friend of his a couple of days ago, an attorney who practices right here in the valley."

Josh watched her as he ate, wondering where in the world this conversation was leading to. He had never seen the kid looking so troubled.

"He found out something about the Canyon-T Ranch, Josh. Something I'd like to verify with you."

Josh put his knife down. "And what's that?"

She told him about her conversation with Paul the day before and how she had refused to believe the part Jeremy had played in the real estate transaction. When she was finished, she searched Josh's eyes. "Is any of this true, Josh?"

He gave her a speculative glance. One didn't need the brain of an Einstein to see how much she wanted him to deny the story. After all, they were talking about her fiancé, a man she trusted and respected, a man she thought was as fair and generous as the press made him out to be. If Josh had thought for one moment that Jeremy was good for her, he might have been tempted to bail the bastard out, for he truly loved that girl like a daughter and wanted to see her happy.

But dammit, any fool could see she had nothing in common with that old fox. And since it was now in his power to make her see that, and perhaps increase his grandson's chances with her, he had no intention of holding back the truth.

"I'm afraid all of it is true, Paige. I knew what Jeremy was up to from the beginning, because shortly after my first call for help five years ago, he came down and made me an offer on my ranch, which of course I turned down. I went back to him many times after that, hoping he'd change his mind about the water. But he didn't. And each time he kept coming back with a higher offer for the Canyon-T. By buying the Smith Ranch and cutting off my water supply, he figures I won't be able to last much longer."

Paige took a bite of flounder although she was no longer hungry. "Why would Jeremy want your ranch?"

"Supposedly, to retire, raise a little cattle."

"You don't sound as if you believe him."

Josh chuckled. "I've known the man for a lot of years, Paige. And I know that when he wants something as badly as he wants my ranch, he's got to have a damn good reason for it. And this retirement crap he fed me is just that—crap."

"Then what's the real reason?"

Josh twirled the ice in his drink. "Years ago, there was a rumor floating around this valley that Jeremy Newman was looking for a site to build a home. No, not a home. A palace, I think the word was—yes, a palace—that would rival the one Hearst built in San Simeon." He shook his head in wonder. "If I had heard that about anyone else, I would have said it was garbage. But knowing Jeremy as I do, I'm inclined to believe it."

So did she, Paige thought, pushing the rest of her lunch away. Building a house like the Hearst castle was a dream Jeremy had shared with her many times in the past. The only part he had failed to mention was that he intended to build it on Josh McKenzie's land.

Her feelings kept vacillating between disappointment and denial. How could the Jeremy she knew be so ruthless? So insensitive to the needs and dreams of another man? A man he claimed to admire so much.

"But surely you can get water elsewhere?" she asked Josh.

He shook his head. "In the last couple of days, Matt and I have traveled up and down this entire valley in search of it. Water just isn't available, Paige. At any price."

She dreaded asking him the next question, but knew she had to. If she were going to talk to Jeremy as she now knew she would, she needed to have all the facts. "Has Jeremy made you another offer since he bought the Smith ranch?"

"He called me the same day he signed the papers. This time, however, his offer went down instead of up."

Paige was silent. She thought about the long evenings she had spent at the ranch, sitting at Josh's feet, listening to his cowboy stories. Ranching was the only thing Josh had ever wanted to do, the only thing he knew. For the last sixty years, it had been his lifeline and an immense source of pride. To give it all up now would kill him.

As if reading her thoughts, Josh reached across the table and took her hand. "Don't you worry about this old cowboy now, you hear? I've got a tough hide. And I've got Matt. Between the two of us, we'll find a way to keep the ranch." He shook her hand. "Come on. Give me a big smile."

She was still smiling and waving as he drove away in his battered Ford pickup. But deep inside, she could already feel the first pinch of helplessness. She knew Jeremy well enough by now to believe that once he had set his eyes on something he wanted, whether it was a work of art or a property, he never let go.

THIRTY

By the time Paige landed at San Francisco Airport that same afternoon, any protective feelings she'd had toward Jeremy earlier had disappeared.

She had tried to maintain her objectivity during the flight up. She had even tried to convince herself that Josh's story might not be entirely true. Not because he had deliberately lied to her, but because he was getting old, and old people sometimes got their facts mixed up.

She had rejected that thought almost immediately. No one was more sane and more sure of his facts than Josh McKenzie.

During the taxi ride from the airport to the house on Pacific Heights, she tried to focus on the many pleasant aspects of her relationship with Jeremy, on his generosity, his attentiveness, his understanding. But each time, a darker picture of the man superimposed itself over that image and she would lose her concentration.

When Chu Seng opened the door, Paige barely gave him time to greet her. "I want to see Mr. Newman, Chu Seng," she said. "Right away."

Moments later, Jeremy was hurrying down the staircase, his expression a mixture of astonishment and concern. "Paige! Chu Seng said you were upset. Why? What happened?"

She waited until he had reached the bottom of the staircase and stood in front of her, before giving him the full brunt of her fury. "How could you do this!"

He stared at her, astounded that so much rage could be directed at him. "How could I do *what*?"

"Buy the Smith ranch and cut off Josh McKenzie's water supply."

Stunned, Jeremy could only look at her. "Who told you that?"

"Then it's true?"

It had to be Josh, he thought bitterly. The bastard had gone to her with his sob story. What the hell was he trying to do? Destroy his relationship with Paige? Did that old meddling fool think she and Matt had a chance now that the prodigal grandson was back?

"Answer me, Jeremy."

Jeremy studied her for a moment, trying to judge how much the old man had told her, how much he could get away with. "Yes, I bought the Smith ranch. But my decision about the water wasn't meant to hurt Josh." He paused, saw that he had her attention, and continued. "I have my own ranch to think about, Paige—horses worth millions of dollars."

"Your horses aren't in jeopardy and you know it. You have more water than they'll ever need. Josh, on the other hand, has nothing. If he loses his cattle, he'll lose his ranch."

"Jesus Christ, Paige! What do you expect me to do? Cure all the ills of the entire valley just because I have more than most people? I'm a businessman. I can't just give everything away everytime someone is in trouble. I'd be bankrupt within a year if I did." He tried to get past her so he could lead the way into the drawing room, but she wouldn't let him.

"Oh, but you do give away a great deal, Jeremy," she said, coming to stand in front of him. "You give to performing arts centers, to universities, to museums, to all sorts of newsworthy organizations. Last year you made the list of the ten most generous living Americans. What was it the *Los Angeles Times* called you? A man of unquestionable conscience and generosity? Where was that generosity when Josh McKenzie came to you for help five years ago? Where was that conscience, that integrity, that total disregard for self when the time came for you to chose between a man's survival and your own selfish needs?''

''Are you forgetting who we're talking about?'' he bellowed, furious that she was siding with the enemy. ''We're talking about the McKenzies—the same people who, a few years ago, accused me of cold-blooded murder.''

''That was Matt,'' she reminded him. ''Not Josh.''

Jeremy gave Paige a long, knowing look. ''What difference does it make? Matt is the one you're thinking about. He's the reason you've embarked on this crusade of yours.''

She ignored the sarcastic remark, refused to let Matt become the issue. ''Is it true you want to buy the Canyon-T Ranch?''

Something inside Jeremy went very still. How in hell had she found out about that? Except for his lawyer and the Solvang realtor they had worked with, no one knew of his plans to buy the McKenzies' property.

''Well, Jeremy?''

Denying it would be futile. Whoever the blabbermouth was, he had been thorough. ''So what if I want to buy Josh's ranch? Is that a crime? Do you think I'm the only one who's ever made him an offer on that land?''

''You don't call trying to destroy a man by driving him to bankruptcy a crime? Or taking away everything he worked for all his life? Leaving him without a shred of dignity?''

''In my circles, we call it business. The kind of business you obviously know nothing about. And for your information, since Josh McKenzie failed to mention it, I offered him thirty million dollars for his property. With that kind of money, a man can buy himself enough dignity to last him a lifetime.''

The callousness of that remark stung her so hard that she took a step backward. She had heard Jeremy cut people down to size many times in the past. But his wrath had never been directed at her—or at someone she cared about. ''That's a despicable thing to say. I thought you

liked Josh. I thought you respected him, respected what
he stood for.''

"I do—"

"Then forget about his ranch and sell him the water
he needs. Or better yet, give it to him. Lord knows you
can afford it.''

The suggestion struck him as so utterly ridiculous that
he laughed. For all her sophistication, Paige could be
hopelessly naive at times. And sentimental. But she
would change. As his wife, she would have to. "I *never*
back down on a business decision, Paige. The sooner you
realize that, the better you and I will . . .''

She never heard the rest of his sentence. Blinded by
tears of pain and disappointment, she pushed him out of
the way and ran out.

The iron double gates were open when Paige arrived
at her father's house that same afternoon. As always at
this time of day, the courtyard was empty and peaceful,
its silence broken only by the chirping of birds and the
rustling of leaves.

Knowing she'd find her father in the back, she circled
the house in the direction of the garden, a fragrant haven
he had created years ago, and where he spent most of his
spare time.

One knee on the ground, Paul was busy trimming several rampant vines from a purple bougainvillea bush. In
his baggy khaki pants and faded blue shirt, he could have
passed for the gardener.

"Hello Daddy.''

He turned around, started to smile, then, seeing the
dispirited expression on Paige's face, he tossed the
sheers aside and stood up. "Oh, darling,'' he said,
closing the distance between them in two quick strides
and taking her hands in his, "you've talked to Josh,
haven't you?''

Paige nodded. "And Jeremy.'' She looked up, her eyes
misting. "It's all true, Daddy. He didn't even try to deny
it.'' Still holding his hand, she let him lead her toward

the terrace. "I owe you an apology," she said, sitting
down. "I behaved abominably yesterday."

"No, you didn't. You behaved exactly the way I expected you to. I attacked the man you loved and you
came to his defense." He leaned toward her in a gentle,
inquiring fashion. "Want to tell me what happened?"

She repeated the conversation she and Jeremy had had
less than twenty-four hours ago. She had gone over it in
her mind a dozen times since yesterday, trying to find
some justification for what he had done to Josh. Each
time, she was left feeling more disillusioned than before.

"What are you going to do?" Paul asked when she
was finished.

She glanced toward the distance, toward the Santa Inez
Mountains, as if seeking an answer from them. "I'm not
sure. Part of me knows I could never be happy with a
man I no longer respect, and another part wants to hold
on to him."

Paul patted her hand. "That, too, is normal, darling."

"I guess what I'm hoping is that he'll change his mind
and reinstate the arrangement Josh had with Arnie
Smith."

"Would that redeem him in your eyes?"

"I don't know. Perhaps." She sighed. "Right now, I
just want to cling to that hope. For Josh's sake."

She was sitting on the deck when Jeremy arrived the
following evening. When she had returned from her father's house yesterday and found Jeremy's message on her
machine saying he had something important to tell her,
her hopes had soared. Were her prayers being answered
after all? Had Jeremy finally come to his senses and re-
considered his decision?

"I see that you've calmed down," Jeremy said, taking
the chair across from her.

Although his tone was slightly patronizing, Paige overlooked it. "You said you had something to tell me?"

"Yes. I want to talk to you about the two of us going
away for a few days, away from pressures and interfer-

ences we don't need. I thought a cruise to Alaska would be nice at this time of year. Unless you'd prefer Marbella.'' He winked, his gaze sheepish and conspiratorial. "You and I had a wonderful time there, remember?''

"You want to go away?'' she repeated, shocked that he could be so casual and lighthearted after all that had happened. "In the middle of a crisis? When we still have so much to resolve?''

He gave her his most confident smile. "There's no crisis. As for whatever you feel needs to be resolved, it can be done away from Santa Barbara.''

Her heart sank, along with her earlier expectations. "You have no intention of changing your mind about Josh, do you? You're still as determined as ever to get your hands on the Canyon-T Ranch.''

"Of course I am. That ranch means everything to me. And I repeat, it's a business decision—one that has nothing to do with us.''

"But it has everything to do with us!'' she cried, standing up. "You know how I feel about Josh—''

"Then I suggest you rethink your priorities, darling.''

Her left eyebrow went up. "*Rethink* my priorities?''

"I've never approved of your relationship with Josh. You know that. Contrary to what you think, the man is far from being the harmless, easygoing cowboy people take him for. He is shrewd and calculating. And,'' he added, his voice brimming with distaste, "he's a McKenzie.''

Slowly shaking her head, Paige continued to watch Jeremy, unable to believe that the man who stood in front of her, telling her who her friends should be, was the same man she had fallen in love with a few months ago. She wondered now if she had ever truly loved him, or if she had simply been infatuated with him, swept away by his charm, flattered by his attention. Looking back, she couldn't remember a single instance when she had said to him, or even to herself, that she loved him.

Yet up to a moment ago a thread of loyalty had still held her bound to him. She had been prepared to listen, to be convinced, to be swept away again. But in a moment of carelessness, his hatred for the McKenzies had prevailed and the carefully constructed mask had fallen off, revealing a cold and ruthless man, a man who would stop at nothing to get what he wanted.

"Josh happens to be a dear and wonderful friend," she snapped, standing up. "And I will not allow you to talk about him that way, or to tell me who I can and cannot see. And before attacking the integrity of a man like Josh McKenzie, you would do well to take a long look at yourself, Jeremy, at the fraud that you are. It took me awhile to see it, but now that I have, it sickens me to think I was foolish enough to be blinded by all the glitter and never saw what was beneath it."

She looked down at the ring on her left finger—the ring he had given her a few days ago as a symbol of love and trust. She had held onto it until this very moment because she had believed in him, believed he loved her enough to do what was right.

Removing it, she pressed it into Jeremy's hand. "Good-bye, Jeremy."

A look of total disbelief appeared on his face. Then, as Paige walked back into the house, locking the sliding doors behind her, Jeremy closed his fist around the ring, turned around and left.

"If you're here to gloat and tell me 'I told you so,' " Paige said to her aunt as Kate walked through the door the following morning, "I don't want to hear it."

Acting happier than Paige had seen her in years, Kate tossed her purse on the kitchen island, walked over to the stove, turned on the burner under the water kettle, and busied herself with cups, saucers, and teabags. "I will do no such thing. But I will not stand by and watch you making yourself miserable over a man who never deserved you."

"I can't help it. I *am* miserable."

"It will pass." Opening a cabinet, Kate pulled out a tin of shortbread cookies and started arranging them on a small plate. When Paul had called her yesterday to tell her the wedding was off, Kate had almost fainted with relief. Two months had passed since the Solstice Parade, and although she had regained control of her emotions and endured her pain with a stoic indifference, deep down she still ached, still yearned, and still feared for Paige.

Now at last this nightmare was over. With Jeremy out of Paige's life—and out of her own—she could finally concentrate on Beauchamp, which she had neglected for so long, and return to a normal life. "Here," she said, handing Paige a cup of tea and a cookie. "This will make you feel better. It always did when you were little."

"How can I feel better when Josh is on the verge of losing his ranch and he won't allow me to help him?"

"I take it he turned down your offer to pay off his loan?"

Paige nodded. "He wouldn't even discuss it. Not that it came as a great surprise, considering that cowboy pride of his. But I had hopes."

It wasn't until later on that evening, as Paige sat huddled in a chair watching the news, that her mood changed abruptly. On the screen, a reporter was interviewing an elderly couple in nearby Goleta. Thanks to an old will that had just resurfaced, Señor and Señora Garcia were now the proud owners of the house in which they had been living for the past thirty years as servants.

The story made Paige think of her friend, Monti Kaluna. A history professor at UCSB, Dr. Kaluna was an expert on old documents and occasionally helped Paige trace old deeds, marriage certificates, and nineteenth-century immigration papers.

Five years ago, Monti had been hailed as a local hero when he discovered several old deeds that had changed the lives of many families throughout the county, deeds no one knew existed.

As she listened to the details, Paige remembered one of Josh's stories about his ancestors, about how his grandfather, Ethan, had formed a close friendship with his neighbor, a land grant owner by the name of Luis

Ortega, who had owned the property now known as Newman's Ranch. The two men had remained friends until Ortega sold his ranch in 1871 and moved to Mexico.

Droughts, although not as severe as the one California was experiencing now, weren't unusual in those days. What if, before Ortega sold his land, he had sold water rights to his friend Ethan? And Josh knew nothing about it?

The possibility that she may have solved Josh's dilemma was so thrilling that it took Paige two hours to fall asleep that night.

The following morning she drove to the Santa Barbara County Courthouse where, for the next three hours, she pored over old records, most of them on microfilm and dating as far back as 1848, when the United States had bought California from Mexico. The transactions were handwritten and the ink had faded, but they were perfectly readable.

She went over each file with minute attention, and although she noted more than a dozen water rights transfers, by the time she had to leave to meet a client, she had found nothing in the name of McKenzie and Ortega.

Driving home that night, she remembered her grandmother once telling her that every problem had its solution. Which meant the solution to Josh's problem was somewhere. All it took was a clear, logical mind to solve it. A mind like Monti's.

THIRTY-ONE

The campus of UCSB, just off State Highway 217, was crowded with students on their way to lunch or to the beach when Paige arrived at twelve noon the following day. She found Monti in the faculty lounge, eating a cheese and tomato sandwich and reading a Teddy Roosevelt biography.

"Hello, Professor."

Monti looked up and grinned, his deep-set black eyes lighting up instantly. "Paige, what a pleasant surprise." He wrapped his unfinished sandwich in a paper napkin, slipped his book into a red knapsack, and stood up. "So," he said, hugging Paige, "what brings my favorite student back to this madhouse?"

"I need help with something, Monti." At his request, she had stopped calling him "Professor" long ago. "But please don't interrupt your lunch on my account."

He waved a hand and quickly discarded the rest of his sandwich. "It wasn't very good, anyway. Cafeteria food hasn't improved much since you were here last." He slung the knapsack over his right shoulder. "Come on," he said, taking her arm. "Let's go for a walk."

Paige nodded and watched him as they made their way out of the building. Monti Kaluna was a tall, lanky man in his early fifties, whose brown, deeply lined face made him look twenty years older. He had the sharp, angular features of his Chumash Indian ancestors, and long black hair pulled back in a ponytail. A widower for the last five years, he divided his time between the university, where he taught history, and the Santa Inez Indian Reservation, where he helped his less fortunate brothers build decent homes to replace their shacks.

"How can I help you?" he asked as they walked along a palm-lined path that ran parallel to the ocean.

Paige told him everything, including the breakup of her engagement to Jeremy. Knowing Monti was another of Matt's fans, she glanced at him to see his reaction. He was smiling.

"What do you think?" she asked when she was finished. "Am I being foolish? Expecting too much?"

Monti's expression was thoughtful.

"What?" she asked, feeling her hopes soar again. "What are you thinking?"

"I'm thinking about research I did for a friend of mine a couple of months ago. It involved a property dispute between two parties and the deed their respective fathers had signed more than seventy years ago—an unrecorded deed."

Paige stopped in her tracks and turned around. "Are unrecorded deeds valid?"

"If they're properly signed and witnessed, yes, they are. Recording is proof of public record only—not proof of validity."

"But if there was a deed, even an unrecorded one, wouldn't Josh know about it?"

Monti shrugged. "Not if his grandfather never mentioned it. Remember, that was a long time ago, Paige. More than a hundred years."

"Do we have a chance of finding it, Monti?"

She could tell by the way his eyes twinkled in the sunlight that the challenge was already working its magic. "I never deal with chances, Paige. Only with facts."

"Then you'll help me?"

"You know I will. But at the same time, I want you to ask Josh to search every nook and cranny in his house. People didn't believe in bank safes in those days, and valuable documents have turned up in the strangest places." They had reached her car and Monti opened the door for her. "This is a very nice thing you're doing for the McKenzies, Paige."

She slid behind the wheel. "Josh is a good friend. I know it's silly, but I feel as if somehow, by associating with Jeremy, I was part of his conspiracy against Josh. I guess that's why it's so important for me to do what I can for him now."

Monti's eyes shone with amusement. "Are you sure Josh is the only reason you're becoming so involved?"

She flashed him a quick look. "What other reason would I have?"

"Matt, perhaps?"

She felt her cheeks color, and quickly put on her sunglasses. "Oh, Monti," she said with a scolding shake of her head. "I see that you're still an incurable romantic."

"Yes, but am I right?"

She turned on the ignition. "No, you're not. Josh is the only man I have on my mind right now."

As she pulled away from the parking lot, she glanced in the rearview mirror and saw that Monti was still standing where she had left him, grinning.

"Liar!" he called.

It took Monti two days to get back to Paige.

"I have good news and I have bad news," he told her when he called her at home on Wednesday evening. "The good news is that when Luis Ortega sold his ranch in 1871, he also sold Ethan the water rights to his spring-fed lake. However, for reasons unknown, those rights were never developed, which may explain why Josh doesn't know anything about them. Over the years, the transaction between the two men was practically forgotten."

"So there was a deed after all!"

"Yes. But, as I suspected, it was never recorded. Ethan may have meant to do it but somehow never got around to it."

"But he must have had a copy."

"I'm sure he did—at one time. But since Josh didn't

find it, it's safe to assume it's been lost. Fortunately, I was able to locate several descendants of the Ortega family. One of them is a Dolores Ortega from San Diego. She's Luis's great-granddaughter and the proud owner of a roomful of old family memorabilia. The deed between Luis and Ethan is one of them.''

"Monti, that's wonderful!''

"Not so fast. By California law, if rights aren't used within five years, they revert back to the original or current owner of the property. And since Ethan never developed those rights, I'm afraid the deed is useless.''

"Oh, no.''

"I'm sorry, Paige. I thought we had the answer there for a while.''

She sighed. "Me too. Thanks anyway, Monti.''

Paige hung up and sat on her kitchen stool for awhile, her hopes draining one by one. After a while, she picked up the phone and called Josh.

Josh stood by the window, gazing at the night sky that blanketed the valley. It had been a little over four hours since Paige had brought him a copy of the deed that granted the Canyon-T Ranch water rights from the former Ortega property. It had been written one hundred and twenty years ago, and yet it was still intact, and so well preserved that it could have been written yesterday.

His heart filling with emotions he seldom felt anymore, Josh glanced at the document again, at the dates; the seals; the strong, wide scrawl at the end of the page—Ethan's signature.

He wasn't surprised that he hadn't known about the deed or the arrangement between the two men. As sharp and capable as Ethan was all his life, in latter years, his mind had wandered elsewhere. At times he had barely been able to remember where and who he was.

As for his father, Daniel, he had been like Adam, more interested in monetary rewards than in working the land. Unlike Adam, however, he had stayed at the ranch and worked with his father, but occasionally he would sail to

Europe or the Far East in search of adventure and come back with stories that had delighted Josh and irritated the hell out of Ethan.

"You know," Josh said to Matt after awhile. "Something about this whole deed business keeps nagging me."

Matt looked up from his newspaper. "What's that, Gramps?"

"My granddaddy may not have been very well educated, but he was a mighty shrewd man. Too shrewd to pass up an opportunity like this one."

"Maybe Ethan had meant to follow up on that agreement and didn't because there was never a need to."

"But that's exactly the point, son. There's *always* a need for water in this area—especially with a ranch this size. And Ethan knew that. Here, listen to this." Holding the deed at arm's length so he could look at it without his glasses, he read: " 'The transfer of water rights together with the right to lay and maintain a conduit.' "

He brought his arm down and looked at Matt. "Doesn't that tell you Ethan was serious about the project? That he and Ortega had talked about it in detail?"

"What are you saying, Gramps?"

"I'm saying there's a pipe somewhere under that land, my boy. And by God, I'm going to find it. Because if we can show the rights were developed after all, that five-year reversion law won't apply and we'll be able to pump all the water we need from Jeremy's lake."

"But if there was a pipe, there'd be water in our lake."

"Not if the pipe is clogged."

For the first time since Paige had come to the ranch with the deed, Matt felt a stirring of excitement. "A blockage," he mused, as if trying to get used to the word. "Of course. A blockage would stop the flow of water."

"You bet it would. We're talking about more than a hundred years. who the hell knows what accumulates in an underground pipe in that much time?"

"So it could have happened any time, ten, twenty, even thirty years ago. But you never noticed anything because the creek was always full and kept feeding your lake."

"Until the drought dried out the creek."

Matt stood up. A moment ago, he had been dead on his feet from a long day on the range with Josh and his men. Now he was so damned keyed up, he doubted he'd get a minute's sleep.

"So," Matt said, grinning. "When do we start digging?"

Leaning against his pickup truck, Josh watched Matt as he drove the John Deere backhoe along the western end of the lake, the end that was closest to Jeremy's property. Although it had been cold when they had first started digging at the break of dawn, the temperature had quickly soared to the low nineties.

Matt, in frayed denim shorts, sat high on the tractor's seat, his bare chest dripping with sweat. From time to time, he'd stop, wipe off his face with the back of his arm, and take a long drink of water from a plastic bottle Josh kept refilling.

Matt's watch told him he had been operating the excavating machine for four straight hours, but it felt more like ten. His shoulders and arms ached from the grueling, repetitive motion of pulling and pushing the control levers, and his throat and mouth were filled with so much dust that no amount of water could quench his thirst.

"Why don't you let me take over for awhile?" Josh asked him at ten-thirty. "Why should you have all the fun?"

Matt shook his head. "If I stop now, I'll never be able to get back to it."

At noon, after six hours of uninterrupted work, Matt had dug a trench that was over a hundred feet long and four feet deep. And there was still no evidence of any underground piping.

"Damn you, Ethan," Josh shouted over the tractor's noise, as he walked back and forth, peering into the freshly dug earth. "I know that pipe's in there. So where the hell did you lay the damn thing?"

At Matt prepared to scoop out another load of dirt and

guided the bucket into the trench, he felt a resistance. Pulling the lever back, he tried again. And again felt the same obstruction.

"God Almighty, I think we got something!" he yelled, jumping down from his seat.

"What? Where?" Josh said, running back as fast as he could.

Matt had already jumped into the excavation, digging the dirt with his bare hands. Josh joined him and in a few moments, they had unearthed it—a clay pipe about twelve inches in diameter, the same kind Spanish padres had used when they had built their missions along the California coast all those years ago.

When Matt was sure this was an actual water conduit and not some buried piece of junk he threw his head back, shook his two fists in the air, and let out a jubilant shout that reverberated over the entire valley.

THIRTY-TWO

"For all your savvy, Mindy Haliday," Paige declared, pushing her sunglasses into her mop of black curls, "you are painfully transparent."

At her friend's request, Paige had met Mindy at Petronella. But the moment she entered the crowded restaurant and saw Matt and his foreman, Rocky, sitting at a table at the other end of the patio, she had seen through Mindy's little ploy.

Mindy fluttered her black eyelashes. "Why Paige, what in the world do you mean by that?"

"Cut the act, Mindy. Matt put you up to this, didn't he?" Paige dipped a carrot stick into Alfonso's famous California yogurt dip and bit an end off. "How did he con you?"

"Matt isn't Jeremy, Paige. He doesn't con people."

"But this little rendezvous was his idea, wasn't it?"

"Yes, but that's because he wants to talk to you and he thought this was the only way he could do it."

"Why does he want to talk to me?"

"I don't know. And I didn't ask."

Paige shook her head. "You always were a sucker for pretty boys."

"I guess that's true," Mindy laughed. Leaning forward, she was suddenly serious. "Look, I know Matt is still a sore subject with you, but do you think you could put your feelings aside long enough to listen to me for just a moment?"

Paige took a sip of her white wine spritzer and gave

Mindy a haughty look. "Why should I? I already know what you're going to say."

"What am I going to say?"

"That now that Jeremy is out of my life, I should give Matt another chance."

"Is that such an outrageous idea?"

"It's an impossible idea. Nothing has changed between Matt and me."

A waiter brought their salad niçoise, and Mindy waited until he was gone before speaking again. "What if I were to tell you something that might change your mind about Matt? About the way you felt toward him near the end of your marriage?"

Paige pushed the anchovies to the side of her plate. "I thought we weren't going to discuss him anymore."

"I never agreed to that." Resting her arms on the table, Mindy leaned forward. "How much do you know about Matt's financial situation?"

Paige shrugged. "We never discussed it."

"Right. Which means you knew nothing about how much money he had, what he spent, or *where* he spent it."

"We didn't have that kind of a marriage, I guess. I did what I wanted with my money and he did the same with his."

"This is going to come as a shock to you, kiddo," Mindy continued. "But Matt didn't inherit the huge fortune from his father so many thought he did. In fact, Adam and Caroline McKenzie were heavily indebted most of their lives. When Adam died, he left nothing in his estate but his New York apartment, which Matt sold to cover the man's debts."

Paige put her fork down. "But I thought . . . Everybody always said . . ."

"That the McKenzies were loaded?" She shook her head. "They weren't. They just acted like it."

"But if Adam left no money, how could Matt afford to keep his mother at the California Trauma Institute for six years? That place costs a fortune."

"He *couldn't* afford it. Which is why he left the FBI and joined Worldwide Investigations shortly after the accident."

From a few tables away, Paige heard Matt's hearty laugh and resisted the impulse to look at him. "How do you know all this? Who have you been talking to?"

"A friend of mine. She works in the comptroller's office at the California Trauma Institute."

"You expect me to pay attention to hospital gossip?"

"It isn't hospital gossip, Paige. These are facts. The only reason Laura told me is because Matt's return brought a flurry of new interest, and because she has a hopeless crush on him. In fact, from what I hear, the entire nursing staff at CTI adored him."

This time Paige glanced toward Matt's table. He was leaning forward talking to Rocky. At the next table, a pretty redhead couldn't take her eyes off him. "I'm well aware of the McKenzie charm, Mindy. You don't have to remind me."

"Charm isn't the only reason Matt was so well thought of. It's what he did for his mother during those six years that won him such devotion from the doctors and nurses." Her voice suddenly earnest, almost passionate, Mindy leaned closer. "Don't you see, Paige? It wasn't that Matt didn't want to leave Worldwide Investigations for you, or that he loved you less than his job. He stayed with the agency because he needed the money."

Paige ate her salad in silence. Nothing Matt had ever done or said during their fourteen-month marriage had given her the slightest indication that money was a problem. He had never refused her anything. The only resistance she had encountered was when she had suggested they move into a larger apartment. He had told her he hated changes and would rather stay where they were. Now, of course, she knew the real reason. He couldn't afford to move.

"If what you're telling me is true," she said, returning her attention to Mindy, "why didn't Matt tell me all this before?"

"God!" Mindy moaned, rolling her eyes. "Am I the only one with brains here? Isn't it obvious that his pride wouldn't let him?"

"So why is he asking you to tell me now? Where is that precious pride all of a sudden?"

Mindy gave an exasperated sigh. "I'm not here as his envoy, you big dope. He has no idea I'm telling you this, or that I even know any of this."

"Hello, ladies."

Paige turned her head and saw Matt standing by their table. He wore pale blue Levi's and a royal blue knit shirt. The brilliant color, combined with his tan and his blond hair, made him look more handsome than ever.

Mindy rose. "If you two will excuse me for a moment? I just remembered a phone call I have to make to a very temperamental client." Not bothering to wait for an answer, she disappeared inside.

"May I?" Matt asked, pointing at the chair Mindy had vacated.

Paige only nodded. She didn't trust herself to speak just yet. She was filled with so many emotions, ranging from sympathy to regret, along with something she didn't dare try to define, that she feared if she spoke, she would probably choke on the first word.

"I asked Mindy to arrange this meeting," Matt confessed.

She took a sip of water and nodded again.

"I suppose I could have just as easily thanked you over the phone, but somehow that didn't feel right." He grinned. "So, thanks, Paige. For everything."

She swallowed, testing her throat. "I did it for Josh."

"I realize that." He was glad to see she didn't look angry anymore, just preoccupied. And soft. So damned soft, it was all he could do not to reach out and touch her, feel the softness, feel that skin come alive and hot, the way it had, for a moment, the night of her Fiesta party.

"I understand you found an underground pipe after

all,'' Paige said, drinking large amounts of water to relieve her dry mouth.

Matt's gray eyes lit up. "Yes. We thought we'd find it all clogged up, but it was clean as a whistle, so we figured the obstruction had to be at the intake—on Jeremy's end—and we started digging there.''

A small smile, the first, tugged at the corner of her mouth. "Jeremy must have been thrilled about that.''

"He wasn't. But he didn't have much of a choice. Not when we showed up with a court order.'' Casually, he reached over and took a small black olive from her plate and ate it. "Anyway, the trouble was well worth it. We found the intake filled with roots, mud, leaves, even a tree stump.''

"I would have loved to have seen Josh's face when you found the pipe.''

Matt laughed. "You wouldn't have recognized him. He was carrying on like a little kid on Christmas morning. I never knew he could jump that high.''

"What happens now?''

"The first step is to have a new intake structure built and the pipes replaced, so the water can flow again. Then we'll start getting the fields in shape so Josh can resume his cattle-feeding operation. And since the bank has agreed to give us an extension on the loan, we should be in fairly good shape by spring.'' He paused, gave her a look so tender that she dropped her fork. "Nothing is going to happen overnight,'' he continued, handing her Mindy's clean fork. "But we're on our way back. Thanks to you.''

She watched him take another olive and smiled again, because he did it so unconsciously, out of habit. He adored black olives. He put them on everything. Black olives and marinara. "I'm glad everything worked out so well for you and Josh.''

Matt glanced at her left hand. "For you too, I see. The wedding's off, huh?'' He had been so happy to learn she was finally free of the jerk that he had considered calling her and telling her about his investigation. But after awhile he had decided against it. He still hadn't made up his mind about Kate and whether he wanted to investigate her or not. If he did, it was best to leave Paige out of it.

"Yes," Paige said in answer to his question. "The wedding is off."

"Then you won't have a problem accepting an invitation, will you?"

She wondered if he heard the sudden, loud thump of her heart. "An invitation from whom?"

"Josh is planning to have a barbecue a couple of weeks from now. He wants you to come." When she didn't answer, he added, "You can't say no because you're the guest of honor. I wasn't supposed to tell you that, so don't mention it to Josh."

"Monti is the one who deserves the recognition."

"Monti won't be forgotten, Paige. I promise you." He would have liked nothing better than to stay here all afternoon and look at her. But he had promised Josh to be there when the engineers and the pipe contractors arrived. "What about the barbecue?" he asked, standing up. "Will you come?"

"I'll think about it."

She watched him walk away, Rocky at his side. Now that she knew the truth about Matt's reasons for staying at Worldwide, there was so much she wanted to tell him, *needed* to tell him. But Petronella, comfortable and familiar as it was, was hardly the place for a serious conversation.

"How did it go?" Mindy asked when she returned to their table.

Paige gave her an innocent look. "How did what go?"

"You know what. Your talk with Matt."

"Oh, that." Paige speared a tomato slice with her fork, and ate it. "He invited me to the ranch for a barbecue."

"That's wonderful! You'll go, won't you?"

"I might." Paige pressed a napkin to her lips before picking up her glass. "For Josh, of course."

"Of course."

* * *

It wasn't until four o'clock that same afternoon, after Matt's meeting with the contractors was over and he had returned to the house, that Nigel walked into the living room, grinning.

"What is it, Nigel?" Matt asked. "From the look on your face one would think Queen Elizabeth herself was coming to tea."

"Better than that, sir," Nigel said, nodding toward the window.

"Really?"

Matt rose from his chair and walked over to where Nigel was standing. Down in the valley, climbing up the winding road toward the Canyon-T Ranch, was Paige's red MG.

THIRTY-THREE

Paige sat in her car for a full five minutes, waiting for the hammering inside her chest to subside before she went to ring the McKenzies' doorbell.

She had made the decision to come and see Matt as she and Mindy had left Petronella's, but it had taken her nearly two hours before she could find the courage to follow through on her brainstorm.

Moments ago, as she drove through San Marco Pass, she had known exactly what she would say to Matt, where she would begin. Now her thoughts were so muddled, she was beginning to wonder if she should be here at all.

At last she stepped out of the car, and as she started across the courtyard, she saw the front door open. Smiling that familiar smile, Matt leaned one shoulder against the door and watched her approach.

"Did you come to deliver your RSVP to the barbecue in person?" he asked amiably.

"No. I came to see you."

His heart began to race. He moved to the side. "Come in."

She turned toward the wide open field behind her. "I'd rather go for a walk instead. If you don't mind."

"I don't mind." He closed the door behind him and together they started walking toward the south pastures, the way they had so many times when they were first married. Paige wore the same yellow sundress she had worn earlier. At the restaurant she had looked sophisticated and remote, but in this pastoral setting she was more like the Paige he had known intimately—sweet and uncomplicated.

"You look like a lady with a very serious problem," he said, unable to tear his eyes from her.

Paige decided to dive right in, as she always did when she found herself in a difficult situation. "I know everything, Matt."

"Mmmm. That's a pretty broad statement. Would you care to elaborate on it?"

"I know that from the moment your mother was injured until the day she died, you were her sole support. And I know that you spent nearly all you made at Worldwide Investigations for her medical care."

With an angry kick, he sent a stone rolling down the road. "Who told you that?"

"That's not important."

"Is it Josh?"

"No. You know he'd never betray you."

"Then how did you find out?"

"Is it true?"

Matt kicked another stone. "My financial situation is my business, Paige."

She ignored the rebuff. "I didn't come here to pry—or to make you feel uncomfortable. I came here because I need answers. And I need to hear them from you."

He remained silent and kept staring straight ahead as they walked. There was a look of fierce pride on his face—one she had seen often but had never really appreciated as much as she did now. He still hadn't given her an answer, but his silence told her all she needed to know. "You should have told me, Matt. I could have helped."

"That's exactly what I didn't want you to do."

"But why not?"

"Because my mother was my responsibility."

They passed an old, dilapidated shed with its red paint half peeled off. "I thought marriage meant sharing everything—the good *and* the bad."

"Not my debts."

"And if the debts had been mine? Would you have expected me to handle the problem all on my own?"

"That's different."

She smiled. The old macho-man syndrome was still alive and well in the Nineties. "Were you ever going to tell me?"

"I almost did once. When I felt you slip away from me after the . . . after we lost our baby. I thought it might make you feel differently toward me, jolt you back somehow." He shook his head. "But each time I tried to talk to you, you were so cold, so distant, I decided it wouldn't change anything."

The words stung. But she deserved them. Nothing could have reached her during those painful weeks after her miscarriage. "I guess I was too wrapped up in my own grief. There were certain words I expected to hear from you and when I didn't, I was convinced you had stopped loving me."

Above them, heavy clouds had gathered, casting an unfamiliar shadow over the valley. "I could never stop loving you, Paige," Matt said softly.

Startled she glanced at him, her heart beating furiously. Did that mean he *still* loved her? "You were pretty quick signing those divorce papers, though," she reminded him.

"I was furious and hurt that you'd do something like that without discussing it with me first. It took me two days to calm down, and although I had signed the papers by then, I decided I'd make one more try to get you back. Even if I had to quit my job to do it."

She stopped walking and turned to look at him. "Would you have done that for me?"

"That's what I came to tell you that day." His jaw tightened and his tone was laced with bitterness. "But you had already left for Marbella."

She laughed then, a laugh that was part joy and part nervous release.

"What's so funny?"

She told him about Marbella, about her decision to

give their marriage one more try, and about how excited she had been during the long flight home. "Then at the airport, when I saw that newspaper picture of you and a blonde woman locked in an embrace that could have melted the state of Alaska, I thought better of it."

He chuckled. "I'm afraid that incident was blown way out of proportion by an overzealous local reporter, Paige. I don't even know who the woman was. Or why she kissed me. After leaving Mindy's shop that day, all I wanted to do was drown my sorrows. Which is exactly what I did. Nothing more."

She had never questioned his honesty. And she didn't question it now. They had reached the top of a knoll and stood shoulder to shoulder looking down at the valley. She waited for him to say something more, to give her an indication that it wasn't too late for them. He didn't. Instead, he kept searching the darkening skies. There had been a few scattered showers in the area during the last couple of days, although nothing serious enough to give valley ranchers any hope that the drought might be over.

"I think we'd better head back," Matt said. "I don't like the looks of those clouds."

He had barely finished his sentence when thunder cracked and an overhead cloud burst, releasing a downpour that drenched them both in an instant. "Come on," he shouted above the noise as he took her hand. "Let's make a run for the shed."

They reached it in a little over a minute. Once inside, Paige fell back against the wall, panting and laughing as she tried to catch her breath.

Matt watched her. Desire rose, swift and potent. With her hair pasted to her head, her face glistening from the rain, and her gorgeous breasts clinging to her wet dress, she had never looked more delectable.

He touched her face, his fingers following the contour of her cheek, her jawline, fluttering across her lips. She opened her eyes and what he saw in them at that moment was such a reflection of his own needs it nearly drove him crazy. Pulling her to him, he kissed her with all the hunger he had kept locked up for two long years.

Paige responded instantly, greedily, her fingers raking through his hair, then interlacing behind his neck. It took her awhile to realize the moaning sounds she heard were coming from her throat.

"God, you feel good," he whispered against her mouth. His hands moved over her entire body, fast and impatient, pushing her dress up, stroking her wet thighs. "Do you know how many times I've fantasized about this moment?"

"No more so than I have," she replied, astounded at the revelation.

His open mouth couldn't get enough of her. He kissed her lips, her throat, the gentle swell of her breasts above the V neckline.

With fingers that shook with need, he reached behind her neck and untied her dress. The bodice fell, baring white, round breasts that begged to be touched, kissed. He took one in each hand, brushing his thumbs against the nipples, watching in fascination as they hardened and came alive, drawing him like a magnet.

When he took a wet tip into his mouth, Paige cried out, the pleasure so fierce that her knees gave way under her. He caught her and held her, gazing down at her. At that moment, she was overwhelmed not only by her love for Matt but by the need to be loved back by him—only him. "Matt! Oh, God, Matt . . ."

"Say it," he whispered as he undressed her. "I've waited two years to hear you say it. Don't stop now."

"I love you," she breathed. "I've never loved anyone but you."

As she spoke, her fingers fumbled with his belt, pulled down the zipper, pushed the wet jeans over his hips. It would be different this time. There would be no tender removal of clothing, no inch-by-inch exploration of each other's body. Later, there would be time for tenderness and rediscovery. Right now, all that mattered was the need, the wanting, their bodies coming together.

Sensing her urgency, Matt slid his hands under her buttocks and lifted her, pulling her legs around him. She was so wet, he slid right into her, plunged deep, and then deeper when she cried out his name. Outside, the storm raged and the thunder roared, but it couldn't match the storm or the passion inside him. It was that passion that drove him now, that sought her lips, her tongue, the very core of her.

Her head thrown back, Paige began to move, pounding her hips against his as she clung to his shoulders. All her thoughts were centered on that part of her body that was joined to him. Nothing else mattered but the excruciating pleasure she experienced with each motion.

When the climax ripped through her, she gasped and reared back, but she didn't loosen her grip. And when the first shudders had passed, when the throbbing had eased off and she was able to breathe again, she buried her head in his shoulder while he held her.

The storm had been brief. They waited it out inside the shed—the love shed, as Matt now called it—and afterward they drove back to Paige's house, where they showered together and slipped into thick dry robes.

Later, as they were contemplating dinner, Paige opened one of her bureau drawers and pulled out a pair of shorts and a T-shirt with the words: "Runners do it with dash," printed on the front and handed them to him.

"Those are mine," Matt exclaimed.

"So they are."

"You told me you had nothing left."

She grinned. "I lied."

They spent a lazy Sunday together, dividing their time between the beach, where they swam and talked, and the bedroom, where they made love and swapped more stories of their two years apart from each other.

"I thought of you almost every day," he confessed as they sat on the beach and watched a flock of pelicans fly over them. "I tried not to, tried to tell myself it was hopeless. But you kept coming back into my mind." He leaned over to kiss her shoulder. "You made my life miserable, woman."

With a small stick, she wrote his name on the warm sand. "What finally made you decide to come back?"

He hesitated. Had he wanted to tell her the truth, this would have been the moment. But he couldn't. Not yet. "The need to be near you," he said. "And knowing that the time had come for me to return home." He was only half-lying. When he and Josh had found that conduit the other day, the experience had been so intense, the gratification so complete, so unlike anything he had ever experienced, that he had known right then that he would be staying.

Paige leaned back on her towel and pulled him down with her. "I'm glad you did."

At six o'clock, while they sat on the upper deck, sipping a very fine Santa Inez Valley Chardonnay, Kate stopped by the house, and at their insistence she agreed to stay for dinner.

"I'm so glad you and Paige are finally back together," Kate told Matt when Paige went inside to prepare the salad. "I never stopped hoping, you know. Even during your darkest moments."

Matt gave her a mocking smile. "You mean you weren't rooting for ole' Jeremy?"

He had made the remark jokingly, expecting her to laugh, but she surprised him by remaining serious and gazing into her drink. "No, I wasn't. Paul and I both tried to tell Paige Jeremy wasn't right for her. But . . ." She shrugged.

"Women in love seldom listen to reason."

At that remark, Kate stiffened. "Paige never loved Jeremy. She was just infatuated with him, with the attention, the power, the Newman mystique." She put her glass down, stood up and walked over to the railing, staring out toward the ocean. "It's that mystique that he created that always won him everything he wanted and helped him get as far as he did.''

Although Matt couldn't see her face, something in the tone of her voice startled him. He couldn't quite make up his mind whether it was hatred or admiration, or a mixture of both.

Intrigued by the change in her, and hopeful she might shed some new information on Jeremy, he came to join her. ''I guess you don't like him very much.''

For a fleeting moment, her eyes closed and her mouth tightened as if she were undergoing a deep and private torment. Lowering his gaze, Matt saw that her hands gripped the railing so tightly that her knuckles had turned white.

When she spoke again, her voice was back to its normal pitch and she was smiling. ''Not many people do.''

To anyone less observant, her brief reaction would have gone unnoticed. To Matt it was a stunning revelation.

Kate had been in love with Jeremy. He was sure of it. It wasn't the infatuation she had mentioned a moment ago on Paige's part. Nor was it the harmless crush Paige had once hinted at when they had been talking about Kate and Jeremy. This was a deep, intense love, which he suspected had caused Kate a great deal of pain.

Looking at her, especially now that she had regained her poise, it was difficult to imagine her losing her head over any man. But as Kate herself had pointed out, Jeremy wasn't just any man.

It wasn't until Matt had left Paige's house and was driving back to the ranch later that night that the full implication of his discovery hit him. If Kate had been secretly in love with Jeremy all those years, how far would she have gone to express that love? And to earn his in return? Would she have helped him acquire the things he treasured most? Even if she had to break the law to do it? Would she have risked her career, her reputation, the respect of her family for the man she loved?

Probably.

Matt's mind was working furiously now. Until today,

Kate had only been a possibility—someone he knew he had to investigate, but was reluctant to because of her closeness to Paige.

Now it was no longer a choice, but a necessity. If Kate had helped Jeremy with some of his illegal acquisitions, she would have the answers, perhaps even the proof he needed to nail the publisher once and for all.

He knew that Kate, like Paige, was a meticulous record keeper, and that every item she had ever sold or purchased was filed on computer disks and could be easily located, if one knew where to look.

She was bound to have a record of her transactions with Jeremy somewhere—legitimate as well as illegitimate. The latter might be filed in code, or protected by a password. But it would be there.

All Matt had to do was find it.

THIRTY-FOUR

Except for an occasional cruising patrol car, the Santa Barbara streets were deserted at this time of night, and getting inside Beauchamp from a side alley had been easy.

Matt's only concern had been the alarm. He had helped Paige open the gallery many times in the past and remembered the combination. But what if it had been changed? To his relief, it hadn't.

Kate kept her disks in a compact box on a wall unit behind her desk. Each disk was labeled and filed alphabetically. Now, sitting in front of her computer, Matt flipped through each file, marveling at the woman's thoroughness. Each of the transactions made during the past twenty-four years was entered, showing the date, the name of her client, the object purchased or sold, its price, and a brief history of the item.

When he had exhausted all possibilities of finding the information he wanted on disks, he began a physical search of the gallery. The personal computer was only ten years old, therefore prior to entering all those names and items into her system, Kate must have had them written down in a ledger, and maybe that ledger was still around.

Ignoring the showroom, he concentrated on Kate's office, which she shared with Paige, and the storeroom where they kept items that hadn't sold, or new items they were preparing to display.

A small closet by the door was filled with boxes neatly stacked on top of one another. But those held nothing of value. On a top shelf were a dozen or so old phone books dating back to the eighties that no one had bothered to throw away.

He looked through each one. It wasn't until he reached for the last two that he saw the box behind them. His heart gave a lurch. It was a slim metal case the size of a shoe box. He pulled it out and, taking a screwdriver from his back pants pocket, he pried the lock open.

Inside was an assortment of memorabilia—faded black and white photographs of an elderly couple, a tarnished baby cup with initials he couldn't read, Kate's parents' marriage and death certificates, and a receipt for a rented prom gown in the name of Miss Katherine Madison.

The last item was a yellowed paper napkin on which a black ink drawing had been hastily sketched. Puzzled, Matt looked at it. Something about the lines connected to one another struck him as odd, somewhat familiar. He turned the napkin around a few times, inspecting the sketch from different angles. It took him almost a full minute to realize what he was looking at.

The drawing of a bomb.

His whole body went numb. His mind, trained to react in an instant, refused to comprehend, to accept. Then, all at once, air was expelled from his body in a long, shuddering breath, and he was able to function again.

He had learned all about bombs during his eleven years with the FBI, and especially while he had worked in the antiterrorism department. This particular bomb was no stranger to him. Smaller than a toiletry bag, it was simple in design and a favorite of terrorists because it could easily be slipped under the seat of an airplane or a car. The weight of a passenger sitting down activated a pressure switch, which in turn started a time-delay circuit designed to send an electric charge to a small blasting cap.

The same bomb that had killed his parents.

He stood there for a long time, staring at the drawing. Through his mind, a series of images flashed at high speed, like an old silent film—images of his mother's car after the accident, with the driver's section blown off; of his father laying on a table at the morgue, his body charred almost beyond recognition; of Jeremy's stunned face when Matt had barged into his house, accusing him of murdering his father.

Paige's words four years ago echoed in his mind. "Aunt Kate never talked about what happened between her and Jeremy that summer of eighty-five. All I know is that it's something so private and painful she can't share it with anyone—not even me."

"That summer of eighty-five."

The bombing of his mother's car had taken place in July of 1985.

His jaw clenched, his heart pounding, Matt put everything back into the box, with the exception of the napkin, and stood up. Then he put the box back on the top shelf with the phone books and closed the door.

Minutes later, he was in his car, heading back toward the ranch. For the next thirty minutes, he asked himself the same question, over and over. Why? Why?

It was four o'clock in the morning when he was finally able to fall asleep.

Early the following morning, his heart cold and his mind razor sharp, Matt drove to Kate's house. He found her fully dressed in a smart khaki suit and comfortable matching pumps.

"Matt, what a pleasant surprise." Although the smile was always genuine, he realized now it never fully extended to her eyes. He had seen that watchful look before, especially when he had stopped at the gallery unexpectedly from time to time, but he had never thought much about it until now.

"Hello, Kate."

Too sharp to miss the sudden change in him, Kate's eyes grew a little warier. But the smile remained. "I was just about to have my second cup of coffee," she said, turning and leading the way into the living room. "Will you join me?"

"I don't think so." He followed her into the familiar

house with its pink and ivory Victorian wallpaper, its woodsy smell of furniture polish, its gleaming hardwood floors. He had always felt comfortable here, at home. "I'd like you to take a look at something."

His arm seemed to weigh a ton, but somehow he managed to reach inside his breast pocket and retrieve a copy he had made of the diagram. He handed it to her.

Under the clever makeup, Kate's cheeks turned white. The welcoming smile faded as a trembling, perfectly manicured hand reached out.

Kate's gaze swept over the diagram. In her chest, her heart pounded so hard she felt dizzy and had to grip the table next to her for support. She looked at Matt, her eyes wide and questioning.

"I found it at the gallery, in a tin box behind a stack of old phone books." There was no need to explain how he had gotten in and why. Not now.

Kate took a trembling breath. That closet had been so full in recent years, they hardly opened it anymore, and she had long forgotten about that box. But dear God, how could she have forgotten that Carlos's diagram was in it?

"Why, Kate?"

Matt's voice was barely audible, yet the anger in it was like a distant, rumbling thunder waiting to explode. Kate sank into a chair. There was no use denying it now. Her initial reaction had told him the truth already.

"I'm so sorry," she whispered. "So very sorry."

Until now, and for Paige's sake, he had hoped it wasn't true, that somehow he had arrived at the wrong conclusions, that another explanation lay just beneath the surface and he was just too close to see it. He sat down in the chair across from hers.

"It was Caroline, wasn't it?" he asked. "Everyone always assumed the bomb was intended for my father, but it wasn't. It was meant for my mother."

Kate didn't answer.

"Why?" he repeated.

It took her a moment to collect her thoughts, to accept the fact that the moment she had dreaded for six long years had finally arrived. And with it, a tremendous, overwhelming sense of relief.

She told him everything—how she had met Jeremy and fallen in love with him, how he had coaxed her into smuggling the St. Petersburg Rose into the country, how other artworks had followed.

With a catch in her voice she told him about the fifteen years she and Jeremy had spent together and how with one phone call he had shattered her dream, discarded her without another thought.

"Something inside me snapped that day." A sob rose to her throat then and she had to press her hand against her mouth to stop it before she could continue. "I remember everything I did, yet there's an unreality to it all, as if someone else had stepped inside me—someone I didn't know—and guided me through all the motions."

As she talked, Matt felt a cold rage sweep over him. He wasn't a violent man. He had never had to kill anyone, had never wanted to. But at this very moment, he could have done it.

"Who made that bomb for you?" he asked, barely recognizing his own voice.

"A man by the name of Carlos Fuente. I met him in South America during one of my trips there."

"Who is he?"

"A jack of all trades—part art trafficker, part drug smuggler, part terrorist. He died a year ago," she added, anticipating his next question.

"Is he the one who drew this diagram?"

She nodded. "It was important for me to know how the bomb worked before I installed it. I forgot I still had it." Carlos had warned her to throw that sketch away as soon as she had familiarized herself with the working mechanism. But she had been in such a daze during those few days that nothing she had done then made any sense.

"Did anyone else help you?" she heard Matt ask.

"No."

The vision, in slow motion, of his parents walking toward their car, of the bomb exploding, sending their bodies flying into the air, was so vivid in his mind that for a moment he thought he was going to be sick. "My God, Kate," he said more to himself than to her. "How could you have done this?"

Tortured eyes looked up. "Jeremy was all I lived for in those days. For fifteen years, everything I did, thought, needed, revolved around him. And when he . . . when she came back . . ."

"Stop it!" He sprang out of his chair. He had heard enough. The authorities would have to handle the rest. But before he called them, he had one more thing to do.

"Where does Jeremy keep his stolen art?" he asked.

She offered no resistance. "At his home, in San Francisco. In a secret basement room."

"Did you keep files of all those acquisitions you made for him over the years?" he asked.

She nodded.

"Where are they?"

The sharp brown eyes narrowed. "Why?"

"Get them," he said.

His harsh tone and the unyielding look in his eyes sent a chill down her back. She stood up. "All right."

She was back in an instant and handed him a small black leatherbound notebook. "It's all in there." Once she had thought of blackmailing Jeremy with this evidence. The need for revenge had been powerful in those early days. But her sense of self-preservation had been stronger.

Matt took the notebook from her. It was a strange, uncomfortable moment. This conspiracy against Jeremy made him feel a little like a traitor, as if by associating with his parents' killer, he was betraying their memory.

The house was suddenly invaded by sounds that seemed to come from another world—the slam of a door, the quick tap of high heels against a hardwood floor, the sound of a happy voice.

"Aunt Kate?" Paige called, hurrying toward the staircase and looking up. "Are you about ready? We don't want to be late for that gallery opening—"

"In here, Paige," Matt said, tucking the notebook into his pants back pocket.

She spun around, her initial expression one of surprise and pleasure. Then, as her gaze took in the ravaged look on Kate's face, the smile disappeared. She took a few slow steps inside the room. "Aunt Kate, what is it? What's wrong?" When Kate didn't answer, she shot Matt a quick, questioning look. "What's going on here?"

Matt met her gaze. "I think you'd better call your father, Paige."

Horrified, Paige stood in her aunt's living room, listening as Kate repeated her story for her benefit and Paul's. The words pierced through her brain with amazing clarity, yet she could not comprehend them. Words like "hatred," "obsession," "madness," and "bomb" made no sense at all.

She knew Kate as a tender, gentle woman, a nonviolent woman, a woman so sensible, practical, and predictable that Eve had once referred to her as "pathetically boring."

Kate cried at weddings and campaigned fiercely against the mistreatment of animals. To this date, and although she could afford a dozen of them, she had never owned or worn a fur coat. To think, or suggest, that she could premeditate such a crime, that she could take a bomb, put it into someone's car, and then go home as if she had just returned from the supermarket, was beyond Paige's imagination.

Paul was the first to break the stunned silence. "Jesus Christ, Kate," he said, raking his fingers through his hair as he paced the room. "What have you done?"

Kate answered with a sob and lowered her head into her hands.

After awhile, the lawyer in him took over. Coming to stand in front of the chair in which his sister-in-law sat, he asked, "Who else knows about this, besides the people in this room?"

Kate didn't look up. "No one."

Paul nodded. "Let's keep it that way. For now. Until further notice, you don't say a word, don't answer a single question without your attorney being present. Do you understand me, Kate?"

"Yes."

He couldn't take his eyes off her. He couldn't believe this woman he knew so well, loved like a sister, had premeditated the murder of an innocent person and then killed in cold blood.

He should have found some compassion in his heart, experienced some need, however small, to help her. It wouldn't be inconceivable for him to want to step down from the bench and take her case. She was family, after all. She had given him and Paige years of love and devotion. He wasn't sure what he would have done without her. Or how Paige would have turned out without Kate's love and patience. Surely, now that she was in trouble, she had a right to expect something in return.

He couldn't do it. He couldn't say the words he knew she waited to hear. He could only look at her, think of what she had done to Matt and Josh. And feel nothing but revulsion.

"I know a lawyer who will take the case," he said, "His name is Don Cheevers. He's very good. I'll call him if you want."

Only a further slumping of Kate's shoulders indicated she had heard him.

A muffled sob to his right made him made turn around. Paige sat on the sofa, her arms wrapped around her. There was such a look of anguish on her face that for a moment Paul was reminded of the little seven-year-old he had held on his lap that Christmas Eve morning as he explained to her that her mother had left them.

He was beside her in an instant and took her hands in his. They felt like ice. All of her seemed frozen in shock.

"I can't believe any of this," she whispered, her tear-filled eyes darting from him to Kate and back to him. "It's like I'm living a nightmare."

"I know." He squeezed her hand. "But we'll get

through this, darling. I promise.'' He glanced toward
Matt and then back at her. ''Right now, don't you think
it's time you talked to Matt? He's been having a pretty
rough time.''

She followed her father's gaze. She had been so caught
up in her own emotions she had forgotten Matt was still
here.

Pushing her own despair aside, she stood up and went
to him. ''Matt. . . ?'' She laid a tentative hand on his
arm.

When he looked at her, his face lost some of its rigid-
ity but the eyes remained cold and distant.

''I'm sorry,'' she whispered.

''You had nothing to do with it.''

''I know. I . . .'' Tears welled up again. But this time
they were for him. ''Let me help?''

Although he heard the pleading in her voice, he was
incapable of reacting to it. A numbness had settled within
him now and, for the moment, that's all he wanted.
''Maybe later.''

He doesn't want me, Paige thought miserably. He can't
even look at me. Before she could turn away, her father
was at her elbow.

''Matt,'' Paul said. ''The district attorney is going to
want to know what you were doing at Beauchamp last
night. Do you want to tell me first?''

He nodded. It wasn't quite how he had planned to do
it. But the choice was no longer his. As he talked, he
was aware that Paige was listening intently. He didn't
look at her. Her reaction when she realized he had come
to California under false pretenses wasn't something he
wished to confront right now.

To his surprise she interrupted him only once, when
he mentioned the shipment from Germany.

''Jeremy told me he had canceled that order.''

''He lied. My contact told me a crate containing, or
supposed to contain, two doll plaster casts, arrived at San
Francisco International Airport on August twelfth and
were delivered to Newman's house the same day.''

Paige waited until he was finished before speaking again. Her voice was calm, her gaze direct. "Tell me something. Did you come to my rescue because you loved me or because you knew I was innocent?"

"Both."

Paul's reaction was more logical. "What about that crate and its contents? Can Paige still be incriminated?"

"Not now that we know Jeremy lied to Paige about it. And not with all the evidence we have against him."

Paul nodded, hesitated a moment as he glanced back at Kate. "Okay," he sighed. "Let's call Cheevers."

Josh's face was grim as he listened to Matt recount the events that had taken place at Kate's house a little over two hours ago. He never interrupted once. Only his eyes, as hard as Matt's, and the occasional tightening of his jaw, betrayed his inner turmoil.

After Matt was finished, Josh walked to the bar, pulled out a shot glass and the Jack Daniels from behind the counter, filled the glass and downed the liquor in one swallow.

When he turned around, his eyes were bright but there was no anger in his voice, only a great sadness. "You know," he said, staring out in space. "Six years ago I wanted to kill the son of a bitch who did this to my boy and to Caroline. And believe me, I would have if they had caught him. But when the police eventually filed the case away with the rest of their unsolved murders, I did the same. It made it easier for me to go on."

He walked back toward the fireplace where Matt stood. "But it's different with you. You've waited six years for this day, and now that it's here, I'm afraid for you. I'm afraid of the anger. I'm afraid you'll lose your sense of priorities."

"Don't ask me not to be angry, Gramps. She killed them in cold blood, dammit! They never had a chance."

Josh felt the prickle of tears behind his eyes. "I'm not saying you can't be angry at Kate, or kick down walls if you need to. I'm saying you've got to get it out of your system quickly. You and Paige can't begin a new life together with this hanging between the two of you. You've got to put it to rest before you see her again. You've got to let justice do its job.''

Matt didn't answer.

''You don't want to lose her, do you, son?''

Matt took a long breath. ''No.''

''Then why don't you go tell her that?''

''Because I need time. I need to be alone. She understands that. She needs time to herself too.''

Josh shook his head. ''Just don't take too long, son.''

It was noon in San Francisco. In his modern, state-of-the-art gym, Jeremy had just finished a strenuous workout and was in a great mood. Earlier today, he had received word from his realtor that a ten-thousand-acre property in Ojai had just been put on the market.

It was smaller than the Canyon-T Ranch, but perfect in every other way. It stood high on a peak overlooking Lake Casitas and commanded one of the most beautiful panoramas in the region.

Jeremy picked up a towel and sponged his face and neck as Lars, his personal trainer, set up the massage table. After the humiliating breakup with Paige, followed by the finding of that damned deed, he deserved a little good news.

He stretched out on the table and closed his eyes as Lars's able fingers began to work the knots in his neck and shoulders. He missed Paige. Since she had walked out of his life a few days ago, he hadn't been able to think of anything else. He had even considered trying to get her back. But he had changed his mind. She had been too angry. And anyway, no woman on earth was worth that kind of aggravation. Not even Paige.

Besides, there were dozens of beautiful women in San Francisco who would be more than willing to take her place. All he had to do was look around.

He had begun to doze off when the intercom next to

him buzzed. Reaching toward it, Jeremy pressed a button. "Yes?"

"Two gentlemen are here to see you, Mr. Newman." There was an unusual tension in Chu Seng's voice. "They're from the district attorney's office."

Jeremy pushed Lars away and jerked to a sitting position. The D.A. was a friend of his. He'd never send anyone here without calling first. Deep in his gut, fear speared a quick warning. "What do they want?"

"I'm not sure, sir. But they have a search warrant."

THIRTY-FIVE

Shortly before noon that day, Kate was taken into custody and formally charged with murder in the first degree. Because the temporary insanity defense no longer existed in California, her lawyer, Don Cheevers, entered a plea of not guilty by reason of total insanity, which, he had explained to Paul, was Kate's best chance for acquittal. Beyond that he could guarantee very little.

"Isn't there anything you can do about her bail?" Paige asked her father that afternoon as he drove her back home. "I can't stand the thought of her being in that awful cell."

"First-degree murder is an unbailable offense, darling. I'm sorry."

Something about the tone of his voice made her turn around. She had noticed that same chill earlier, when she had questioned the insanity plea, but had been too distraught to bring it up. "What is it, Daddy? You're acting as if you don't care what happens to Aunt Kate. I know she did a terrible thing, but we can't abandon her now. Not after all she did for us."

Paul stopped his car in front of Paige's front door and sat staring at the ocean. "I don't plan to abandon her, Paige. It's just that some of my findings about your aunt are forcing me to look at her in an altogether different light."

"What sort of findings?"

"Her obsession with Jeremy, for one. It didn't end with Adam McKenzie's death, you see. It continued long after that, through Jeremy's relationship with you."

"Did Aunt Kate tell you that?"

"No. She told Dr. Harris. He is the criminal psychiatrist Don hired to evaluate Kate and help him with his defense."

Paige shrugged. "All right. So she still loved Jeremy. I can't say I'm surprised about that. And you shouldn't be, either. Not after hearing how she felt about him during the fifteen years they were together."

His face grim, Paul turned to look at her. "Would you be as understanding if I told you she recently attempted to kill him?"

The shock made Paige whip around in her seat. "Kill Jeremy? Dear Lord! When?"

"At the Solstice Parade two months ago. She bought a mask, donned a costume, and joined the parade, intending to shoot Jeremy with her .38 revolver before the two of you reached Alameda Park."

"She was going to kill him right there? In broad daylight? In front of thousands of witnesses?" Paige's voice was muffled and she felt ill, but her gaze remained steady.

"She hoped the crowd would work in her favor. But it didn't. When she joined the parade on Micheltorena Street, a ring of dancers took hold of her and wouldn't let her go. By the time she got away, you and Jeremy had disappeared."

Paige leaned back against the car seat as visions of a masked Kate stalking them through the crowd flashed through her head. "I never suspected the torment she was going through . . . never realized . . ." She stopped, unable to finish her sentence, feeling more and more as if she was talking about a stranger instead of her beloved aunt.

"That's because she was very good—most of the time—at keeping her emotions under control. But when you told her Jeremy had proposed and you had accepted, she lost control, the same way she lost control when he left her for Caroline."

A sob caught in Paige's throat. "Why didn't she tell me? We could have talked about it. I could have helped."

Paul shook his head. "Reasoning wouldn't have done any good, darling. Not in her case."

"Why not?"

"According to Dr. Harris, Kate was totally traumatized that day, to the point that she was no longer able to distinguish right from wrong." His face solemn, Paul took Paige's hand. "What I'm trying to tell you," he said gently. "Is that Kate's emotions and frame of mind were so erratic that afternoon, and so distorted, that if she hadn't been interrupted by those dancers, she could have just as easily killed you."

Stunned, Paige stared at him. Every inch of her wanted to reject that last remark as totally ludicrous. Kate would never harm her. Kate loved her, had raised her and sheltered her all her life. Then, more objectively, she remembered small incidents that had taken place over the years—Kate's repeated warnings against Jeremy, her angry reaction at his growing interest in Paige. Once or twice, she had even caught her aunt's unsmiling eyes on her, caught that disturbing, slightly haunted look, which Kate, when questioned, always blamed on a difficult client or some other problem.

Had she been thinking . . . even then . . . ?"

"How could this happen?" Paige asked, running trembling fingers through her hair. "How could such a warm, intelligent, sensible woman allow herself to lose control over a man?"

Paul rolled down the window and took a slow, cleansing breath. "Dr. Harris believes Kate's difficult childhood is probably to blame for many of her problems. The pain and terror she suffered as a little girl, the hatred she developed for her abusive father and couldn't release. It all built up over the years, like a volcano waiting to erupt." He sighed. "It's a very complicated matter, darling. And I'm afraid that in or out of prison, Kate is going to need help."

As Paige watched her father drive away a few moments later, a shiver ran through her from head to toe at the thought of what might have happened at the parade. Her feelings, tried beyond their limits, kept vacillating among love, sorrow and loathing.

"I've never felt so lost," she told Mindy that evening when her friend stopped by. "So out of touch with reality."

"You don't have to fight this battle alone, you know. Matt is there for you, and you can be there for him. Why don't the two of you talk about this?"

"Matt doesn't want to hear from me right now."

"Nonsense. He's torn, that's all. Just like you are. But staying in your separate corners is only going to make matters worse."

"He said he would call me."

"But he hasn't, has he? And since you're so miserable, why don't *you* call? Who says *he* has to be the one?"

In spite of her low spirits, Paige smiled. "Still defending Matt's cause, I see."

Mindy shrugged. "I just know a good man when I see one."

By the time Paige was getting ready for bed that night, Matt still hadn't called. She told herself he needed time, that if his love for her had survived the last two years, it would survive this. But as she lay awake and thought about the distant look in his eyes earlier, her heart filled with a cold fear. She would give him until tomorrow evening. If he hadn't called by then, she would take Mindy's advice and go to the ranch. This nonsense had lasted long enough.

The following morning, twenty-four hours after the ordeal had begun, Paige stopped at her father's house to find out the latest development on Kate's case. Paul was on the terrace, finishing his cornflakes and talking into the phone at the same time.

"That was Don Cheevers," he told her after he hung up. "The trial has been set for Tuesday, September tenth, and will be heard by Judge Serano, who's a very fine judge." He paused. "The D.A. is asking for the death penalty."

Paige closed her eyes. Although she had expected it,

the words seemed unreal, the outcome unthinkable. "Couldn't Don get him to agree to a plea bargain?"

Paul shook his head. "No. However, there is a fair chance that even with a guilty verdict, the jury will reject the death penalty, which means the sentencing will be up to the judge."

"What kind of a sentence are we talking about then?"

Paul shrugged. The penalty for first-degree murder is death or life imprisonment without possibility of parole. But in many cases, the court has the discretion to order a much lesser sentence."

"Would you?"

"Don't put me on the spot, Paige."

"I need to know."

Paul sighed. "She killed two people. Some might be tempted to call it a crime of passion. Others will call it temporary insanity." He shook his head. "In my courtroom, it would amount to cold-blooded, premeditated murder. She wouldn't walk out of there with less than fifteen years to life—no parole."

Paul saw Paige's brave front falter. The last twenty-four hours had taken their toll on his beautiful daughter. Her face was pale and drawn and the dark circles under her eyes told of a long, sleepless night.

She had worshipped Kate. Perhaps more than she had worshipped Ann. But like him, Paige possessed a deep sense of justice and an abhorrence of violence. Her love for Matt, and knowing the anguish he was going through, only made the problem more complicated.

"Have you talked to Matt recently?" he asked.

Paige looked away. Out in the yard three squirrels chased each other, fighting over the platter of sunflower seeds Maria put out every morning. It was comforting to see that for some, life went on as usual. "Not yet. If I don't hear from him by this evening, I'll drive out to the ranch."

Paul squeezed her hand. "That's my girl."

He was interrupted by the ring of the telephone.

Reaching out, Paul picked up the receiver. "Paul Granger here."

"Judge Granger," the man at the other end said. "This is Edward Branigan. I'm an attorney and need to talk to Miss Kate Madison right away. I tried her home, but there's no answer."

"My sister-in-law isn't available right now," Paul said curtly. "And for the record, she already has an attorney."

"I'm not a practicing attorney, Mr. Granger. Not anymore. I live in Rome. I'm a friend of Marcello and Ann Ludicci. *Was* a friend," he corrected.

Paul sat up. "Has something happened to Ann?"

The man's voice grew much more subdued. "Ann passed away this afternoon."

Paul fell back against his chair. Although time and bitterness had eroded his love for Ann, hearing about her death brought an unexpected but familiar ache to his heart. "Oh, dear God!"

"What, Dad? What is it? What happened to Ann?"

Paul silenced her with his raised hand. "How . . . ?"

"She died of a brain tumor. She had been ill for some time."

"Kate never mentioned it to me."

"Miss Madison didn't know. No one knew—except myself. That's the way Ann wanted it."

"My sister-in-law is undergoing a difficult time right now," Paul explained. "I would prefer if she heard about Ann from the family. If you don't mind."

"That will be fine. And perhaps you could do something else for me? Ann had one last wish before she died—that her daughter, Paige, come to Rome for the funeral."

Paul glanced at Paige. "I don't know if that will be possible. The family is . . . well, we're all—"

"Please, Judge Granger. This is terribly important. Ann asked me to do everything in my power to convince her daughter to come."

Paul sighed. "All right, Mr. Branigan. I'll tell her.

Why don't you give me your phone number so we can call you back?'' He jotted down the information on a yellow pad in front of him. ''Got it. Thanks for calling. Good-bye.''

''That was Ann's attorney in Rome,'' Paul said, meeting Paige's questioning gaze. ''Your mother died earlier today.''

Paige delivered the news to Kate herself. Because of Paul's position in the community and the nature of the visit, she had been allowed to meet Kate in the privacy of her cell.

It was the first time she had faced her aunt since learning how she had stalked her and Jeremy at the parade. But whatever awkwardness she had felt initially vanished in the wake of her aunt's grief.

''I'm very sorry,'' Paige said, experiencing no pain of her own. ''I know how close the two of you were.''

Kate nodded and raised her head. ''I wish now I had gone to see her when she invited me a couple of months ago.''

''You didn't know.''

''I should have guessed something was wrong. She was more insistent than usual, telling me about the Sicilian fishing village where she and Marcello had spent their summers, and how anxious she was to show it to me.'' Fresh tears pressed behind her eyelids. ''But I was too damned concerned about my own problems to notice hers.''

Taking the handkerchief Paige handed her, she wiped her eyes. ''You'll go, won't you, Paige?'' she asked, looking up. ''You'll go to your mother's funeral?''

Paige, who had expected the request and was prepared for it, shook her head. ''No, Aunt Kate. I can't leave at a time like this. And anyway, why would I want to go to Ann's funeral? You know how I feel about her.''

Saddened by her niece's cold, dispassionate tone, Kate asked, ''Don't you feel anything? Regret? Compassion? Some love buried deep within you?''

Paige looked at the dull gray wall across the room and said nothing.

With a sigh, Kate stood up. Many times during the last four years, she had been tempted to break her promise to Ann and tell Paige and Paul the truth. Only the fear of losing her sister all over again had stopped her.

But there was nothing to stop her now. Ann's secret had been kept quiet long enough.

"I think it's time you knew the truth about your mother," she said. Before Paige had a chance to protest, she raised her hand. "No, Paige. I won't be brushed aside this time. This is something you should have heard four years ago when your mother came to your wedding. But you wouldn't let her tell you, so now you'll have to listen to me." Ignoring Paige's exasperated sigh, Kate's gaze remain steady. "Ann was blackmailed into leaving Santa Barbara."

Paige's first impulse was to laugh. Had Kate completely lost her mind? Did she think for one minute she'd fall for such a preposterous story?

She studied her aunt for a moment, remembering her father's warning about her erratic behavior, trying to decide what might be going through her head. In the end, it was the calm and determined look in Kate's eyes that convinced her she might be telling the truth. "Who would want to blackmail Ann?" she asked. "And why?"

Sounding like her old self again, Kate told her everything. She told her about Ann's struggle when she had first arrived in New York, about her job at Lolita's and her dream to be on Broadway. And she told her how, eight years after Ann's marriage to Paul, Eve had found out the truth and threatened to expose her if she didn't leave Santa Barbara immediately.

"Ann fought her with all the strength she had," Kate continued, seeing her niece's body grow rigid under the shock. "But she was no match for Eve, no match for that woman's hatred and determination."

For a long time, Paige remained silent, unable to deal with the wave of emotions that threatened to engulf her.

The thought that her mother, the beautiful, elegant, refined woman she had loved and idolized for seven years, had been a prostitute, was so shattering, that she couldn't see or feel anything beyond that. Not even anger toward her grandmother.

"Why didn't Ann tell Dad the truth?" she asked, reliving the pain of those first few days twenty-four years ago all over again. "Why didn't she believe in his love? In our strength as a family?"

"Because she was terrified of the consequences."

"So she ran away. Like a coward."

"Oh, Paige, don't say that. It took more courage to leave you than you'll ever imagine."

Paige went to stand in front of a table where a photograph of herself was prominently displayed. It had been taken on her eighth birthday, only a few months after Ann's abrupt departure. Anxious to impress all her friends, Eve had pulled out all the stops that day, hiring a circus act to entertain the more than one hundred guests, most of whom Paige hardly knew. She had hated every minute of it but hadn't said a word for fear of making her grandmother angry.

It wasn't until several years later that Paige had learned to stand up to her. Why hadn't Ann done the same?

Behind her, Kate lay a hand on her shoulder. "I know I have hurt you deeply," she murmured in that gentle tone Paige had always found so soothing. "That I have done things for which you'll never be able to forgive me. Therefore, I have no right to ask anything of you. But you must go to Rome, Paige. You must go and say goodbye to your mother. Because if you don't, you'll never forgive yourself."

THIRTY-SIX

Rome in August was stifling, Paige thought, as she arrived in the Italian capital. With so many restaurants, movie theaters, newsstands, and even pharmacies closed down for the month, parts of the city, especially the small, sun-baked piazzas where the fountains had been turned off, looked like ghost towns.

But Villa Assumpta, located at the end of a lovely, tree-lined avenue on the Aventine Hill, was a cool and inviting haven. From the Benedetto da Maiano fountain inside the front gates, to the cantilevered staircase that led to the second and third floor, the villa was a study in wealth, beauty, and taste.

Ed Branigan, who had met Paige at the airport, had been anxious for Paige to feel at home.

"The staff would love to have you stay at the house," he told her. There are more than twelve guest rooms. I'm sure you'll find one suitable."

She had turned down the offer, explaining she felt more comfortable in a downtown hotel.

She liked Ed Branigan. He was in his early seventies, with eyes as blue as hers and white hair, which, judging from his heavily freckled face, must have been a fiery shade of red when he was younger.

Although he had made no secret that he knew all about her relationship with her mother, his attitude was cordial. After a few moments in his company, she felt totally at ease with him and understood why he had been a friend of the Ludiccis for so long.

The following morning, Ann was buried next to her

husband, Marcello, in a family plot on the villa's grounds. Although Paige no longer felt the deep, burning hatred for her mother she had known for the past twenty-four years, she was still too overwhelmed by what she had learned recently to experience the pain that seemed to be expected of her.

She wished her father was here with her. But although he too now knew the truth, he had declined to accompany her.

"You're the one she wanted there," he had told her with a sad, faraway look in his eyes. "I prefer to go later. After Kate's trial."

After the services, a few of the Ludiccis' close friends stopped at the villa to offer Paige their condolences.

"Signora Ludicci—very good person," a frail, tiny woman in black told her in halting English. She patted her heart for emphasis. "Like daughter to me."

Others came to her, all with something kind to say about Ann.

"Your mother was well liked around these parts," Ed told Paige as both stood on the terrace saying good-bye to the last guest.

"Yes, I can see that."

Back inside, Paige watched Noemi, her mother's private maid, clear away the remains of the light buffet lunch she had served earlier. Her eyes were red and downcast.

"Was Noemi close to my mother?" Paige asked.

"Very. Ann was good to all the servants and they worshipped her." As an afterthought, he asked, "Would you like to see the rest of the house? The view from upstairs is one not to be missed."

Paige had hoped to do a little sightseeing, perhaps even some shopping, but the fierce heat had changed her mind. "Why not?" she said with a shrug.

They walked through rooms that were lavishly furnished and filled with flowers and sunshine. Each had a name chosen after a color and was decorated throughout in that theme.

"You mother loved this house," Ed said as he played tour guide. "Not at first, though. At first, she hated it."

"Why?"

"She was intimidated by it, felt awkward—a little like an intruder."

"From what my aunt told me, I thought Marcello had made her feel as if this house belonged to her—right from the beginning."

"Oh, he did. He was wonderful to her. It was the history of the house Ann found overwhelming. She told me once, half-jokingly, of course, that the ghosts of Marcello's ancestors roamed those halls, spying on her, waiting for her to make a mistake."

"Yes," Paige said, remembering Kate's comments about Eve's chilling welcome when Ann had moved into the Grangers' house years ago. "Ann was always a little insecure in that respect."

He gave her a puzzled look. "Do you always call your mother Ann?"

Her hands behind her back, Paige stood in front of a superb copperplate map of Italy by Abraham Ortelius. With the setting sun slanting over it, the brown and gold hues took on a new patina, a new richness. "I was very young when she left me, Mr. Branigan. Somehow, the word 'mother' went with her."

Ignoring the slight pursing of the attorney's lips, she stopped on the threshold of a large room decorated in various shades of blue and filled with magnificent Italian antiques. "This is lovely," she said.

"Your mother called it The Blue Salon. It was her favorite room. She spent a lot of time here, listening to music, having tea. Sometimes she and Marcello played cards—over there," he added, pointing in the general direction of a sofa and chair by a blue-tiled fireplace.

Ed caught Paige's indifferent expression and sighed at her lack of enthusiasm. He had sensed her reluctance to be here from the moment he had greeted her at the airport. Of course, knowing what he knew about her past relationship with Ann, he had expected it. But he had hoped that after the funeral, and once she walked through the house, through the rooms that were still so alive with Ann's presence, she'd mellow a little, shed that stiffness he found so unnatural in a beautiful young woman such as she.

The only change in her was when the opened the ballroom's double doors.

"Dear Lord, what is *that*?"

"The ballroom."

Although Paige had visited many sumptuous homes over the years, this room, unlike any other she had ever seen, took her breath away. Decorated in gold and ivory, it reminded her of the palatial ballrooms she had seen at Versailles.

It was immense, featuring three fireplaces, a dozen palladian windows, and as many crystal chandeliers. On the ceiling was a fresco by Giovanni Battista Crosato, illustrating episodes from the life of Alexander the Great.

"This is where Marcello and his family used to entertain," Ed explained when he saw her gaze drift over the gold-inlaid boiserie and the gold and white marble floor. "But when Ann arrived, the lavish parties stopped."

"You mean they never used this room again?"

"Oh, on the contrary. Ann used it more than ever before. But instead of entertaining heads of state and European society, she invited local orphans."

"Orphans?"

Ed nodded. "She was a generous benefactor of one of Rome's largest orphanages, and organized many parties for the children throughout the year. But it was at Christmastime that this room really came alive. Personally, Ann hated the holiday because it brought her so many painful memories. But she loved Christmas for the children, whom she adored and showered with presents."

As Paige walked around the room with him, she could almost hear the sound of laughter and Christmas music echo from the ancient walls. Memories stirred within her and she was reminded of their own Christmases at home, of all the times she had sat in front of the huge blue spruce, listening to her mother's melodious voice as she told her about a jolly, wonderful man named Santa Claus.

"You make her sound like a saint," she said, caught off guard by her sudden bout of nostalgia.

"Do I? I'm sorry. That wasn't my intention." He closed the doors. "She'd be very upset if she knew I was trying to influence you in any way."

Paige turned, raised an eyebrow. "Influence me about what?"

He hesitated, wondering if she was ready for what he had to tell her next. Probably not. But he couldn't put it off any longer. He had made a promise to Ann and he intended to keep it. "About her will. Your mother left you everything, Mrs. Mckenzie. This house, its contents, her entire fortune."

Paige hadn't expected that. A generous inheritance perhaps, even a few mementos, but certainly, in view of all that had happened, no more than that. "Everything?" she repeated.

"Everything. Except for a trust fund she left to the orphanage, and a few items for Miss Madison, the Ludicci estate is yours."

She shook her head. "I can't accept it."

"Mrs. Mckenzie, I don't think you fully realize the size of the estate. One does not turn down several million dollars without a valid reason."

"I have a valid reason, Mr. Branigan. Contrary to what my mother may have thought, I have no rights to this house or to the money. For all practical purposes, Ann and I were strangers. I didn't even like her. What kind of a person would I be if I accepted her money now?"

"But Ann put no conditions on his inheritance, demanded nothing in return. She left it to you simply because she loved you."

Paige didn't reply.

"Look, I'm not going to pressure you about this." The attorney stopped on the second floor landing and leaned against an intricately carved railing. "I promised your mother I wouldn't. I will, however, ask you to fulfill one term of her will.''

"I thought you weren't going to pressure me.''

"This has nothing to do with the actual inheritance.''

Paige sighed. "All right. What is it?''

"As it happens, Ann had anticipated your refusal. However, it was her final wish that you accept the contents of one room, take them back to California with you, and hold them for a period of three months. If, after that period, you still felt the same, you would be free to dispose of those contents, and the rest of your inheritance, any way you wished.''

"That's an odd request. What room was she talking about?''

"Her studio on the third floor. You do know that your mother was a successful artist? At least here in Italy.''

"Yes, I'm aware of that.'' She frowned. "I thought most of her work was on consignment in a Roman gallery.''

"It is. What's in her studio now isn't for sale. It's something she started when she found out how ill she was. She did it for you, Mrs. McKenzie, so you would know a mother's love is forever.''

"I don't understand.''

"You will.'' He pointed at the staircase. "The studio is on the third floor. You can't miss it.''

Paige glanced up, hesitated. Was that some sort of trick? Would she find a room filled with such treasures, such fabulous antiques, that she, as a lover of great art, would be forced to accept them?

She started to turn down Branigan's offer. She hated games. And she hated being here. She had fulfilled her duty, hadn't she? She had come to her mother's funeral. What more did they want from her?

Something in the lawyer's eyes—a gentle challenge perhaps? stopped her. She shrugged. Why not? She had seen so many rooms in the last half hour, would one more matter?

"All right,'' she said, amused by the look of relief on

the lawyer's face. "I'll go take a look." She started to climb the long curving staircase, then, realizing he wasn't following her, she stopped and turned around. "Aren't you coming?"

He shook his head. "It's best if you do this alone, Mrs. McKenzie. I'll be downstairs—in the Blue Salon."

He had been right to say she wouldn't be able to miss it. The studio door was open, and as she stood in the doorway, she was immediately drenched in bright Roman sunlight that poured from the tall, palladian windows.

Paige stepped inside and caught her breath.

All around her were magnificent canvases that exploded with color and life, paintings of children, of family gatherings, of holiday celebrations that stunned and dazzled the senses.

The brilliant profusion of reds, oranges, blues, and greens, reminded Paige of Gauguin's South Sea paintings, while the touching storytelling quality in each canvas was more reminiscent of Renoir.

Paintings, some barely dry, were everywhere—hung on the walls, stacked against them, propped up on easels and even spread out on the floor.

At first, all she could see was the incredible burst of colors, the sure strokes, the clever use of shadow and light. But as she took a closer look, as she started walking around the room, pulling some of the paintings away from the wall and studying them, she realized there was a familiarity about them she hadn't noticed at first.

It wasn't until she found herself face to face with one in particular that she realized, with a gasp, that the little girl in the pigtails, waiting for her school bus, was her.

She had long forgotten that day, but now she remembered it vividly. It had been a warm September morning, her first day of school. She had been filled with mixed feelings—anticipation, joy, pride. And fear. In a few clever strokes of her brush, Ann had captured it all in the little girl's face—her face.

There were others—paintings of her at the beach,

building a sand castle while Ann watched; another of
Paige and her Girl Scout troop, taking an oath. There
was her first dance recital, a family picnic, her graduation from high school and college, her wedding to Matt.

There were five wedding scenes in all, each beautiful
and moving. But it was the largest one she found the
most poignant. She and Matt had just come out of the
church, hand in hand. They were laughing as they gazed
into each other's eyes, so obviously in love. In the background, removed from the happy moment, was a woman
in a beautiful, shimmering green suit. Her two hands,
balled into fists, were pressed against her mouth as if to
stifle a cry.

Paige felt the beginning of a sob rise in her own throat.
She swallowed quickly. Her hands trembling, she let the
canvas fall back against the others. She wanted to run
out of here, out of this room. She wanted to return to the
safety of her own home. Instead, she stood in the middle
of Ann's studio and kept turning around, slowly, to take
it all in.

A woman had just died. Yet this room radiated life and
joy. Each painting was a celebration, a tribute to all the
mothers and daughters of this world, a tribute her own
mother had told from the deepest part of her heart.

Her throat dry and her heart pounding, Paige tore her
eyes away from the paintings and focused them on the
rest of the room. She saw a paint-splattered smock hanging on a hook, a CD player on a shelf, tin cans filled
with brushes, tubes of paint scattered everywhere, some
squeezed flat, others still half-full. Near one of the windows was a drawing board with a sketch on it.

Intrigued to see what her mother had been preparing
to paint next, Paige approached the table. It was a pencil
sketch of a beautiful woman in a lavish evening gown.
Next to her, smiling and holding the woman's hand, was
a little girl, dressed in the same elegant gown, her black
curls combed in that same glamorous, tousled upsweep.

Paige stifled a gasp. It was their Christmas portrait.
The portrait Paige had destroyed.

The pain hit her all at once, swift, unexpected, ravaging. It pierced through her heart with such force, her upper body bent under the weight. Her head fell into her hands and she sobbed, deep, wrenching sobs she couldn't control. "Oh, Mama," she cried, her heart tearing as she heard herself say the beloved name at last. "Mama, I'm sorry. I'm so sorry."

She was aware of two strong hands on her shoulders. Ed Branigan must have heard her cry. But she didn't care. Nothing could stop the outpouring of grief now.

"I thought you might be in need of a friendly shoulder," a familiar voice whispered in her ear.

She whirled around. Through the blur of tears, she saw Matt standing in front of her, his expression solemn, but warm, comforting.

For a moment, she was incapable of uttering a single word. She touched his cheek, as if to reassure herself that she wasn't dreaming. Overcome with joy and grief, she tried to smile. "You're here," she said at last, touching his cheek. "You're really here."

"I came as soon as I heard."

"I . . . wanted to call you. I was going to come to the ranch, but then Mr. Branigan called and . . ."

"Shhh. I know. I was a fool. But I'm here now." He opened his arms and she fell into them, burying her face against his chest as he murmured soothing, loving words. How different it felt to cry in the arms of the man you loved, she thought.

"Oh, Matt, Mama died all alone," she whispered as she dried her tears.

"No." He stroked her hair as his gaze swept over the room and its incredible contents. "She died with her thoughts full of you, full of her love for you."

"A love I didn't return."

"Do you love her now?"

"Yes. Oh, yes. But now it's too late."

Taking her face in his hands, Matt wiped her tears with his thumbs. "It's never too late, darling." He smiled. "Look at us."

THIRTY-SEVEN

Paige and Matt decided to stay in Rome a few days longer in order to arrange for the shipment of Ann's paintings to Santa Barbara. Much to Noemi's pleasure, they agreed to move out of their hotel and into Villa Assumpta, where the devoted housekeeper could pamper them the way she had pampered Ann and Marcello all those years.

Both agreed not to discuss Kate, the trial, or whatever might be happening back home. They talked only about themselves and their plans for the future—their future.

"I thought it might be a good idea to keep Villa Assumpta," Paige told Matt as Noemi served them breakfast on the terrace the following morning. "That way, we could use it as a vacation home and let my father use it as well, if he wants, and of course, Mindy and Larry, and Josh." She filled their cups with strong, black coffee. "Or do you think we should sell it?"

"I think you should do whatever makes you happy."

She smiled. "That's easy. Being with you makes me happy. And," she added with a mocking smile, "having you help me with difficult decisions would make me very happy."

Putting his cup down, Matt glanced around him, at the elegant surroundings, the spectacular view, the majestic gardens, a bit formal for his own tastes but beautiful just the same. Villa Assumpta wasn't just a lovely piece of history, it was her mother's home, the mother whose love Paige had just rediscovered. Later perhaps she might be able to part with it. For the moment, she needed to keep it.

"Well, since you're asking my opinion, I think you should hold on to it. I wouldn't mind coming here from time to time and letting Noemi spoil us. And if we let all our friends and relatives do the same, think what that will do for our popularity."

Looking smug, Paige picked up a thick slice of toasted Italian bread from a silver basket and spread some of Noemi's blackberry jam on it. "Would you like to come here for our honeymoon?"

Matt pushed his sunglasses into his hair and leaned forward, arms on the table. His gray eyes sparkled with amusement. "By honeymoon, you mean that period that immediately follows a wedding?"

Paige laughed. "Yes."

"Why, darling. Is this a proposal?"

"It could be. Are you shocked?"

Matt kept grinning. "Not at all. I'm a liberated man. It's just that . . ."

Paige lowered her toast. "What?"

"Well . . . I have to . . . you know, think about your proposal for a while. After all, I can't make an important decision like this without giving it—"

He never got a chance to finish. Leaning across the table, Paige smeared blackberry-lathered toast over Matt's startled face.

The following morning, on a whim, they flew to Venice. But it was crowded and noisy, and in this heat the tepid waters smelled foul. After a Campari at Florian's and a romantic lunch at a trattoria near the Rialto, they came back to Rome and kept cool in the villa's olympic-size pool.

Now, on their last night at the Ludicci estate, Paige stood in front of the bathroom mirror. She had changed into a red, lacy teddy and was wondering if she was overdoing this seduction bit.

Earlier that day she and Matt had been shopping on Via Condotti when Matt had spotted the sexy teddy in a window and told her she'd look great in it.

Later, while he was finishing his drink at a nearby

café, she had run back to the store and bought the garment, eager to make their last night in the eternal city special.

"Not bad actually," she murmured, turning back and forth and glancing over her shoulder to check the view from the back. "A little obvious perhaps, but so what?"

With a flush of anticipation, for she had thought about this moment since early afternoon, she walked back into the bedroom and stopped in her tracks. Matt was stretched out on the double bed, sound asleep.

Paige was overwhelmed with tenderness. While she had been dozing off by the pool, making last-minute arrangements with Ed Branigan and sipping ice-cold lemonade, Matt had been supervising the movers and helping them carry the paintings into the truck. Later, he had chopped a cord of firewood—enough to last Noemi through the winter—and carried it into the shed. No wonder the poor darling was exhausted.

Well, he would just have to wake up, wouldn't he? Because she wasn't about to waste this expensive trinket on herself.

Moving silently toward the bed, she came to kneel by Matt's side and study him for a moment. In repose, his features were relaxed, the mouth slightly open, the lines around it not as pronounced. There was a look of youthfulness about him now, a vulnerability she had never noticed before and found touching.

My Sir Galahad, she thought, gently stroking his hair. Like the heroes of her childhood, he had jumped on his horse and dashed to her rescue, braving the villains, ready to fight them all with only one weapon—his love for her.

How could she have resisted him?

Resting her arms on the edge of the bed, she leaned forward and pressed her lips to his. Matt slept on. Was he truly tired, she wondered, pulling back and watching him suspiciously. Or was she losing her touch?

She kissed him again. This time she was rewarded with a moan. "Mmmm. More."

More what?"

He stirred but kept his eyes closed. "Kiss," he said in a sleepy voice. "More kiss."

She did as he asked, not once but several times. In between kisses she traced the contour of his mouth with her tongue and nibbled at his lower lip. She knew from the rapid beat of his heart that he was no longer sleeping but prolonging the game. "You like that?" she asked, not letting on she had discovered his ruse.

"Yes," he murmured, still feigning sleep. "I like."

Her hand moved slowly down his chest, trailed across his flat stomach, sank into the thick triangle of dark blond hair, and stopped. So did Matt's breathing. Swallowing a rising giggle, Paige let her fingers slide lower until she reached his erection. "So you're not asleep after all, are you?" she asked, closing her hand around him.

Matt's lusty laugh filled the room. Wrapping two strong arms around her, he pulled her on top of him. "Hell, no. I've been watching you for ages." He took a handful of her hair and brought her face to him. "I thought you'd never come to bed."

"Pervert."

"What do you expect? There you are, prancing around in that thing driving me crazy. How can a man sleep?"

"Does that mean you like my teddy?"

"Love it. And it looks a lot better on you than on that skinny window mannequin. Too bad you're not going to keep it on long."

She chuckled. "You have no idea how to take this off."

"Oh, really?" His hand moved down her back, over the swell of her buttocks, reached between her thighs and with a quick tug, he unsnapped the flimsy garment. In an instant he had it off her.

"Now," he said, cupping her breasts and lifting his head to lick a tender nipple. "What were you saying?"

"I forgot."

He continued to kiss and tease, and when his mouth moved back to hers, she took it greedily, rolling with him over the bed, entangling her legs with his, opening her thighs. Matt gritted his teeth. It would be so easy to slide into her now, to feel her moist tightness surround him, to surrender to the magic and climb with her. But she wasn't ready. He wanted her to reach that point where her control began to slip. He wanted to see those cool beautiful eyes turn hot and dreamy and know the heat was only for him.

Under his touch, her skin grew warmer, and in her mouth he could already taste the passion. It flowed into him, engulfing him until he wanted, needed, to touch her everywhere—breasts, hips, buttocks, the tender skin between her thighs.

As her flesh, hot and wet, opened to him, he let his finger slide inside her. Almost immediately her body began to respond, to writhe, to demand more.

"Ah, yes." As Matt entered her, Paige sighed with relief. This was what she wanted, to be filled, to be led into this frenzied dance, to be carried to that special place she had only known in his arms, the only place she wanted to be.

Knowing she would reach it soon, her hands went searching for his hands. And found them, clasped them while she climbed from rise to rise until she reached the top. As she tightened her hold, shuddering, crying out his name, she felt his own passion, hot and flowing, inundate her.

They held each other for a while, and talked, until the sound of cicadas coming in from the open window lulled them into a deep sleep.

Matt was awakened by bright sunlight piercing through his closed lids and cool lips pressing against his own.

"If you have any idea about me missing breakfast," he teased, opening one eye. "Forget it. I'm famished. Especially since I can smell Noemi's *fritelle* from here." Hearing no answer, he opened both eyes.

Paige stood at the side of the bed, looking delectable in a long, flowing white robe. In her hands, she held a breakfast tray, complete with coffee, freshly squeezed orange juice, and hot apple fritters Noemi made by the dozens now that she knew Matt loved them so much.

"Why do I have the feeling we're going to miss our plane?" he asked, moving aside so Paige could climb back in bed with him, and taking the tray from her hands.

"If so, we'll take another plane. You like my surprise?"

He reached for the coffee, took a sip and nodded. "Love it. But as it so happens, I have a surprise of my own."

Paige bit into a fritter and watched him pull out a small black box from the bedside table.

"For you, *bella signorina*," he said, handing it to her with a flourish.

Paige opened the box. Nestled in black satin was an exquisite square-cut emerald ring surrounded by tiny diamonds. "Oh, Matt, it's beautiful." She looked up, her eyes misting. "When in the world did you have time to buy this?"

"I didn't. It belonged to my mother. It was her engagement ring, and the only piece of jewelry I kept." He gave her a hesitant look. "Do you like it? If you don't, say so and we'll get something else in Santa Barbara or—"

She touched her fingers to his lips. "I love it, darling. It's perfect. And I'm so touched you gave it to me."

"Caroline would have liked that."

When they took off from da Vinci Airport that afternoon, cuddled together and sipping champagne, they already looked like newlyweds.

THIRTY-EIGHT

When Paige and Matt landed in Los Angeles on August twenty-third, the "Newman Art Scandal," as the press had labeled it, was the subject of every conversation and the headline of every newspaper and tabloid across the nation.

Mindy, the ever-diligent taxi driver, came to pick them up at LAX and briefed them on what had taken place while they were gone.

Besides Turkey, which in recent years had suffered a rash of art thefts and wished to set an example, several museums across the country and abroad had filed suits against Jeremy and the many art dealers he had implicated in the scandal.

At home, American people had reacted with equal outrage. Unhappy that the man they had respected and trusted for so many years had betrayed them, San Franciscans demonstrated for days in front of the Newman Museum, forcing it to close. Throughout the city, important advertisers, convinced the *San Francisco Globe* no longer projected the right image for their products, canceled ads not only in the *Globe* but in all Newman-owned magazines and radio and television stations.

"He's hired one of the best attorneys in the country to defend him," Mindy said as she merged onto the crowded Ventura Freeway. "So he might get off with a relatively light sentence. But professionally and publicly, the man is finished. Washed out. There's talk the *Globe* is going to be sold and that he'll move to Ojai until his trial. But for the moment, Jeremy Newman is living in seclusion in his San Francisco home. No one has seen or heard from him in days.''

Mindy smiled and glanced at Paige, who sat next to her. ''The mighty do fall hard, don't they?''

Paige stared out the window in silence. After awhile, she asked, ''How's Aunt Kate?''

''Hanging in there. I went to see her a couple of days ago. But my visit seemed to make her nervous, so I didn't stay long.'' Reaching out, she squeezed her friend's hand. ''She'll be glad to see you, though.''

An hour later, Mindy pulled her Ford Taurus station wagon to a stop in front of Paige's house. ''Pardon the quick exit,'' she said, not getting out of the car. ''But my sweetie is due home in a little over six hours, and I need to make myself gorgeous.''

''Does that mean I'm not going to see you for a week?'' Paige shouted as her friend backed out of the driveway.

Mindy honked her horn twice in answer.

Although Paul told Paige and Matt he couldn't predict how long Kate's trial would last, and there was no reason for them not to get married right away, Paige remained adamant in her decision to wait until the trial was over before setting a wedding date.

''You understand, don't you?'' she asked Matt the day after she visited her aunt in jail. ''This nightmare won't really be behind us until I know what will happen to Kate.''

Matt took her hand and kissed it. ''I understand.''

Reopening the gallery and facing the public while splashy headlines continued to attract attention, was difficult, but Paige managed to get through it. In the wake of the adverse publicity, however, Beauchamp had suffered a tremendous blow.

Although Kate had told Paige she would not be back at Beauchamp, even if found not guilty, many indignant clients had said good-bye and closed their accounts.

"Today was a disaster," Paige told Matt when he came to pick her up one evening in early September. "I just lost Mr. Bloom."

"You'll get through this, Paige."

"Not this time."

He saw the frown line between her brows deepen and tried to jolt her back with the kind of challenge he knew she couldn't resist. "I've never known you to be a quitter."

Understanding what he was trying to do, she gave him a small smile. "Sometime one's strength lies in the ability to recognize when to quit."

"True." His heart ached for her. All her life Paige had been a pioneer, unafraid of challenges, undeniably daring. Her innovative ideas, together with her guts and dedication to excellence, had brought Santa Barbara, and Beauchamp, to the world's attention. He had no doubt she'd get back on her feet. But Beauchamp wouldn't.

"Perhaps after the trial is over, things will settle down. People forget, you know." He didn't believe it, but right now, those were the words Paige needed to hear.

She shook her head. "I doubt it. And so does Kate." She paused. "She wants me to put the gallery up for sale."

Matt watched her turn the page of her appointment calendar to the following day. It was blank. "How do you feel about that?"

Paige was pensive for a moment. "I don't really know. It's not that I *can't* run the gallery by myself. But the question is: Do I want to?"

"I suppose it will be different now." Matt glanced at a George IV ladies' writing desk Paige had acquired last month. A few weeks ago, this desk would have been bought in the blink of an eye. He turned back to her. "Would you consider getting another gallery? Something a little less nerve-racking?"

She snapped the book shut and came to stand in front of him. "As a matter of fact," she said, with the hint of a smile on her lips. "On my way to the ranch the other day, I saw a very pretty shop filled with attractive crafts—pottery, a few paintings, some jewelry. I think I might enjoy running something small and unpretentious like that.'' She stroked his arms. ''Of course, that would mean I'd be spending less time traveling, less time worrying about art traffickers, thieves, *or* nosy investigators who might cramp my style.''

''Mmmm. Those are the worst kind.''

''Some are.'' She wrapped her arms around his neck. ''What I'm saying is that I want to do something that will allow me to spend more time with you—now that you've decided to become a native again.''

Matt wrapped his arms around her waist and pulled her to him. ''In that case, why not take up ranching? We could use another strong, able body right now. What, with fences that need fixing, barns that need painting, new cattle that need branding . . . Or better yet, you could set up a chuckwagon kitchen for hungry cowboys . . .''

She shut him up with a kiss.

Kate's trial lasted three weeks. Although Matt had chosen to stay away, Paige, sitting directly behind her aunt, had been there every day.

Don Cheevers, an accomplished, rather flamboyant courtroom lawyer, who looked more like a wealthy rancher than an attorney, presented a brilliant defense. Bringing tears to the eyes of one of the female jurors, he cited Kate's exemplary life prior to the murder, her deeply disturbed emotional state at the time of the bombing, and the corrupt, ruthless man who had driven her to the brink of despair.

The prosecutor, however, painted an altogether different picture of Kate. He referred to her as cold-blooded, violent, and vengeful, a woman who had sought the help of a well-known terrorist, and who, for three days, had plotted a brutal murder and then carried it out, killing not one innocent person, but two.

Dozens of witnesses were called to the stand—medical experts, bomb experts, character witnesses, and even

Jeremy Newman, who, under Don's clever cross-examination, revealed a devious, self-centered side of himself no one had ever seen in public.

Through the entire court proceedings, Kate sat quietly, staring at her hands, never looking at the jury, or at the judge, sometime ignoring her lawyer's whispered questions until he repeated them to her.

On September thirtieth, the jury, comprised of eight men and four women, found Kate guilty of murder in the first degree. As Paul had predicted however, in the second phase of the trial, that same jury rejected the death penalty.

Taking into consideration the special circumstances Don Cheevers had brought up during his defense, Judge Serano later sentenced Kate to fifteen years to life imprisonment, and had recommended that she undergo psychiatric treatment while in prison.

"This is for the best, darling," Paul said to Paige when he was finally able to pull her away from Kate. "She'll be taken care of, and if her treatment is successful, as I'm sure it will be, she'll be eligible for parole in fifteen years."

Paige cried in Matt's arms that night. Her heart ached for the aunt she had worshipped and for the years of solitude Kate would have to face. I'll never forget what you did for me, Aunt Kate, Paige vowed silently as she settled deeper into Matt's arms. And I'll never abandon you. Then she fell asleep.

It was another spectacular day in Santa Barbara. The fog had drifted out to sea early, leaving the noon sky a cloudless, brilliant blue.

Although only a handful of people had been invited to the wedding, the sidewalks outside the Santa Barbara County Courthouse where Paige and Matt were being married, were jammed with the curious and with newspaper and television reporters.

The ceremony over, Paige stood outside, holding Matt's arm, while a few feet away, Paul and Tom Di-

Maggio, who had flown from New York with his wife
Joan to be the best man, snapped pictures. This time,
setting aside her indifference to big-name couturiers,
Paige had pulled out all the stops by wearing a stunning
Karl Lagerfeld white cotton bouclé suit, white lacy
stockings, and Ann Klein slingback pumps.

"Have I told you how ravishing you look today, Mrs.
McKenzie?" Matt whispered in Paige's ear.

"I don't believe so, Mr. McKenzie."

"Paige!" her father called. "Look this way, will you,
darling? That's it. Now smile."

"So ravishing," Matt continued, ignoring the dozens
of questions reporters hurled at them. "That I can hardly
wait to get you home, peel that suit from your body, and
make mad, passionate love to you."

"That's three hours from now." Paige saw Tom aim
his camera and flashed another smile.

"Don't remind me," Matt groaned.

She waited until a lady judge and good friend of her
father's had wished them both a lifetime of love and happiness, before adding, "However, if excitement is what
you want, I have something that might tide you over until
we do get home."

Pulling away from her, Matt pretended to be shocked.
"Paige Elizabeth McKenzie. Are you implying we sneak
behind the courthouse for a quickie?"

Paige giggled. "Sorry to disappoint, darling, but that's
not what I had in mind."

"Oh. Then what exactly *did* you have in mind?"

She leaned into him. "An announcement."

Although Paul and Tom continued to give them instructions, Matt was no longer listening to them. Something in Paige's voice demanded his immediate attention.
He turned to look at her, saw the gleam in her eyes, the
parted lips, the look of sheer, undiluted joy.

Afraid to hope, he searched her beautiful face for an
answer to his unspoken question. "What are you trying
to tell me?" he asked at last.

Striking another cheek-to-cheek pose for her father,

Paige whispered. ''I'm pregnant, Matt. We're going to have a baby.''

At those words, Matt let out a whoop that nearly brought traffic to a stop. Then, under the eyes of a cheering crowd, Matt McKenzie took his bride in his arms and kissed her.